Lineberger Memorial Library

THE LOEB CLASSICAL LIBRARY

FOUNDED BY JAMES LOEB 1911

EDITED BY

JEFFREY HENDERSON

THEOPHRASTUS
CHARACTERS

HERODAS
MIMES

SOPHRON AND OTHER
MIME FRAGMENTS

LCL 225

THEOPHRASTUS
CHARACTERS

HERODAS
MIMES

SOPHRON AND OTHER
MIME FRAGMENTS

EDITED AND TRANSLATED BY
JEFFREY RUSTEN
I. C. CUNNINGHAM

HARVARD UNIVERSITY PRESS
CAMBRIDGE, MASSACHUSETTS
LONDON, ENGLAND
2002

First Edition, 1929
Second Edition, with new text and translation of
Theophrastus and Herodas, 1993
Third Edition, adding Sophron and
Other Mime Fragments, 2002

LOEB CLASSICAL LIBRARY® is a registered trademark
of the President and Fellows of Harvard College

CIP data available from the Library of Congress

ISBN 0-674-99603-8

CONTENTS

PREFATORY NOTE

This volume is a thoroughly revised and considerably altered version of the edition that was published in 1993. The text and translation of Theophrastus' *Characters* and of Herodas' *Mimes* have been corrected and revised by Jeffrey Rusten and Ian Cunningham respectively. Dr. Cunningham has added an edition and translation of the mimes of Sophron of Syracuse and of fragments of popular mime dating from the 2nd century B.C. to the 5th century A.D. The 1929 edition of Cercidas and the Choliambic Poets with translation by A. D. Knox that was included in the 1993 volume is omitted here; of the poets in Knox's collection, Hipponax and Ananius are now included in the volume of Greek Iambic Poetry edited and translated by D. E. Gerber.

THEOPHRASTUS
CHARACTERS

EDITED AND TRANSLATED BY
JEFFREY RUSTEN

PREFACE

Theophrastus' *Characters* is a pleasant little book for
the casual reader, but an enormously difficult one for the
scholar; I would guess that most of its editors, even the
likes of Casaubon, Korais, Immisch and company, and
Diels, have begun their work with relish and confidence,
but concluded with an apologetic feeling that there was
much more to be done. I am certainly no exception. The
manuscript tradition of the work is perhaps the most corrupt among classical Greek authors, almost every other
sentence requiring some emendation. To produce a text
that can be translated and read requires adopting more
conjectures than a proper critical edition might normally
allow. Such a full edition—and a repertory of conjectures
—is very much needed, but not to be sought here: my
notes on the Greek text are normally restricted to record-
ing conjectures by modern scholars, and are thus very limited; manuscript readings are reported at all only in these
cases, and are usually taken from Immisch's 1923 Teubner
edition, which I judged to be most accurate.

Many allusions in the *Characters* to the daily life of
Athens require explanation; so when necessary I have
not hesitated to annotate the translation more (on 16, "Superstition," *much* more) than may be customary for a
Loeb volume. My translations of the individual titles were

chosen to suit the descriptions ("Griping," "Sponging," "Chiseling") rather than to render a single Greek word; but the Additional Notes give an account of each trait's literal meaning, and its treatment in ancient literature.

For the section numbers within each character I follow the standard numeration (Steinmetz, Navarre, Immisch), rather than Diels' Oxford Classical Text.

For advice and suggestions I owe thanks to many more than I could name. But I cannot pass over Peter Bing, who lent me his notes from what must have been fascinating lectures on the *Characters* by the late Konrad Gaiser; William Fortenbaugh, not only for the splendid new edition of the fragments of Theophrastus but also for comments and hints on the Introduction; Rudolf Kassel, who introduced me to the dissertation on the *Characters* by Markus Stein, who in turn generously allowed me to use it in advance of publication and made countless acute corrections of my own work; and, especially, Zeph Stewart, for many hours of careful reading of my results, and painstaking criticism combined with unfailing encouragement.

Ithaca, New York   Jeffrey Rusten
August 1992

The reprint of 2002 has allowed the opportunity for some corrections and updates, deriving especially from Robin Lane Fox, "Theophrastus' *Characters* and the Historian," *Proceedings of the Cambridge Philological Society* 42 (1996) 127–170, and from James Diggle (who is now preparing a new editon of the *Characters* with commentary).

INTRODUCTION

Theophrastus' range of interests almost matched that of his teacher Aristotle, from great works on botany,[1] studies on winds, weather, and many other topics in natural science, to logic and metaphysics, rhetoric and poetics, politics and ethics.[2] He would doubtless be astonished to learn that he is best remembered today for a little book only marginal to these studies and preserved only in a mutilated, perhaps abbreviated, form. Yet his *Characters* became a paradigm for European literature, and in the seventeenth and eighteenth centuries found translators and imitators in England, France, and Germany.

Before turning to its relatively recent influence, however, we must first look at its author's career, the character of the book itself, and its affinities with ancient ethical, comic, and rhetorical writings, as well as several difficult (perhaps insoluble) problems: how the book came into being, why the text is in such lamentable condition, and to what extent the method and substance of this book can

---

[1] *Inquiry into Plants*, ed. and tr. A. Hort (2 vols., Loeb Classical Library, 1916); *De Causis Plantarum*, ed. and tr. B. Einarson and G. K. K. Link (3 vols., Loeb Classical Library, 1976–1990).

[2] See the bibliography in Wehrli, "Der Peripatos" 475–476. (For abbreviations and works cited by author or short title only see the Bibliography.)

be reconciled with what we know of the philosopher Theophrastus himself.

THEOPHRASTUS

Theophrastus was born in Eresus, on the island of Lesbos, ca. 370 B.C. He may have studied philosophy earlier, but at least by the age of 25 he began to work with Aristotle, who after the death of Plato had left Athens for the patronage of Hermias at Assos, a town near Theophrastus' home.[3] Hermias was executed by the Persians in 341; the young man followed his master first to Macedonia and the court of Philip, then joined him on his return to Athens after 334, where he was recognized as Aristotle's preeminent student and designated successor.

Theophrastus' residence in Athens coincided with a turbulent period in its political history,[4] some of which is mirrored in the *Characters*. Despite the power of Macedonia, the city remained democratic, under the leadership of Lycurgus, until his death in 324.[5] The subsequent death of Alexander himself threw all into confusion, beginning with the Athenian uprising against Alexander's regent Antipater

[3] For speculations on this period see Konrad Gaiser, *Theophrast in Assos* (Abhandlungen der Heidelberger Akademie der Wissenschaften, 1985.3). See in general the sketch of the lives of Aristotle (by H. Flashar) and Theophrastus in Wehrli, "Der Peripatos" 230–234, 477, and Theophr. fr., Introd. pp. 1–2.

[4] See W. S. Ferguson, *Hellenistic Athens* (London 1911) chapters 1–3, Claude Mossé, *Athens in Decline* (London 1973) chapter 5.

[5] F. Mitchel, "Lykourgan Athens, 388–322," *Semple Lectures*, series 2 (Cincinnati 1970).

in 322 (when Aristotle himself withdrew again from Athens, leaving his school behind, and died in Euboea). Athens' defeat by Antipater led to a new oligarchic constitution under the Athenian conservative Phocion, with a limitation on the number of citizens.[6] But then Antipater's death (319) produced a further struggle among his heirs, and the remnants of Alexander's family, for control of Greece: his designated successor Polyperchon, in partnership with Alexander's half-brother Philip III Arridaios, proclaimed the autonomy of all Greek states in exchange for their support. Democratic forces in Athens rallied to him, and Phocion was executed. But Polyperchon's power waned, and in 317 Antipater's son Cassander assumed control of Athens, which he placed under the control of Demetrius of Phaleron, a student of Aristotle and staunch supporter of Theophrastus. Demetrius fled to Egypt in 307, and Theophrastus was driven for a year into exile;[7] but after his return he remained firmly established as the head of the most popular philosophical school in Athens until his death ca. 285 B.C.

STYLE, STRUCTURE, AND SETTING OF THE CHARACTERS

As preserved in the medieval manuscripts, the *Characters* consist of: a *Table of Contents* and a *Preface* explaining the

---

[6] L. A. Trittle, *Phocion the Good* (London 1988).

[7] Through a decree against non-Athenian heads of schools, moved by a certain Sophocles of Sounion. J. P. Lynch, *Aristotle's School* (Berkeley 1972) 103–104, Theophr. fr 1.38; cf. Alexis *PCG* fr. 99, with the commentary of W. G. Arnott (Cambridge 1996) 858–859.

genesis and purpose of the whole collection; and *thirty chapters*, each with:

1) *Title*: a single-word personality trait, always ending in -ια;

2) *Definition* in abstract terms of this quality;

3) *Description*, the longest part of each chapter, introduced with the formula "the X man is the sort who . . .," and continuing in a series of infinitives giving characteristic actions;

4) *Epilogue* (in some cases) in a more rhetorical style, with moralizing generalizations.

It is certain that two of these elements—the preface and the epilogues—are not by Theophrastus himself, being later (perhaps much later) additions to the text. Of the definitions, one (the first) is certainly a later addition, and several others which seem irrelevant to the descriptions they introduce, or seem to be taken from other sources, are probably interpolations as well. (For the reasons behind these assumptions, see pages 30–32 below.)

What remains at the heart of the work are the descriptions, which are priceless for several reasons. First, because of their style. Theophrastus was a master of Greek rhetoric both in theory and practice—he received his name ("the divine speaker") from it, being originally called Tyrtamus (fr. 5A-6)—but here he disregards its constraints: there is no avoidance of hiatus, no logical or rhetorical figures or structures. An introductory formula "X is the sort who . . ." (τοιοῦτός τις, οἷος . . .)[8] leads to an

---

[8] For the style compare *PCG* Antiphanes fr. 166.6, and the treatise on letter writing ascribed to a certain Demetrius (R. Kassel, *Kleine Schriften* [Berlin 1991] 420–421).

infinitive containing the characteristic act— usually quali-
fied by a series of participles giving the circumstances—
followed by another participle and infinitive, and then another and another (sometimes interrupted with δεινὸς καί
. . . "he is also apt to . . .") until the description ends. Not all
scholars have found this style pleasing, and the attempt to
account for its singularity has led to theories that it springs
from lecture notes or a personal sketchbook, or even that it
is the work of an excerptor, or a forgery utterly unrelated
to Theophrastus; the only certain conclusion is that it is
unique in Greek literature.[9]

Second, the setting is anything but timeless or idealiz-
ing, being unmistakably the Athens of the last few decades
of the fourth century B.C., whose customs, institutions,
and prejudices form the backdrop of every character's actions. Only the fragments of contemporary Athenian comedies offer an equal insight into the city's daily life.

Finally, the descriptions are equally distinctive as literary portraiture.[10] They are never generalizations, but catalogues of vivid detail (some indeed so distinctive that they
are difficult to interpret). We learn, for example, the exact
words of the obsequious man, the boor, or the babbler,
which gods the superstitious man placates on which
days, how the chiseler avoids school fees, how the rumor-

[9] Critics of its monotony include R. Porson and H. Sauppe
(see Gomperz 5), but most others have been more generous: see
especially Pasquali, "Sui caratteri" 47–56.

[10] For the background see Ivo Bruns, *Das literarische Porträt
der Griechen im fünften und vierten Jahrhundert* (Berlin 1896);
comparisons between Theophrastus and the portraiture of
Lysippus in T. B. L. Webster, *Art and Literature in Fourth Century Athens* (London 1956) 124–133.

monger or the garrulous man finds an audience and the ungenerous man avoids one, which market vendors the shameless man franchises, how much he makes each day, and where he carries his earnings.

DATE OF THE *CHARACTERS*

Numerous allusions in the *Characters* themselves seem to offer hints about when they were composed.[11] The most tantalizing clue is in the gossip spread by the rumor-monger in *Characters* 8: he claims that Polyperchon and "the King" have defeated and captured Cassander, and that the current Athenian leadership is worried. C. Cichorius thought this rumor suited best the situation in Athens in late 319, when a decree of the new regent Polyperchon had encouraged Athens to restore its democracy, and Cassander appeared weak;[12] in that case the king will have been Philip Arridaios, and the worried Athenian leader, Phocion (Plutarch, *Phocion* 32.1, Diodorus 18.55–56).

Cichorius went on to argue that other chronological indications are consistent with 319 as well: thus *Characters* 23 assumes that the famine at Athens and the campaigns of Alexander are over, but that Antipater is still alive and in Macedon, which points to 326–3, 322-1, or 319. There is

[11] On dating *Characters* see A. Boegehold, "The Date of Theophrastus' *Characters*," *Transactions of the American Philological Association* 90 (1959) 15–19; Stein, *Definition und Schilderung* 21–45; Robin Lane Fox, "Theophrastus' *Characters* and the Historian," *PCPS* 42 (1995) 127–170 (especially 134–138).

[12] See C. Cichorius, Introduction to the edition of the Leipzig Philological Society, lvii–lxii.

mention of liturgies (23.6, 26.6), which were abolished by Demetrius of Phaleron (317–307) and not reinstated thereafter. The complaints of the authoritarian in *Characters* 26 seem to have been composed under a democracy—as do the democratic sentiments of the patron of scoundrels (29.5). But the fact that in 26.2 commissioners are being elected rather than chosen by lot (cf. Aristotle, *Constitution of Athens* 56.4) suggests a date after 322.[13]

But recent scholarship has endorsed other candidates for "the king" of *Characters* 8[14] and Cichorius' insistence that all 30 sketches were composed in 319 seems somewhat doubtful. It is intrinsically just as plausible that different characters have different dramatic dates, and the various sketches may have been composed over a period of 10–15 years.[15]

There are other features of the *Characters* which recall anecdotal evidence on the life and school of Theophrastus.

[13] See Boegehold in TAPA 90:18, and Stein, *Definition und Schilderung.*

[14] Alexander IV, or Heracles, in which case the nervous current ruler of Athens will be Demetrius of Phaleron (and in any case the story is a lie). A detailed review of all the possibilities in Stein, *Definition und Schilderung* 21–36. Christian Habicht, *Athens from Alexander to Anthony* (Cambridge MA 1997) 123, prefers 317 B.C.; Lane Fox 309.

[15] This seems a reasonable assumption, particularly since 319 was a year of constant crisis in Athens; the attempted prosecution of Theophrastus by the democrat Hagnonides (Diogenes Laertius 5.37) may belong to this year also (Boegehold in TAPA 90:17). Habicht suggests "the years 324–315 should be accepted as reasonable boundaries." Lane Fox (PCPS 43:138) suggests even wider boundaries, from the lifetime of Alexander to 309.

He and his students dressed rather well, and had a reputation for high living;[16] it is therefore noteworthy that there are four varieties of stinginess, but none of extravagance (see the Additional Notes on *Characters* 9). His elegant manners and sophistication were well known; and we find in this work a number of types who lack social graces or make themselves foolish in society (see Additional Notes on *Characters* 4). He discussed sacrifice at length elsewhere (fr. 584A–585), and constantly employs it here to illustrate his types (9.2, 12.11, 15.5, 16 *passim*, 17.1, 21.7, 21.11, 22.4, 27.5); his father was a fuller, a trade with which his characters often have dealings (18.6, 22.8, 30.10; for the prominence of this craft in *De Causis Plantarum* see Einarson and Link, Introd. viii note a).

THE *CHARACTERS* AND
ANCIENT LITERATURE[17]

Ethics

The meanings of ancient Greek χαρακτήρ are derived from an original sense of an *inscribing* (χαράσσειν) onto a surface: the *imprint* on a coin, the *form* of a letter, often the *style* of an author for rhetorical analysis.[18] "Character" in the modern sense is *not* one of its meanings—the Greek

---

16 Stein, *Definition und Schilderung* cites Teles fr. 30 Hense, Theophr. fr. 12, 23, Lycon fr. 7, 8, 14 Wehrli.

17 For the concept in general see the survey in C. B. R. Pelling (ed.), *Characterization and Individuality in Greek Literature* (Oxford 1990).

18 See A. Koerte, "ΧΑΡΑΚΤΗΡ," *Hermes* 64 (1928) 69–86.

word for "character" is usually ἦθος[19]—and if it were not firmly established, Theophrastus' title might better be rendered "traits." Basic to his whole enterprise is the notion that individual good or bad traits of character may be isolated and studied separately, a notion formulated most memorably by his teacher Aristotle in the *Nicomachean Ethics* Book 2:[20] for each range of emotion (fear, anger) or sphere of action (wealth, honor), Aristotle defines moral virtue and vice (ἀρετὴ καὶ κακία ἠθική, literally "excellence and badness of character") by their relation to the middle: too large or small an amount is to be avoided as a vice, and only by remaining between the extremes can one attain virtue.[21]

Although Aristotle would not reduce moral behavior to a formula,[22] he is nonetheless able to apply this doctrine to

[19] For examples of the various Greek terms for character see O. Thimme, Φύσις, τρόπος, ἦθος (Diss. Göttingen, 1935).

[20] Among earlier philosophic descriptions of vices are Plato's account of character types which parallel forms of government in *Republic* VIII, and the literature of national characters (Boeotian, Spartan, etc.) based ultimately on the sort of climatological determinism in the Hippocratic *Airs, Waters, Places*: see M. Goebel, *Ethnica* (Diss. Breslau 1915).

[21] This in turn is related to Greek popular wisdom that avoidance of extremes is best: Nisbet-Hubbard on Horace, *Odes* II.10.5, Hermann Kalchreuter, *Die* ΜΕΣΟΤΗΣ *bei und vor Aristoteles* (Diss. Tübingen, 1911), H.-J. Mette, "ΜΗΔΕΝ ΑΓΑΝ," *Kleine Schriften* (ed. A. Mette and B. Seidensticker, Frankfurt 1988) 1–38.

[22] See W. F. R. Hardie, "Virtue Is a Mean," chapter 7 in *Aristotle's Ethical Theory* (second ed. Oxford 1980).

THEOPHRASTUS

a wide range of traditionally named virtues and vices of character (*Nicomachean Ethics* 1107a33–1108b7):[23]

ἔλλειψις (deficiency)	μεσότης (mean)	ὑπερβολή (excess)
*δειλός (coward)	ἀνδρεία (courage)	θρασύς (rash)
*ἀναίσθητος (unable to feel)	σωφροσύνη (temperance)	ἀκολασία (intemperance)
*ἀνελευθερία (lack of generosity)	ἐλευθεριότης (generosity)	ἀσωτία (profligacy)
μικροπρεπεία (niggardliness)	μεγαλοπρεπεία (magnificence)	βαναυσία (vulgarity)
μικροψυχία (pusillanimity)	μεγαλοψυχία (magnanimity)	χαυνότης (vanity)
ἀφιλότιμος (unambitious)	φιλότιμος (ambitious-good)	φιλότιμος (ambitious-bad)
ἀοργησία (passivity)	πραότης (gentleness)	ὀργιλότης (irascibility)
*εἰρωνεία (self-deprecation)	ἀλήθεια (truthfulness)	*ἀλαζονεία (boastfulness)
*ἀγροικία (boorishness)	εὐτραπελία (wit)	βωμολοχία (buffoonery)
δύσερις (quarrelsomeness)	φιλία (friendliness)	*ἄρεσκος (obsequious)
δύσκολος (bad-tempered)	φιλία (friendliness)	*κόλαξ (flatterer)
*ἀναίσχυντος (shameless)	αἰδήμων (polite)	καταπλήξ (bashful)
ἐπιχαιρεκακία (spitefulness)	νέμεσις (righteous indignation)	φθόνος (enviousness)

14

Aristotle goes on in Books 3 and 4 (1115a6–1128b33) to describe almost all of these virtues and vices in detail. Although considerably more abstract, his descriptions of individual vices, both here and in the parallel discussions in the *Eudemian Ethics* (2.1220b21–1221b3, 3.1228a23–1234b11) and the Pseudo-Aristotelian *Magna Moralia* (1.1190b9–1193a37), seem to be precursors of some of the *Characters* (see the Additional Notes on individual characters); it is easy to imagine Theophrastus' work as inspired by his teacher's approach to vices.

Peripatetic authors after Theophrastus wrote works in a similar style. A fragment of Satyrus' "On Characters" condemning profligacy is preserved by Athenaeus (4.168c). Extensive quotations from Ariston of Keos, "On Relieving Arrogance," are given by Philodemus, *On Vices* Book 10 (for text and translation see the Appendix); their style and use of detail show a remarkable resemblance to the *Characters*. Lycon's description of a drunkard is quoted by Rutilius Lupus 2.7 (Lycon fr. 26 Wehrli). Other treatments of vice owe something to character writing as well: Seneca and Plutarch[24] are the most obvious examples, but also evidently Posidonius (fr. 176 Kidd).

---

[23] The listing here is based on the *Nicomachean Ethics*; there is a slightly different list in exactly this format in *Eudemian Ethics* 1120b38ff. I give the abstract noun when Aristotle uses one, otherwise the adjective; an asterisk means it is found also in the *Characters*.

[24] He wrote essays *On Garrulity, How to Tell a Flatterer From a Friend, On Superstition, On Meddling, On the Love of Money,* and *On Extravagant Self-Praise*.

15

Comedy and Satire

For all their ethical basis, Theophrastus' sketches—especially in extended scenes like "Idle Chatter" (3), "Rumor-Mongering" (8), or "Cowardice" (25)—quite obviously have comic affinities as well. Characterization by type was already an important feature in Aristophanes,[25] but it was the comedy of the fourth century which brought stock characters to the fore:[26] the flattering parasite, the greedy or mistrustful old man, the shameless pimp or the braggart soldier. The remains of comedies of this period (or their Roman adaptations) offer instructive parallels to the behavior of Theophrastus' characters,[27] and the titles of fourth-century plays now lost suggest that traits of character were sometimes central (those with an asterisk are in Theophrastus also): *The Boor* (Ἄγροικος), *The Mistrustful Man* (Ἄπιστος), The Glutton (Ἄπληστος), The Profligate (Ἄσωτος), *The Superstitious Man* (Δεισιδαίμων), The Grouch (Δύσκολος), *The Flatterer* (Κόλαξ), *The Griper* (Μεμψίμοιρος), The Loner (Μονότροπος), The Meddler (Πολυπράγμων), The Miser (Φιλάργυρος), The Busybody (Φιλοπράγμων).

Menander, the greatest author of New Comedy, has

[25] W. Süss, "Zur Komposition der altattischen Komödie," *Rheinisches Museum* 63 (1908) 12–38, R. G. Ussher, "Old Comedy and 'Character': Some Comments," *Greece and Rome* 24 (1977) 71–79.

[26] H.-G. Nesselrath, *Die attische mittlere Komödie* (Berlin 1991) 280–330.

[27] R. L. Hunter, *The New Comedy of Greece and Rome* (Cambridge 1985) 148–151.

even been claimed as Theophrastus' student.[28] Not only does he appear to echo several other Theophrastan works in his writing, he manipulates his characters with as much skill as Theophrastus—in fact, even more skill, which prompts caution in assuming any direct influence. His philosophizing passages, impressive in themselves, are often given an ironic turn when put in the mouths of unsuitable characters. His stock characters too (especially soldiers and prostitutes) may often surprise us by transcending their limitations.[29]

Satire and comedy were often linked by ancient theorists,[30] and here too there are occasional resemblances to the *Characters*, especially in the vivid portraits by Hipponax, Herodas, Phoenix, and Cercidas. Other such sketches are found in the poem by Semonides of Amorgos (seventh century B.C.) on types of women: their various vices (e.g., filthiness, cunning, extravagance) are explained by their creation from animals (e.g., the pig, fox, horse) or other elements (the sea). Only the industrious woman,

[28] The imperial writer Pamphile (*FHG* III fr. 10) as quoted by Diogenes Laertius 5.36; for a detailed examination of the tradition of Menander as philosopher see Konrad Gaiser, "Menander und der Peripatos," *Antike und Abendland* 13 (1967) 8–40.

[29] For the "philosophical" passages—note especially the slave Onesimos' garbled psychological theory, *Epitrepontes* 1092–1099—see Gaiser (preceding note); for the stock characters, Nesselrath (above n. 26) 333, and Wilamowitz' oft-repeated dictum (R. Kassel, *Kleine Schriften* [Berlin 1991], 508 n. 6): "Theophrastus gives us types; Menander gives us people."

[30] Horace, *Satires* 1.4, *Prolegomena* to Comedy p. 3 Koster.

created from the bee, is praiseworthy.[31] Among Roman
satirists, Horace discusses greed (1.2, 2.2), and offers an
extensive portrait of a bore (1.9); Martial (3.63) defines the
bellus homo with a Theophrastan eye for detail, and Juvenal skewers the miser (14.126–134). The diatribes of
Teles adapt some of the same techniques, and Lucian even
shows a direct knowledge of the *Characters*.[32]

Rhetoric[33]

Character sketching could also be an important weapon in
court: Aristotle's account of moral traits in the *Ethics* is
complemented by a rhetorical discussion of the contrast-
ing traits of the old and young in *Rhetoric* 2.12–14.[34] Just as
La Bruyère saw that fictitious characters could be mixed
with the literary portrait of a real individual, so the ancient
rhetorical tradition demanded exercises in character
drawing as practice for historical portraits from life. Called
χαρακτηρισμοί or ἠθολογίαι, these seem to have been
standard exercises in all rhetorical training, and are mentioned by Cicero (*Topica* 83), and Quintilian (1.9.3);[35] a

31 Semonides fr. 7 West; H. Lloyd-Jones, *Females of the Spe-*
cies (London 1975); Walter Marg, *Der Charakter in der Sprache*
der frühgriechischen Dichtung (Würzburg 1938).

32 M. D. MacLeod, *Mnemosyne* 27 (1974) 75–76.

33 See in general Wilhelm Süss, *Ethos: Studien zur älteren*
griechischen Rhetorik (Leipzig 1910).

34 A. Dyroff, *Der Peripatos über das Greisenalter* (Studien zur
Geschichte und Kultur des Altertums 21.3, Paderborn 1939).

35 Probably also by Suetonius, *De Grammaticis* 4.

fine sample of a braggart is given by the *Rhetorica ad Herennium* 4.50–51.64. They led not only to portraits like Cicero's *In Pisonem*, but also the famous sketches of historical figures in Sallust and Tacitus.[36]

PURPOSE OF THE *CHARACTERS*

The authenticity of the *Characters* as a work of Theophrastus, although doubted (without argument) by scholars as distinguished as Porson, Haupt, Vettorio, and Valckenaer, is as good as proved, as we have seen, by its allusions to Theophrastus' lifetime. Yet it is easy to see why it was suspected: the work's subject and its execution seem as alien to the philosopher's other work as its style.

Theophrastus' motive for writing the *Characters* might be sought in his ethical works, where several fragments offer connections, for example, the attested title "On Characters" (Περὶ ἠθῶν fr. 436.1); or fr. 465, where he notes how much care is devoted to the choice of a city, friends, even the route for a journey, while the more important choice of a way of life is left to chance; or fr. 449A, on virtue and vice, which closely resembles Aristotle—we have seen that the division of the *Characters* into traits, and even some of their names, recalls the *Nicomachean Ethics* as well.

---

[36] The most detailed introduction (although it slights rhetorical influence) is Christopher Gill, "The Question of Character-Development: Plutarch and Tacitus," *Classical Quarterly* 33 (1983) 469–487. For later parallels see David Nichol Smith, *Characters from the Histories and Memoirs of the Seventeenth Century* (Oxford 1918).

But the differences between the *Nicomachean Ethics* and the *Characters* are even more obvious. The latter deals only with faults, while Aristotle is far more interested in virtues than in vices; Aristotle develops an argument about virtue as a mean, which is then illustrated with specific examples from spheres like reactions to danger, behavior with money, treatment of other individuals, leading to extended consideration of the virtues of justice and friendship; the *Characters*, on the other hand, are utterly lacking in analysis, their order of presentation apparently random—traits relating to money, friendship, or talk are not treated together, or compared in any way.

Most importantly, the *motives* behind the characters' actions are not discussed.[37] Much of the behavior detailed here—things like charging compound interest and late fees for loans, hiring flute girls for dinner parties, dedicating skulls of sacrificed cows, shirking payments for public service, seeking purification after incurring pollution— is in fact very close to normal, and well-attested for Athens of the fifth and fourth centuries. If the *Characters* are to offer ethical instruction, we need an analysis such as Terence (probably following Menander) puts in the mouth of Micio (*Adelphi* 821–825):

> multa in homine, Demea,
> signa insunt ex quibus coniectura facile fit,

---

[37] See especially W. Fortenbaugh, "Die Charaktere Theophrasts," *Rheinisches Museum* 118 (1975) 64. The opening definitions of each character are completely inadequate as indications of motive, and their authenticity is in any case suspect (see below at note 54).

duo quom idem faciunt, saepe ut possis dicere
'hoc licet inpune facere huic, illi non licet.'
non quo dissimilis res sit, sed quo is qui facit.

>   In a person, Demeas, there are many
> clues that lead to an obvious conclusion. Thus
> even though two people behave the same, you can
>   usually say
> "this man can get away with it—that one can't."
> Not because the behavior is different, but because
>   the *person* is.

Thus support is lacking for the idea that the *Characters* is a series of excerpts made from Theophrastus' ethical writings,[38] or was written to illustrate them.

Some have suggested its purpose was not ethical at all. One alternative candidate is comedy.[39] Since there are no examples of virtue in the *Characters*, we are reminded of Aristotle's dictum (*Poetics* 1449a32, cf. 1448a1–5) that the depiction of people we do not take seriously (φαυλότεροι) is the province of comedy. Aristotle and his successors wrote frequently on the techniques and ethical implications of comedy. Their exact views are far from clear, but the so-called "Tractatus Coislinianus," which has peripatetic affinities,[40] lists in section XII three "characters of

[38] Formulated by Sonntag (see p. 30 below), but refuted by Gomperz, "Über die Charaktere Theophrasts," 4–8.

[39] R. G. Ussher, "Old Comedy and ' Character' ," *Greece and Rome* 24 (1977) 71–79; W. Fortenbaugh, "Theophrast über den komischen Charakter," *Rheinisches Museum* 124 (1981) 245–260.

[40] Most recently and fully R. Janko, *Aristotle on Comedy* (London 1984) and Nesselrath (above n. 26) 102–162.

comedy" (ἤθη κωμῳδίας), the βωμολοχικά, ἀλαζονικά, and εἰρωνικά ("buffoons, braggarts, and tricksters"), two of which appear in the *Characters* (1, 23), the other in Aristotle (*Nicomachean Ethics* 1108a24). Works "On Comedy" and "On the Ridiculous" are ascribed to Theophrastus himself (frs. 709–710), as well as a definition of the genre (fr. 708).

Another suggested purpose is rhetorical instruction.[41] There is no doubt that this is the use to which the work was eventually put; indeed it owes its very survival to its inclusion among the handbooks of the schools; but we have no trace in the rhetorical writings of Theophrastus (fr. 667–707) that he treated characterization, nor in the *Characters* themselves that they have such a purpose; it might indeed seem to be ruled out if the title ἠθικοὶ χαρακτῆρες in Diogenes Laertius 5.47 is correct.

What ultimately defeats any attempt to find an ethical, comic, or rhetorical basis in the *Characters* is the fact that there is no trace in them of structure or analysis at all. Like any other work of fictional literature—and unlike any other work of Theophrastus—the *Characters* are presented as pure entertainment. The question is therefore not the work's purpose so much as its style, and here three

[41] O. Immisch, *Philologus* 11 (1898) 193–212, Süss, *Ethos* (above n. 33) 167, A. Rostagni, *Rivista di filologia* 48 (1920) 417–443, D. Furley, *Symbolae Osloenses* 30 (1953) 56–60, S. Trenkner, *The Greek Novella in the Classical Period* (Cambridge 1958) 147–154, Fortenbaugh, "Theophrastus, the *Characters* and Rhetoric," chapter 3 in *Rutgers University Studies in Classical Humanities* 6 (1993).

scholars have made complementary suggestions: 1) Gomperz (11–13), that the *Characters* bear the same relation to Theophrastus' ethical works as the sketchbook of a painter does to finished paintings—he compared the connection of Aristotle's *Constitution of Athens* to the *Politics*, his *Homeric Problems* to the *Poetics*; in the school of Aristotle, such preliminary collections of materials were published, though they would not be today; 2) Pasquali ("Sui caratteri" 51–3) points to the radically unusual style, which he regards as an experimental publication based on lectures; 3) Gaiser[42] also suggested the lecture hall, as the place where the giving of information, moral instruction, and entertainment intersect.

Indeed Theophrastus' public lectures seem to have been enormously popular and entertaining: Diogenes Laertius 5.37 tells us that he had 2000 students (cf. Theophrastus fr. 15), and Hermippus (fr. 51 Wehrli = Theophrastus fr. 12) that he punctuated his lectures with gestures, citing in particular his mimicry of a glutton. Some other works of Theophrastus, known only from fragments, may have been as lively ("On Marriage," fr. 486), and the peripatetic school after him interested itself in a wide range of popular and practical ethical questions in an anecdotal style.[43]

---

[42] To my knowledge this suggestion was never published; I know it from notes on his Tübingen lectures on the *Characters* lent me by Peter Bing.

[43] Wehrli, "Peripatos" 467–469. The ethical fragments of Theophrastus (fr. 436–579) include "On Drunkenness," "On Pleasure," and "Piety."

HISTORY OF THE TEXT

Medieval Manuscripts

The most valuable individual manuscripts are:[44]

A = *Parisinus graecus* 2977, XI cent.
B = *Parisinus graecus* 1983, X–XI cent.

Both A and B contain *Characters* 1–15, the proem and the table of contents (for 1–15 only); in both manuscripts, the text of *Character* 30.5–16 is wrongly appended to *Character* 11.[45]

V = *Vaticanus graecus* 110, XIII cent., which only begins with *Character* 16, yet it alone continues to the end of *Character* 30 (29–30.5 were first edited from this manuscript by Amaduzzi in 1786).[46]

Since the text of 30.5–16 is (incorrectly) added by AB after *Character* 11, for the final sentences of the work we may compare AB and V, which reveals that at least here (al-

---

[44] The clearest and most thorough account of the medieval manuscripts is by Immisch, pp. viii–lii of the Philological Society of Leipzig edition.

[45] For detailed accounts of both these manuscripts see H. Rabe, *Rheinisches Museum* 67 (1912) 323–332, W. Abraham in Studemund, *Jahrbücher für classische Philologie* 1885 (31) 759–772, and E. Matelli, *Scrittura e civiltà* 13 (1989) 329–386.

[46] The writing is indistinct, and heavily abbreviated; see the photograph of fol. 253 r/v (*Characters* 16–21) in R. Merkelbach und H. van Thiel, *Griechisches Leseheft zur Einführung in Paläographie und Textkritik* (Göttingen 1965) no. 5 pp. 15–16.

though not necessarily elsewhere) AB gives in many cases a *shorter* text, but often a *better* one than V.

The simplest approach to reconstructing this phase of their transmission is the assumption that an original manuscript a was divided into two parts (1–15, 16–30) and copied separately; the branch of the tradition containing *Characters* 1–15 found a fragment (perhaps the final page detached) containing *Character* 30.5–16 from an abridged text, and re-copied this where it was thought to belong, at the end of *Character* 11.[47] Thus the accompanying stemma (page 26).

All manuscripts *later* than A, B, and V are divided into three groups:[48]

C, consisting of 7 manuscripts (XV–XVI cent.) containing *Characters* 1–28: Immisch pp. ix–xiii.

D, consisting of 6 manuscripts (XIV–XVI cent.) containing *Characters* 1–23: Immisch pp. xiii–xviii.

E, consisting of 32 manuscripts (XIII–XVI cent.) which never contained more than *Characters* 1–15: Immisch pp. xix–xxv.

[47] On the other hand AB is *not* derived from an abridgment for 1–15, as shown by the papyri (see below).

[48] N. G. Wilson, *Scriptorium* 16 (1962) 96–8, extends this list of manuscripts from published library catalogues: yet among the manuscripts he designates as new, nos. 3, 20, 24, and 55 were already known to Immisch (the first three only in his Teubner edition of 1923); whereas nos. 19, 34, and 63 (none designated "new") have to my knowledge never been mentioned before.

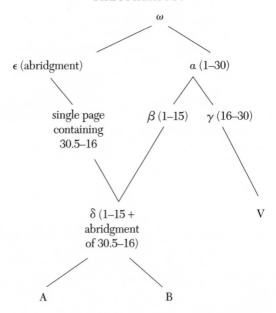

The transmission of these later families C, D, and E is more complicated: E, containing *Characters* 1–15, appears to derive from A and B, and therefore to have no independent value. The families C and D, however, derive from A and B only for the first 15 characters; after that, they copy 16–23 or 16–28 from another source, which is however not identical with V, since when V was discovered it proved to have a significantly longer text in many passages.[49] Therefore C and D must have derived *Characters* 16ff from an abridged manuscript also, producing the following stemma:

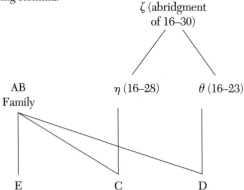

ζ (abridgment
of 16–30)

AB
Family

η (16–28)   θ (16–23)

E   C   D

The ultimate source of the abridgment ζ remains in dispute. Diels (followed by Stein, *Definition und Schilderung*, and most modern editors) believed it to be entirely derived from V, so that CD would possess no independent

[49] These so-called "additamenta Vaticana" are printed in bold type in the apparatus of the Philological Society of Leipzig edition and Immisch's 1923 Teubner edition. Steinmetz 38–41 suggested that the abridgments were carried out in the thirteenth century by Maximus Planudes, whom we know to have reworked the rhetorical corpus in A and B (H. Rabe, *Rheinisches Museum* 67 [1912] 332–337).

value; Immisch (Leipzig edition pp. xxxvi–lii, Teubner edition pp. iii–iv, followed by Pasquali and Steinmetz) maintained that occasionally C and D preserved an independent tradition.

Finally, there exists an epitome of *Characters* 1–21 in "M" (*Monacensis graecus* 505, XV cent.), which agrees mostly with B in 1–15, mostly with V in 16–21.

Papyri and Testimonia

The text offered by the medieval manuscripts of the *Characters* may be the most corrupt of any major work of Greek antiquity; yet the fragments found on papyrus suggest that it is more or less that already fixed by the first century B.C.:

P. Hamb. 143 (I B.C., *Characters* 7–8), M. Gronewald *Zeitschrift für Papyrologie und Epigraphik* 35 (1979) 21–2.

P. Herc. 1457 (I B.C., Philodemus *On flattery* citing *Character* 5). For this and other possible citations of Theophrastus among the Herculaneum papyri see Eiko Kondo, "I ' caratteri' di Teofrasto nei papiri ercolanesi," *Cronache ercolanesi* 1 (1971) 73–86, with the corrections of T. Dorandi and M. Stein, "Der älteste Textzeuge für den APECKOC des Theophrast," *ZPE* 100 (1994) 1–16.

P. Oxy. 699 (A.D. III) offers an epitome of *Characters* 25–6.

In the twelfth century the *Characters* was mentioned (and perhaps imitated, see N. G. Wilson, *Scholars of By-*

zantium [London 1983] 200–201) by Eustathius on *Iliad* 12.276 (p. 931.18) and Tzetzes, *Chiliades* 9.941.

Earliest Transmission

We have seen that the date of the *Characters* is only roughly known, while the purpose for which it was written and the earliest stages of its textual history are shrouded in mystery. But it is obvious why the work survived: every single medieval manuscript which contains it is derived from collections of treatises on rhetoric (whose central authors were Hermogenes and Aphthonius), so that it must owe its preservation to a decision to make it part of a rhetorical corpus, doubtless as an aid to the description of character. This must have occurred by the ninth century, perhaps considerably earlier.[50]

In the process of being included in rhetorical corpora, the *Characters* was prone to being shortened in transmission: as we have seen, many of the medieval manuscripts of 16–30 are presumed to derive from abridgments, and there exist two epitomes, M and P. Oxy. 699.

Yet at other stages of its history, the work was prey to expansion as well, and here the motive seems to have been to adapt the work not to rhetoric, but to moralizing instruction in ethics.[51] The evidence for these expansions is entirely subjective, since even the earliest papyri offer more or less the same sort of text we have today. Yet there can be

[50] Immisch, Philological Society of Leipzig edition, xxix–xxxv.
[51] Immisch, Philological Society of Leipzig edition, xxxvi.

little doubt that some parts of the *Characters* as we have them are later additions, of three kinds:

The Proem. Even beyond its chronological absurdities and fatuous repetitions, the introductory essay now preserved in all manuscripts gives a completely false picture of the work that is to follow. For details see the note *ad loc.* It was first shown to be a later insertion by Carl Gottlieb Sonntag, *Dissertatio in prooemium characterum Theophrasti* (Leipzig 1787).

Epilogues are appended to several *Characters* (1.7, 2.13, 3.5, 6.10, 8.10–14, 10.14, 26.6, 28.7, 29.6). The *Characters* themselves, as we have seen, employ a simple and repetitive style to describe the specific actions of a single individual. In these epilogues, by contrast, a florid style and the tendency to moralize and generalize (and consequent use of the plural) betray immediately that they are alien. They are usually considered Byzantine, although not necessarily by the same hand as the proem.[52]

Definitions are prefixed to every character: their style is uncompromisingly abstract, and they are composed of a limited number of recurring elements;[53] there are often problems in reconciling them with the character description which follows—at worst they flatly contradict it, at best they are irrelevant or offer only a partial introduction to the character described. (It is therefore especially unfortunate that they come first, since they lead the reader to

[52] Gomperz 4; Immisch, Philological Society of Leipzig edition, xxxv; Pasquali, "Sui caratteri" 67–69.

[53] For example, ὡς ὅρῳ/τύπῳ (περι)λαβεῖν in 1, 5, 9, 20, cf. 14; δόξει/δόξειεν ἂν εἶναι in 1, 4, 7, 13, 16, 23, 25, 26, 27.

try to match what follows to their formula, rather than reading the description itself.) Most suspicious is the fact that several separate collections of definitions (ethical and otherwise) circulated in antiquity, some of them falsely attributed to famous names: Pseudo-Plato, *Definitions*, Pseudo-Aristotle, *On Virtues and Vices*, and the Stoic definitions of emotions collected in *SVF* III p. 92–102. Some of the definitions in the *Characters* correspond closely either with these collections (*Characters* 5, 7, 9, 12, 16) or with a formula in Aristotelian ethical writings (*Character* 1): since they seem less at home in Theophrastus, it is probable that in at least some cases the *Characters* were "improved" by the addition of definitions from these and other collections.[54]

On the other hand, there are two strong arguments against athetizing the definitions as a group: 1) the Theophrastan imitations of Ariston of Keos in the third/second century B.C. (see the Appendix) begin with definitions as well (although much more apt ones than in Theophrastus); and 2) three of the definitions (*Char.* 2, 6, 26) are attested in papyri. If *all* the definitions in the *Characters* are post-

---

[54] The first to suggest the definitions were not Theophrastan was Hanow; the case was made more strongly by Gomperz, and more recently by Stein, *Definition und Schilderung*. On the pseudo-platonic and other definitions see Ernst A. Schmidt, *Aristoteles über die Tugend* (Berlin 1965 = Aristoteles *Werke*, ed. E. Grumach XVIII.1) 27, 140, who however proceeds from the assumption that the definitions in *Characters* are genuine. Pasquali's suggestion ("Sui caratteri," 85) that Theophrastus himself borrowed from the collections of definitions seems on chronological and intellectual grounds unlikely.

Theophrastan additions, their interpolation must have taken place extremely early.[55]

Conclusions

After working backward to investigate the history of the text, we may now speculate at a positive account of its origins and transmission until its republication in the Renaissance.

I. (ca. 325–315 B.C.) Composition of the *Characters* by Theophrastus, in an experimental style; the publication was perhaps based on lectures. (There is no reason to believe the *Characters* was one of the "lost" works of Theophrastus edited by Andronicus in the first century B.C., on which see Theophrastus fr. 37–41; but it also seems clear that the work never received the kind of scholarly attention in Alexandria that was accorded to Plato or the historians.)

II. (III–II B.C.) At least some definitions added from other sources (Ps-Plato, *Definitions*, Ps-Aristotle, *On Virtues and Vices*. *Characters* known to peripatetics Lykon, Satyros, and Ariston.

III. (I B.C.) *Characters* known to Philodemus.

---

[55] Pasquali ("Sui caratteri" 76) suggests that some of the definitions and titles have been meddled with, others not. As far as titles go (they all end in -ια), there seems reason to be skeptical when they do not match the character, being used elsewhere in a different sense: εἰρωνεία (1), ἀπόνοια (6), ἀναισχυντία (9), ἀναισθησία (14), ἀηδία (20), ὀλιγαρχία (26).

IV. (Roman empire) Beginnings of use in Roman rhetorical instruction (*Rhetorica ad Herennium*, Cicero, Quintilian): occasional epitomization (P. Oxy. 699).

V. (Later Roman empire) Proem and epilogues added to stress the work's ethical importance.

VI. (Early middle ages) Inclusion of *Characters* in the corpus of rhetorical treatises dominated by Hermogenes and Aphthonius.

VII. (IX–XI cent.) Separation of *Characters* 1–15 from 16–30; major manuscripts produced.

VIII. (Later middle ages) *Characters* mentioned by Tzetzes, Eustathius, Planudes.

THE *CHARACTERS* AND EUROPEAN LITERATURE

The *Characters* had a small but persistent influence on European literature[56] even before the seventeenth century, through the tradition of rhetorical instruction: as we have seen, several ancient rhetorical works include character sketches in the Theophrastan style, and the *Characters* itself owes its very survival into the middle ages solely to its inclusion among the rhetorical treatises of Hermogenes and Aphthonius, doubtless as a model of character depiction. Galleries of such rhetorical portraits can be found already in the prologue to *The Canterbury Tales* or the

[56] For what follows see especially Smeed, *Theophrastan Character*. There are selections from all these writings in Aldington, *A Book of Characters*.

Seven Deadly Sins in *Piers Plowman*, or Sebastian Brant's *Ship of Fools*.[57]

Although parts of it were edited as early as 1527, it was the great edition and commentary of Isaac Casaubon in 1592[58] that brought the *Characters* wider attention; his multiple corrections of the text, and commentary illustrating the background of the sketches in the life of ancient Athens, made it possible to read it with understanding for the first time. The seed it contained could fall on fertile soil: Rabelais and Cervantes had introduced new literary forms, Erasmus and others had adapted and popularized the writings of Lucian and Juvenal,[59] Montaigne had written in the Senecan manner on the components of character, and Thomas Chapman and Ben Jonson were beginning to exploit the ancient medical theory of humors to produce characters for the comic stage.[60]

[57] Smeed, *Theophrastan Character* 6–19.

[58] See Rudolf Pfeiffer, *History of Classical Scholarship* II (Oxford 1976) 120–123. (The detailed and idiosyncratic biography by Mark Pattison, *Isaac Casaubon*, second ed. Oxford 1892, largely ignores Casaubon's scholarship.) Casaubon's commentary remained standard for nearly two centuries. His first edition contained only *Characters* 1–23; 24–28 were added in 1599; 29–30 were first included in the edition by J. C. Amaduzzi, 1786.

[59] Christopher Robinson, *Lucian and His Influence in Europe* (London 1979); Gilbert Highet, *Juvenal the Satirist* (Oxford 1954) 206–218; R. M. Alden, *The Rise of Formal Satire in England Under Classical Influence* (Philadelphia 1899).

[60] Chapman's *A Humorous Days' Mirth* (in 1597) and Jonson's *Every Man in His Humour* (1598) show no direct knowledge of the *Characters*, but the character sketches spoken by Mercury and Cupid in *Cynthia's Revels* (1600) are obviously modeled on

The idea of an individual essay devoted to the description of a single psychological type was an instant success. The first to imitate it was Joseph Hall, Bishop of Norwich and later of Exeter, who not surprisingly stressed its moral aspects; his own *Characters* (first published in London in 1608) were more abstract, moralizing, and rhetorical than Theophrastus, and (following the preface, which he did not know to be spurious) included characters of virtue as well as of vice.

Hall's book itself inspired imitations for the rest of the seventeenth century; but most of these were more interested in vice (and entertainment) than in virtue and moral instruction. Apart from individual sketches issued as pamphlets or incorporated into other books, two other English collections of this period stand out. In 1614 there appeared a book of 21 characters (expanded to 83 in subsequent editions) by the late Sir Thomas Overbury and "other learned gentlemen" (among them Webster, Dekker, and Donne), often employing extravagant wordplay and metaphor, which extend the genre to reflect contemporary English life—there are characters not only of vices and virtues but trades ("The Ostler") and national types ("The Dutchman"). Then in 1628 John Earle's *Microcosmography* retained the wide range of subjects treated in Overbury, but returned to a more relaxed, less mannered style.

Hall, Overbury, and Earle provided the models for innumerable others throughout the seventeenth century in

Theophrastus; see E. C. Baldwin, "Ben Jonson's Indebtedness to the Greek Character-Sketch," *Modern Language Notes* 16 (1901) 385–396.

England, where character writing became a standard exercise, as prescribed by Ralph Johnson, *The Scholar's Guide* (1665):[61]

A Character

A Character is a witty and facetious description of the nature and qualities of some person, or sort of people.

RULES *for making it*

1. Choose a subject, *viz.* such a sort of men as will admit a variety of observation, such be, drunkards, usurers, liars, tailors, excise-men, travellers, peddlers, merchants, tapsters, lawyers, an upstart gentleman, a young Justice, a Constable, an Alderman, and the like.

2. Express their natures, qualities, conditions, practices, tools, desires, aims or ends, by witty Allegories, or Allusions, to things or terms in nature, or art, of like nature and resemblance, still striving for wit and pleasantness, together with tart nipping jerks about their vices or miscarriages.

3. Conclude with some witty and neat passage, leaving them to the effect of their follies or studies.

Among the characters from this period are extensive collections by Samuel Butler and Richard Flecknoe.[62]

   In France, Hall's *Characters* had been translated as early as 1610, but English character-writing had little in-

---

[61] Quoted by Smeed, *Theophrastan Character* 36.
[62] Aldington, *Book of Characters* 269–333, 390–4.

fluence on the great work of Jean de La Bruyère:[63] he began with a translation of Theophrastus, and continued with
his own updating, a collection of aphorisms, reflective essays, and character sketches; the latter combine elements
of Theophrastus with the then-fashionable literary "portrait": a description (usually flattering) of an unnamed figure from contemporary society, the game being to guess
the name, although "keys" were often published separately. Thus La Bruyère's characters have classical names
(Menalcas, Theophilus) rather than traits, and while they
mostly illustrate moral failings, some of them are clearly
based on real individuals as well—his work also attracted
the writers of keys. The most original of all modern character writers, La Bruyère offered an ingenious combination:
a classical model; a new twist to the genre of the "portrait";
a critical but vivid and entertaining picture of his own contemporaries; and a simplicity and precision of style which
matches La Rochefoucauld even more than Theophrastus.

In eighteenth-century England the work of La Bruyère
became more influential than the mannered formulas of
the Overbury collection, and the character found still another home in the coffeehouse periodical: *The Tatler* and
Spectator regularly featured sketches by Joseph Addison
and Richard Steele, ranging from moralizing abstraction
(e.g., Steele's "Women's Men") to accumulations of telling
detail for a single individual ("Sir Roger de Coverley,"

---

[63] *Les Caractères de Thèophraste traduits du grec avec les
Caractères ou les Moeurs de ce Siècle*, first edition 1688, subse-
quently expanded until the ninth edition of 1696. See Smeed,
Theophrastan Character chapter 2.

"Will Honeycomb"); in the *Rambler* and *Idler* Samuel Johnson followed suit.[64] The character was further adapted to use in published sermons, and to verse epistles by Alexander Pope.[65]

The writing of characters was never again to be practiced so widely, or with as much originality, as in the seventeenth and eighteenth centuries; but the nineteenth saw its migration—through such preparatory works as Dickens' *Sketches by Boz* (1836) or Thackeray's *The Book of Snobs* (1846)—to the realm of the novel, and collections of sketches were published by George Eliot (*The Impressions of Theophrastus Such*, 1879) and Trollope.[66]

Surveying such a variety of forms, purposes, and styles, we may be inclined to conclude that little remains of Theophrastus' original work apart from its brief scope and a certain concern with typology; that is why the most recent collection of characters, Elias Canetti's *Der Ohrenzeuge: Fünfzig Charaktere* (*The Earwitness: Fifty Characters*, 1974), is so striking. It contains brief essays, in no particular order, giving details of the behavior of unnamed individuals, each dominated by a single trait. The foibles of Canetti's characters are exaggerated to almost grotesque proportions, e.g. *Der Verlierer* (*The Man Who Loses Things*):

[64] Aldington, *Book of Characters* 422–476. For the influence of these periodicals on German-language characters see Smeed, *Theophrastan Character* 82–113.

[65] Benjamin Boyce, *The Character-Sketches in Pope's Poems* (Durham, North Carolina 1962).

[66] Smeed, *Theophrastan Character* 225–262.

He manages to lose everything. He starts with small things. He has a lot to lose. There are so many good places to lose things.

Pockets—he has them specially made for losing. Children, running after him on the street—"Hey, Mister!" all around him. He smiles contentedly, never bends down. He must be careful not to find anything again. No matter how many of them run after him, he won't bend down. If it's lost, it's lost. Isn't that why he brought it along? And yet, why does he still have so many things? Shouldn't he be running out of them? Are they inexhaustible? They are, but no one sees that. He seems to have a huge house full of little objects, and it seems impossible to get rid of them all. . . .

The surreal effect is new; but in their simplicity and use of striking detail and his utter silence about these peoples' motives, and his purpose in writing them—there is no preface—Canetti's *Characters* revert almost completely to the Theophrastan form.[67]

---

[67] Smeed *Theophrastan Character* 130–131, who also gives (367–368) numerous examples of character sketches from popular literature in England of the 1960's and 70's, to which could be added even a popular song: "A Dedicated Follower of Fashion" (The Kinks, 1966).

Modern scholarly literature with an implicit similarity in approach to Theophrastus might be sought in, e.g. the typologies of Jungian psychologists, the trait-theory of Gordon Allport (*Personality*, New York 1937, chapter 3), or sociologists who delineate types (see the essays collected in Lewis A. Coser, ed., *The Pleasures of Sociology*, New York 1980, 232ff).

BIBLIOGRAPHY

Manuscripts

A = *Parisinus graecus* 2977, XI cent., containing *Characters* 1–15.

B = *Parisinus graecus* 1983, X–XI cent., containing *Characters* 1–15.

V = *Vaticanus graecus* 110, XIII cent., containing *Characters* 16–30.

M = *Monacensis graecus* 505, XV cent., an epitome of *Characters* 1–21.

C = a family of 7 manuscripts (XV–XVI cent.) containing *Characters* 1–28.

D = a family of 6 manuscripts (XIV–XVI cent.) containing *Characters* 1–23.

E = a family of 32 manuscripts (XIII–XVI cent.) which never contained more than *Characters* 1–15.

c, d, e = at least one manuscript of the families C, D, or E.

P. Hamb. 143 (I B.C.), containing *Characters* 7–8

P. Herc. 1457 (I B.C.), Philodemus *On flattery* citing *Character* 5

P. Oxy. 699 (A.D. III), an epitome of *Characters* 25–6.

Abbreviations

FGrHist	*Die Fragmente der griechischen Historiker*, ed. Felix Jacoby, Berlin-Leiden 1922–.
FHG	*Fragmenta historicorum graecorum*, ed. Carl and Theodor Müller, 5 vols. Paris 1841–1870.
LSJ	H. G. Liddell and R. Scott, *A Greek-English Lexicon*, 9th ed. revised by Sir Henry Stuart Jones, Oxford 1925–1940.
Paroem. Graec.	E. Leutsch and F. Schneidewin, *Corpus paroemiographorum graecorum*, 2 vols., Göttingen 1839–1851.
PCG	R. Kassel and C. Austin, *Poetae comici Graeci*, Berlin 1983–.
RE	Pauly and Wissowa, *Real-enzyclopädie der classischen Altertumswissenschaft*, Stuttgart 1894–1979.
SVF	J. von Arnim (ed.), *Stoicorum veterum fragmenta*, 4 vols. Leipzig 1905–1924.
Theophr. fr.	W. M. Fortenbaugh, P. M. Huby, R. W. Sharples, D. Gutas, *Theophrastus of Eresus: Sources for His Life, Writings, Thought and Influence*, Philosophia Antiqua 54, 2 vols. Leiden 1992.
Wehrli	F. Wehrli, *Die Schule des Aristoteles, Texte und Kommentar*, 10 vols. and 2 supplements, Basel 1967–1978. (Cited for the fragments of peripatetic philosophers.)

BIBLIOGRAPHY

Selected Editions and Commentaries

Casaubon, Isaac *Theophrasti notationes morum*, 3rd ed. Lyon 1617.

Korais, Adamantios *Les caractères de Theophraste*, Paris 1799.

Foss, H. E. *Theophrasti Characteres* (Bibliotheca Teubneriana) Leipzig 1858.

Philological Society of Leipzig (M. Bechert, C. Cichorius, A. Giesecke, R. Holland, J. Ilberg, O. Immisch, R. Meister, W. Ruge), *Theophrasts Charaktere*, edited with translation and commentary, Leipzig 1897.

Diels, Hermann *Theophrasti Characteres* (Oxford Classical Texts) Oxford 1909.

Navarre, Octave *Theophraste, Caractères* (Association Guillaume Budé) Paris 1920.

Immisch, Otto *Theophrasti Characteres* (Bibliotheca Teubneriana) Leipzig 1923.

Edmonds, J. M. *The Characters of Theophrastus* (Loeb Classical Library; with Herodes, Cercidas and the Choliambic Poets) London 1929.

Ussher, R. G. *The Characters of Theophrastus*, edited with an Introduction, Commentary and Index, 2nd ed. London 1993.

Steinmetz, Peter *Theophrast, Charaktere*, edited with commentary, 2 vols., Munich 1960–62.

Selected Books and Articles

Aldington, Richard *A Book of Characters*, New York, 1924.

Fortenbaugh, William "Die Charaktere Theophrasts," *Rheinisches Museum* 118 (1975) 62–82.

Gomperz, Theodor "Über die Charaktere Theophrasts," *Sitzungsberichte der kaiserlichen Akademie der Wissenschaften*, Vienna, ph.-hist. Klasse, Vol. 117.10 (1889).

Gordon, G. S. "Theophrastus and His Imitators" 49–86 in Gordon (ed.), *English Literature and the Classics*, Oxford 1912.

Hanow, F. *De Theophrasti characterum libello*, Diss. Bonn, 1858.

Kondo, Eiko "I 'caratteri' di Teofrasto nei papiri ercolanesi," *Cronache ercolanesi* 1 (1971) 73–86.

Robin Lane Fox, "Theophrastus' *Characters* and the Historian," *Proceedings of the Cambridge Philological Society* 42 (1996) 127–170.

Pasquali, Giorgio "Sui *caratteri* di Teofrasto," 47–96 in *Scritti filologici*, ed. F. Bornmann, G. Pascucci, S. Timpanaro, with an introduction by A. La Penna, Florence 1986 (originally in *Rassegna italiana di lingue e letterature classiche* 1 [1918] 73–79, 124–150, 2 [1919] 1–21).

Smeed, J. W. *The Theophrastan 'Character': the History of a Literary Genre*, Oxford 1985.

Stein, Markus *Definition und Schilderung in den Theophrasts Charaktaren (Beiträge zur Altertumskunde* 28) Stuttgart 1992.

Ussher, R. G. "Some Characters of Athens, Rome and England," *Greece and Rome* 13 (1966) 64–78.

Wehrli, F. "Der Peripatos bis zum Beginn der römischen Kaiserzeit," 459–599 in H. Flashar (ed.), *Die Philosophie der Antike* III: *ältere Akademie, Aristoteles, Peripatos* (=Friedrich Überweg, *Grundriss der Geschichte der Philosophie*, Antike vol. 3, new ed. Basel 1983).

Wilson, N. G. "The Manuscripts of Theophrastus," *Scriptorium* 16 (1962) 96–102.

ΧΑΡΑΚΤΗΡΕΣ

ΧΑΡΑΚΤΗΡΕΣ	CHARACTERS[1]
1. ΕΙΡΩΝΕΙΑ	Dissembling[2]
2. ΚΟΛΑΚΕΙΑ	Flattery
3. ΑΔΟΛΕΣΧΙΑ	Idle Chatter
4. ΑΓΡΟΙΚΙΑ	Boorishness
5. ΑΡΕΣΚΕΙΑ	Obsequiousness
6. ΑΠΟΝΟΙΑ	Shamelessness
7. ΛΑΛΙΑ	Garrulity
8. ΛΟΓΟΠΟΙΙΑ	Rumor-Mongering
9. ΑΝΑΙΣΧΥΝΤΙΑ	Sponging
10. ΜΙΚΡΟΛΟΓΙΑ	Pennypinching
11. ΒΔΕΛΥΡΙΑ	Obnoxiousness
12. ΑΚΑΙΡΙΑ	Bad Timing
13. ΠΕΡΙΕΡΓΙΑ	Overzealousness
14. ΑΝΑΙΣΘΗΣΙΑ	Absent-mindedness
15. ΑΥΘΑΔΕΙΑ	Grouchiness
16. ΔΕΙΣΙΔΑΙΜΟΝΙΑ	Superstition
17. ΜΕΜΨΙΜΟΙΡΙΑ	Griping
18. ΑΠΙΣΤΙΑ	Mistrust
19. ΔΥΣΧΕΡΕΙΑ	Squalor
20. ΑΗΔΙΑ	Bad Taste
21. ΜΙΚΡΟΦΙΛΟΤΙΜΙΑ	Petty Ambition

[1] This traditional translation of the title is not accurate: the Greek equivalent for our "character" is ἦθος; a better translation for χαρακτῆρες would be "Traits" (Diogenes Laertius 5.47 gives the title as ἠθικοὶ χαρακτῆρες, "Character traits"). See Introd. p. 11.

[2] The colloquial titles describe the sort of behavior actually depicted in each sketch, rather than translate the trait names in Greek, which are sometimes suspect (see Introd. n. 55); for the literal meanings of the Greek trait names, see the Additional Notes.

[ΠΡΟΘΕΩΡΙΑ[1]

(1) ἤδη μὲν καὶ πρότερον πολλάκις ἐπιστήσας τὴν διάνοιαν ἐθαύμασα, ἴσως δὲ οὐδὲ παύσομαι θαυμάζων, τί γὰρ δήποτε, τῆς Ἑλλάδος ὑπὸ τὸν αὐτὸν ἀέρα κειμένης καὶ πάντων τῶν Ἑλλήνων ὁμοίως παιδευομένων, συμβέβηκεν ἡμῖν οὐ τὴν αὐτὴν τάξιν τῶν τρόπων ἔχειν. (2) ἐγὼ γάρ, ὦ Πολύκλεις, συνθεωρήσας ἐκ πολλοῦ χρόνου τὴν ἀνθρωπίνην φύσιν καὶ βεβιωκὼς ἔτη ἐνενήκοντα ἐννέα, ἔτι δὲ ὡμιληκὼς πολλαῖς τε καὶ παντοδαπαῖς φύσεσι καὶ παρατεθεαμένος ἐξ ἀκριβείας πολλῆς τούς τε ἀγαθοὺς τῶν ἀνθρώπων καὶ τοὺς φαύλους ὑπέλαβον δεῖν συγγράψαι, ἃ ἑκάτεροι αὐτῶν ἐπιτηδεύουσιν ἐν τῷ βίῳ. (3) ἐκθήσω δέ σοι κατὰ γένος ὅσα τε τυγχάνει γένη τρόπων τούτοις προσκείμενα[2] καὶ ὃν τρόπον τῇ οἰκονομίᾳ χρῶνται· ὑπολαμβάνω γάρ, ὦ Πολύκλεις, τοὺς υἱεῖς ἡμῶν βελτίους ἔσεσθαι καταλειφθέντων αὐτοῖς ὑπομνημάτων τοιούτων, οἷς παραδείγμασι χρώμενοι αἱρήσονται τοῖς εὐσχημονεστάτοις συνεῖναί τε καὶ ὁμιλεῖν, ὅπως μὴ καταδεέστεροι ὦσιν αὐτῶν.

---

[1] Prooemium totum del. Sonntag.
[2] e: προκείμενα codd.

48

[PREFACE[1]

(1) Before now I've often wondered, when I thought about it, and perhaps will never cease to wonder why, even though Greece lies in the same climate and all Greeks are educated the same way, it happens that we do not have the same composition of character. (2) After a life of ninety-nine years,[2] long observation of human nature, and furthermore an acquaintance with many natures of all types and a detailed study of men both superior and inferior, I have come to believe, Polycles,[3] that I ought to write about how both groups normally behave in their lives.

(3) I shall set forth for you one by one which classes of character are attached to these people and how they manage; for I believe, Polycles, that our sons will be better if such writings are bequeathed to them, which they can use as a guide in choosing to associate with and become close to the finest men, so as not to fall short of their standard.

[1] This fatuous and repetitive preface has long been recognized as a later addition to the *Characters* (see Introd. p. 30). Steinmetz (volume 2, p. 32) speculates it was composed outside Greece in the fifth century A.D.   [2] In fact, Theophrastus died at 85 (Diogenes Laertius 5.40), and the *Characters* was most likely composed ca. 325–315 B.C. when he was around 50.

[3] His identity is not known; there was a Macedonian general by this name (Diodorus Siculus 18.38.2).

(4) τρέψομαι δὲ ἤδη ἐπὶ τὸν λόγον. σὸν δὲ παρακολουθῆσαί τε ὀρθῶς τε καὶ εἰδῆσαι, εἰ ὀρθῶς λέγω. πρῶτον μὲν οὖν ποιήσομαι τὸν λόγον ἀπὸ τῶν τὴν εἰρωνείαν ἐζηλωκότων, ἀφεὶς τὸ προοιμιάζεσθαι καὶ πολλὰ περὶ τοῦ πράγματος λέγειν. (5) καὶ ἄρξομαι πρῶτον ἀπὸ τῆς εἰρωνείας καὶ ὁριοῦμαι αὐτήν, εἴθ᾽ οὕτως τὸν εἴρωνα διέξειμι, ποῖός τίς ἐστι καὶ εἰς τίνα τρόπον κατενήνεκται· καὶ τὰ ἄλλα δὴ τῶν παθημάτων, ὥσπερ ὑπεθέμην, πειράσομαι κατὰ γένος φανερὰ καθιστάναι.]

ΕΙΡΩΝΕΙΑΣ Α΄

(1) [ἡ μὲν οὖν εἰρωνεία δόξειεν ἂν εἶναι, ὡς τύπῳ λαβεῖν, προσποίησις ἐπὶ χεῖρον πράξεων καὶ λόγων,][1] ὁ δὲ εἴρων (2) τοιοῦτός τις, οἷος προσελθὼν τοῖς ἐχθροῖς ἐθέλειν λαλεῖν [οὐ μισεῖν]·[2] καὶ ἐπαινεῖν παρόντας οἷς ἐπέθετο λάθρα, καὶ ⟨οἷς δικάζεται,⟩[3] τούτοις συλλυπεῖσθαι ἡττωμένοις· καὶ συγγνώμην δὲ ἔχειν τοῖς αὐτὸν κακῶς λέγουσι καὶ ⟨γελᾶν⟩[4] ἐπὶ τοῖς καθ᾽ ἑαυτοῦ λεγομένοις. καὶ (3) πρὸς τοὺς ἀδικουμένους καὶ ἀγανακτοῦντας πράως διαλέγεσθαι· καὶ τοῖς ἐντυγχάνειν κατὰ σπουδὴν βουλομένοις προστάξαι ἐπανελθεῖν. (4) καὶ μηδὲν ὧν πράττει ὁμολογῆσαι, ἀλλὰ φῆσαι βουλεύεσθαι καὶ προσποιήσασθαι

---

[1] del. Hanow, Gomperz, Stein.   [2] del. Ussing.
[3] suppl. Kassel.   [4] suppl. Darvaris.

(4) I shall now turn to my story; it is your task to follow it correctly, and see whether it is told correctly as well. I shall speak first of those who affect dissembling, dispensing with preliminaries and details about the topic. (5) I shall begin with dissembling and define it, then describe the dissembler as to his qualities and how he is inclined; and I will attempt to render clear the rest of the emotions type by type, as I promised.]

1. DISSEMBLING

(1) [Dissembling, to put it in outline, would seem to be a false denigration of one's actions and words.][1] The dissembler is the sort (2) who goes up to his enemies and is willing to chat with them. He praises to their faces those whom he has attacked in secret, and commiserates with people he is suing if they lose their case. He is forgiving to those who slander him, and laughs at anything said against him. (3) With people who have been wronged and are outraged his conversation is mild,[2] and those who urgently seek a meeting with him he bids to come back later. (4) He admits to nothing that he is actually doing, but says he is thinking it

[1] This introductory definition is derived from Aristotle, *Nicomachean Ethics* 1108a21ff, 1108a11, *Eudemian Ethics* 1233b39–1234a1. Like some other definitions in the *Characters* (see Introd.), it is probably a later addition to the text: it describes well the irony of Socrates (see Additional Notes), but not the character that follows here.

[2] That is, he does not share their outrage; cf. Xenophon, *Anabasis* I.5.14.

ἄρτι παραγεγονέναι [καὶ ὀψὲ γενέσθαι αὐτὸν][5] καὶ
μαλακισθῆναι. (5) καὶ πρὸς τοὺς δανειζομένους καὶ
ἐρανίζοντας ‹φῆσαι ὡς χρημάτων ἀπορεῖ, καὶ πωλῶν
τι φῆσαι›[6] ὡς οὐ πωλεῖ καὶ μὴ πωλῶν φῆσαι πωλεῖν·
καὶ ἀκούσας τι μὴ προσποιεῖσθαι, καὶ ἰδὼν φῆσαι μὴ
ἑορακέναι, καὶ ὁμολογήσας μὴ μεμνῆσθαι καὶ τὰ μὲν
σκέψεσθαι φάσκειν, τὰ δὲ οὐκ εἰδέναι, τὰ δὲ θαυμάζειν, τὰ δ᾽ ἤδη ποτὲ καὶ αὐτὸς οὕτως διαλογί-
σασθαι. (6) καὶ τὸ ὅλον δεινὸς τῷ τοιούτῳ τρόπῳ τοῦ
λόγου χρῆσθαι· "οὐ πιστεύω·" "οὐχ ὑπολαμβάνω·"
"ἐκπλήττομαι·" καὶ "λέγεις αὐτὸν ἕτερον γεγονέναι·"
"καὶ μὴν οὐ ταῦτα πρὸς ἐμὲ διεξῄει·" "παράδοξόν μοι
τὸ πρᾶγμα·" "ἄλλῳ τινὶ λέγε·" "ὅπως δὲ σοὶ ἀπιστήσω
ἢ ἐκείνου καταγνῶ, ἀπορροῦμαι·" "ἀλλ᾽ ὅρα, μὴ σὺ
θᾶττον πιστεύεις."

(7) [τοιαύτας φωνὰς καὶ πλοκὰς καὶ παλιλλογίας
εὑρεῖν ἔστι τῶν εἰρώνων. τὰ δὴ τῶν ἠθῶν μὴ ἁπλᾶ
ἀλλ᾽ ἐπίβουλα φυλάττεσθαι μᾶλλον δεῖ ἢ τοὺς
ἔχεις.][7]

ΚΟΛΑΚΕΙΑΣ Β΄

(1) [τὴν δὲ κολακείαν ὑπολάβοι ἄν τις ὁμιλίαν

---

[5] del. Kassel.
[6] lacunam statuit Salmasius: φῆσαι ὡς χρημάτων ἀπορεῖ
Kassel, καὶ πωλῶν (τι add. Kassel) φῆσαι Ast.
[7] epilogum del. editores.

over, and pretends that he just arrived, and behaves like a coward.[3] (5) To those seeking a loan or a contribution[4] he says he's short of cash, and if he is selling something says that he is not, and if he's not, says that he is. If he has heard something, he pretends he hasn't, and says he hasn't seen something when he has, and if he has made an agreement he doesn't remember it. He says about some things that he will look into them, about others that he doesn't know, about others that he is surprised, about others that once in the past he had thought that way himself too.[5] (6) And in general he is apt to employ phrases like this: "I don't believe it." "I don't think so." "I'm astonished." And "you're telling me he's become a different person." "That's by no means what he told me." "The business is a mystery to me." "Save your words for someone else." "I do not see how I can doubt you—nor condemn him, either." "Be careful you don't make up your mind too quickly."

(7) [Such are the phrases, dodges and contradictions it is characteristic of dissemblers to invent. When natures are not open, but contriving, one must be more cautious of them than of vipers.]

2. FLATTERY

(1) [You might call flattery talk that is shameful, but also

---

[3] The text may not be sound; but if it is, the verb is used not of illness (so most translators), but of irresolution in battle (cf. LSJ μαλακίζω).   [4] For ἔρανος see on 15.7.

[5] But does so no longer. Usually translated "he had already come to the same conclusion," which would be an anomaly in this list of responses.

αἰσχρὰν εἶναι, συμφέρουσαν δὲ τῷ κολακεύοντι,]¹ τὸν
δὲ κόλακα τοιοῦτόν τινα, (2) ὥστε ἅμα πορευόμενον
εἰπεῖν· "ἐνθυμῇ, ὡς ἀποβλέπουσι πρὸς σὲ οἱ ἄνθρωποι; τοῦτο δὲ οὐθενὶ τῶν ἐν τῇ πόλει γίνεται πλὴν σοί·"
"ηὐδοκίμεις χθὲς ἐν τῇ στοᾷ·" πλειόνων γὰρ ἢ
τριάκοντα ἀνθρώπων καθημένων καὶ ἐμπεσόντος λόγου, τίς εἴη βέλτιστος, ἀφ᾽ αὑτοῦ ἀρξαμένους πάντας
ἐπὶ τὸ ὄνομα αὐτοῦ κατενεχθῆναι.

(3) καὶ ἅμα τοιαῦτα λέγων ἀπὸ τοῦ ἱματίου ἀφελεῖν
κροκύδα, καὶ ἐάν τι πρὸς τὸ τρίχωμα τῆς κεφαλῆς ὑπὸ
πνεύματος προσενεχθῇ ἄχυρον, καρφολογῆσαι. καὶ
ἐπιγελάσας δὲ εἰπεῖν· "ὁρᾷς; ὅτι δυοῖν σοι ἡμερῶν οὐκ
ἐντετύχηκα, πολιῶν ἔσχηκας τὸν πώγωνα μεστόν,
καίπερ εἴ τις καὶ ἄλλος πρὸς τὰ ἔτη ἔχεις μέλαιναν
τὴν τρίχα."

(4) καὶ λέγοντος δὲ αὐτοῦ τι τοὺς ἄλλους σιωπᾶν
κελεῦσαι καὶ ἐπαινέσαι δὲ ἀκούοντος, καὶ ἐπισημή-
νασθαι δέ, εἰ παύεται,² "ὀρθῶς," καὶ σκώψαντι ψυχρῶς
ἐπιγελάσαι τό τε ἱμάτιον ὦσαι εἰς τὸ στόμα ὡς δὴ οὐ
δυνάμενος κατασχεῖν τὸν γέλωτα. (5) καὶ τοὺς ἀπαντῶντας ἐπιστῆναι κελεῦσαι, ἕως ἂν αὐτὸς παρέλθῃ.

(6) καὶ τοῖς παιδίοις μῆλα καὶ ἀπίους πριάμενος
εἰσενέγκας δοῦναι ὁρῶντος αὐτοῦ, καὶ φιλήσας δὲ

---

¹ del. Hanow, Gomperz, Stein (videtur citare sine nomine
auctoris Philodemus in libro περὶ κολακείας, P. Herc. 222 et
1082, v. T. Gargiulo, *Cronache ercolanese* 11 (1981) 103–127).

² Ast: παύσεται codd.

profitable to the flatterer.][1] The flatterer is the sort (2) to say, as he walks along, "Do you notice how people are looking at you? This does not happen to anyone in the city except you." "They praised you yesterday in the stoa"; and he explains that when more than thirty people were sitting there and a discussion arose about who was the best, at his own suggestion they settled on his man's name.

(3) While he says more like this, he picks a flock of wool from his man's cloak and, if some chaff in the wind lands on the hair on his head, harvests it, and says with a laugh, "You see! Since I haven't seen you for two days, you've got a beard full of grey hairs—although your hair is black for your years, if anyone's is."[2]

(4) He tells everyone else to keep quiet while his man is saying something, and praises him when he is listening, and if he should pause, adds an approving "You're right!" If he makes a tasteless[3] joke, he laughs at it and pushes his cloak into his mouth to show he can't contain his laughter. (5) He commands everyone who approaches to stand still until his man has passed by.

(6) To his children he brings apples and pears he has bought and, while his man is watching, presents them and

[1] The introductory definition, although twice mentioned (without Theophrastus' name) in fragments of Philodemus, *On Flattery*, is probably a later insertion which has partly replaced the original first sentence. The notion that the flatterer's motive is profit is derived from Aristotle, *Nicomachean Ethics* 1108a26, 1127a7, but is irrelevant here.

[2] The flatterer usually plucks the grey hairs from his patron's beard (cf. *PCG* Aristophanes fr. 416, 689, *Knights* 908).

[3] Literally "frigid," but cf. *PCG* Eupolis fr. 261 and Timocles fr. 19, Demosthenes 18.256, Theophr. fr. 686.

εἰπεῖν· "χρηστοῦ πατρὸς νεόττια." (7) καὶ συνωνού-
μενος ἐπικρηπῖδας τὸν πόδα φῆσαι εἶναι εὐρυθμότε-
ρον τοῦ ὑποδήματος. (8) καὶ πορευομένου πρός τινα
τῶν φίλων προδραμὼν εἰπεῖν ὅτι "πρὸς σὲ ἔρχεται,"
καὶ ἀναστρέψας ὅτι "προσήγγελκά σε." (9) ἀμέλει δὲ
καὶ τὰ ἐκ γυναικείας ἀγορᾶς διακονῆσαι δυνατὸς
ἀπνευστί.

(10) καὶ τῶν ἑστιωμένων πρῶτος ἐπαινέσαι τὸν
οἶνον καὶ παραμένων εἰπεῖν· "ὡς μαλακῶς ἐσθίεις,"
καὶ ἄρας τι τῶν ἀπὸ τῆς τραπέζης φῆσαι "τουτὶ ἄρα
ὡς χρηστόν ἐστι·" καὶ ἐρωτῆσαι μὴ ῥιγοῖ, καὶ εἰ
ἐπιβάλλεσθαι βούλεται, καὶ εἴ τι³ περιστείλῃ αὐτόν,
καὶ μὴν ταῦτα λέγων πρὸς τὸ οὖς προσκύπτων⁴ δια-
ψιθυρίζειν· καὶ εἰς ἐκεῖνον ἀποβλέπων τοῖς ἄλλοις
λαλεῖν. (11) καὶ τοῦ παιδὸς ἐν τῷ θεάτρῳ ἀφελόμενος
τὰ προσκεφάλαια αὐτὸς ὑποστρῶσαι. (12) καὶ τὴν
οἰκίαν φῆσαι εὖ ἠρχιτεκτονῆσθαι καὶ τὸν ἀγρὸν εὖ
πεφυτεῦσθαι καὶ τὴν εἰκόνα ὁμοίαν εἶναι.

(13) [καὶ τὸ κεφάλαιον τὸν κόλακα ἔστι θεάσασθαι
πάντα⁵ καὶ λέγοντα καὶ πράττοντα ᾧ χαριεῖσθαι ὑπο-
λαμβάνει.]⁶

---

³ Petersen: ἔτι A, ἔτὶ B.

⁴ Valckenaer: προσπίπτων A^corr. B.

⁵ πᾶν Cobet, πάντη Diels, sed cf. Xen. *Cyr.* 8.2.25 (πάντα
ὅτου δεῖ), Kühner-Gerth II.1.56.

⁶ epilogum del. editores.

kisses the children and says "Chips off the excellent old block!"[4] (7) When he joins him in shopping for overshoes, he says that his foot is more symmetrical than the sandal. (8) When he is going to see one of his friends, he runs ahead and says "He is coming to your house!" Then he runs back and says "I have announced you." (9) You can be sure he is also capable of doing his errands from the women's market[5] without stopping for breath.

(10) He is the first of the dinner guests to praise the wine, and keeps it up by saying "How luxuriously you dine!" He takes up something from the table and says "This is really good!"[6] He asks whether his man is chilly, and whether he wants him to put a blanket on him, and whether he should wrap something around his man's shoulders; and yet he says all this in a whisper, leaning forward toward his ear. He keeps an eye on his man while speaking to others. (11) At the theater he takes the cushions away from the slave, and tucks them under his man personally. (12) He says that his house has been well laid-out, and his farm well cultivated, and his portrait a perfect resemblance.[7]

(13) [And the sum is that the flatterer is on the lookout for everything in word or deed by which he thinks he will curry favor.]

[4] The proverbial phrase is literally "chicks of their father" (Aristophanes, *Birds* 767), to which the flatterer adds a further complimentary adjective.   [5] Pollux, *Onomasticon* 10.18 says this name is used by Menander (*PCG* fr. 344) for a place where one could buy household furnishings.   [6] Cf. *PCG* Alexis fr. 15.8, Antiphanes fr. 238.   [7] Since classical Greek portraits tended toward ideal beauty, this is a handsome compliment.

ΑΔΟΛΕΣΧΙΑΣ Γ´

(1) ἡ δὲ ἀδολεσχία ἐστὶ μὲν διήγησις λόγων μακρῶν καὶ ἀπροβουλεύτων, ὁ δὲ ἀδολέσχης τοιοῦτός ἐστιν, (2) οἷος, ὃν μὴ γινώσκει, τούτῳ παρακαθεζόμενος πλησίον πρῶτον μὲν τῆς αὐτοῦ γυναικὸς εἰπεῖν ἐγκώμιον· εἶτα ὃ τῆς νυκτὸς εἶδεν ἐνύπνιον, τοῦτο διηγήσασθαι· εἶθ᾿ ὧν εἶχεν ἐπὶ τῷ δείπνῳ τὰ καθ᾿ ἕκαστα διεξελθεῖν. (3) εἶτα δὴ προχωροῦντος τοῦ πράγματος λέγειν, ὡς πολὺ πονηρότεροί εἰσιν οἱ νῦν ἄνθρωποι τῶν ἀρχαίων, καὶ ὡς ἄξιοι γεγόνασιν οἱ πυροὶ ἐν τῇ ἀγορᾷ, καὶ ὡς πολλοὶ ἐπιδημοῦσι ξένοι, καὶ τὴν θάλατταν ἐκ Διονυσίων πλόιμον εἶναι, καὶ εἰ ποιήσειεν ὁ Ζεὺς ὕδωρ πλεῖον, τὰ ἐν τῇ γῇ βελτίω ἔσεσθαι, καὶ ὅτι ἀγρὸν εἰς νέωτα γεωργήσει, καὶ ὡς χαλεπόν ἐστι τὸ ζῆν, καὶ ὡς Δάμιππος μυστηρίοις μεγίστην δᾷδα ἔστησεν, καὶ "πόσοι εἰσὶ κίονες τοῦ Ὠιδείου," καὶ "χθὲς ἤμεσα," καὶ "τίς ἐστιν ἡμέρα τήμερον;" καὶ ὡς Βοηδρομιῶνος μέν ἐστι τὰ μυστήρια, Πυανοψιῶνος δὲ τἀπατούρια, Ποσιδεῶνος δὲ <τὰ>¹ κατ᾿ ἀγροὺς Διονύσια. (4) κἂν ὑπομένῃ τις αὐτόν, μὴ ἀφίστασθαι.²

(5) [παρασείσαντα δὴ δεῖ τοὺς τοιούτους τῶν ἀνθρώπων καὶ διαράμενον ἀπαλλάττεσθαι, ὅστις ἀπύρευτος βούλεται εἶναι· ἔργον γὰρ συναρκεῖσθαι τοῖς

¹ suppl. Casaubon.
² κἂν . . . ἀφίστασθαι ante καὶ ὡς Βοηδρομιῶνος codd.: transposuit Schneider.

3. IDLE CHATTER

(1) Idle chatter is engaging in prolonged and aimless talk. The idle chatterer is the sort (2) who sits right down beside someone he doesn't know, and starts out by speaking in praise of his own wife; then he recounts the dream he had the night before; then he relates the details of what he had for dinner. (3) Then, as matters progress, he says that people nowadays are much more wicked than they used to be; that wheat is a bargain in the marketplace; that there are lots of foreigners in town, and that the sea lanes have been open since the festival of Dionysus. And that if it rains more, the soil will be better; that he intends to start a farm next year, and that it's hard to make a living; and that Damippos dedicated the biggest torch at the mysteries.[1] "How many pillars are there in the Odeion?"[2] "Yesterday I threw up!" "What day is it today?" And that the mysteries are in the month Boedromion, and the Apatouria in Pyanepsion, and the country Dionysia in Poseideon. (4) And if you put up with him, he doesn't stop!

(5) [Men like this you must flee at top speed[3] if you want to stay unscathed; it is hard to stand people who don't care

---

[1] Initiates carried torches in the procession from Athens to Eleusis, and evidently private individuals could dedicate representations of them in the Eleusinian sanctuary: G. Mylonas, *Eleusis* (Princeton 1961) 204.

[2] An indoor music hall constructed under Pericles, with many interior columns; see Plutarch, *Pericles* 13.9 (with the commentary of Philip Stadter).

[3] Literally "swinging (your arms) and stretching (your legs) wide."

μήτε σχολὴν μήτε σπουδὴν διαγινώσκουσιν.][3]

ΑΓΡΟΙΚΙΑΣ Δ΄

(1) ἡ δὲ ἀγροικία δόξειεν ἂν εἶναι ἀμαθία ἀσχήμων, ὁ δὲ ἄγροικος τοιοῦτός τις, (2) οἷος κυκεῶνα πιὼν εἰς ἐκκλησίαν πορεύεσθαι (3) καὶ τὸ μύρον φάσκειν οὐδὲν τοῦ θύμου ἥδιον ὄζειν· (4) καὶ μείζω τοῦ ποδὸς τὰ ὑποδήματα φορεῖν· (5) καὶ μεγάλῃ τῇ φωνῇ λαλεῖν· (6) καὶ τοῖς μὲν φίλοις καὶ οἰκείοις ἀπιστεῖν, πρὸς δὲ τοὺς αὑτοῦ οἰκέτας ἀνακοινοῦσθαι περὶ τῶν μεγίστων. καὶ τοῖς παρ' αὑτῷ ἐργαζομένοις μισθωτοῖς ἐν ἀγρῷ πάντα τὰ ἀπὸ τῆς ἐκκλησίας διηγεῖσθαι. (7) καὶ ἀναβεβλημένος ἄνω τοῦ γόνατος καθιζάνειν ὥστε τὰ γυμνὰ αὑτοῦ φαίνεσθαι.[1] (8) καὶ ἐπ' ἄλλῳ μὲν μηδενὶ ⟨μήτε εὐφραίνεσθαι⟩[2] μήτε ἐκπλήττεσθαι ἐν ταῖς ὁδοῖς, ὅταν δὲ ἴδῃ βοῦν ἢ ὄνον ἢ τράγον, ἑστηκὼς θεωρεῖν. (9) καὶ προαιρῶν[3] δέ τι ἐκ τοῦ ταμιείου δεινὸς φαγεῖν, καὶ ζωρότερον πιεῖν. (10) καὶ τὴν σιτοποιὸν πειρῶν λαθεῖν, κᾆτ' ἀλέσας

---

[3] epilogum del. editores.

[1] ὥστε τὰ γυμνὰ αὑτοῦ φαίνεσθαι del. Darvaris, fortasse recte, cf. 20.9 [ὥστε εἶναι ψυχρόν].

[2] μήτε suppl. editores, εὐφραίνεσθαι Kassel: θαυμάζειν De.

[3] Casaubon: προαίρων codd.

---

[1] The κυκεὼν was a mixture of grains, liquids (wine, milk, water, honey, oil) and spices, drunk by the poorer classes: N. J. Rich-

whether you are busy or free.]

4. BOORISHNESS

(1) Boorishness would seem to be an embarrassing lack of sophistication. The boor is the sort (2) who drinks a posset[1] before going to the assembly, (3) and claims that perfume smells no sweeter than thyme. (4) He wears sandals that are too big for his feet. (5) He talks in too loud a voice.[2] (6) He is wary of friends and family, but asks advice from his servants on the most important matters. He describes to hired laborers in the field all the proceedings of the city assembly. (7) He sits down with his cloak hitched up above his knee, thereby revealing his nakedness.[3] (8) He doesn't enjoy or gawk at anything else on the street—yet stands in rapt attention at the sight of a cow, an ass, or a goat. (9) He is apt to eat the food as he is taking it out of the storeroom. He drinks his wine too strong.[4]

(10) He seduces his cook without anyone's knowing,

ardson, *The Homeric Hymn to Demeter* (Oxford 1974) 344. The boor does not care how strongly his breath smells of thyme (which in antiquity was a much stronger herb than today; see *PCG* Pherecrates fr. 177).

[2] For a "barnyard voice" cf. *PCG* Cratinus fr. 371.

[3] He isn't wearing anything underneath; cf. *PCG* Philetairus fr. 18, and the illustrations in the Leipzig Edition of the *Characters*, p. 26, and A. Dieterich, *Pulcinella* (Leipzig 1897) 119.

[4] Athenaeus 423d-f cites many parallels to show that ζωρότερον (first in Homer, *Iliad* 9.203) means "with more wine and less water." He also notes that Theophrastus in a treatise *On Drunkenness* (=fr. 574) dissents with an interpretation ("mixed") that cannot be applied here.

μετ᾽ αὐτῆς ⟨μετρεῖν⟩[4] τοῖς ἔνδον πᾶσι καὶ αὐτῷ τὰ
ἐπιτήδεια. (11) καὶ ἀριστῶν δὲ ἅμα τοῖς ὑποζυγίοις
ἐμβαλεῖν. (12) καὶ τὴν θύραν ὑπακοῦσαι[5] αὐτός, καὶ
τὸν κύνα προσκαλεσάμενος καὶ ἐπιλαβόμενος τοῦ
ῥύγχους εἰπεῖν· "οὗτος φυλάττει τὸ χωρίον καὶ τὴν
οἰκίαν."

(13) καὶ [τὸ][6] ἀργύριον δὲ παρά του λαβὼν ἀποδο-
κιμάζειν, λίαν ⟨γὰρ⟩[7] μολυβρὸν[8] εἶναι, καὶ ἕτερον
ἀνταλλάττεσθαι.[9] (14) καὶ εἰ ⟨τῳ⟩[10] ἄροτρον ἔχρησεν
ἢ κόφινον ἢ δρέπανον ἢ θύλακον, ταῦτα τῆς νυκτὸς
κατὰ ἀγρυπνίαν ἀναμιμνησκόμενος ⟨ἀπαιτεῖν⟩.[11] (15)
καὶ εἰς ἄστυ καταβαίνων ἐρωτῆσαι τὸν ἀπαντῶντα,
πόσου ἦσαν αἱ διφθέραι καὶ τὸ τάριχος καὶ εἰ τήμερον
[ὁ ἀγὼν][12] νουμηνίαν ἄγει, καὶ εἰπεῖν εὐθὺς ὅτι βούλεται καταβὰς ἀποκείρασθαι καὶ ἐν βαλανείῳ δὲ ᾆσαι
καὶ εἰς τὰ ὑποδήματα δὲ ἥλους ἐγκροῦσαι καὶ τῆς
αὐτῆς ὁδοῦ παριὼν κομίσασθαι παρ᾽ Ἀρχίου τοῦ
ταρίχους.[13]

4 suppl. Casaubon.　　5 Casaubon: ἐπακοῦσαι codd.
6 suspectum habuit Stein (cf. 14.8).
7 suppl. Eberhard.
8 Diels: μὲν λυπρὸν ABce, μὲν λυπηρὸν cDe.
9 Cobet: ἅμα ἀλλάττεσθαι codd.
10 Diels: καὶ εἰ τὸ A, καὶ ὁ CDe, καὶ τὸ B, καὶ εἰς τὸ e.
11 suppl. Casaubon.
12 del. Edmonds.
13 Sylburg: τοὺς ταρίχους codd. verba καὶ ἐν βαλανείῳ—
ἐγκροῦσαι fortasse aut post τοῦ ταρίχους ponenda aut
secludenda sunt.

62

but then joins her in grinding up the daily ration of meal and handing it out to himself and the whole household.[5] (11) While he is eating his breakfast, he feeds his plough-animals. (12) He answers the door himself, then calls his dog, grabs his snout and says "This fellow looks out for our property and household."

(13) He rejects a silver coin that he gets from someone because it looks too much like lead, and trades for another.[6] (14) And if he has lent someone a plough, basket, sickle or sack, he asks for it back in the middle of the night, because he just remembered it while he couldn't sleep. (15) And when he is going into town, he asks anyone he meets about the price of hides and salt fish, and whether today is the first of the month,[7] and he says right away that when he reaches town he wants to get a haircut, do some singing at the baths, hammer some nails into his shoes,[8] and while he's going in that direction pick up some salt fish at Archias'.

[5] He is so smitten that he joins her in work the master should not be doing (cf. 30.11).

[6] The text is corrupt; as emended here, the rustic cares more about the appearance than the value of his money, despite the higher value of the older (and less shiny) silver coins. Cf. Aristophanes, *Frogs* 718ff, Plautus, *Casina* 9.

[7] A market-day, Aristophanes, *Knights* 43, *Wasps* 171.

[8] Evidently to stick the soles back on (cf. 22.11).

ΑΡΕΣΚΕΙΑΣ Ε΄

(1) [ἡ δὲ ἀρέσκειά ἐστι μέν, ὡς ὅρῳ περιλαβεῖν, ἔντευξις οὐκ ἐπὶ τῷ βελτίστῳ ἡδονῆς παρασκευαστική,]¹ ὁ δὲ ἄρεσκος ἀμέλει τοιοῦτός τις, (2) οἷος πόρρωθεν προσαγορεῦσαι² καὶ ἄνδρα κράτιστον εἴπας³ καὶ θαυμάσας ἱκανῶς, ἀμφοτέραις ταῖς χερσὶν ἀψάμενος⁴ μὴ ἀφιέναι καὶ μικρὸν προπέμψας⁵ καὶ ἐρωτήσας, πότε αὐτὸν ὄψεται, ἐπαινῶν⁶ ἀπαλλάττεσθαι.

(3) καὶ παρακληθεὶς δὲ πρὸς δίαιταν μὴ μόνον ᾧ πάρεστι⁷ βούλεσθαι ἀρέσκειν, ἀλλὰ καὶ τῷ ἀντιδίκῳ, ἵνα κοινός τις⁸ εἶναι δοκῇ. (4) καὶ ‹πρὸς›⁹ τοὺς ξένους δὲ εἰπεῖν ὡς δικαιότερα λέγουσι τῶν πολιτῶν.

(5) καὶ κεκλημένος δὲ ἐπὶ δεῖπνον κελεῦσαι καλέσαι τὰ παιδία τὸν ἑστιῶντα, καὶ εἰσιόντα φῆσαι σύκου ὁμοιότερα εἶναι τῷ πατρί, καὶ προσαγόμενος φιλῆσαι καὶ παρ' αὑτὸν καθίσασθαι,¹⁰ καὶ τοῖς μὲν

---

¹ del. Hanow, Gomperz, Stein.   ² προσαγορεύσας codd.
(προαγορεύσας A):]ρευσαι ut videtur P. Herc. 1457.

³ εἴπα[ς P. Herc. 1457: εἰπὼν codd.

⁴ τα[ῖ]ς χε[ρσ]ὶν [. . .]μεν[. .] μὴ P. Herc. 1457, ut videtur,
supplevit Stein: ταῖς χερσὶ μὴ ἀφιέναι codd.

⁵ μικρ[ὸ]ν [̣] . . προπέμψας P. Herc. 1457.

⁶ ὄψε]ται ἐπαινῶν P. Herc. 1457 (quod coniecerat Needham): ὄψεται ἔτι αἰνῶν ABCe, ὄψεται ἔτι ἐπαινῶν De.

⁷ δίαιτα[ν μὴ μόνον τούτῳ ᾧ] πάρεστ[ιν P. Herc. 1457, ut
videtur, sed de pronomine cf. 13.5, 18.6 (Stein).   ⁸ εἷς AB
(εἷς om. CDE): τις (quod iam coniecerat Pauw) P. Herc. 1457,
Durandi et Stein ZPE 100 (1994) 8.

5. OBSEQUIOUSNESS

(1) [Obsequiousness, to put it in a definition, is a manner of behavior that aims at pleasing, but not with the best intentions.][1] You can be sure that the obsequious man is the sort (2) who greets you from a distance,[2] then, after calling you "your excellency" and expressing great respect, detains you by grabbing you with both hands, walks along a little farther, asks when he will see you again, and calls out compliments as he leaves.

(3) When he is asked to join an arbitration board, he wants to gratify not only the man whose side he is on, but his opponent too, so that he'll appear to be a neutral party.[3] (4) He tells foreigners that they have a better case than his fellow-citizens.

(5) When he is invited to dinner, he asks his host to call in the children and, when they come, says "Spit 'n' image of their dad!"[4] He hugs and kisses them and sits them down beside him; some he joins in a game, himself shouting out

[1] Probably adapted from the definition of flattery in Pseudo-Plato, *Definitions* 415e9 (cf. *Gorgias* 465a).

[2] As prescribed in Menander, *Dyskolos* 105. With the whole scene cf. Horace, *Satires* 1.9.4, Plautus, *Aulularia* 114–6.

[3] For a private arbitration one member of the board had to be acceptable to both sides as an impartial tie-breaker, but each disputant could choose any (equal) number of judges. See Douglas M. MacDowell, *Law in Classical Athens* (London 1978) 203–206.

[4] Literally "more like their father than a fig (is like another)." For the proverb see *Paroem. Graec.* I.293 and Herodas 6.60.

9 suppl. Casaubon.
10 Cobet: καθίστασθαι AB, καθίσαι CDe.

συμπαίζειν αὐτὸς λέγων· "ἀσκός, πέλεκυς," τὰ δὲ ἐπὶ
τῆς γαστρὸς ἐᾶν καθεύδειν ἅμα θλιβόμενος. ‹...›[11]

(6) ‹...› καὶ πλειστάκις δὲ ἀποκείρασθαι καὶ τοὺς
ὀδόντας λευκοὺς ἔχειν καὶ τὰ ἱμάτια δὲ χρηστὰ μετα-
βάλλεσθαι καὶ χρίσματι ἀλείφεσθαι. (7) καὶ τῆς μὲν
ἀγορᾶς πρὸς τὰς τραπέζας προσφοιτᾶν, τῶν δὲ
γυμνασίων ἐν τούτοις διατρίβειν, οὗ ἂν οἱ[12] ἔφηβοι
γυμνάζωνται, τοῦ δὲ θεάτρου καθῆσθαι, ὅταν ᾖ θέα,
πλησίον τῶν στρατηγῶν. (8) καὶ ἀγοράζειν αὑτῷ μὲν
μηδέν, ξένοις δ᾽ εἰς Βυζάντιον ἐπιστάλματα[13] καὶ
Λακωνικὰς κύνας εἰς Κύζικον καὶ μέλι Ὑμήττιον εἰς
Ῥόδον, καὶ ταῦτα ποιῶν τοῖς ἐν τῇ πόλει διηγεῖσθαι.

(9) ἀμέλει δὲ καὶ πίθηκον θρέψαι δεινὸς καὶ τίτυρον
κτήσασθαι καὶ Σικελικὰς περιστερὰς καὶ δορκαδείους
ἀστραγάλους καὶ Θουριακὰς τῶν στρογγύλων ληκύ-
θους καὶ βακτηρίας τῶν σκολιῶν ἐκ Λακεδαίμονος καὶ
αὐλαίαν Πέρσας ἐννυφασμένην[14] καὶ παλαιστρίδιον

11 lacunam indicavit Casaubon (continuat P. Herc. 1457).
12 P. Herc. 1457: om. codd.   13 οἶνον pro ἐπιστάλματα
Naber conferens [Dem.] 35.35, alii alia.   14 αὐλαίαν
ἔχουσαν Πέρσας ἐννυφασμένους codd., α]ὐλαίας Πέρσας
ἐν[υφασ]μεν[ο]υς P. Herc. 1457: corr. Herwerden et Cobet.

5 Evidently part of a children's game, no longer known.
6 Cf. Catullus 39, Paroem. Graec. I.159, PCG Alexis fr. 103.20.
7 He is choosing the spots where the greatest crowd will be
watching.   8 The word may be corrupt, but perhaps he sends
the equivalent of a "gift-certificate" to a local merchant.

"wineskin" and "ax";[5] others he lets fall asleep on his stomach even though they are crushing him . . .

⟨From a different character (see Additional Notes)⟩

(6) . . . He gets frequent haircuts and keeps his teeth white,[6] and discards cloaks that are still good, and anoints himself with perfumed oil. (7) In the marketplace he goes frequently to the moneychangers; among gymnasia he spends his time at those where the ephebes work out; in the theater, whenever there is a show, he sits next to the generals.[7] (8) He buys nothing for himself, but for foreigners he buys letters of commission[8] for Byzantium, and Laconian dogs for Kyzikos, and Hymettos honey for Rhodes, and as he does so tells everybody in town about it.[9]

(9) You can be sure he is apt to keep a pet monkey, and buys a pheasant,[10] and some Sicilian pigeons,[11] and dice made from gazelle horns,[12] and oil flasks from Thurii of the rounded sort, and walking sticks from Sparta of the twisted sort,[13] and a tapestry embroidered with pictures of Persian

[9] For the fame of Laconian hunting-dogs cf. Aristotle, *History of Animals* 608a25; for honey from Mt. Hymettos, Gow and Page on *Hellenistic Epigrams: The Garland of Philip* (Cambridge 1968) 2265.

[10] So D'Arcy W. Thompson, *Glossary of Greek Birds* (Cambridge 1936) 282, although other identifications of the *tityros* are possible.

[11] See Arnott on Alexis *PCG* fr. 58.

[12] See Herodas 3.19; they are mentioned frequently in papyrus documents as items of great value.

[13] See Aristophanes, *Birds* 1281–3, Plutarch, *Nicias* 19.6.

κόνιν ἔχον καὶ σφαιριστήριον. (10) καὶ τοῦτο περιὼν
χρηννύναι[15] τοῖς σοφισταῖς,[16] τοῖς ὁπλομάχοις, τοῖς
ἁρμονικοῖς ἐνεπιδείκνυσθαι·[17] καὶ αὐτὸς ἐν ταῖς ἐπι-
δείξεσιν ὕστερον ἐπεισιέναι ἐπὰν συγκαθῶνται ἵν'
ἄλλος ἄλλῳ εἴπῃ τῶν θεωμένων[18] ὅτι "τούτου ἐστὶν ἡ
παλαίστρα."

ΑΠΟΝΟΙΑΣ ϛ΄

(1) ἡ δὲ ἀπόνοιά ἐστιν ὑπομονὴ αἰσχρῶν ἔργων καὶ
λόγων, ὁ δὲ ἀπονενοημένος τοιοῦτός τις, (2) οἷος
ὀμόσαι ταχύ, κακῶς ἀκοῦσαι, λοιδορηθῆναι δυναμέ-
νοις,[1] τῷ ἤθει ἀγοραῖός τις καὶ ἀνασεσυρμένος καὶ
παντοποιός. (3) ἀμέλει δυνατὸς καὶ[2] ὀρχεῖσθαι νήφων
τὸν κόρδακα καὶ προσωπεῖον ἔχων ἐν κωμικῷ χορῷ.[3]
  (4) καὶ ἐν θαύμασι δὲ τοὺς χαλκοῦς ἐκλέγειν καθ'

---

[15] χρηννύναι (quod habet, ut videtur, P. Herc. 1457) Foss:
χρὴ νῦν ἀεί ABe.   [16] τοῖς φιλοσόφοις (quod non habet P.
Herc. 1457) ante τοῖς σοφισταῖς codd.

[17] Cobet (quod habet, ut videtur, P. Herc. 1457): ἐπιδείκ-
νυσθαι codd.

[18] ἔπεισιν ἐπὶ τῶν θεωμένων πρὸς τὸν ἕτερον ὅτι AB,
εἰπεῖν ἐπὶ . . . πρὸς ἕτερον ὅτι CDe: vestigia P. Herc. 1457 sic
interpretatus est Stein: ἐπει[σιέναι ἐπὰν] συγκαθων[ται ἵ]ν'
[ἄλλος ἄλλωεἴ]πῃ τῶν θεω[μ]έν[ω]ν ὅτι.

[1] Foss: δυνάμενος codd.

[2] ὀμόσαι ταχὺ . . . δυνατὸς καὶ del. Diels.

[3] καὶ προσωπεῖον . . . χορῷ del. Navarre.

soldiers,[14] and his own little arena (complete with sand) and handball court. (10) The last of these he goes around lending to sophists, military instructors, and musicians to perform in; and during their shows he himself is the last to enter after they are seated, so that the audience will say to each other[15] "That's the man the arena belongs to!"

6. SHAMELESSNESS

(1) Shamelessness is a tolerance for doing and saying unseemly things.[1] The shameless man is the sort (2) who takes an oath too readily, ruins his reputation, vilifies the powerful, in his character is like a market-vendor, coarse and ready for anything.[2] (3) You can be sure he is capable of even dancing the *kordax*[3] while sober, and while wearing a mask in a comic chorus.

(4) At street fairs[4] he goes around and collects coppers

[14] See *PCG* Hipparchus fr. 1.4.   [15] The text of the medieval manuscripts here is nonsense; the translation is based on a speculative reconstruction of the Herculaneum papyrus.

[1] The definition is alluded to by Philodemus, *On Flattery* (M. Gigante and G. Indelli, *Cronache ercolanesi* 8 [1978] 130), but may still be a post-Theophrastan addition (see Introd. p. 30).

[2] This section and start of the next use an adjectival style alien to the rest of the *Characters*, and may be a later addition.

[3] A lewd dance sometimes included in comedies (see Aristophanes, *Clouds* 540); for the assumption that one danced only when drunk see 12.14. The end of the sentence ("and while wearing . . .") offers no sense in this context—it may be a marginal explanation of the dance which has found its way into the text.

[4] Literally "marvels," a mixture of puppet shows, magic tricks, skits, and animal fights; see W. Kroll, *RE* Suppl. VI.1281.

ἕκαστον παριὼν καὶ μάχεσθαι τούτοις τοῖς τὸ σύμ-
βολον φέρουσι, καὶ προῖκα θεωρεῖν ἀξιοῦσι. (5) δεινὸς
δὲ καὶ πανδοκεῦσαι καὶ πορνοβοσκῆσαι καὶ τελωνῆ-
σαι καὶ μηδεμίαν αἰσχρὰν ἐργασίαν ἀποδοκιμάσαι,
ἀλλὰ κηρύττειν, μαγειρεύειν, κυβεύειν, (6) τὴν μητέ-
ρα⁴ μὴ τρέφειν, ἀπάγεσθαι κλοπῆς, τὸ δεσμωτήριον⁵
πλείω χρόνον οἰκεῖν ἢ τὴν αὐτοῦ οἰκίαν.

(7) [καὶ τοῦτο ἂν εἶναι δόξειε τῶν περισταμένων
τοὺς ὄχλους καὶ προσκαλούντων, μεγάλῃ τῇ φωνῇ καὶ
παρερρωγυίᾳ λοιδορουμένων καὶ διαλεγομένων πρὸς
αὐτούς, καὶ μεταξὺ οἱ μὲν προσίασιν, οἱ δὲ ἀπίασι
πρὶν ἀκοῦσαι αὐτοῦ, ἀλλὰ τοῖς μὲν τὴν ἀρχήν, τοῖς δὲ
συλλαβήν, τοῖς δὲ μέρος τοῦ πράγματος λέγει, οὐκ
ἄλλως θεωρεῖσθαι ἀξιῶν τὴν ἀπόνοιαν αὐτοῦ ἢ ὅταν ᾖ
πανήγυρις.]⁶

(8) ἱκανὸς δὲ καὶ δίκας τὰς μὲν φεύγειν, τὰς δὲ
διώκειν, τὰς δὲ ἐξόμνυσθαι, ταῖς δὲ παρεῖναι ἔχων
ἐχῖνον ἐν τῷ προκολπίῳ καὶ ὁρμαθοὺς γραμματιδίων
ἐν ταῖς χερσίν. (9) οὐκ ἀποδοκιμάζειν⁷ δὲ οὐδ᾽ ἅμα
πολλῶν ἀγοραίων στρατηγεῖν καὶ εὐθὺς τούτοις δα-
νείζειν καὶ τῆς δραχμῆς τόκον τρία ἡμιωβόλια τῆς
ἡμέρας πράττεσθαι καὶ ἐφοδεύειν τὰ μαγειρεῖα, τὰ

4 κυβεύειν. <δεινὸς δὲ καὶ> τὴν μητέρα Meier.
5 δεσμωτήριον: κέραμον M (de carcere schol. Hom. Il.
5.387).　　6 del. editores.
7 Meier: ἀποδοκιμάζων codd.

from each individual, and fights with those who already have a ticket or claim they can watch without paying. (5) He is apt to keep an inn or run a brothel or be a tax collector, and he rejects no disgraceful occupation, but works as an auctioneer, a cook, a gambler. (6) He lets his mother starve, is arrested for theft, and spends more time in jail than at home.

(7) [And this[5] would seem to be the character of those who gather crowds around them and give a harangue, railing in a loud and cracked voice and arguing with them. Meanwhile some of them are coming in, some are leaving before they hear him; yet he manages to say the beginning to some, a word or two to others, a part of his message to others, in the conviction that the only place for his shamelessness to be displayed is among a crowd.]

(8) In court he is capable of being now a defendant, now a plaintiff, now taking an oath for a postponement,[6] now showing up for trial with a potful of evidence[7] in the fold of his cloak and sheaves of memoranda in his hands. (9) He doesn't even have any qualms about being the leader of a group of street vendors, while at the same time giving them quick loans and charging one and a half obols per drachma per day interest,[8] and making the rounds of

[5] I.e., shamelessness; but this whole paragraph is so different in style (use of the plural, finite verbs instead of infinitives, rhetorical tone) as to be almost certainly a later addition.

[6] MacDowell, *Law in Classical Athens* 208.

[7] All the documentation in a case was deposited in a pot in the court (Aristotle, *Constitution of Athens* 53.2); this man has brought his own.

[8] Twenty-five percent interest each day.

ἰχθυοπώλια, τὰ ταριχοπώλια, καὶ τοὺς τόκους ἀπὸ τοῦ
ἐμπολήματος εἰς τὴν γνάθον ἐκλέγειν.

(10) [ἐργώδεις δέ εἰσιν οἱ τὸ στόμα εὔλυτον ἔχοντες
πρὸς λοιδορίαν καὶ φθεγγόμενοι μεγάλῃ τῇ φωνῇ, ὡς
συνηχεῖν αὐτοῖς τὴν ἀγορὰν καὶ τὰ ἐργαστήρια.][8]

ΛΑΛΙΑΣ Ζ΄

(1) [ἡ δὲ λαλιά, εἴ τις αὐτὴν ὁρίζεσθαι βούλοιτο, εἶναι
ἂν δόξειεν ἀκρασία τοῦ λόγου·][1] ὁ δὲ λάλος τοιοῦτός
τις, (2) οἷος τῷ ἐντυγχάνοντι εἰπεῖν, ἂν ὁτιοῦν πρὸς
αὐτὸν φθέγξηται, ὅτι οὐθὲν λέγει καὶ ὅτι αὐτὸς πάντα
οἶδεν καὶ, ἂν ἀκούῃ αὐτοῦ, μαθήσεται· καὶ μεταξὺ δὲ
ἀποκρινομένῳ ἐπιβάλλειν εἴπας "σὺ μὴ ἐπιλάθῃ, ὃ
μέλλεις λέγειν," καὶ "εὖ γε, ὅτι με ὑπέμνησας," καὶ "τὸ
λαλεῖν ὡς χρήσιμόν που," καὶ "ὃ παρέλιπον," καὶ
"ταχύ γε συνῆκας τὸ πρᾶγμα," καὶ "πάλαι σε παρετή-
ρουν, εἰ ἐπὶ τὸ αὐτὸ ἐμοὶ κατενεχθήσῃ·" καὶ ἑτέρας
ἀρχὰς τοιαύτας πορίσασθαι, ὥστε μηδὲ ἀναπνεῦσαι
τὸν ἐντυγχάνοντα.

(3) καὶ ὅταν γε τοὺς καθ᾽ ἕνα ἀπογυμνώσῃ, δεινὸς
καὶ ἐπὶ τοὺς ἀθρόους [καὶ][2] συνεστηκότας πορευθῆναι
καὶ φυγεῖν ποιῆσαι μεταξὺ χρηματίζοντας. (4) καὶ εἰς

---

[8] epilogum del. editores.
[1] del. Hanow, Gomperz, Stein.
[2] del. Meineke.

the stalls where they sell hot food and fresh or salted fish, and tucking into his cheek[9] the interest he's made from his business.

(10) [They are tiresome, these people who have a ready tongue for abuse, and who speak in such a loud voice that the marketplace and workshops resound with them.]

7. GARRULITY

(1) [Garrulity, should you like to define it, would seem to be an inability to control one's speech.][1] The garrulous man is the sort (2) who says to anyone he meets that he is talking nonsense—no matter what that man may tell him—and that he knows it all himself, and if he listens, he'll find out about it. And as the other tries to answer, he keeps interrupting and says, "Now don't forget what you intend to say!" and "Good of you to remind me of that!" and "How nice to be able to talk!" "That's something I left out!" and "You're quick to grasp the point!" and "I've been waiting all this time to see whether you would come around to my view!"[2] He tries to give himself more openings like these, so that the man who meets him can't even catch his breath.

(3) Once he has finished off individuals, he is apt to move against whole formations and put them to flight in the midst of their business. (4) He goes into the schools

[9] The poor man's way of carrying money when shopping, see *PCG* Aristophanes fr. 3.   [1] The definition seems derived from Pseudo-Plato, *Definitions* 416a23.

[2] Even when he agrees with the other, the talkative man uses these phrases to cut back into the conversation.

τὰ διδασκαλεῖα δὲ καὶ εἰς τὰς παλαίστρας εἰσιὼν
κωλύειν τοὺς παῖδας προμανθάνειν· [τοσαῦτα καὶ
προσλαλεῖ[3] τοῖς παιδοτρίβαις καὶ διδασκάλοις.][4]

(5) καὶ τοὺς ἀπιέναι φάσκοντας δεινὸς προπέμψαι
καὶ ἀποκαταστῆσαι εἰς τὰς οἰκίας.[5] (6) καὶ πυθο-
μένοις[6] ⟨τὰ ἀπὸ⟩[7] τῆς ἐκκλησίας ἀπαγγέλλειν, προσ-
διηγήσασθαι δὲ καὶ τὴν ἐπ᾽ Ἀριστοφῶντος τότε
γενομένην [τοῦ ῥήτορος][8] μάχην καὶ τὴν Λακεδαι-
μονίοις ὑπὸ Λυσάνδρου, καὶ οὓς ποτε λόγους αὐτὸς
εἴπας εὐδοκίμησεν ἐν τῷ δήμῳ, καὶ κατὰ τῶν πληθῶν
γε ἅμα διηγούμενος κατηγορίαν παρεμβαλεῖν, ὥστε
τοὺς ἀκούοντας ἤτοι ἐπιλαβέσθαι[9] ἢ νυστάξαι ἢ
μεταξὺ καταλιπόντας ἀπαλλάττεσθαι.

(7) καὶ συνδικάζων δὲ κωλῦσαι κρῖναι καὶ συν-
θεωρῶν θεάσασθαι καὶ συνδειπνῶν φαγεῖν, καὶ λέγειν
ὅτι "χαλεπόν μοι[10] ἐστὶν σιωπᾶν," καὶ ὡς ἐν ὑγρῷ
ἐστιν ἡ γλῶττα, καὶ ὅτι οὐκ ἂν σιωπήσειεν, οὐδ᾽ εἰ τῶν
χελιδόνων δόξειεν εἶναι λαλίστερος. (8) καὶ σκωπτό-
μενος ὑπομεῖναι καὶ ὑπὸ τῶν αὑτοῦ παιδίων, ὅταν
αὐτὰ[11] ἤδη καθεύδειν βουλόμενον[12] κωλύῃ[13] λέγοντα
ταῦτα, "λαλεῖν τι ἡμῖν, ὅπως ἂν ἡμᾶς ὕπνος λάβῃ."

---

3 Diels: προσλαλεῖν codd.   4 del. Diels coll. 8.14 οὕτως
καὶ καταπονοῦσι.   5 Ribbeck: ἐκ τῆς οἰκίας AB.

6 Foss: πυθόμενος codd.   7 suppl. Kayser (cf. 4.6).

8 ut glossema del. Fischer: τῶν ῥητόρων Casaubon.

9 Foss: ἐπιλαθέσθαι codd.   10 Kassel e P. Hamb. 143: τῷ
λάλῳ codd.   11 dubitanter conieci: αὐτὸν codd.

12 c: βουλόμενα AB.   13 Hartung: κελεύῃ codd.

and wrestling grounds and prevents the boys from making progress with their studies. [That is how much he talks to their trainers and teachers.]

(5) When people say they must go, he is apt to keep them company, or see them back home. (6) He reports what has happened in the assembly to people who ask him, but adds to his account as well the battle in the year of Aristophon[3] and that of the Spartans under Lysander,[4] and the speeches by which he himself gained a public reputation, and as he tells his story he interjects a condemnation of the masses, so that his hearers interrupt him, or doze off, or go away and leave before he finishes.

(7) When he is among them, he prevents jurors from reaching a verdict, an audience from watching the show, and dinner guests from getting anything to eat, and he remarks "it's hard for me to keep still," and how mobile the tongue is, and that he simply couldn't be quiet, not even if he might appear to chatter more than the swallows.[5] (8) He puts up with being mocked even by his own children when he wants them to go to bed right now, and they stop him by saying this: "Talk to us a little, so we can get to sleep."[6]

---

[3] Aristophon was archon of Athens in 330/29, but no suitable battle is known. Casaubon suggested that this was a political rather than military battle, between Demosthenes and Aeschines in the speeches *On the Crown* and *Against Ctesiphon* in 330; but see Hermann Wankel, *Demosthenes' Kranzrede* (Heidelberg 1976) 29–30.

[4] Again the battle cannot be identified; Lysander was a Spartan general 408–395.

[5] *Paroem. Graec.* II.183.

[6] The text is uncertain.

ΛΟΓΟΠΟΙΑΣ Η´

(1) ἡ δὲ λογοποιία ἐστὶ σύνθεσις ψευδῶν λόγων καὶ
πράξεων, ὧν ‹...›[1] βούλεται ὁ λογοποιῶν, ὁ δὲ λογο-
ποιὸς τοιοῦτός τις, (2) οἷος ἀπαντήσας τῷ φίλῳ εὐθὺς
καταβαλὼν τὸ ἦθος καὶ μειδιάσας ἐρωτῆσαι "πόθεν
σύ;" καὶ "λέγεις τι;" καὶ "πῶς ἔχεις;" πρὸ τοῦ δ᾽ εἰπεῖν
ἐκεῖνον "καλῶς"[2] ἐπιβαλὼν "ἐρωτᾷς[3] μὴ λέγεταί τι
καινότερον; καὶ μὴν ἀγαθά γέ ἐστι τὰ λεγόμενα." (3)
καὶ οὐκ ἐάσας ἀποκρίνασθαι εἰπεῖν· "τί λέγεις; οὐθὲν
ἀκήκοας; δοκῶ μοί σε εὐωχήσειν καινῶν λόγων." (4)
καὶ ἔστιν αὐτῷ ἢ στρατιώτης ἢ παῖς Ἀστείου τοῦ
αὐλητοῦ ἢ Λύκων ὁ ἐργολάβος παραγεγονὼς ἐξ αὐτῆς
τῆς μάχης, οὗ φησιν ἀκηκοέναι· αἱ μὲν οὖν ἀναφοραὶ
τῶν λόγων τοιαῦταί εἰσιν αὐτῷ, ὧν οὐθεὶς ἂν ἔχοι
ἐπιλαβέσθαι.[4] (5) διηγεῖται δὲ τούτους φάσκων λέγειν,
ὡς Πολυπέρχων καὶ ὁ βασιλεὺς μάχῃ νενίκηκε, καὶ
Κάσανδρος ἐζώγρηται. (6) καὶ ἂν εἴπῃ τις αὐτῷ, "σὺ
δὲ ταῦτα πιστεύεις;" φήσει· τὸ πρᾶγμα βοᾶσθαι γὰρ
ἐν τῇ πόλει, καὶ τὸν λόγον ἐπεντείνειν, καὶ πάντας[5]
συμφωνεῖν, ταὐτὰ γὰρ λέγειν περὶ τῆς μάχης, καὶ
πολὺν τὸν ζωμὸν γεγονέναι. (7) εἶναι δ᾽ ἑαυτῷ καὶ
σημεῖον τὰ πρόσωπα τῶν ἐν τοῖς πράγμασιν· ὁρᾶν
γὰρ αὐτῶν πάντων μεταβεβληκότα. λέγει δ᾽, ὡς καὶ

---

[1] ‹πιστεύεσθαι› suppl. Diels, ‹διασπείρων σεμνύνεσθαι›
Navarre.   [2] sic vestigia P. Hamb. 143 interpretatur Gronewald: περὶ τοῦδε εἰπεῖν καινὸν καὶ ὡς codd.
[3] Kassel: ἐρωτᾶν codd.

8. RUMOR-MONGERING

(1) Rumor-mongering is the invention of untrue reports and events about which the monger wants ⟨. . .⟩. The rumor-monger is the sort (2) who, when he meets his friend, immediately relaxes his expression[1] and asks with a laugh, "Where have you been? Do you have anything to tell me? How's it going?" But before the man can say "I'm fine," he interrupts him: "You ask if there's any news? Actually, you know, the reports are rather good." (3) And without allowing an answer, he says "What? You haven't heard *anything*? It looks like I'll be giving you a feast of the latest news." (4) He has got a man he says he's heard just back from the battle itself, a soldier, or a slave of Asteios the flute-player, or Lykon the contractor—he has ways of vouching for his stories that no one can refute. (5) He relates, as he claims these people told him, that Polyperchon and the king were victorious in a battle, and Cassander has been taken prisoner.[2] (6) And if you say to him "Do *you* believe it?" he will say he does, because it's the talk of the city, and the discussion is intensifying; all the people are in unison since they tell the same story about the battle; it was a huge bloodbath, (7) and he has proof in the faces of the political leaders, since he notices they are all changed. And he says he

---

[1] For καταβάλλειν in this sense see Van Leeuwen on Aristophanes, *Wasps* 655.

[2] For the possible historical situation of this (untrue) rumor see Introd. pp. 10–11.

---

4 Casaubon: ἐπιλαθέσθαι codd.

5 Casaubon: πάντα codd.

παρακήκοε παρὰ τούτοις κρυπτόμενόν τινα ἐν οἰκίᾳ, ἤδη πέμπτην ἡμέραν ἥκοντα ἐκ Μακεδονίας, ὃς πάντα ταῦτα οἶδε.

(8) καὶ πάντα διεξιὼν πως[6] οἴεσθαι πιθανῶς σχετλιάζειν[7] λέγων· "δυστυχὴς Κάσανδρος· ὦ ταλαίπωρος· ἐνθυμῇ τὸ τῆς τύχης; ἀλλ' οὖν ἰσχυρὸς γενόμενος." (9) καὶ "δεῖ δ' αὐτόν σε μόνον εἰδέναι." πᾶσι δὲ τοῖς ἐν τῇ πόλει προσδεδράμηκε λέγων.

(10) [τῶν τοιούτων ἀνθρώπων τεθαύμακα, τί ποτε βούλονται λογοποιοῦντες· οὐ γὰρ μόνον ψεύδονται, ἀλλὰ καὶ ἀλυσιτελῶς ἀπαλλάττουσι. (11) πολλάκις γὰρ αὐτῶν οἱ μὲν ἐν τοῖς βαλανείοις περιστάσεις ποιούμενοι τὰ ἱμάτια ἀποβεβλήκασιν, οἱ δ' ἐν[8] τῇ στοᾷ πεζομαχίᾳ καὶ ναυμαχίᾳ νικῶντες ἐρήμους δίκας ὠφλήκασιν. (12) εἰσὶ δ' οἳ καὶ πόλεις τῷ λόγῳ κατὰ κράτος αἱροῦντες παρεδειπνήθησαν. (13) πάνυ δὴ ταλαίπωρον αὐτῶν ἐστι τὸ ἐπιτήδευμα. ποίᾳ γὰρ οὐ στοᾷ, ποίῳ δὲ ἐργαστηρίῳ, ποίῳ δὲ μέρει τῆς ἀγορᾶς οὐκ ἐνημερεύουσιν ἀπαυδᾶν ποιοῦντες τοὺς ἀκούοντας; (14) οὕτως καὶ καταπονοῦσι ταῖς ψευδολογίαις.][9]

[6] Diels: πῶς codd.
[7] οἴεσθε cDE, σχετλιάζει D.
[8] δ' ἐν CDe: δὲ AB.
[9] τῶν τοιούτων . . . ταῖς ψευδολογίαις del. editores.

also overheard that someone who knows the whole story has been kept hidden by them in a private house since he came to town four days ago from Macedonia.

(8) And as he tells his story, he somehow believes[3] he is persuasively indignant when he says, "Miserable Cassander! Poor fellow! You see what Fortune can do? Well, he had his power once." (9) and "You must keep it to yourself." But he has run up to everyone in town with the news.

(10) [I wonder what such people hope to gain from their rumor-mongering; not only do they tell lies, they also end up no better off for it. (11) Those who draw a circle of hearers in the baths often have their cloaks stolen, and those who are victorious by land and sea in the stoa lose court-cases forfeited for failure to appear. (12) Some of them capture cities in an all-out talk-fight, but go without their dinner. (13) Their behavior is sad indeed, for in what stoa, or what workshop, or what part of the market do they not pass the day exhausting those who listen to them? (14) That is how they persevere in telling lies.][4]

---

[3] The rumor-monger abandons his glee at the supposed fall of Cassander and ends with an evocation of pity. The text may be corrupt beyond repair; the reading adopted here assumes that the construction reverts to the typical string of infinitives begun in §2 and interrupted with §6.

[4] This whole paragraph, beginning in the first person, with tenses and constructions unlikely for fourth-century Greek, and rhetorical questions alien to the *Characters*, is certainly one of the later epilogues.

ΑΝΑΙΣΧΥΝΤΙΑΣ Θ´

(1) [ἡ δὲ ἀναισχυντία ἐστὶ μέν, ὡς ὅρῳ λαβεῖν, καταφρόνησις δόξης αἰσχρᾶς[1] ἕνεκα κέρδους,][2] ὁ δὲ ἀναίσχυντος τοιοῦτος, (2) οἷος πρῶτον μὲν ὂν ἀποστερεῖ πρὸς τοῦτον ἀπελθὼν δανείζεσθαι, εἶτα θύσας τοῖς θεοῖς αὐτὸς μὲν δειπνεῖν παρ᾽ ἑτέρῳ, τὰ δὲ κρέα ἀποτιθέναι ἁλσὶ πάσας, (3) καὶ προσκαλεσάμενος τὸν ἀκόλουθον δοῦναι ἀπὸ τῆς τραπέζης ἄρας κρέας καὶ ἄρτον καὶ εἰπεῖν ἀκουόντων πάντων "εὐωχοῦ, Τίβειε."

(4) καὶ ὀψωνῶν δὲ ὑπομιμνήσκειν τὸν κρεωπώλην, εἴ τι χρήσιμος αὐτῷ γέγονε, καὶ ἑστηκὼς πρὸς τῷ σταθμῷ μάλιστα μὲν κρέας, εἰ δὲ μή, ὀστοῦν εἰς τὸν ζωμὸν ἐμβαλεῖν, καὶ ἐὰν μὲν λάβῃ, εὖ ἔχει, εἰ δὲ μή, ἁρπάσας ἀπὸ τῆς τραπέζης χολίκιον ἅμα γελῶν ἀπαλλάττεσθαι.

(5) καὶ ξένοις δὲ αὐτοῦ θέαν ἀγοράσας μὴ δοὺς τὸ μέρος συνθεωρεῖν,[3] ἄγειν δὲ καὶ τοὺς υἱεῖς εἰς τὴν ὑστεραίαν καὶ τὸν παιδαγωγόν. (6) καὶ ὅσα ἐωνημένος

---

[1] Kassel: αἰσχροῦ codd.　　[2] del. Hanow, Gomperz, Stein.
[3] Cobet: θεωρεῖν codd.

---

[1] The definition is too vague to suit the following description, and seems derived from Pseudo-Plato, *Definitiones* 416a14.

[2] The meat of the sacrifical animal was normally given to guests and the household in a feast on a holy day (W. Burkert, *Homo Necans*, Berkeley 1983, 6–7)—this man goes to another's feast instead.

9. SPONGING

(1) [Sponging, to put it in a definition, is a disregard for a bad reputation for the sake of gain.][1] The sponger is the sort (2) who, in the first place, goes back to a man he is holding out on and asks for a loan; second, after performing a sacrifice to the gods he salts and stores away the meat, and goes to dinner at another's;[2] (3) he invites his slave along too, and gives him meat and bread he takes from the table and says in everyone's hearing "Enjoy yourself, Tibeios."[3]

(4) When he goes shopping, he reminds the butcher of any favor he has done him, then stands by the scale and throws in[4] preferably some meat, otherwise a bone for the soup, and if he gets it, good, otherwise he grabs some tripe from the table with a laugh as he goes away.

(5) When he buys theater tickets for his guests[5] he goes to the show too without paying his share; the next day, he brings along his children and the slave who takes care of them. (6) If anyone makes a purchase at a bargain price, he

---

[3] A name of Paphlagonian slaves (Strabo 7.304), often in Menander (*Heros* 21 and *Perinthia* 3 Sandbach, *PCG* fr. 172, 241). For giving slaves a taste, cf. Athenaeus 4.128d–e; but often in such cases the slave's task was to hide the food and take it home for later (Martial 2.37, 3.23, 7.16, *Anth. Pal.* 11.205).

[4] After the weighing: he wants it for nothing.

[5] With money they have given him. Since they make no objection the first time, he is even more brazen for the following day's show.

ἄξιά τις φέρει, μεταδοῦναι κελεῦσαι καὶ αὑτῷ. (7) καὶ
ἐπὶ τὴν ἀλλοτρίαν οἰκίαν ἐλθὼν δανείζεσθαι κριθάς,
ποτὲ δὲ ἄχυρα, καὶ ταῦτα τοὺς χρήσαντας ἀναγκάσαι
ἀποφέρειν πρὸς αὑτόν.

(8) δεινὸς δὲ καὶ πρὸς τὰ χαλκεῖα τὰ ἐν τῷ
βαλανείῳ προσελθὼν καὶ βάψας ἀρύταιναν βοῶντος
τοῦ βαλανέως αὐτὸς αὑτοῦ καταχέασθαι καὶ εἰπεῖν,
ὅτι λέλουται, ἀπιὼν †κἀκεῖ† "οὐδεμία σοι χάρις."

ΜΙΚΡΟΛΟΓΙΑΣ Ι´

(1) ἔστι δὲ ἡ μικρολογία φειδωλία τοῦ διαφόρου ὑπὲρ
τὸν καιρόν, ὁ δὲ μικρολόγος τοιοῦτός τις, (2) οἷος ἐν
τῷ μηνὶ ἡμιωβόλιον ἀπαιτεῖν ἐπὶ τὴν οἰκίαν. (3) καὶ
συσσιτῶν ἀριθμεῖν τὰς κύλικας, πόσας ἕκαστος
πέπωκε, καὶ ἀπάρχεσθαι ἐλάχιστον τῇ Ἀρτέμιδι τῶν
συνδειπνούντων. (4) καὶ ὅσα μικροῦ τις πριάμενος
λογίζεται, πάντα φάσκειν εἶναι <...>[1] (5) καὶ οἰκέτου
χύτραν[2] ἢ λοπάδα κατάξαντος εἰσπρᾶξαι ἀπὸ τῶν
ἐπιτηδείων. (6) καὶ τῆς γυναικὸς ἐκβαλούσης τρί-

---

[1] lacunam statuit Holland, e.g. <τιμιώτερα καὶ ἀποδοκι-
μάζειν> Stein.   [2] post χύτραν add. εἶναι AB.

---

[6] Used as filling material, or mixed with grain: W. K. Pritchett,
Hesperia 25 (1956) 182–183.

[7] For the apparatus and procedure see René Ginouvès,
Βαλανευτική: *Recherches sur le bain dans l'antiquité grecque*
(Paris 1962) 205, 214. Only the proverbially outspoken (Ginouvès

asks to be given a share too. (7) He goes to other people's houses and borrows barley, sometimes chaff,[6] and makes the lenders deliver it to him besides.

(8) He is apt to go up to the hot-water tanks at the baths, draw a ladle-full and rinse himself, as the bath attendant screams at him, and say, as he goes away, "I've already had my bath—no thanks to you!"[7]

10. PENNYPINCHING

(1) Pennypinching is an immoderate sparing of expense. The pennypincher is the sort (2) who stipulates the repayment of a half-cent "within the month, to his house."[1] (3) When he is sharing a dinner he reckons up how many glasses each has drunk;[2] his initial offering to Artemis[3] is smaller than any other at the table. (4) When someone has bought goods for him at a bargain price and presents his bill, he says they are too expensive, and rejects them.[4] (5) When a servant breaks a clay pot or serving dish, he deducts it from his daily rations. (6) And if his wife drops a

212) bath attendant (who has lost his fee) has the nerve to object to the sponger's tricks.

[1] The text is very condensed and may be corrupt.

[2] He demands a complete reckoning of each glass before he pays his share of the bill after dinner; cf. *PCG* Alexis fr. 15.

[3] The initial offering was a libation of wine; evidently the dining-group has Artemis as its patron.

[4] Some of the text must be missing; the last part of the sentence translated here is a speculative reconstruction (cf. *PCG* Ephippus fr. 15).

χαλκον οἷος μεταφέρειν τὰ σκεύη καὶ τὰς κλίνας καὶ τὰς κιβωτοὺς καὶ διφᾶν τὰ καλύμματα. (7) καὶ ἐάν τι πωλῇ, τοσούτου ἀποδόσθαι, ὥστε μὴ λυσιτελεῖν τῷ πριαμένῳ.

(8) καὶ οὐκ ἂν ἐᾶσαι οὔτε συκοτραγῆσαι ἐκ τοῦ αὑτοῦ κήπου οὔτε διὰ τοῦ αὑτοῦ ἀγροῦ πορευθῆναι οὔτε ἐλαίαν ἢ φοίνικα τῶν χαμαὶ πεπτωκότων ἀνελέσθαι.

(9) καὶ τοὺς ὅρους δ' ἐπισκοπεῖσθαι ὁσημέραι εἰ διαμένουσιν οἱ αὐτοί. (10) δεινὸς δὲ καὶ ὑπερημερίαν πρᾶξαι καὶ τόκον τόκου. (11) καὶ ἑστιῶν δημότας μικρὰ τὰ κρέα κόψας παραθεῖναι. (12) καὶ ὀψωνῶν μηθὲν πριάμενος εἰσελθεῖν. (13) καὶ ἀπαγορεῦσαι τῇ γυναικὶ μήτε ἅλας χρηννύειν[3] μήτε ἐλλύχνιον μήτε κύμινον μήτε ὀρίγανον μήτε ὀλὰς μήτε στέμματα μήτε θυηλήματα, ἀλλὰ λέγειν ὅτι τὰ μικρὰ ταῦτα πολλά ἐστι τοῦ ἐνιαυτοῦ.

(14) [καὶ τὸ ὅλον δὲ τῶν μικρολόγων καὶ τὰς ἀργυροθήκας ἔστιν ἰδεῖν εὐρωτιώσας καὶ τὰς κλεῖς ἰωμένας καὶ αὐτοὺς δὲ φοροῦντας ἐλάττω τῶν μηρῶν[4] τὰ ἱμάτια καὶ ἐκ ληκυθίων μικρῶν πάνυ ἀλειφομένους καὶ ἐν χρῷ κειρομένους καὶ τὸ μέσον τῆς ἡμέρας ὑποδουμένους καὶ πρὸς τοὺς γναφεῖς διατεινομένους ὅπως τὸ ἱμάτιον αὐτοῖς ἕξει πολλὴν γῆν, ἵνα μὴ ῥυπαίνηται ταχύ.][5]

3 Foss: χρωννύειν codd.
4 A (ante correctionem) et e: μικρῶν A (corr.) et BDe, μετρῶν C.   5 epilogum del. editores.

three-penny piece, he is capable of moving the dishes, couches, and chests, and searching in the floorboards. (7) If he sells something, he charges so much that the buyer can't recover his price of purchase.

(8) He doesn't allow eating of figs from his own garden, or passage through his field, or picking up of an olive or date that has fallen on the ground.

(9) He inspects his property markers daily to see if they remain the same. (10) He is apt to charge a late fee and compound interest. (11) When he gives a dinner for his precinct,[5] he serves the meat cut into tiny portions. (12) When he goes shopping, he returns home without buying anything. (13) He forbids his wife to lend out salt, or a lampwick, or cumin, or oregano, or barley groats, or garlands, or sacrifical cakes, maintaining that these small items add up to a lot over the course of a year.

(14) [In general, pennypinchers like to see their money boxes moldy and the keys to them rusty, and they themselves wear cloaks that don't cover their thighs, rub themselves down from tiny oil flasks,[6] have their heads shaved,[7] put on their shoes at midday, and insist to the cleaners that their cloaks get a lot of earth[8] so that they won't get dirty again quickly.][9]

---

[5] Lit. "his deme," the members of his local voting-district: David Whitehead, *The Demes of Attica* (Princeton 1986) 152.

[6] At the baths (30.8 note).

[7] To save money on haircuts.

[8] Fuller's clay: Hugo Blümner, *Technologie und Terminologie der Gewerbe und Künste* (2nd ed. Leipzig 1912) 1.176.

[9] The change in style and the switch to the plural among other things suggest that this closing paragraph is a later addition.

ΒΔΕΛΤΡΙΑΣ ΙΑ´

(1) οὐ χαλεπὸν δέ ἐστι τὴν βδελυρίαν διορίσασθαι· ἔστι γὰρ παιδιὰ ἐπιφανὴς καὶ ἐπονείδιστος, ὁ δὲ βδελυρὸς τοιοῦτος, (2) οἷος ἀπαντήσας γυναιξὶν ἐλευθέραις ἀνασυράμενος δεῖξαι τὸ αἰδοῖον. (3) καὶ ἐν θεάτρῳ κροτεῖν, ὅταν οἱ ἄλλοι παύωνται, καὶ συρίττειν, οὓς ἡδέως θεωροῦσιν οἱ λοιποί· καὶ ὅταν σιωπήσῃ τὸ θέατρον, ἀνακύψας ἐρυγεῖν ἵνα τοὺς καθημένους ποιήσῃ μεταστραφῆναι. (4) καὶ πληθούσης τῆς ἀγορᾶς προσελθὼν πρὸς τὰ κάρυα ἢ τὰ μύρτα ἢ τὰ ἀκρόδρυα ἑστηκὼς τραγηματίζεσθαι ἅμα τῷ πωλοῦντι προσλαλῶν· καὶ καλέσαι δὲ τῶν παρόντων ὀνομαστί τινα, ᾧ μὴ συνήθης ἐστί· (5) καὶ σπεύδοντας δέ ποι[1] ὁρῶν περιμεῖναι κελεῦσαι· (6) καὶ ἡττωμένῳ δὲ μεγάλην δίκην ἀπιόντι ἀπὸ τοῦ δικαστηρίου προσελθὼν[2] συνησθῆναι.

(7) καὶ ὀψωνεῖν ἑαυτῷ[3] καὶ αὐλητρίδας μισθοῦσθαι καὶ δεικνύειν δὲ τοῖς ἀπαντῶσι τὰ ὠψωνημένα καὶ παρακαλεῖν ἐπὶ ταῦτα· (8) καὶ διηγεῖσθαι προσστὰς πρὸς κουρεῖον ἢ μυροπώλιον ὅτι μεθύσκεσθαι μέλλει.

ΑΚΑΙΡΙΑΣ ΙΒ´

(1) [ἡ μὲν οὖν ἀκαιρία ἐστὶν ἐπίτευξις ⟨χρόνου⟩[1]

---

[1] Casaubon: που codd.   [2] Cobet: προσελθεῖν καὶ codd.
[3] Casaubon: ἑαυτὸν codd.
[1] suppl. Ruge.

11. OBNOXIOUSNESS

(1) It is not difficult to define obnoxiousness: it is joking that is obvious and offensive. The obnoxious man is the sort (2) who, when he meets respectable women, raises his cloak and exposes his genitals. (3) In the theater he claps after others have stopped, and hisses the actors whom the others enjoy watching. When the audience is silent he rears back and belches, to make the spectators turn around. (4) When the agora is crowded he goes to the stands for walnuts, myrtleberries, and fruits, and stands there nibbling on them while talking with the vendor. He calls out by name to someone in the crowd with whom he's not acquainted. (5) When he sees people hurrying somewhere he tells them to wait. (6) He goes up to a man who has lost an important case and is leaving the court, and congratulates him.

(7) He goes shopping for himself and hires flute girls,[1] and he shows his purchases to anyone he meets and invites them to share. (8) He stands by the barber shop or perfume seller and relates that he intends to get drunk.

12. BAD TIMING

(1) [Bad timing is a usage of time which causes pain to

---

[1] Women who were expected to provide music (and sometimes sex) for a dinner party; cf. 20.9 and C. G. Starr, *Parola del passato* 34 (1978) 401–410.

λυποῦσα τοὺς ἐντυγχάνοντας,][2] ὁ δὲ ἄκαιρος τοιοῦτός
τις, (2) οἷος ἀσχολουμένῳ προσελθὼν ἀνακοινοῦσθαι.
(3) καὶ πρὸς τὴν αὑτοῦ ἐρωμένην κωμάζειν πυρέτ-
τουσαν. (4) καὶ δίκην ὠφληκότα ἐγγύης προσελθὼν
κελεῦσαι αὑτὸν ἀναδέξασθαι. (5) καὶ μαρτυρήσων
παρεῖναι τοῦ πράγματος ἤδη κεκριμένου. (6) καὶ κεκλημένος εἰς γάμους τοῦ γυναικείου γένους κατηγο-
ρεῖν. (7) καὶ ἐκ μακρᾶς ὁδοῦ ἥκοντα ἄρτι παρακαλεῖν
εἰς περίπατον.

(8) δεινὸς δὲ καὶ προσάγειν ὠνητὴν πλείω διδόντα
ἤδη πεπρακότι. (9) καὶ ἀκηκοότας καὶ μεμαθηκότας
ἀνίστασθαι ἐξ ἀρχῆς διδάξων.[3] (10) καὶ πρόθυμος δὲ
ἐπιμεληθῆναι ἃ μὴ βούλεταί τις γενέσθαι, αἰσχύνεται
δὲ ἀπείπασθαι. (11) καὶ θύοντας καὶ ἀναλίσκοντας
ἥκειν τόκον ἀπαιτήσων. (12) καὶ μαστιγουμένου οἰκέτου παρεστὼς διηγεῖσθαι ὅτι καὶ αὑτοῦ ποτε παῖς
οὕτως πληγὰς λαβὼν ἀπήγξατο. (13) καὶ παρὼν διαί-
τῃ συγκρούειν, ἀμφοτέρων βουλομένων διαλύεσθαι.
(14) καὶ ὀρχησόμενος ἅψασθαι ἑτέρου μηδέπω μεθύ-
οντος.

those you happen to meet.][1] The man with bad timing is the sort (2) who goes up to someone who is busy and asks his advice. (3) He sings love songs to his girlfriend when she has a fever. (4) He goes up to a man who has just had to forfeit a security deposit in court and asks him to stand bail for him. (5) He shows up to give testimony after the case has already been decided. (6) If he's a guest at a wedding, he launches into a tirade against women.[2] (7) When a man has just returned from a long journey, he invites him to go for a walk.

(8) He is apt to bring in to a man who has already completed a sale a buyer who will pay more. (9) After people have listened and understand, he stands up to explain all over again. (10) He is zealous in seeing to things that you don't desire, but are embarrassed to refuse. (11) When people are consuming a sacrifice, he comes to ask for interest on his loan. (12) When a slave is being beaten he stands watching and tells the story of how a slave of his once hanged himself after being beaten in just this way. (13) When he is on an arbitration board[3] he exacerbates the dispute, when what both sides desire is a reconciliation. (14) When he wants to dance, he grabs a partner who is still sober.[4]

[1] This extremely abstract definition appears to be adapted from the definition of its opposite ("good timing") in Pseudo-Plato, *Definitiones* 413c12.

[2] Cf. the tirade in Theophrastus, *On Marriage* (fr. 486).

[3] See on 5.3.

[4] Cf. 6.3.

ΠΕΡΙΕΡΓΙΑΣ ΙΓ΄

(1) ἀμέλει ⟨ἡ⟩[1] περιεργία δόξει εἶναι προσποίησίς τις λόγων καὶ πράξεων μετὰ εὐνοίας, ὁ δὲ περίεργος τοιοῦτός τις, (2) οἷος ἐπαγγέλλεσθαι ἀναστὰς ἃ μὴ δυνήσεται. (3) καὶ ὁμολογουμένου τοῦ πράγματος δικαίου εἶναι ἐντείνας[2] ἐλεγχθῆναι. (4) καὶ πλείω δὲ ἐπαναγκάσαι τὸν παῖδα κεράσαι ἢ ὅσα δύνανται οἱ παρόντες ἐκπιεῖν.

(5) καὶ διείργειν τοὺς μαχομένους καὶ οὓς οὐ γινώσκει. (6) καὶ ἀτραποῦ ἡγήσασθαι, εἶτα μὴ δύνασθαι εὑρεῖν οἷ[3] πορεύεται. (7) καὶ τὸν στρατηγὸν προσελθὼν ἐρωτῆσαι πότε μέλλει παρατάττεσθαι, καὶ τί μετὰ τὴν αὔριον παραγγελεῖ. (8) καὶ προσελθὼν τῷ πατρὶ εἰπεῖν, ὅτι ἡ μήτηρ ἤδη καθεύδει ἐν τῷ δωματίῳ. (9) καὶ ἀπαγορεύοντος τοῦ ἰατροῦ ὅπως μὴ δώσει οἶνον τῷ μαλακιζομένῳ, φήσας βούλεσθαι διάπειραν λαμβάνειν εὖ ποτίσαι[4] τὸν κακῶς ἔχοντα. (10) καὶ γυναικὸς δὲ τελευτησάσης ἐπιγράψαι ἐπὶ τὸ μνῆμα τοῦ τε ἀνδρὸς αὐτῆς καὶ τοῦ πατρὸς καὶ τῆς μητρὸς καὶ αὐτῆς τῆς γυναικὸς τοὔνομα καὶ ποδαπή ἐστι, καὶ προσεπιγράψαι ὅτι οὗτοι πάντες χρηστοὶ ἦσαν.

(11) καὶ ὀμνύναι μέλλων εἰπεῖν πρὸς τοὺς περιεστηκότας, ὅτι "καὶ πρότερον πολλάκις ὀμώμοκα."

---

[1] suppl. Buecheler.   [2] Immisch: ἔν τινι στάς codd.
[3] Casauboń: οὗ codd.
[4] Foss: εὐτρεπίσαι codd.

13. OVERZEALOUSNESS

(1) You can be sure overzealousness will seem to be a well-intentioned appropriation of words and actions. The overzealous man is the sort (2) who gets up and promises to do things he won't be able to carry out. (3) When people are in agreement that his cause is just, he becomes too intense and loses the case. (4) He forces the servant to mix more wine than the company can drink.

(5) He tries to stop fights even between strangers to him.[1] (6) He leads the way down a path, but then can't find the way to where he is going.[2] (7) He goes up to the general and asks him when he will take the field, and what his orders are going to be the day after tomorrow. (8) He goes up to his father and tells him that his mother is already asleep in their bedroom. (9) Even though the doctor forbids giving any wine to a sick man, he says he wants to do an experiment, and soaks the poor fellow with it. (10) If a woman dies, he inscribes on her tomb the names of her husband, her father and mother, and herself and place of birth, and adds that they were *all* "fine persons."[3]

(11) When he is going to swear an oath he says to the bystanders, "I've sworn oaths many times before."[4]

---

[1] As does the cook in Menander, *Samia* 383ff.

[2] The proverb was "don't take a path when you have a road" (*Paroem. Graec.* I.437).   [3] In Attic funerary inscriptions Athenian women were rarely listed with more than their names, and χρηστός (literally "good") was limited to slaves (Lane Fox 149–150).   [4] Cf. Menander *PCG* fr. 96. Swearing to the truth of something undocumented (Harrison, *Law of Athens* II, Oxford 1971, 150–152) was a last resort, not to be taken lightly.

ΑΝΑΙΣΘΗΣΙΑΣ ΙΔ΄

(1) ἔστι δὲ ἡ ἀναισθησία, ὡς ὅρῳ εἰπεῖν, βραδυτὴς ψυχῆς ἐν λόγοις καὶ πράξεσιν, ὁ δὲ ἀναίσθητος τοιοῦτός τις, (2) οἷος λογισάμενος ταῖς ψήφοις καὶ κεφάλαιον ποιήσας ἐρωτᾶν τὸν παρακαθήμενον· "τί γίνεται;" (3) καὶ δίκην φεύγων καὶ ταύτην εἰσιέναι μέλλων ἐπιλαθόμενος εἰς ἀγρὸν πορεύεσθαι. (4) καὶ θεωρῶν ἐν τῷ θεάτρῳ μόνος καταλείπεσθαι καθεύδων. (5) καὶ πολλὰ φαγὼν καὶ τῆς νυκτὸς ἐπὶ θάκου ἀνιστάμενος[1] ὑπὸ κυνὸς τῆς τοῦ γείτονος δηχθῆναι. (6) καὶ λαβὼν ⟨τι⟩[2] καὶ ἀποθεὶς αὐτός, τοῦτο ζητεῖν καὶ μὴ δύνασθαι εὑρεῖν. (7) καὶ ἀπαγγέλλοντος αὐτῷ ὅτι τετελεύτηκέ τις αὐτοῦ τῶν φίλων, ἵνα παραγένηται, σκυθρωπάσας καὶ δακρύσας εἰπεῖν· "ἀγαθῇ τύχῃ."

(8) δεινὸς δὲ καὶ ἀπολαμβάνων ἀργύριον ὀφειλόμενον μάρτυρας παραλαβεῖν. (9) καὶ χειμῶνος ὄντος μάχεσθαι τῷ παιδὶ ὅτι σικύους οὐκ ἠγόρασεν. (10) καὶ τὰ παιδία ἑαυτοῦ παλαίειν ἀναγκάζων καὶ τροχάζειν εἰς κόπον ἐμβάλλειν. (11) καὶ ἐν ἀγρῷ αὐτὸς φακῆν ἕψων δὶς ἅλας εἰς τὴν χύτραν ἐμβαλὼν ἄβρωτον ποιῆσαι. (12) καὶ ὕοντος τοῦ Διὸς εἰπεῖν †ἡδύ γε τῶν ἄστρων νομίζει, ὅτι δὴ καὶ οἱ ἄλλοι λέγουσι πίσσης† (13) καὶ λέγοντός τινος· "πόσους οἴει κατὰ τὰς Ἱερὰς

[1] post ἀνιστάμενος lacunam statuerunt editores, fortasse recte ⟨τῆς νυκτὸς καὶ codd., transp. Salmasius⟩.
[2] add. M.

14. ABSENT-MINDEDNESS

(1) Absent-mindedness, to say it in a definition, is slowness of soul in words and deeds. The absent-minded man is the sort (2) who, when he has made a calculation with an abacus and determined the total, asks the person sitting by him, "What's the answer?" (3) If he is a defendant, and intends to appear in court, he forgets and goes to the country. (4) If he's in the audience at the theater, he falls asleep and is left behind alone. (5) If he eats too much and gets up at night to go to the toilet, he is bitten by his neighbor's dog.[1] (6) When he's received something and put it away himself, he looks for it and can't find it. (7) If it's reported to him that one of his friends has died, so he should attend the funeral, he makes a sad face and says weepingly, "Let's hope it's for the best!"

(8) When he receives money that is owed to him, he is apt to ask for a receipt.[2] (9) Despite its being winter he quarrels with his servant because he didn't buy cucumbers. (10) He forces his children to practice wrestling and running until he drives them to exhaustion. (11) When he is cooking himself bean-soup in the field, he adds salt to the pot twice, and makes it inedible. (12) When it rains, he says "He thinks it sweet from the stars," which others in fact say "from pitch."[3] (13) If someone says to him "How many bodies do you suppose have been carried out for

[1] The text seems abbreviated: instead of the outhouse he wanders into the watchdog's pen.

[2] Literally "secure witnesses."

[3] The Greek text of this sentence is corrupt beyond repair.

πύλας ἐξενηνέχθαι νεκρούς;" πρὸς τοῦτον εἰπεῖν·
"ὅσοι ἐμοὶ καὶ σοὶ γένοιντο."

ΑΥΘΑΔΕΙΑΣ ΙΕ΄

(1) ἡ δὲ αὐθάδειά ἐστιν ἀπήνεια ὁμιλίας ἐν λόγοις, ὁ
δὲ αὐθάδης τοιοῦτός τις, (2) οἷος ἐρωτηθείς· "ὁ δεῖνα
ποῦ ἐστιν;" εἰπεῖν· "πράγματά μοι μὴ πάρεχε." (3) καὶ
προσαγορευθεὶς μὴ ἀντιπροσειπεῖν. (4) καὶ πωλῶν τι
μὴ λέγειν τοῖς ὠνουμένοις πόσου ἂν ἀποδοῖτο, ἀλλ᾽
ἐρωτᾶν "τί εὑρίσκει;" (5) καὶ τοῖς τιμῶσι καὶ πέμπου-
σιν εἰς τὰς ἑορτὰς εἰπεῖν, ὅτι οὐκ ἂν γένοιτο διδόμενα.
(6) καὶ οὐκ ἔχειν συγγνώμην οὔτε τῷ ῥυπώσαντι[1]
αὑτὸν ἀκουσίως οὔτε τῷ ὤσαντι οὔτε τῷ ἐμβάντι. (7)
καὶ φίλῳ δὲ ἔρανον κελεύσαντι εἰσενεγκεῖν εἰπών, ὅτι
οὐκ ἂν δοίη, ὕστερον ἥκειν φέρων καὶ λέγειν, ὅτι
ἀπόλλυσι καὶ τοῦτο τὸ ἀργύριον. (8) καὶ προσπταίσας
ἐν τῇ ὁδῷ δεινὸς καταράσασθαι τῷ λίθῳ. (9) καὶ
[ἀναμεῖναι][2] οὐκ ἂν ὑπομείναι[3] πολὺν χρόνον οὐθένα.
(10) καὶ οὔτε ᾆσαι οὔτε ῥῆσιν εἰπεῖν οὔτε ὀρχήσασθαι
ἂν ἐθελήσειεν·[4] (11) δεινὸς δὲ καὶ τοῖς θεοῖς μὴ ἐπεύ-
χεσθαι.

---

[1] Foss (cf. Seneca *de beneficiis* 6.9.1): ἀπώσαντι codd.
[2] del. Reiske.   [3] ὑπομείναι (optativum) Casaubon,
Ussing: ὑπομεῖναι (infinitivum) codd.
[4] Petersen: ἠθέλησε(ν) AB, θελῆσαι CDe.

burial at the sacred gate?"[4] He says to him, "May you and I have as many!"

15. GROUCHINESS

(1) Grouchiness is verbal hostility in social contacts. The grouch is the sort (2) who, when asked "Where is so-and-so?" responds "don't bother me." (3) If someone speaks to him he doesn't answer. (4) If he is selling something, he doesn't tell customers how much he would sell it for, but asks "What will it fetch?"[1] (5) If people honor him by sending him some of the food on a festival day,[2] he tells them not to expect anything in return. (6) If anyone splashes him accidentally or jostles him or steps on his foot, he won't forgive him. (7) After first refusing to give to a friend who has asked him to contribute to a loan,[3] he comes to him later and brings it, but adds that he is throwing his money away again. (8) If he stumbles on the street, he is apt to curse the stone. (9) He isn't likely to wait very long for anyone. (10) He won't sing or recite a speech or dance.[4] (11) He is apt to ask for nothing—even from the gods.

[4] Perhaps in a time of plague, or after a military disaster (for the sacred gate see Plutarch, *Sulla* 14.3). He answers as if he had been asked something like "how much money do you suppose x has?"   [1] For this meaning see LSJ εὑρίσκω V.

[2] For the custom cf. 17.2 below, and Aristophanes, *Acharnians* 1049, Menander, *Samia* 403, *PCG* Ephippus fr. 15.11.

[3] In its financial sense, ἔρανος was a loan put together from multiple contributors (cf. 1.5, 17.9, 22.9, 23.6; MacDowell in Demosthenes, *Against Medias* 101), sometimes interest-free (and therefore a friendly gesture), but not always.

[4] At a banquet.

THEOPHRASTUS

ΔΕΙΣΙΔΑΙΜΟΝΙΑΣ Ιϛ´

(1) [ἀμέλει ἡ δεισιδαιμονία δόξειεν ἂν εἶναι δειλία πρὸς τὸ δαιμόνιον,][1] ὁ δὲ δεισιδαίμων τοιοῦτός τις, (2) οἷος †ἐπιχρωνῆν[2] ἀπονιψάμενος τὰς χεῖρας καὶ περιρρανάμενος ἀπὸ ἱεροῦ δάφνην εἰς τὸ στόμα λαβὼν οὕτω τὴν ἡμέραν περιπατεῖν. (3) καὶ τὴν ὁδὸν ἐὰν ὑπερδράμῃ γαλῆ, μὴ πρότερον πορευθῆναι ἕως διεξέλθῃ τις ἢ λίθους τρεῖς ὑπὲρ τῆς ὁδοῦ διαβάλῃ. (4) καὶ ἐὰν ἴδῃ ὄφιν ἐν τῇ οἰκίᾳ, ἐὰν παρείαν, Σαβάζιον[3] καλεῖν, ἐὰν δὲ ἱερόν, ἐνταῦθα ἡρῷον[4] εὐθὺς ἱδρύσασθαι.

(5) καὶ τῶν λιπαρῶν λίθων τῶν ἐν ταῖς τριόδοις παριὼν ἐκ τῆς ληκύθου ἔλαιον καταχεῖν καὶ ἐπὶ γόνατα πεσὼν καὶ προσκυνήσας ἀπαλλάττεσθαι. (6)

---

1 del. Hanow, Gomperz, Stein.   2 ἐπὶ Χόων Foss, ἐπιδὼν κορώνην Usener, ἐπιτυχὼν ἐκφορᾷ Bolkestein.

3 Schneider: Σαβάδιον codd.

4 Duebner: ἱερῶον (ι in rasura) V, om. CD.

---

1 The definition resembles one found in Stoic writings (SVF III p. 98.42, p. 99.13) and is probably interpolated from another source.   2 The word in the text is nonsense, and various changes have been proposed, e.g. "when it is ' Pitchers'" (a festival of the dead, see Burkert, *Homo Necans* 218–222), "when he sees a crow," or "when he meets a funeral procession."

3 For weasels as bad luck cf. Aristophanes, *Ecclesiazousai* 792, *Paroem. Graec.* I.230.

4 A Phrygian god often identified with Dionysus, imported to Athens in the fifth century B.C.; Demosthenes gives a detailed ac-

16. SUPERSTITION

(1) [You can be sure superstition would seem to be coward-ice about divinity.][1] The superstitious man is the sort (2) who < . . .>[2] washes his hands, sprinkles himself with water from a shrine, puts a sprig of laurel in his mouth and walks around that way all day. (3) If a weasel crosses his path[3] he goes no further until someone passes between them, or he throws three stones over the road. (4) If he sees a snake in his house, he invokes Sabazios[4] if it is a cheek snake, but if it is a holy one[5] he immediately founds a hero shrine on the spot.

(5) When he passes the oiled stones[6] at the crossroads, he drenches them with olive oil from his flask,[7] kneels and prostrates himself before he departs. (6) If a mouse eats a

count of how he was worshipped in *On The Crown* 18.259–260, and describes handling snakes of the variety mentioned here, which were harmless (Aelian, *Nature of Animals* 8.12).

[5] This variety of snake was poisonous (Aristotle, *History of Animals* 8.607a30). "Heroes" were potentially harmful spirits of the dead: Walter Burkert, *Greek Religion*, tr. John Raffan (Oxford and Cambridge, Mass. 1985) 206–207. Compare the snake in the fraudulent hero-cult of Heraclides of Pontus, Diog. Laert. 5.89 = fr. 16 Wehrli. Plato, *Laws* X.909e3–910a6 condemns the establishment of private shrines to avert bad luck.

[6] For the anointing of stones see Homer, *Odyssey* 3.406–11; Tibullus I.1.11–12; W. Burkert, *Structure and History in Greek Mythology and Ritual* (Berkeley 1979) 162 n.20; Frazer on Pausanias 10.24.6. Worshipping them is ridiculed by Lucian, *Alexander* 30; Arnobius, *Adv. nationes* I.39; Clement of Alexandria, *Stromateis* 7.4.26.

[7] The one he carries for the baths, see on 30.8.

καὶ ἐὰν μῦς θύλακον ἀλφίτων διαφάγῃ, πρὸς τὸν
ἐξηγητὴν ἐλθὼν ἐρωτᾶν τί χρὴ ποιεῖν, καὶ ἐὰν ἀπο-
κρίνηται αὐτῷ ἐκδοῦναι τῷ σκυτοδέψῃ ἐπιρράψαι, μὴ
προσέχειν τούτοις, ἀλλ᾽ ἀποτραπεὶς ἐκθύσασθαι.⁵

(7) καὶ πυκνὰ δὲ τὴν οἰκίαν καθᾶραι δεινὸς Ἑκάτης
φάσκων ἐπαγωγὴν γεγονέναι. (8) κἂν γλαῦκες βαδί-
ζοντος αὐτοῦ ‹ἀνακράγωσι›,⁶ ταράττεσθαι καὶ εἴπας
"Ἀθηνᾶ κρείττων," παρελθεῖν οὕτω. (9) καὶ οὔτε ἐπι-
βῆναι μνήματι οὔτ᾽ ἐπὶ νεκρὸν οὔτ᾽ ἐπὶ λεχὼ ἐλθεῖν
ἐθελῆσαι, ἀλλὰ τὸ μὴ μιαίνεσθαι συμφέρον αὑτῷ
φῆσαι εἶναι.

(10) καὶ ταῖς τετράσι δὲ καὶ ταῖς ἑβδόμαις προ-
στάξας οἶνον ἕψειν τοῖς ἔνδον, ἐξελθὼν ἀγοράσαι
μυρσίνας, λιβανωτόν, πόπανα⁷ καὶ εἰσελθὼν εἴσω
στεφανοῦν⁸ τοὺς Ἑρμαφροδίτους ὅλην τὴν ἡμέραν.

(11) καὶ ὅταν ἐνύπνιον ἴδῃ, πορεύεσθαι πρὸς τοὺς
ὀνειροκρίτας, πρὸς τοὺς μάντεις, πρὸς τοὺς ὀρνιθο-
σκόπους, ἐρωτήσων, τίνι θεῶν ἢ θεᾷ εὔχεσθαι δεῖ. καὶ

---

5 Bernard: ἐκλύσασθαι codd.
6 suppl. Foss: ταράττεται V, corr. Korais.
7 Foss: λιβανωτῶν πίνακα V.
8 Siebenkees: στεφανῶν codd.

---

8 For an account of a Hekate-exorcism see Sophron fr. 4 below, and Robert Parker, *Miasma* (Oxford 1983) 223–224.
9 Thompson, *Glossary of Greek Birds* 78.   10 He extends
legitimate rules of purity (see West on Hesiod, *Works and Days*
750; Burkert, *Greek Religion* 378 nn. 30–31) to avoid attending fu-
nerals, or even seeing his wife after childbirth.   11 Boiling

98

hole in a sack of barley, he visits the theologian and asks what he should do; if the answer is to give it to the tailor to be patched he pays no attention, but hurries off and performs an expiation.

(7) He is apt to purify his house frequently, claiming Hekate has bewitched it.[8] (8) If owls hoot[9] as he passes by he becomes agitated, and says "mighty Athena!" before he goes on. (9) He refuses to step on a gravestone, view a corpse or visit a woman who has given birth, and says it's the best policy for him not to incur pollution.[10]

(10) On the fourth and the seventh of every month he orders his household to boil some wine,[11] then goes out and buys myrtle, frankincense, and cakes,[12] comes back home and spends all day putting wreaths on the Hermaphrodites.[13]

(11) Whenever he has a dream, he visits the dream analysts or the prophets or the omen-readers to ask to which god or goddess[14] he should pray. He goes to the Initiators

wine made it sweeter, see MacDowell on Aristophanes, *Wasps* 878, *PCG* Plato Comicus fr. 164. [12] The first is to make wreaths (Aristophanes, *Wasps* 861), the others to burn as a sacrifice (Menander, *Dyskolos* 449–50). [13] If the text is sound, he seems to spend too much time and money on a regular household offering. The word "Hermaphroditos" first occurs here (it is also the title of a comedy by the third-century writer Posidippus, and found in a votive inscription perhaps of the fourth century B.C.): rather than the androgynous god of later mythology, the plural may designate a variety of the neighborhood portrait-busts known as "herms" with female and male faces on opposites sides. See *Lexicon Iconographicum Mythologiae Classicae* V (Zurich 1991) 269. [14] A prayer formula: J. Alvar, "Materiaux pour l'étude de la formule *sive deus sive dea*," *Numen* 32 (1985) 236–273.

THEOPHRASTUS

τελεσθησόμενος πρὸς τοὺς Ὀρφεοτελεστὰς κατὰ
μῆνα πορεύεσθαι μετὰ τῆς γυναικός, ἐὰν δὲ μὴ σχο-
λάζῃ ἡ γυνή, μετὰ τῆς τίτθης καὶ τῶν παιδίων. (12)
καὶ τῶν περιρραινομένων ἐπὶ θαλάττης ἐπιμελῶς
δόξειεν ἂν εἶναι. (13) κἄν ποτε ἐπίδῃ σκορόδῳ ἐστεμ-
μένον⁹ τῶν ἐπὶ ταῖς τριόδοις, ἀπελθὼν κατὰ κεφαλῆς
λούσασθαι καὶ ἱερείας καλέσας σκίλλῃ ἢ σκύλακι
κελεῦσαι αὐτὸν περικαθᾶραι. (14) μαινόμενον δὲ¹⁰
ἰδὼν ἢ ἐπίληπτον φρίξας εἰς κόλπον πτύσαι.

MEMΨIMOIPIAΣ IZ´

(1) ἔστι δὲ ἡ μεμψιμοιρία ἐπιτίμησις παρὰ τὸ προσ-
ῆκον τῶν δεδομένων, ὁ δὲ μεμψίμοιρος τοιόσδε τις, (2)
οἷος ἀποστείλαντος μερίδα τοῦ φίλου εἰπεῖν πρὸς τὸν
φέροντα· "ἐφθόνησέν¹ μοι τοῦ ζωμοῦ καὶ τοῦ οἰναρίου
οὐκ ἐπὶ δεῖπνον καλέσας." (3) καὶ ὑπὸ τῆς ἑταίρας
καταφιλούμενος εἰπεῖν· "θαυμάζω εἰ σὺ καὶ ἀπὸ τῆς
ψυχῆς οὕτω με φιλεῖς." (4) καὶ τῷ Διὶ ἀγανακτεῖν, οὐ

⁹ Foss: ἐστεμμένων V.   ¹⁰ Blaydes: τε codd.
¹ Pauw: ἐφθόνησας V.

15 Itinerant priests, cf. Plato *Republic* 364b–e, W. Burkert,
Ancient Mystery Cults (Cambridge, Mass. 1987) 33. Evidently
the presence of a woman was required.   16 For the purifying
powers of salt water see Robert Parker, *Miasma* 226–227.

17 Crossroads were repositories of religious pollution, including the bodies of murderers: S. I. Johnston, "Crossroads," *Zeit-*

100

of Orpheus[15] every month to be inducted with his wife—if she has no time, he takes his children and their wet-nurse. (12) When people are sprinkling themselves carefully at the seaside,[16] he would seem to be among them. (13) If he ever notices someone at the crossroads wreathed in garlic[17] he goes away, takes a shower, summons priestesses and orders a deluxe purification by sea onion[18] or dog.[19] (14) If he sees a madman or epileptic he shudders, and spits down at his chest.[20]

17. GRIPING

(1) Griping is unsuitable criticism of what one has been given. The griper is a type such as this, (2) who, when his friend has sent him part of the meat from a sacrifice,[1] says to the delivery boy, "by not inviting me to the dinner, he did me out of the soup and wine." (3) When he is being kissed by his mistress, he says "I wonder whether you really love me that much in your heart." (4) He is annoyed

schrift für Papyrologie und Epigraphik 88 (1991) 222–224. As it is today, garlic was a protection against evil spirits (cf. Persius 5.188), so that he immediately suspects danger.

[18] Also called "squill"; credited with apotropaic powers, *PCG* Cratinus fr. 250.2; Theophrastus, *Inquiry into Plants* 7.13.4; John Scarborough, "The Pharmacology of Sacred Plants, Herbs, and Roots," in *Magika Hiera*, ed. C. A. Faraone and D. Obbink (New York 1991) 146–148.   [19] Killed and rubbed around the bodies of those to be purified: Plutarch, *Roman Questions* 280B–C, 290D; N. J. Zaganiaris, "Sacrifices de chiens dans l'antiquité classique," Πλάτων 27 (1975) 322–329; *PCG* Aristophanes fr. 209.   [20] The ancient Greek equivalent of knocking on wood (see Gow on Theocritus 6.39).   [1] Cf. 15.5.

THEOPHRASTUS

διότι ὕει, ἀλλὰ διότι ὕστερον. (5) καὶ εὑρὼν ἐν τῇ ὁδῷ
βαλλάντιον εἰπεῖν· "ἀλλ᾽ οὐ θησαυρὸν εὕρηκα οὐδέ-
ποτε." (6) καὶ πριάμενος ἀνδράποδον ἄξιον καὶ πολλὰ
δεηθεὶς τοῦ πωλοῦντος· "θαυμάζω," εἰπεῖν, "ὅ τι ὑγιὲς
οὕτω ἄξιον ἐώνημαι." (7) καὶ πρὸς τὸν εὐαγγελιζό-
μενον ὅτι "υἱός σοι γέγονεν" εἰπεῖν ὅτι "ἂν προσθῇς
'καὶ τῆς οὐσίας τὸ ἥμισυ ἄπεστιν,' ἀληθῆ ἐρεῖς." (8)
καὶ δίκην² νικήσας καὶ λαβὼν πάσας τὰς ψήφους
ἐγκαλεῖν³ τῷ γράψαντι τὸν λόγον ὡς πολλὰ παραλε-
λοιπότι τῶν δικαίων. (9) καὶ ἐράνου εἰσενεχθέντος
παρὰ τῶν φίλων καὶ φήσαντός τινος· "ἱλαρὸς ἴσθι,"
"καὶ πῶς;" εἰπεῖν, "ὅτι δεῖ τἀργύριον ἀποδοῦναι
ἑκάστῳ καὶ χωρὶς τούτων χάριν ὀφείλειν ὡς εὐεργε-
τημένον;"

ΑΠΙΣΤΙΑΣ ΙΗ΄

(1) ἔστιν ἀμέλει ἡ ἀπιστία ὑπόληψίς τις ἀδικίας κατὰ
πάντων, ὁ δὲ ἄπιστος τοιοῦτός τις, (2) οἷος ἀπο-
στείλας τὸν παῖδα ὀψωνήσοντα ἕτερον παῖδα πέμπειν
τὸν πευσόμενον πόσου ἐπρίατο. (3) καὶ φέρων αὐτὸς
τὸ ἀργύριον [καὶ]¹ κατὰ στάδιον καθίζων ἀριθμεῖν
πόσον ἐστίν. (4) καὶ τὴν γυναῖκα τὴν αὑτοῦ ἐρωτᾶν
κατακείμενος εἰ κέκλεικε τὴν κιβωτόν, καὶ εἰ σεσή-
μανται τὸ κυλιούχιον, καὶ εἰ ὁ μοχλὸς εἰς τὴν θύραν
τὴν αὐλείαν ἐμβέβληται· καὶ ἂν ἐκείνη φῇ, μηδὲν

² Casaubon: νίκην V.   ³ Stephanus: ἐγκαλεῖ V.

with Zeus not because it is raining, but because it rained too late. (5) If he finds a wallet in the road, he says, "well, I still haven't ever found a treasure." (6) If he buys a slave at a good price, after much haggling with the seller, he says "I wonder how sound the merchandise can be if I got it so cheap." (7) To the bearer of the good news "you have a son!" he replies, "if you add ' half of your property is gone,' you'll be telling the truth." (8) If he wins a court case, even by a unanimous vote, he criticizes his lawyer for leaving out many valid arguments. (9) If his friends get together a loan for him,[2] and someone says "Congratulations!" he says "Why? Because I've got to pay the money back to each of you, and be grateful besides, as if you'd done me a favor?"

18. MISTRUST

(1) You can be sure that mistrust is an assumption that one is being wronged by everyone. The mistrustful man is the sort (2) who, when he has dispatched his slave to do the shopping, sends another one to find out how much he paid. (3) Even though he carries his money himself,[1] he sits down every hundred yards and counts how much he has. (4) When he is lying in bed he asks his wife whether she has locked up the money chest, whether the cupboard has been sealed, and whether the bolt is in place on the front

---

[2] See on 15.7.

[1] Normally a slave would carry it (Plautus, *Pseudolus* 170, *Menaechmi* 265), cf. 23.8.

---

[1] del. Needham.

ἧττον αὐτὸς ἀναστὰς γυμνὸς ἐκ τῶν στρωμάτων καὶ
ἀνυπόδητος τὸν λύχνον ἅψας ταῦτα πάντα περιδρα-
μὼν ἐπισκέψασθαι καὶ οὕτω μόλις ὕπνου τυγχάνειν.
(5) καὶ τοὺς ὀφείλοντας αὐτῷ ἀργύριον μετὰ μαρτύ-
ρων ἀπαιτεῖν τοὺς τόκους, ὅπως μὴ δύνωνται[2] ἔξαρνοι
γενέσθαι. (6) καὶ τὸ ἱμάτιον δὲ ἐκδοῦναι δεινὸς οὐχ ὃς
<ἂν>[3] βέλτιστα ἐργάσηται, ἀλλ᾽ οὗ ἂν ᾖ ἄξιος ἐγγυη-
τὴς [τοῦ κναφέως].[4] (7) καὶ ὅταν ἥκῃ τις αἰτησόμενος
ἐκπώματα, μάλιστα μὲν μὴ δοῦναι, ἂν δ᾽ ἄρα τις
οἰκεῖος ᾖ καὶ ἀναγκαῖος, μόνον οὐ πυρώσας καὶ στήσας καὶ σχεδὸν ἐγγυητὴν λαβὼν χρῆσαι.[5] (8) καὶ τὸν
παῖδα δὲ ἀκολουθοῦντα κελεύειν αὐτοῦ ὄπισθεν μὴ
βαδίζειν ἀλλ᾽ ἔμπροσθεν, ἵνα φυλάττῃ αὐτὸν[6] μὴ ἐν
τῇ ὁδῷ ἀποδρᾷ.[7] (9) καὶ τοῖς εἰληφόσι τι παρ᾽ αὐτοῦ
καὶ λέγουσι "πόσου, κατάθου· οὐ γὰρ σχολάζω πω,"
εἰπεῖν[8] "μηδὲν πραγματεύου· ἐγὼ γάρ, <ἕως>[9] ἂν σὺ
σχολάσῃς, συνακολουθήσω."

ΔΥΣΧΕΡΕΙΑΣ ΙΘ´

(1) ἔστι δὲ ἡ δυσχέρεια ἀθεραπευσία σώματος λύπης
παρασκευαστική, ὁ δὲ δυσχερὴς τοιοῦτός τις, (2) οἷος
λέπραν ἔχων καὶ ἀλφὸν καὶ τοὺς ὄνυχας μεγάλους

[2] Jebb: δύναιντο codd.   [3] suppl. Diels. (ὃς Salmasius: ὡς
codd.)   [4] Ast: ὅταν ᾖ codd.   [5] Schneider: χρήσει codd.
[6] Needham: αὐτῷ vel αὑτῷ codd.
[7] φυλάττῃ . . . ἀποδρᾷ Hirschig: φυλάττηται . . . ἀπο-
δράσῃ codd.

door; and even if she says yes he gets out of bed anyway, naked and barefoot, lights the lamp and runs around checking all these, and only then can he get some sleep. (5) When people owe him money he takes the witnesses with him when he collects the interest, so they won't be able to deny the debt. (6) He is apt to give his cloak not to the man who does the best work, but the one whose bondsman is worth the most.[2] (7) Whenever someone comes to him to borrow drinking cups he prefers not to give them at all, but if it is a relative or close friend he makes the loan only after practically testing their composition and weight, and nearly asking for someone to guarantee replacement costs. (8) When his slave is attending him he tells him not to walk behind but in front, so he can watch to make sure he doesn't run away.[3] (9) To those who are buying something from him and say "Add it up and put it down to my account; I don't have time yet," he says "Don't go to any trouble; I'll stay with you until you have time."[4]

19. SQUALOR

(1) Squalor is a neglect of one's body which produces distress. The squalid man is the sort (2) who goes around in a leprous and encrusted state, with long fingernails, and says

---

[2] He assumes his clothing is going to be lost or ruined.

[3] As in Plautus, *Curculio* 487.

[4] The text is uncertain.

---

[8] Madvig: πέμπειν codd.

[9] suppl. Madvig.

περιπατεῖν καὶ φῆσαι ταῦτα εἶναι αὐτῷ συγγενικὰ
ἀρρωστήματα· ἔχειν γὰρ αὐτὸν καὶ τὸν πατέρα καὶ
τὸν πάππον, καὶ οὐκ εἶναι ῥᾴδιον αὐτῶν[1] εἰς τὸ γένος
ὑποβάλλεσθαι. (3) ἀμέλει δὲ δεινὸς καὶ ἕλκη ἔχειν ἐν
τοῖς ἀντικνημίοις καὶ προσπταίσματα ἐν τοῖς δακτύ-
λοις καὶ μὴ θεραπεῦσαι ἀλλ᾽ ἐᾶσαι θηριωθῆναι· καὶ
τὰς μασχάλας δὲ θηριώδεις καὶ δασείας ἔχειν ἄχρι
ἐπὶ πολὺ τῶν πλευρῶν, καὶ τοὺς ὀδόντας μέλανας καὶ
ἐσθιομένους [ὥστε δυσέντευκτος εἶναι καὶ ἀηδής.][2]

(4) καὶ τὰ τοιαῦτα· ἐσθίων ἀπομύττεσθαι· θύων ἅμ᾽
ἀδαξᾶσθαι·[3] προσλαλῶν ἀπορρίπτειν ἀπὸ τοῦ στόμα-
τος· ἅμα πιὼν ἐρυγγάνειν.[4] (5) ἀναπόνιπτος[5] ἐν τοῖς
στρώμασι μετὰ τῆς γυναικὸς αὐτοῦ κοιμᾶσθαι. (6)
ἐλαίῳ σαπρῷ ἐν βαλανείῳ χρώμενος ὄζεσθαι.[6] (7) καὶ
χιτωνίσκον παχὺν καὶ ἱμάτιον σφόδρα λεπτὸν καὶ
κηλίδων μεστὸν ἀναβαλλόμενος εἰς ἀγορὰν ἐξελθεῖν.
‹...›[7]

(8) καὶ εἰς ὀρνιθοσκόπου τῆς μητρὸς ἐξελθούσης
βλασφημῆσαι. (9) καὶ εὐχομένων καὶ σπενδόντων
ἐκβαλεῖν[8] τὸ ποτήριον καὶ γελάσαι ὡς τεράστιόν τι
πεποιηκώς· (10) καὶ αὐλούμενος δὲ κροτεῖν ταῖς χερσὶ
μόνος τῶν ἄλλων καὶ συντερετίζειν καὶ ἐπιτιμᾶν τῇ

---

[1] Meister: αὐτὸν V.   [2] ut glossema del. Immisch.
[3] Diels: θύων ἅμα δ᾽ ἄρξασθαι V, θύων ἀρξάμενος CD.
[4] Stein: προσερυγγάνειν codd.
[5] Badham: ἀναπίπτοντος V.   [6] Petersen: σφύζεσθαι V,
χρίεσθαι c, χρᾶσθαι c, χρῆσθαι d.
[7] lacunam stat. edd., qui §8–11 aliena esse viderunt.

these are all inherited illnesses; he has them like his father and grandfather before him, so it won't be easy to smuggle an illegitimate child into *their* family! (3) You can be sure he is apt to have sores on his shins, whitlows on his fingers, which he doesn't treat but lets fester. His armpits might belong to an animal, with hair extending most of the way down his sides. His teeth are black and decayed.

(4) And things like this: he wipes his nose while eating, scratches himself while sacrificing, shoots spittle from his mouth while talking, belches while drinking. (5) He sleeps in bed with his wife without washing.[1] (6) Because he uses rancid oil in the baths, he smells.[2] (7) He goes out to the market wearing thick underwear, and a very thin cloak full of stains.

<From a different character (see Additional Notes)>

(8) . . . When his mother goes out to the omen reader, he curses.[3] (9) When people are praying and pouring libations, he drops his drinking cup and laughs, thinking he's performed a marvel. (10) When he is listening to a flute performance he is the only one of the group to clap his hands, and he hums along and asks the flute girl accusingly

---

[1] For washing after dinner and before bed cf. Aristophanes, *Ecclesiazousai* 419, *Wasps* 1217, Plato, *Symposium* 223d.

[2] Cf. 30.8.

[3] She is worried about offending the gods (cf. 16.11), but her son deliberately offends them.

---

[8] Casaubon: ἐμβαλεῖν codd.

αὐλητρίδι, τί οὕτω ταχὺ ἐπαύσατο·[9] (11) καὶ
ἀποπτύσαι δὲ βουλόμενος, ὑπὲρ τῆς τραπέζης προσ-
πτύσαι τῷ οἰνοχόῳ.

ΑΗΔΙΑΣ Κ

(1) ἔστι δὲ ἡ ἀηδία, ὡς ὅρῳ περιλαβεῖν, ἔντευξις
λύπης ποιητικὴ ἄνευ βλάβης, ὁ δὲ ἀηδὴς τοιοῦτός τις,
(2) οἷος ἐγείρειν ἄρτι καθεύδοντα εἰσελθών, ἵνα αὐτῷ
λαλῇ. (3) καὶ ἀνάγεσθαι δὴ μέλλοντας κωλύειν, (4)
καὶ[1] προσελθὼν δεῖσθαι ἐπισχεῖν, ἕως ἂν περιπα-
τήσῃ.

(5) καὶ τὸ παιδίον τῆς τίτθης ἀφελόμενος, μασώ-
μενος σιτίζειν αὐτὸς καὶ ὑποκορίζεσθαι ποππύζων καὶ
πανουργότερον[2] τοῦ πάππου καλῶν. (6) καὶ ἐσθίων δὲ
ἅμα διηγεῖσθαι ὡς ἐλλέβορον πιὼν ἄνω καὶ κάτω
καθαρθείη καὶ ζωμοῦ τοῦ παρακειμένου ἐν τοῖς ὑπο-
χωρήμασιν αὐτῷ μελαντέρα ⟨εἴη⟩[3] ἡ χολή. (7) καὶ
ἐρωτῆσαι δὲ δεινὸς ἐναντίον τῶν οἰκείων· "εἴπ', ὦ[4]
μάμμη, ὅτ' ὤδινες καὶ ἔτικτές με, τίς ἡμέρα;" (8) †καὶ
ὑπὲρ αὐτῆς δὲ λέγειν ὡς ἡδύ ἐστι, καὶ ἀμφότερα δὲ
οὐκ ἔχοντα οὐ ῥᾴδιον ἄνθρωπον λαβεῖν,† (9) καὶ ὅτι
ψυχρὸν ὕδωρ ἐστὶ παρ' αὐτῷ λακκαῖον, καὶ ὡς κῆπος
λάχανα πολλὰ ἔχων καὶ ἁπαλὰ [ὥστε εἶναι ψυχρὸν][5]

[9] Ribbeck: τί οὐ ταχὺ παύσαιτο V, μὴ ταχὺ παυσαμένη
CD.   [1] inter καὶ et προσελθὼν lacunam statuit Stein.
[2] Schneider: πανουργιῶν V.   [3] suppl. Hanow.

why she stopped so quickly. (11) When he wants to spit, he spits over the table and hits the wine pourer.

20. BAD TASTE

(1) Bad taste, to put it in a definition, is a manner of behavior which produces distress without injury. The man with bad taste is the sort (2) who goes in and wakes up a man who is just asleep, to have a chat. (3) He delays people when they are about to set sail, (4) and ‹. . .›[1] goes up to a man and asks him to wait until he takes his walk.

(5) He takes his baby from its wet-nurse, chews its food[2] and feeds it himself, gurgles[3] in baby-talk, and says "You're a bigger rascal than your daddy!" (6) While eating he relates that he's drunk some hellebore that cleaned him inside out, and that the bile in his stool was blacker than the soup that is on the table. (7) He is apt to ask in front of the household, "Tell me, mommy, when you were in labor and giving birth to me, what day was it?" (8) He says about her that it is sweet, and that it isn't easy to find a man who doesn't have them both,[4] (9) and that he has a cistern of cold water at his house, and a garden with lots of fresh vegetables, and a cook who prepares dishes well, and that his

---

[1] Some words may have fallen out of the text in this sentence.

[2] Nurses chewed the baby's food first to soften it (Aristophanes, *Knights* 717, *RE* XVII.1493).   [3] Literally, "says 'pop'" to attract its attention (see Gow on Theocritus 5.89).

[4] The text of this sentence is corrupt beyond repair.

---

[4] Diels: εἶπον V.

[5] ut glossema del. Bloch.

καὶ μάγειρος εὖ τὸ ὄψον σκευάζων, καὶ ὅτι ἡ οἰκία
αὐτοῦ πανδοκεῖόν ἐστι· μεστὴ γὰρ ἀεί· καὶ τοὺς φίλους αὐτοῦ εἶναι τὸν τετρημένον πίθον· εὖ ποιῶν γὰρ
αὐτοὺς οὐ δύνασθαι ἐμπλῆσαι.

(10) καὶ ξενίζων δὲ δεῖξαι τὸν παράσιτον αὐτοῦ
ποῖός τίς ἐστι τῷ συνδειπνοῦντι· καὶ παρακαλῶν δὲ
ἐπὶ τοῦ ποτηρίου εἰπεῖν, ὅτι "τὸ τέρψον τοὺς παρόντας
παρεσκεύασται," καὶ ὅτι "αὐτήν," ἐὰν κελεύσωσιν, "ὁ
παῖς μέτεισι παρὰ τοῦ πορνοβοσκοῦ ἤδη, ὅπως[6] πάντες ὑπ' αὐτῆς αὐλώμεθα καὶ εὐφραινώμεθα."

ΜΙΚΡΟΦΙΛΟΤΙΜΙΑΣ ΚΑ

(1) ἡ δὲ μικροφιλοτιμία δόξει εἶναι ὄρεξις τιμῆς
ἀνελεύθερος, ὁ δὲ μικροφιλότιμος τοιοῦτός τις, (2) οἷος
σπουδάσαι ἐπὶ δεῖπνον κληθεὶς παρ' αὐτὸν τὸν καλέ-
σαντα κατακείμενος δειπνῆσαι. (3) καὶ τὸν υἱὸν ἀπο-
κεῖραι ἀγαγὼν εἰς Δελφούς, (4) καὶ ἐπιμεληθῆναι δέ,
ὅπως αὐτῷ ὁ ἀκόλουθος Αἰθίοψ ἔσται.

(5) καὶ ἀποδιδοὺς μνᾶν ἀργυρίου καινὸν [ποιῆσαι][1]
ἀποδοῦναι. (6) καὶ κολοιῷ δὲ ἔνδον τρεφομένῳ δεινὸς
κλιμάκιον πρίασθαι καὶ ἀσπίδιον χαλκοῦν ποιῆσαι, ὃ
ἔχων ἐπὶ τοῦ κλιμακίου ὁ κολοιὸς πηδήσεται.

(7) καὶ βοῦν θύσας τὸ προμετωπίδιον ἀπαντικρὺ

---

6 Siebenkees: πῶς codd.
1 del. Pauw.

house is like a hotel, since it's always overflowing, and that his friends are like a pitcher full of holes, since he can never seem to fill them up with his favors.

(10) When he is giving a party he points out to his dinner-companion how impressive his lackey is. While they are drinking he says by way of challenge, "The delight of the guests has been arranged"; if they bid it, "The servant will go and fetch her right now from the pimp, so she can pipe us all to happiness."[5]

21. PETTY AMBITION

(1) Petty ambition will seem to be an ignoble desire for prestige. The man of petty ambition is the sort (2) who, when invited for dinner, takes care to eat reclining next to the host himself. (3) For the ceremony of cutting his son's hair, he takes him to Delphi.[1] (4) He takes care to have an Ethiopian attendant.

(5) When he pays back a debt of one mina, he does it in brand-new coin. (6) He is apt to keep a jackdaw as a housepet, and buy it a little ladder and make it a tiny bronze shield to hold as the bird hops up the ladder.[2]

(7) When he has sacrificed an ox he nails up its skull fac-

[5] Perhaps a double entendre, Lane Fox p. 122, J. Henderson, *The Maculate Muse* [New Haven 1975] 184–185); but cf. *PCG* Philetaerus fr. 18.1.

[1] It was customary for youths coming of age to dedicate their hair to a local deity (Burkert, *Greek Religion* 70, 373–374 n. 29); this man has his son imitate Theseus (Plutarch, *Theseus* 5.1).

[2] For vase paintings of pet birds wearing helmets and shields see J. D. Beazley, *Classical Review* 43 (1949) 42–43.

τῆς εἰσόδου προσπατταλεῦσαι στέμμασι μεγάλοις περιδήσας, ὅπως οἱ εἰσιόντες ἴδωσιν ὅτι βοῦν ἔθυσε. (8) καὶ πομπεύσας δὲ μετὰ τῶν ἱππέων τὰ μὲν ἄλλα πάντα δοῦναι τῷ παιδὶ ἀπενεγκεῖν οἴκαδε, ἀναβαλλόμενος δὲ θοἰμάτιον ἐν τοῖς μύωψι κατὰ τὴν ἀγορὰν περιπατεῖν.

(9) καὶ κυναρίου δὲ Μελιταίου τελευτήσαντος αὐτῷ, μνῆμα [ποιῆσαι]² καὶ στηλίδιον ποιήσας ἐπιγράψαι "Κλάδος Μελιταῖος." (10) καὶ ἀναθεὶς δακτυλίδιον χαλκοῦν ἐν τῷ Ἀσκληπιείῳ τοῦτο ἐκτρίβειν, στεφανοῦν, ἀλείφειν ὁσημέραι. (11) ἀμέλει δὲ καὶ διοικήσασθαι παρὰ τῶν συμπρυτάνεων,³ ὅπως ἀπαγγείλῃ τῷ δήμῳ τὰ ἱερά, καὶ παρεσκευασμένος λαμπρὸν ἱμάτιον καὶ ἐστεφανωμένος παρελθὼν εἰπεῖν· "ὦ ἄνδρες Ἀθηναῖοι, ἐθύομεν οἱ πρυτάνεις [τὰ ἱερά]⁴ τῇ Μητρὶ τῶν θεῶν τὰ Γαλάξια,⁵ καὶ τὰ ἱερὰ καλά, καὶ ὑμεῖς δέχεσθε τὰ ἀγαθά." καὶ ταῦτα ἀπαγγείλας ἀπιὼν διηγήσασθαι οἴκαδε τῇ ἑαυτοῦ γυναικὶ ὡς καθ' ὑπερβολὴν εὐημερεῖν.⁶

ΑΝΕΛΕΥΘΕΡΙΑΣ ΚΒ΄

(1) ἡ δὲ ἀνελευθερία ἐστὶν ἀπουσία τις φιλοτιμίας

---

² del. Pauw.   ³ Madvig: συνδιοικήσασθαι (-οικίσασθαι V) . . . πρυτανέων codd.   ⁴ del. Schneider.

⁵ Wilamowitz: τὰ γὰρ ἄξια V, τὰ ἄξια CD.

⁶ εὐημέρει Needham, sed cf. Kühner-Gerth II.357.3b (Fischer, Stein).

ing his front door and wreathes it with large garlands,[3] so that people coming in will see that he's sacrificed an ox. (8) When he has ridden in the cavalry parade[4] he gives his slave everything else to carry home, but walks around the market in his spurs, wearing his riding cloak.

(9) When his Maltese dog[5] dies, he builds it a monument and inscribes on a plaque "Klados of Malta." (10) If he dedicates a bronze ring in the sanctuary of Asclepius, he polishes it, garlands it, and anoints it every day. (11) You can be sure that as council president he obtains from his colleagues the job of reporting the sacrifice, and going to the podium in a white robe and garland and saying "Men of Athens, we presidents of the council have sacrificed the *Galaxia*[6] to the Mother of the gods; the omens are propitious, and we bid you accept their favorable outcome."[7] After making this announcement he goes home and gives a report to his wife of his stupendous success.

22. LACK OF GENEROSITY

(1) Lack of generosity is an absence of pride when expense

---

[3] An ox was an expensive sacrifice for an individual (Menander, *Dyskolos* 474; Herodas 4.16; *PCG* Posidippus fr. 28.19; Strato fr. 1.20). For the custom of hanging the wreathed skull of the sacrificial ox (usually in a sanctuary) see Burkert, *Greek Religion* 92, 372 n. 93.   [4] See *RE* XXI.1904ff.

[5] One of the most expensive dogs one could own: Virginia T. Leitch, *The Maltese Dog: A History of the Breed* (2nd ed. D. Carno, New York 1970) 10–22.   [6] Literally "milk-festival," after the mash of barley and milk dedicated then: L. Deubner, *Attische Feste* (Berlin 1932) 216.   [7] A formula attested [Dem.] *Proem* 54, cf. *PCG* Alexis fr. 267.3.

δαπάνην ἐχούσης,[1] ὁ δὲ ἀνελεύθερος τοιοῦτός τις, (2)
οἷος νικήσας τραγῳδοῖς ταινίαν ξυλίνην ἀναθεῖναι τῷ
Διονύσῳ ἐπιγράψας μόνον[2] αὑτοῦ τὸ ὄνομα.

(3) καὶ ἐπιδόσεων γινομένων ἐκ τοῦ δήμου, σιωπᾶν
ἢ ἀναστὰς[3] ἐκ τοῦ μέσου ἀπελθεῖν. (4) καὶ ἐκδιδοὺς
αὑτοῦ θυγατέρα τοῦ μὲν ἱερείου πλὴν τῶν ἱερέων τὰ
κρέα ἀποδόσθαι, τοὺς δὲ διακονοῦντας ἐν τοῖς γάμοις
οἰκοσίτους μισθώσασθαι.

(5) καὶ τριηραρχῶν τὰ τοῦ κυβερνήτου στρώματα
αὑτῷ[4] ἐπὶ τοῦ καταστρώματος ὑποστορέννυσθαι, τὰ
δὲ αὑτοῦ ἀποτιθέναι. (6) καὶ τὰ παιδία δὲ δεινὸς μὴ
πέμψαι εἰς διδασκάλου ὅταν ᾖ Μουσεῖα,[5] ἀλλὰ φῆσαι
κακῶς ἔχειν, ἵνα μὴ συμβάλωνται. (7) καὶ ἐξ ἀγορᾶς
δὲ ὀψωνήσας τὰ κρέα αὐτὸς φέρειν ⟨ἐν ταῖς χερσὶν
καὶ⟩[6] τὰ λάχανα ἐν τῷ προκολπίῳ. (8) καὶ ἔνδον

---

[1] Schweighäuser: περιουσία τις ἀπὸ φιλοτιμίας δαπάνην
ἔχουσα codd. (definitionem del. Hanow, Gomperz, Stein).

[2] anonymus apud Hanow: μὲν V.

[3] Schwarz: ἀναστὰς σιωπᾶν ἢ V (σιωπᾶ cD, σιωπῶν c).

[4] Meier: στρῶμα ταὐτὸν V.

[5] post ὅταν ᾖ iterat V τοῦ ἀποτιθέναι καὶ τὰ παιδία: del.
Meier.

[6] Navarre (*Revue des études anciennes* 20 [1918] 218).

---

[1] The definition requires extensive emendation, and may in
any case be a later addition (see Introd. p. 30); it resembles [Aristotle,] *Virtues and Vices* 1251b13.

[2] The wealthiest citizens were required to act as *choregus*
(producer) and pay for dramatic productions; if the play won the

is involved.[1] The ungenerous man is the sort (2) who, if he wins the tragedy competition, dedicates to Dionysus a strip of wood with only his own name written on it.[2]

(3) When emergency contributions[3] are announced in an assembly, he either remains silent or gets up and leaves their midst. (4) When he marries off his daughter, he sells the meat from the sacrifice except for the priests' share, and hires staff for the wedding feast who must bring their own dinners.

(5) When he is captaining a ship[4] he spreads his helmsman's bedding on deck for himself, and puts away his own. (6) He is apt not to send his children to the teacher's for the annual pageant,[5] but say they are sick, so they will not have to bring presents. (7) When he goes shopping he carries the meat home from the market in his hands, with the vegetables in the fold of his cloak.[6] (8) When he is having his

competition, they often dedicated an elaborate monument in a public place (Arthur Pickard-Cambridge, *The Dramatic Festivals of Athens*, revised by John Gould and D. M. Lewis, Oxford 1988, 77–78). The ungenerous man's meager plaque (like some choregic dedications actually preserved) does not even add the customary names of the poet, the play, actors, or the tribe he represented.

[3] In times of crisis the wealthiest citizens were asked to pledge voluntary payments (ἐπιδόσεις) to the government: W. Kendrick Pritchett, *The Greek State at War* II (Berkeley 1974) 110 n. 286.

[4] The wealthy citizen who provided money for a warship became its captain: J. S. Morrison and J. F. Coates, *The Athenian Trireme* (Cambridge 1986) 109, 121–127, 130.

[5] Literally "the festival of the Muses" (cf. Aeschines 1.10).

[6] Delivery boys (LSJ προὔνεικοι) could be hired cheaply.

μένειν, ὅταν ἐκδῷ θοἰμάτιον πλῦναι.[7] (9) καὶ φίλου
ἔρανον συλλέγοντος καὶ διειλεγμένου αὐτῷ, προσιόν-
τα προϊδόμενος ἀποκάμψας ἐκ τῆς ὁδοῦ τὴν κύκλῳ
οἴκαδε πορευθῆναι.

(10) καὶ τῇ γυναικὶ δὲ τῇ ἑαυτοῦ προῖκα εἰσ-
ενεγκαμένῃ μὴ πρίασθαι θεράπαιναν, ἀλλὰ μισθοῦσθαι εἰς τὰς ἐξόδους ἐκ τῆς γυναικείας παιδίον τὸ
συνακολουθῆσον.[8] (11) καὶ τὰ ὑποδήματα παλιμπήξει
κεκαττυμένα φορεῖν καὶ λέγειν, ὅτι "κέρατος οὐδὲν
διαφέρει." (12) καὶ ἀναστὰς τὴν οἰκίαν καλλῦναι καὶ
τὰς κλίνας ἐκκορίσαι.[9] (13) καὶ καθεζόμενος παρα-
στρέψαι τὸν τρίβωνα, ὃν αὐτὸν[10] φορεῖ.

ΑΛΑΖΟΝΕΙΑΣ ΚΓ

(1) ἀμέλει δὲ ἡ ἀλαζονεία δόξει εἶναι προσποίησίς[1] τις
ἀγαθῶν οὐκ ὄντων, ὁ δὲ ἀλαζὼν τοιοῦτός τις, (2) οἷος
ἐν τῷ διαζεύγματι ἑστηκὼς διηγεῖσθαι ξένοις ὡς
πολλὰ χρήματα αὐτῷ[2] ἐστιν ἐν τῇ θαλάττῃ· καὶ περὶ
τῆς ἐργασίας τῆς δανειστικῆς διεξιέναι ἡλίκη, καὶ
αὐτὸς ὅσα εἴληφε καὶ ἀπολώλεκε· καὶ ἅμα ταῦτα
πλεθρίζων πέμπειν τὸ παιδάριον εἰς τὴν τράπεζαν,
δραχμῆς αὐτῷ κειμένης.

[7] Hirschig: ἐκπλῦναι V.   [8] Korais, Schneider: συνακο-
λουθῆσαν (-ῆσον perperam Siebenkees) V.

[9] Casaubon: ἐκκορῆσαι V, ἐκκορύσαι CD.

[10] Münsterberg: αὐτός V.   [1] Auber: προσδοκία codd.

[2] Lycius: αὐτοῖς codd.

116

cloak cleaned, he doesn't leave the house.[7] (9) If a friend is soliciting a loan[8] and has discussed it with him, he veers out of his path whenever he sees him approaching, and takes a roundabout way home.

(10) Even though his wife brought him a dowry, he doesn't buy her a slave-girl, but rents from the women's market[9] a slave to go along when she leaves the house. (11) He wears shoes with soles that have been stuck back on, and says "They wear like iron."[10] (12) As soon as he wakes up he cleans the house, and picks the fleas off the couches.[11] (13) When he sits down he pulls aside his cheap cloak, even though it's the only thing he's wearing.[12]

23. FRAUDULENCE

(1) You can be sure fraudulence will seem to be a pretence of nonexistent goods. The fraud is the sort (2) who stands on the breakwater[1] and tells strangers how much of his money is invested in shipping; he goes into detail about the extent of his moneylending business, and the size of his profits and losses; and while he exaggerates these, he sends his slave to the bank because a drachma is on deposit for him there.[2]

---

[7] He owns only one cloak.   [8] See on 15.7.

[9] See on 2.9.   [10] Literally "they are no different from horn," proverbial for its hardness (Lucian, *True History* I.14, *Alexander* 21).   [11] Instead of having a servant to do it.

[12] That is, he tries to protect his cheapest clothing ($\tau\rho\acute{\iota}\beta\omega\nu$, see *RE* VIA.2416–17), even when this means sitting on his bare buttocks (cf. 4.7).   [1] For the meaning of $\delta\iota\acute{\alpha}\zeta\epsilon\nu\gamma\mu\alpha$ see *RE* V.355.   [2] That is, he is actually so poor he must withdraw even the smallest sum immediately.

(3) καὶ συνοδοιπόρου δὲ ἀπολαῦσαι ἐν τῇ ὁδῷ δεινὸς λέγων, ὡς μετ᾽ Ἀλεξάνδρου[3] ἐστρατεύσατο, καὶ ὡς αὐτῷ εἶχε, καὶ ὅσα λιθοκόλλητα ποτήρια ἐκόμισε· καὶ περὶ τῶν τεχνιτῶν τῶν ἐν τῇ Ἀσίᾳ ὅτι βελτίους εἰσὶ τῶν ἐν τῇ Εὐρώπῃ ἀμφισβητῆσαι· καὶ ταῦτα φῆσαι,[4] οὐδαμοῦ ἐκ τῆς πόλεως ἀποδεδημηκώς. (4) καὶ γράμματα δὲ εἰπεῖν ὡς πάρεστι παρ᾽ Ἀντιπάτρου τριττὰ δὴ λέγοντα παραγενέσθαι αὐτὸν εἰς Μακεδονίαν· καὶ διδομένης αὐτῷ ἐξαγωγῆς ξύλων ἀτελοῦς ὅτι ἀπείρηται, ὅπως μηδ᾽ ὑφ᾽ ἑνὸς συκοφαντηθῇ, "περαιτέρω φιλοσοφεῖν προσῆκε τοῖς Μακεδόσι." (5) καὶ ἐν τῇ σιτοδείᾳ[5] δὲ ὡς πλείω ἢ πέντε τάλαντα αὐτῷ γένοιτο τὰ ἀναλώματα διδόντι τοῖς ἀπόροις τῶν πολιτῶν, ἀνανεύειν γὰρ οὐ δύνασθαι.

(6) καὶ ἀγνώτων δὲ παρακαθημένων κελεῦσαι θεῖναι τὰς ψήφους ἕνα αὐτῶν καὶ ποσῶν[6] κατὰ χιλιάδας[7] καὶ κατὰ μίαν καὶ προστιθεὶς πιθανῶς ἑκάστοις τούτων ὀνόματα ποιῆσαι καὶ δέκα τάλαντα· καὶ τοῦτο φῆσαι[8] εἰσενηνέχθαι εἰς ἐράνους αὐτῷ[9] καὶ τὰς τρι-

---

3 Auber: μετὰ Εὐάνδρου codd.

4 Korais: ψηφῆσαι V.

5 Casaubon: σποδιᾷ V, σποδία ΞΔ.

6 Goez: πόσων V, ποσοῦν αὐτὰς CD.

7 ἑξακοσίας V, ἑξακοσίους CD: χιλίας Wilamowitz (errorem ratus e compendio X ortum), sed χιλιάδας correctius esse docet P. Keyser, *Classical Journal* 81 (1986) 231–2.

8 Lycius: φῆσας codd.

9 Foss: αὐτῶν codd.

(3) On a journey he is apt to put one over on a travel companion by relating how he campaigned with Alexander, and how Alexander felt about him, and how many jewel-studded goblets he got, and arguing that the craftsmen in Asia are better than those in Europe (he says all this even though he's never been out of town). (4) He says that he's got no less than three letters from Antipater summoning him to visit Macedonia, and that he has declined a grant to him for the duty-free export of timber, because he refuses to be prey to even one informer—"The Macedonians should have been smarter than that!"[3] (5) And that during the food shortage[4] his expenses in giving to destitute citizens amounted to more than five talents—he just can't bring himself to say no.

(6) When people he doesn't know are sitting beside him, he asks one of them to move the stones for him, and doing the addition from the thousands column to the ones[5] and convincingly supplying names for each of these sums, he actually reaches ten talents; and says that these are just

[3] I.e., smarter than to think he could be bribed with such a poor gift. He claims to have turned down a lucrative contract, much sought-after by Athenian politicians (Andoc. 2.11, R. Meiggs, *Trees and Timber in the Ancient Mediterranean World*, Oxford 1982, 126) because he feared prosecution for trading with an enemy state (MacDowell, *Law in Classical Athens* 62–63, 158–159).

[4] In Athens, 330–326: see Wankel on Demosthenes *On the Crown* 491, Mikhail Rostovtzeff, *Social and Economic History of the Hellenistic World* (Oxford 1941) 95.

[5] The Greek abacus had columns for counting-stones numbered 1000, 500, 100, 50, 10, 5 and 1: for its use see Mabel Lang, "Herodotus and the Abacus," *Hesperia* 26 (1957) 271–287.

ηραρχίας εἰπεῖν ὅτι οὐ τίθησιν οὐδὲ τὰς λειτουργίας ὅσας λελειτούργηκε.

(7) καὶ προσελθὼν δ᾽ εἰς τοὺς ἵππους τοὺς ἀγαθοὺς τοῖς πωλοῦσι προσποιήσασθαι ὠνητιᾶν. (8) καὶ ἐπὶ τὰς κλίνας ἐλθὼν ἱματισμὸν ζητῆσαι εἰς δύο τάλαντα καὶ τῷ παιδὶ μάχεσθαι, ὅτι τὸ χρυσίον οὐκ ἔχων αὐτῷ ἀκολουθεῖ. (9) καὶ ἐν μισθωτῇ οἰκίᾳ οἰκῶν φῆσαι ταύτην εἶναι τὴν πατρῴαν πρὸς τὸν μὴ εἰδότα, καὶ διότι μέλλει πωλεῖν αὐτὴν διὰ τὸ ἐλάττω εἶναι αὐτῷ πρὸς τὰς ξενοδοχίας.

ΥΠΕΡΗΦΑΝΙΑΣ ΚΔ΄

(1) ἔστι δὲ ἡ ὑπερηφανία καταφρόνησίς τις πλὴν αὑτοῦ τῶν ἄλλων, ὁ δὲ ὑπερήφανος τοιόσδε τις, (2) οἷος τῷ σπεύδοντι ἀπὸ δείπνου ἐντεύξεσθαι φάσκειν ἐν τῷ περιπατεῖν. (3) καὶ εὖ ποιήσας μεμνῆσθαι φάσκειν. (4) καὶ βιάζεσθαι[1] ἐν ταῖς ὁδοῖς τὰς διαίτας κρίνειν ἐντυχὼν[2] τοῖς ἐπιτρέψασι. (5) καὶ χειροτονούμενος ἐξόμνυσθαι τὰς ἀρχάς, οὐ φάσκων σχολάζειν. (6) καὶ προσελθεῖν πρότερος οὐδενὶ θελῆσαι. (7) καὶ τοὺς πωλοῦντάς τι ἢ μεμισθωμένους δεινὸς κελεῦσαι ἥκειν πρὸς αὑτὸν ἅμ᾽ ἡμέρᾳ. (8) καὶ ἐν ταῖς ὁδοῖς πορευόμενος μὴ λαλεῖν τοῖς ἐντυγχάνουσι, κάτω κεκυφώς, ὅταν δὲ αὐτῷ δόξῃ, ἄνω πάλιν. (9) καὶ ἑστιῶν

---

1 Foss: βιάζειν codd.
2 Foss: ἐν τοῖς ἐπιτρέψασι codd.

his loans to friends;[6] he's not counting the warships, nor the public events he's paid for.[7]

(7) He goes up to the high-priced horse market and pretends to the sellers that he wants to buy. (8) Going to the clothing-vendors, he picks out a wardrobe totalling two talents, then quarrels with his servant because he came along without bringing any gold coins.[8] (9) When he is living in a rented house, he tells someone who doesn't know that it belongs to his family, and that he intends to sell it because it's too small for him for entertaining.

24. ARROGANCE

(1) Arrogance is a sort of contempt for anyone other than oneself. The arrogant man is a type such as this, (2) who says to a man in a hurry that he'll meet him after dinner while he takes his walk. (3) If he does a favor, he says to remember it. (4) If he meets disputants on the street, he forces them to decide their arbitration.[1] (5) If elected to office he takes an oath to avoid serving, claiming lack of time.[2] (6) He won't make the first approach to anyone. (7) He is apt to tell salesmen or employees to come to his house first thing next morning. (8) As he walks down the street he avoids speaking to passers-by by casting his eyes down, then back up again when it suits him. (9) When he

6 See on 15.7.

7 See on 26.6.

8 Cf. 18.3.

1 For private arbitrations see on 5.3.

2 One could avoid office with a sworn statement of ill-health (Demosthenes 19.124).

τοὺς φίλους αὐτὸς μὴ συνδειπνεῖν, ἀλλὰ τῶν ὑφ᾽
αὑτόν τινι συντάξαι αὐτῶν ἐπιμελεῖσθαι.

(10) καὶ προαποστέλλειν δέ, ἐπὰν πορεύηται, τὸν
ἐροῦντα, ὅτι προσέρχεται.[3] (11) καὶ οὔτε ἐπ᾽ ἀλειφό-
μενον αὐτὸν οὔτε λουόμενον οὔτε ἐσθίοντα ἐᾶσαι[4] ἂν
εἰσελθεῖν.

(12) ἀμέλει δὲ καὶ λογιζόμενος πρός τινα τῷ παιδὶ
συντάξαι τὰς ψήφους διωθεῖν[5] καὶ κεφάλαιον ποιή-
σαντι γράψαι αὐτῷ εἰς λόγον. (13) καὶ ἐπιστέλλων μὴ
γράφειν ὅτι "χαρίζοιο ἄν μοι," ἀλλ᾽ ὅτι "βούλομαι
γενέσθαι," καὶ "ἀπέσταλκα πρὸς σὲ ληψόμενος," καὶ
"ὅπως ἄλλως μὴ ἔσται," καὶ "τὴν ταχίστην."

ΔΕΙΛΙΑΣ ΚΕ΄

(1) ἀμέλει δὲ ἡ δειλία δόξειεν ἂν εἶναι ὕπειξίς τις
ψυχῆς ἔμφοβος, ὁ δὲ δειλὸς τοιοῦτός τις, (2) οἷος
πλέων τὰς ἄκρας φάσκειν ἡμιολίας εἶναι· καὶ κλύ-
δωνος γενομένου ἐρωτᾶν εἴ τις μὴ μεμύηται τῶν
πλεόντων· καὶ τοῦ κυβερνήτου ἀνακύπτων μὲν πυν-
θάνεσθαι εἰ μεσοπορεῖ καὶ τί αὐτῷ δοκεῖ τὰ τοῦ θεοῦ,
καὶ πρὸς τὸν παρακαθήμενον λέγειν ὅτι φοβεῖται ἀπὸ
ἐνυπνίου τινός· καὶ ἐκδὺς διδόναι τῷ παιδὶ τὸν χιτω-
νίσκον· καὶ δεῖσθαι πρὸς τὴν γῆν προσάγειν αὐτόν.

(3) καὶ στρατευόμενος δὲ ⟨τοῦ⟩[1] πεζοῦ ἐκβοηθοῦν-

---

[3] Schneider: προέρχεται V, ἔρχεται C.
[4] Casaubon: ἐάσας codd.   [5] διαθεῖναι Sheppard.

entertains his friends he doesn't join them at dinner himself, but orders one of his subordinates to see to them.

(10) When he goes somewhere he sends someone ahead to say that he's on his way. (11) He won't let anyone in when he's oiling himself, bathing, or eating.

(12) You can be sure that when he's reckoning accounts with someone he tells his slave to clear the counters[3] and find the total, and write it in his account. (13) When he sends a commission he doesn't write "would you be so kind as to . . ." but rather "I want this done" and "I've sent to you to pick up . . ." and "no deviations" and "immediately."

25. COWARDICE

(1) You can be sure that cowardice would seem to be a sort of fearful yielding of the soul. The coward is the sort (2) who, when at sea, says that the cliffs are pirate ships. When a wave hits, he asks whether anyone on board has not been initiated.[1] Of the helmsman he first pops up and asks whether he is halfway, and how he thinks the heavens look, and says to the man sitting beside him that his fear is the result of some dream. He strips off his shirt and hands it to his slave;[2] he begs to be put ashore.

(3) When he is on military service and the infantry is

[3] On the abacus see on 23.6. He is so busy that he has his slave perform the whole transaction.

[1] The mysteries at Samothrace promised special protection for seafarers: Burkert, *Ancient Mystery Cults* 15–16.

[2] To ready himself to swim.

---

[1] suppl. Wilamowitz.

τος προσκαλεῖν πάντας[2] κελεύων πρὸς αὐτὸν στάντας
πρῶτον περιδεῖν, καὶ λέγειν ὡς ἔργον διαγνῶναί ἐστι
πότεροί εἰσιν οἱ πολέμιοι. (4) καὶ ἀκούων κραυγῆς καὶ
ὁρῶν πίπτοντας εἰπεῖν πρὸς τοὺς παρεστηκότας ὅτι
τὴν σπάθην λαβεῖν ὑπὸ τῆς σπουδῆς ἐπελάθετο,
τρέχειν ἐπὶ τὴν σκηνήν, τὸν παῖδα ἐκπέμψας κελεύειν
προσκοπεῖσθαι ποῦ εἰσιν οἱ πολέμιοι, ἀποκρύψαι αὐτὴν ὑπὸ τὸ προσκεφάλαιον, εἶτα διατρίβειν πολὺν
χρόνον ὡς ζητῶν.[3] (5) καὶ ἐν τῇ σκηνῇ ὁρῶν τραυμα-
τίαν τινὰ προσφερόμενον τῶν φίλων προσδραμὼν καὶ
θαρρεῖν κελεύσας ὑπολαβὼν φέρειν. καὶ τοῦτον θερα-
πεύειν καὶ περισπογγίζειν καὶ παρακαθήμενος ἀπὸ
τοῦ ἕλκους τὰς μυίας σοβεῖν καὶ πᾶν μᾶλλον ἢ
μάχεσθαι τοῖς πολεμίοις. καὶ τοῦ σαλπιστοῦ δὲ τὸ
πολεμικὸν σημήναντος καθήμενος ἐν τῇ σκηνῇ
⟨εἰπεῖν⟩.[4] "ἄπαγ' ἐς κόρακας· οὐκ ἐάσει τὸν ἄνθρωπον
ὕπνου λαβεῖν πυκνὰ σημαίνων." (6) καὶ αἵματος δὲ
ἀνάπλεως ἀπὸ τοῦ ἀλλοτρίου τραύματος ἐντυγχάνειν
τοῖς ἐκ τῆς μάχης ἐπανιοῦσι καὶ διηγεῖσθαι ὡς
κινδυνεύσας· "ἕνα σέσωκα τῶν φίλων." καὶ εἰσάγειν
πρὸς τὸν κατακείμενον σκεψομένους [τοὺς δημότας][5]
τοὺς φυλέτας καὶ τούτων ἅμ' ἑκάστῳ διηγεῖσθαι, ὡς
αὐτὸς αὐτὸν ταῖς ἑαυτοῦ χερσὶν ἐπὶ σκηνὴν ἐκόμισεν.

ΟΛΙΓΑΡΧΙΑΣ Κϛ'

(1) δόξειεν δ' ἂν εἶναι ἡ ὀλιγαρχία φιλαρχία τις
ἰσχύος καὶ[1] κέρδους γλιχομένη, ὁ δὲ ὀλιγαρχικὸς

attacking he calls to everyone and orders them to stand
near him first and reconnoitre, and says that their task is to
discern which ones are the enemy. (4) When he hears a tu-
mult and sees men falling, he says to those beside him that
in his haste he forgot to take his sword, and runs to his tent,
sends his attendant out and orders him to spy out the enemy's location, hides the sword under the pillow, then
wastes a long time pretending to look for it. (5) When from
his tent he sees one of his friends brought in wounded, he
runs up to him, bids him be brave, picks him up and carries
him; then he takes care of him, sponges him off, sits at his
side shooing the flies off his wound—anything rather than
fight the enemy. When the trumpeter sounds the charge,
he sits in his tent and says "Go to hell! He won't let a man
get any sleep with his endless signalling!" (6) Drenched in
blood from another man's wound, he meets the men returning from battle and tells the story as if he'd been in
danger: "I saved one of our friends." Then he leads the
members of his tribe inside to view him lying there, while
he tells each one that he personally brought him into the
tent with his own hands.

26. AUTHORITARIANISM

(1) Authoritarianism would seem to be a desire for office
that covets power and profit. The authoritarian is the sort

---

² sic refinxi: στρατευόμενος δὲ προσκαλεῖν πάντας πρὸς
αὑτὸν καὶ στάντας C, στρατευόμενος δὲ πεζοῦ ἐκβοηθοῦντός
τε προσκαλεῖν κελεύων πρὸς αὑτὸν στάντας V.

³ Schneider: ζητεῖν V.　　⁴ suppl. Schneider.

⁵ del. Diels.　　　¹ P. Oxy. 699: ἰσχυρῶς V, ἰσχυροῦ C.

τοιοῦτος, (2) οἷος τοῦ δήμου βουλευομένου,[2] τίνας τῷ
ἄρχοντι προσαιρήσονται[3] τῆς πομπῆς τοὺς συνεπι-
μελησομένους, παρελθὼν ἀποφήνασθαι[4] ὡς δεῖ αὐτο-
κράτορας τούτους εἶναι, κἂν ἄλλοι προβάλλωνται
δέκα, λέγειν "ἱκανὸς εἷς ἐστι, τοῦτον δὲ" ὅτι "δεῖ
ἄνδρα εἶναι·" καὶ τῶν Ὁμήρου ἐπῶν τοῦτο ἓν μόνον
κατέχειν, ὅτι "οὐκ ἀγαθὸν πολυκοιρανίη, εἷς κοίρανος
ἔστω," τῶν δὲ ἄλλων μηδὲν ἐπίστασθαι·

(3) ἀμέλει δὲ δεινὸς τοῖς τοιούτοις τῶν λόγων[5]
χρήσασθαι, ὅτι "δεῖ αὐτοὺς ἡμᾶς συνελθόντας περὶ
τούτων βουλεύσασθαι, καὶ ἐκ τοῦ ὄχλου καὶ τῆς
ἀγορᾶς ἀπαλλαγῆναι, καὶ παύσασθαι ἀρχαῖς πλη-
σιάζοντας καὶ ὑπὸ τούτων οὕτως ὑβριζομένους ἢ
τιμωμένους," ‹καὶ›[6] ὅτι "ἢ τούτους δεῖ ἢ ἡμᾶς οἰκεῖν
τὴν πόλιν."

(4) καὶ τὸ μέσον δὲ τῆς ἡμέρας ἐξιὼν καὶ τὸ ἱμάτιον
ἀναβεβλημένος καὶ μέσην κουρὰν κεκαρμένος καὶ
ἀκριβῶς ἀπωνυχισμένος σοβεῖν τοὺς τοιούτους λόγους τραγῳδῶν·[7] (5) "διὰ τοὺς συκοφάντας οὐκ
οἰκητόν ἐστιν ἐν τῇ πόλει," καὶ ὡς "ἐν τοῖς δικαστηρίοις δεινὰ πάσχομεν ὑπὸ τῶν δεκαζομένων,"[8] καὶ
ὡς "θαυμάζω[9] τῶν πρὸς τὰ κοινὰ προσιόντων τί
βούλονται," καὶ ὡς "ἀχάριστόν ἐστι ‹τὸ πλῆθος καὶ
ἀεὶ›[10] τοῦ νέμοντος καὶ διδόντος," καὶ ὡς αἰσχύνεται
ἐν τῇ ἐκκλησίᾳ, ὅταν παρακάθηταί τις αὐτῷ λεπτὸς

² Casaubon: βουλομένου codd.   ³ Schneider: προαιρή-
σονται V.   ⁴ Schneider: ἀποφήνας ἔχει codd.

(2) who, when the people are debating which people to choose to assist the chief magistrate with the procession, takes the podium and says they need to have absolute power; if other speakers propose ten of them, he says "One is plenty—but he has to be a real man!" He remembers only one line of Homer—he doesn't know a single thing about the rest: "More than one leader is bad; let one alone be our ruler."[1]

(3) You can be sure he is apt to say things like these: "We ought to get together by ourselves and make decisions about this, and be rid of the rabble and the marketplace, and stop depending on them as we do for reward or rejection when we compete for public offices"; and "Either they must run the city or we must!"

(4) At midday he goes out with his cloak arranged about him, hair cut to a moderate length, fingernails expertly trimmed, and struts along intoning speeches like this: (5) "With the informers, life in the city has become unbearable!" "What the bribe-takers in the courts are doing to us is a crime!" "I wonder what the men getting involved in politics are after." "The common people show no gratitude; they always follow anyone with a handout or a gift." He says that he is ashamed in the assembly when some scrawny, unwashed type sits beside him. (6) And "When

---

[1] *Iliad* 2.204, Aristotle, *Politics* 1292a13.

---

5 Casaubon: ὀλίγων V.   6 suppl. Ussing.
7 Herwerden: τὴν τοῦ ὠδίω V (τὴν τοῦ Ὠιδείου Preller).
8 Meier: δικαζομένων codd.
9 Schneider: θαυμάζων V.
10 suppl. Ast.

καὶ αὐχμῶν· (6) καὶ εἰπεῖν· "πότε παυσόμεθα ὑπὸ τῶν
λειτουργιῶν καὶ τῶν τριηραρχιῶν ἀπολλύμενοι;" καὶ
ὡς μισητὸν τὸ τῶν δημαγωγῶν γένος, τὸν Θησέα
πρῶτον φήσας τῶν κακῶν τῇ πόλει γεγονέναι αἴτιον·
τοῦτον γὰρ ἐκ δώδεκα πόλεων εἰς μίαν καταγαγόντα
λῦσαι τὰς[11] βασιλείας· καὶ δίκαια αὐτὸν παθεῖν· πρῶτον γὰρ αὐτὸν ἀπολέσθαι ὑπ' αὐτῶν·

[καὶ τοιαῦτα ἕτερα πρὸς τοὺς ξένους καὶ τῶν πολιτῶν τοὺς ὁμοτρόπους καὶ ταὐτὰ προαιρουμένους.][12]

ΟΨΙΜΑΘΙΑΣ ΚΖ´

(1) [ἡ δὲ ὀψιμαθία φιλοπονία δόξειεν ἂν εἶναι ὑπὲρ τὴν
ἡλικίαν,][1] ὁ δὲ ὀψιμαθὴς τοιοῦτός τις, (2) οἷος ῥήσεις
μανθάνειν ἑξήκοντα ἔτη γεγονὼς καὶ ταύτας λέγων
παρὰ πότον ἐπιλανθάνεσθαι. (3) καὶ παρὰ τοῦ υἱοῦ
μανθάνειν τὸ "ἐπὶ δόρυ"[2] καὶ "ἐπὶ ἀσπίδα" καὶ "ἐπ'
οὐράν." (4) καὶ εἰς ἡρῷα[3] συμβάλλεσθαι τοῖς μειρα-
κίοις ⟨καὶ⟩[4] λαμπάδα τρέχειν. (5) ἀμέλει δὲ κἄν που

---

11 Kayser: λυθείσας βασίλ' V.   12 del. Diels.
1 del. Hanow, Gomperz, Stein.   2 τὸ ἐπὶ Schneider: ἐπὶ
τὸ codd.   3 Schneider: ἥρωα V.   4 suppl. Ast.

---

2 Literally "liturgies and trierarchies" required of the wealthiest citizens: J. K. Davies, *Athenian Propertied Families* (Oxford
1971) xvii–xxxi.

3 The so-called συνοικισμός of Attika (Thucydides 2.15,
FGrHist 328 Philochorus F 94, with Jacoby's commentary).

will we be delivered from the deathgrip of being forced to pay for public events and warships?"[2] "How loathsome the breed of demagogues is!" adding that the originator of the city's troubles was Theseus, since he reduced it to a unit instead of twelve cities[3] and broke up the monarchy; but he got what he deserved, since he was the first one they killed.[4]

[He says more of this sort to foreigners, and to those citizens who share his character and political preferences.][5]

27. REJUVENATION

(1) [Rejuvenation would seem to be an enthusiasm for work[1] inappropriate to one's age.] The rejuvenated man is the sort (2) who, after turning sixty, memorizes passages, but when he is reciting at a drinking party can not remember them.[2] (3) From his son he learns "right face" and "left face" and "about face."[3] (4) For the hero-festivals, he contributes to the boys, and runs in the relay races.[4] (5) If he is

---

[4] There was a tradition that Theseus was ostracized from Athens, Theophrastus fr. 638.

[5] The epilogue is a later addition; see Introd. p. 30.

[1] φιλοπονία is a quality for which ephebes are often praised (*Inscriptiones Graecae* II² 900.17, 1039.48–9), but it does not apply to all the behavior described below, and this definition is probably a later addition.   [2] Cf. Philocleon's mangling of the drinking songs in Aristophanes, *Wasps* 1225ff.

[3] Literally "to the spear," "to the shield," and "to the tail" (Pollux 1.129, and frequently in Xenophon), commands from the military training of ephebes.

[4] Torch races are attested for festivals of Ajax and Theseus (*Inscriptiones Graecae* II² 956.6, 1011.54).

κληθῇ εἰς Ἡράκλειον, ῥίψας τὸ ἱμάτιον τὸν βοῦν
αἴρεσθαι[5] ἵνα τραχηλίσῃ.

(6) καὶ προσανατρίβεσθαι εἰσιὼν[6] εἰς τὰς παλαίστρας. (7) καὶ ἐν τοῖς θαύμασι τρία ἢ τέτταρα πληρώ-
ματα ὑπομένειν τὰ ᾄσματα ἐκμανθάνων. (8) καὶ τελού-
μενος τῷ Σαβαζίῳ σπεῦσαι ὅπως καλλιστεύσῃ παρὰ
τῷ ἱερεῖ.

(9) καὶ ἐρῶν ἑταίρας[7] καὶ κριοὺς προσβάλλων ταῖς
θύραις πληγὰς εἰληφὼς ὑπ᾽ ἀντεραστοῦ δικάζεσθαι.
(10) καὶ εἰς ἀγρὸν ἐφ᾽ ἵππου ἀλλοτρίου κατοχούμενος
ἅμα μελετᾶν ἱππάζεσθαι καὶ πεσὼν τὴν κεφαλὴν
κατεαγέναι.

(11) καὶ ἐν δεκαδισταῖς[8] συνάγειν τοὺς μεθ᾽ αὑτοῦ
συναύξοντας. (12) καὶ μακρὸν ἀνδριάντα παίζειν πρὸς
τὸν ἑαυτοῦ ἀκόλουθον. (13) καὶ διατοξεύεσθαι καὶ
διακοντίζεσθαι τῷ τῶν παιδίων παιδαγωγῷ καὶ ἅμα
μανθάνειν παρ᾽ αὐτοῦ <παραινεῖν>,[9] ὡς ἂν καὶ ἐκείνου
μὴ ἐπισταμένου. (14) καὶ παλαίων δ᾽ ἐν τῷ βαλανείῳ
πυκνὰ ἕδραν στρέφειν, ὅπως πεπαιδεῦσθαι δοκῇ.

---

[5] Meier: αἱρεῖσθαι V.   [6] Ast: εἰπὼν V.
[7] Schneider: ἱερᾶς V.   [8] Wilhelm: ἕνδεκα λιταῖς V.
[9] suppl. Hanow.

---

[5] As the ephebes do at some sacrifices (*Inscriptiones Graecae*
I³ 82.29, II² 1028.10, *Supplementum Epigraphicum Graecum* 15
(1958) 104).   [6] See on 6.4.

[7] The precise context is unknown. For Sabazios see on 16.4.

[8] Fighting over prostitutes is pardoned in the young (Dem.

invited to a shrine of Heracles somewhere, you can be sure he will throw off his cloak and try to lift the bull[5] to twist its neck.

(6) He goes into the wrestling schools and challenges them to a match. (7) At street fairs[6] he sits through three or four shows, trying to learn the songs. (8) When he is being inducted into the cult of Sabazios he wants the priest to judge him the most handsome.[7]

(9) He becomes infatuated with a prostitute, uses a battering ram on her door and gets a beating from her other lover—then takes him to court.[8] (10) While he is riding on a borrowed horse in the country he tries to practice fancy horsemanship at the same time, but falls and hurts his head.

(11) Among the members of a monthly club[9] he plans the attendance of his fellow financial sponsors. (12) He plays "long statue"[10] against his own attendant. (13) He competes in archery and the javelin against his childrens' teacher, and suggests that the teacher, as if he were not an expert, take lessons from him. (14) When he wrestles at the baths, he often twists his hips so that he will look well-trained.[11]

54.14, Micio in Terence, *Adelphoe*), but not the old (Philokleon in *Wasps*): Dover, *Greek Popular Morality* (Oxford 1974) 103. For the impropriety of older men consorting with prostitutes see *PCG* Pherekrates fr. 77. A similar court case—except that the prostitute is a young male—is found in Lysias' 3rd Oration.

[9] Lit. "Tenth-day men," for the day of the month on which they celebrated. The rest of the sentence remains unexplained.

[10] The game is otherwise unknown.   [11] Hip movements were a specialty of Argive wrestlers: Theocritus 24.111.

(15) καὶ ὅταν ὦσιν ἐγγὺς γυναῖκες,[10] μελετᾶν ὀρχεῖσθαι αὐτὸς αὑτῷ τερετίζων.

ΚΑΚΟΛΟΓΙΑΣ ΚΗ΄

(1) ἔστι δὲ ἡ κακολογία ἀγωγὴ ψυχῆς[1] εἰς τὸ χεῖρον ἐν λόγοις, ὁ δὲ κακολόγος τοιόσδε τις, (2) οἷος ἐρωτηθείς· "ὁ δεῖνα τίς ἐστιν;" ὀγκοῦσθαι[2] καθάπερ οἱ γενεαλογοῦντες· "πρῶτον ἀπὸ τοῦ γένους αὐτοῦ ἄρξομαι. τούτου ὁ μὲν πατὴρ ἐξ ἀρχῆς Σωσίας ἐκαλεῖτο, ἐγένετο δὲ ἐν τοῖς στρατιώταις Σωσίστρατος, ἐπειδὴ δὲ εἰς τοὺς δημότας ἐνεγράφη, ⟨Σωσίδημος⟩.[3] ἡ μέντοι μήτηρ εὐγενὴς Θρᾷττά ἐστι· καλεῖται γοῦν ἡ ψυχὴ Κρινοκόρακα· τὰς δὲ τοιαύτας φασὶν ἐν τῇ πατρίδι εὐγενεῖς εἶναι. αὐτὸς δὲ οὗτος ὡς ἐκ τοιούτων γεγονὼς κακὸς καὶ μαστιγίας."

(3) καὶ κακῶς[4] δὲ πρός τινα εἰπεῖν· "ἐγὼ δήπου τὰ τοιαῦτα οἶδα, ὑπὲρ ὧν σὺ πλανᾷ[5] πρὸς ἐμέ." κἀπὶ[6] τούτοις διεξιών· "αὗται αἱ γυναῖκες ἐκ τῆς ὁδοῦ τοὺς παριόντας συναρπάζουσι," καὶ "οἰκία τις αὕτη τὰ σκέλη ἠρκυῖα· οὐ γὰρ οἷον λῆρός ἐστι, τὸ λεγόμενον,

[10] ὦσι . . . γυναῖκ . . . μελετᾶν V: supplevit Meister.

[1] ἀγὼν τῆς ψυχῆς codd.: ἀγωγὴ Casaubon, τῆς del. Edmonds.   [2] Diels: οὐκοῦνδε V, om. C.

[3] suppl. Meier.   [4] Siebenkees: κακῶν V.

[5] Schneider: πλανᾶς V.

[6] Immisch (praeeunte Casaubon): καὶ codd.

(15) And when women are nearby he practices a chorus dance, humming to himself.

28. SLANDER

(1) Slander is a tendency of the soul toward derogatory talk. The slanderer is the sort (2) who, when asked "Who is such-and-such?" becomes pompous like the genealogers:[1] "Let me begin at the beginning, with his lineage. This man's father was originally named Sosias, but became Sosistratos in the army, and after he had been enrolled as a citizen, Sosidemos. However, his mother was noble— a noble Thracian, that is.[2] The darling[3] is called 'Krinokoraka—women like that pass for noble where he comes from. As you'd expect coming from such stock, he's a villain and a scoundrel."

(3) He says to someone as an insult, "Of course I know the sort of things for which you are wandering to me."[4] And then beyond this, as he goes into detail: "These women snatch men passing by from the street." And "This house practically has its legs in the air. That's not just a joke, you know, the old saying, they really copulate in the streets

---

[1] Usually a genealogy lists the names of various ancestors: this list gives the aliases of a single man; "Sosias," common in comedies, suggests that he started as a slave. For changing one's name to bolster a claim of citizenship see Lane Fox 158–159 n. 16.

[2] Considered by the Greeks a wild and uncultured people (Aristophanes, *Acharnians*, 141–171 and Euripides, *Hecuba*).

[3] Literally "soul," a term of endearment suggesting she had many lovers.   [4] The text here makes little sense, even with emendations. In what follows, the topic has shifted to the women of a particular family.

ἀλλ' ὥσπερ αἱ κύνες[7] ἐν ταῖς ὁδοῖς συνέχονται," καὶ "τὸ ὅλον ἀνδρολάλοι τινές," καὶ "αὐταὶ τὴν θύραν τὴν αὔλειον ὑπακούουσι."

(4) ἀμέλει δὲ καὶ κακῶς λεγόντων ἑτέρων συνεπιλαμβάνεσθαι εἴπας·[8] "ἐγὼ δὲ τοῦτον τὸν ἄνθρωπον πλέον πάντων μεμίσηκα· καὶ γὰρ εἰδεχθής τις ἀπὸ τοῦ προσώπου ἐστίν· ἡ δὲ πονηρία — οὐδὲν ὅμοιον· σημεῖον δέ· τῇ γὰρ ἑαυτοῦ γυναικὶ τάλαντα εἰσενεγκαμένη προῖκα, ἐξ οὗ[9] παιδίον αὐτῷ γεννᾷ, τρεῖς χαλκοῦς εἰς ὄψον δίδωσι καὶ τῷ ψυχρῷ λούεσθαι ἀναγκάζει τῇ τοῦ Ποσειδῶνος ἡμέρᾳ."

(5) καὶ συγκαθήμενος δεινὸς περὶ τοῦ ἀναστάντος εἰπεῖν καὶ ἀρχήν γε εἰληφὼς[10] μὴ ἀποσχέσθαι μηδὲ τοὺς οἰκείους αὐτοῦ λοιδορῆσαι. (6) καὶ πλεῖστα περὶ τῶν <αὑτοῦ>[11] φίλων καὶ οἰκείων [κακὰ εἰπεῖν,][12] καὶ περὶ τῶν τετελευτηκότων κακῶς λέγειν, ἀποκαλῶν παρρησίαν καὶ δημοκρατίαν καὶ ἐλευθερίαν καὶ τῶν ἐν τῷ βίῳ ἥδιστα τοῦτο ποιῶν.

(7) [οὕτως ὁ τῆς διδασκαλίας ἐρεθισμὸς μανικοὺς καὶ ἐξεστηκότας ἀνθρώπους τοῖς ἤθεσι ποιεῖ.][13]

ΦΙΛΟΠΟΝΗΡΙΑΣ ΚΘ

(1) ἔστι δὲ ἡ φιλοπονηρία ἐπιθυμία κακίας, ὁ δὲ

---

[7] anonymus apud Ast: γυναῖκες V.   [8] Cobet: εἴπου V.
[9] Immisch: ἐξ ἧς V.   [10] Schneider: εἰληφότος V.
[11] suppl. Herwerden.

like dogs." And "They'll always talk to men." And "These women answer their own front door!"[5]

(4) You can be sure that when others are engaging in slander he will join in, saying "I loathe this man more than anyone; he has a quite hateful-looking face; his wickedness is unequalled, and I'll prove it: his wife brought him thousands in dowry, but ever since she bore him a son, she gets from him three coppers for her shopping, and he makes her bathe in cold water on Poseidon's day."[6]

(5) When he is sitting in a group he is apt to start talking about whoever has just left and, once started, not refrain from reviling even his family. (6) He maligns most his own friends and household, and the dead, passing off his slander as free speech, democracy or openness, and taking more pleasure in it than anything in his life.

(7) [That is how the stimulus for learning makes men mad and distraught in their personality.][7]

29. PATRONAGE OF SCOUNDRELS

(1) Patronage of scoundrels is a predilection for evil. The

---

[5] Anyone respectable would have had someone to answer the door (cf. 4.12, Aristophanes, *Peace* 979, *Thesm.* 792, Menander fr. 592).   [6] Presumably this was in the cold month Poseideon (December-January).

[7] For the interpolated epilogue (probably displaced from the preceding character) see Introd. p. 30.

---

[12] del. Hanow.

[13] epilogum byzantinum capitis prioris (ὀψιμαθία) huc inepte insertum agnovit Hanow.

φιλοπόνηρός ἐστι τοιόσδε τις, (2) οἷος ἐντυγχάνειν
τοῖς ἡττημένοις καὶ δημοσίους ἀγῶνας ὠφληκόσι καὶ
ὑπολαμβάνειν, ἐὰν τούτοις χρῆται, ἐμπειρότερος γε-
νήσεσθαι καὶ φοβερώτερος.

(3) καὶ ἐπὶ τοῖς χρηστοῖς εἰπεῖν, "ὡς φαίνεται,"[1] καὶ
φῆσαι ὡς οὐδείς ἐστι χρηστός, καὶ ὁμοίους πάντας
εἶναι, καὶ ἐπισκῶψαι[2] δέ, ὡς χρηστός ἐστι.

(4) καὶ τὸν πονηρὸν δὲ εἰπεῖν ἐλεύθερον, ἐὰν βού-
ληταί τις εἰς πεῖραν ἐλθεῖν,[3] καὶ τὰ μὲν ἄλλα ὁμολο-
γεῖν ἀληθῆ ὑπὲρ αὐτοῦ λέγεσθαι ὑπὸ τῶν ἀνθρώπων,
ἔνια δὲ ἀγνοεῖν· φῆσαι γὰρ αὐτὸν εὐφυῆ καὶ φιλέ-
ταιρον καὶ ἐπιδέξιον· καὶ διατείνεσθαι δὲ ὑπὲρ αὐτοῦ,
ὡς οὐκ ἐντετύχηκεν ἀνθρώπῳ ἱκανωτέρῳ·

(4a) καὶ εὔνους δὲ εἶναι αὐτῷ[4] ἐν ἐκκλησίᾳ λέγοντι
ἢ ἐπὶ δικαστηρίῳ κρινομένῳ· καὶ πρὸς τοὺς καθημένους[5] δὲ εἰπεῖν δεινός, ὡς οὐ δεῖ τὸν ἄνδρα, ἀλλὰ τὸ
πρᾶγμα κρίνεσθαι· καὶ φῆσαι αὐτὸν κύνα εἶναι τοῦ
δήμου, φυλάττειν γὰρ αὐτὸν τοὺς ἀδικοῦντας· καὶ
εἰπεῖν ὡς "οὐχ ἕξομεν τοὺς ὑπὲρ τῶν κοινῶν συν-
αχθεσθησομένους, ἂν τοὺς τοιούτους προώμεθα." (5)
δεινὸς δὲ καὶ προστατῆσαι φαύλων καὶ συνηγορῆσαι[6]
ἐν δικαστηρίοις ἐπὶ πονηροῖς πράγμασιν καὶ κρίσιν
κρίνων ἐκδέχεσθαι τὰ ὑπὸ τῶν ἀντιδίκων λεγόμενα
ἐπὶ τὸ χεῖρον.

---

[1] Diels: γίνεται V.   [2] Nast: ἐπισκῆψαι V.
[3] supplevit Naber: π . . . . . V.   [4] Meier: τῷ codd.
[5] Meier: προσκαθήμενος V.   [6] Immisch: συνεδρεῦσαι
codd.

patron of scoundrels is a type such as this, (2) who seeks
out losers in court and those convicted in public trials, and
imagines that with their friendship he will become more
experienced and formidable.

(3) About those called "good"[1] he says "apparently,"
and says "No one is good," and that all people are the same,
and ridicules "How good he is."

(4) About a wicked man, if someone wants to examine
him, he says that he is a gentleman, and admits the truth of
the rest of what is said about him by people, but some
points he does not believe, since he says the man is good at
heart, loyal, and fair; he exerts himself on his behalf, stat-
ing he's never met a more capable man.

(4a) He supports him when he is speaking in the assembly or a defendant in court, and to the judges he is apt to
say: "You must judge the case, and not the man." He claims
he is a watchdog for the public,[2] since he is vigilant against
wrongdoers. "If we abandon men like this, we won't have
anyone left to join in the struggle for the public interest."
(5) He is apt to come to the defense of riff-raff, testify
for the defence in cases involving the wicked and, when
judging a dispute, react negatively to what is said by both
parties.

---

[1] E.g., The oligarchic politician Phocion, who received the
title χρηστός by public decree (*Suda* s.v. Φρύνων καὶ Φιλο-
κράτης, Diod. 17.15.2); but the text of this sentence is probably
corrupt.

[2] Cf. Plutarch, *Demosthenes* 23.4, R. A. Neil on Aristophanes,
Knights 1017.

(6) [καὶ τὸ ὅλον ἡ φιλοπονηρία ἀδελφή ἐστι τῆς πονηρίας. καὶ ἀληθές ἐστι τὸ τῆς παροιμίας, τὸ ὅμοιον πρὸς τὸ ὅμοιον πορεύεσθαι.][7]

ΑΙΣΧΡΟΚΕΡΔΕΙΑΣ Λ´

(1) ἡ δὲ αἰσχροκέρδειά ἐστιν ἐπιθυμία[1] κέρδους αἰσχροῦ, ἔστι δὲ τοιοῦτος ὁ αἰσχροκερδής, (2) οἷος ἑστιῶν[2] ἄρτους ἱκανοὺς μὴ παραθεῖναι· (3) καὶ δανείσασθαι παρὰ ξένου παρ᾽ αὐτῷ καταλύοντος. (4) καὶ διανέμων μερίδας φῆσαι δίκαιον εἶναι διμοιρίαν[3] τῷ διανέμοντι δίδοσθαι καὶ εὐθὺς αὐτῷ νεῖμαι. (5) καὶ οἰνοπωλῶν κεκραμένον τὸν οἶνον τῷ φίλῳ ἀποδόσθαι. (6) καὶ ἐπὶ θέαν τηνικαῦτα πορεύεσθαι ἄγων τοὺς υἱεῖς, ἡνίκα προῖκ᾽ ἀφιᾶσιν οἱ θεατρῶναι.

(7) καὶ ἀποδημῶν δημοσίᾳ τὸ μὲν ἐκ τῆς πόλεως ἐφόδιον οἴκοι καταλιπεῖν, παρὰ δὲ τῶν συμπρεσβευτῶν δανείζεσθαι· καὶ τῷ ἀκολούθῳ μεῖζον φορτίον ἐπιθεῖναι ἢ δύναται φέρειν καὶ ἐλάχιστα ἐπιτήδεια τῶν ἄλλων παρέχειν· καὶ ξενίων τὸ μέρος τὸ αὐτοῦ ἀπαιτήσας ἀποδόσθαι.

---

[7] epilogum del. editores.
[1] Cobet: περιουσία V.
[2] Korais: ἐσθίων V.
[3] Petersen: δίμοιρον ("two-thirds") Amaduzzi; διμοίρῳ V.

(6) [In general, patronage of scoundrels is evil's close relative. What the proverb says is true: like travels with like.[3]]

30. CHISELING

(1) Chiseling is a desire for tawdry gain. The chiseler is the sort (2) who doesn't serve enough bread when he gives a feast. (3) He asks for a loan from an out-of-town guest who is staying at his house. (4) When distributing shares[1] he asserts that it is fair for a double share to be given to the distributor, and awards it immediately to himself. (5) If he sells wine, he sells a watered-down wine to his friend.[2] (6) He goes to the theater—and brings his sons—only when the theater managers[3] have remitted the entrance fee.

(7) When traveling abroad at public expense, he leaves his public travel-funds behind at home, and asks for loans from his fellow ambassadors. He burdens his attendant with a greater load than he can carry, and yet gives him fewer provisions than any others. He asks for his own share of the gifts they receive[4] and sells it.

---

[3] Never preserved in quite this form, but cf. Homer, *Od.* 17.218, Aristotle, *Rhet.* 1371b15, *Nicomachean Ethics* 1155a34.

[1] The word is vague enough to cover portions of meat at a sacrifice (cf. 17.2), contributions of food to a joint dinner, or even financial returns from a commercial enterprise.

[2] The Greeks mixed water with wine when they drank it, but did not purchase it already watered.

[3] Evidently those who leased rights to produce plays; see Pickard-Cambridge, *The Dramatic Festivals of Athens* 266.

[4] "Guest-gifts" here are presumably those given to the embassy by its foreign hosts.

(8) καὶ ἀλειφόμενος ἐν τῷ βαλανείῳ καὶ εἰπών
"σαπρόν γε τὸ ἔλαιον ἐπρίω, ὦ παιδάριον"[4] τῷ ἀλλο-
τρίῳ ἀλείφεσθαι. (9) καὶ τῶν εὑρισκομένων χαλκῶν
ἐν ταῖς ὁδοῖς ὑπὸ τῶν οἰκετῶν δεινὸς ἀπαιτῆσαι τὸ
μέρος, κοινὸν εἶναι φήσας τὸν Ἑρμῆν. (10) καὶ θοἰμάτιον[5] ἐκδοῦναι πλῦναι καὶ χρησάμενος παρὰ γνωρί-
μου ἐφελκύσαι πλείους ἡμέρας, ἕως ἂν ἀπαιτηθῇ. (11)
καὶ τὰ τοιαῦτα· Φειδωνείῳ μέτρῳ τὸν πύνδακα εἰσκε-
κρουμένῳ[6] μετρεῖν αὐτὸς τοῖς ἔνδον τὰ ἐπιτήδεια
σφόδρα ἀποψῶν.

(12) ὑποπρίασθαι φίλου δοκοῦντος πρὸς τρόπου τι
ὠνεῖσθαι, εἶτα λαβὼν ἀποδόσθαι.[7] (13) ἀμέλει δὲ καὶ
χρέος ἀποδιδοὺς τριάκοντα μνῶν ἔλαττον τέτταρσι
δραχμαῖς ἀποδοῦναι.

(14) καὶ τῶν υἱῶν δὲ μὴ πορευομένων εἰς τὸ

---

4 Reiske: τῷ παιδαρίῳ AB, παιδ'ρ V.

5 Meineke: ἱμάτιον V.

6 εἰσ- vel ἐγκεκρουσμένῳ (sic) Casaubon (ad char. 11):
πύνδακα ἐκκεκρουμένῳ AB, π δακ κεκρου μενω V.

7 locus desperatus: ὑποπριάσθαι φίλου δοκοῦντος πρὸς
τρόπου πωλεῖσθαι V, ὑποπρίασθαι φίλου ἐπιλαβὼν ἀποδόσθαι AB (τι ὠνεῖσθαι, εἶτα λαβὼν Naber).

---

5 Every visitor to the baths would carry a personal flask of oil
with which to wash himself by rubbing it on and scraping off again;
see Ginouvès, Βαλανευτική 214.

6 Lucky finds were called "gifts of Hermes"; for the use of this
phrase to justify sharing them see Menander, *Epitrepontes* 284,

(8) When rubbing himself down in the bath, he exclaims "Stupid boy, you've bought oil that is rancid!" and uses someone else's.[5] (9) He is apt to ask for his own share of any coins that are found in the street by his slaves, citing the proverb "Hermes is impartial."[6] (10) He sends out his cloak to be cleaned and, borrowing one from an acquaintance, hangs onto it[7] for several extra days, until he is asked for it back. (11) And things like this: he measures out provisions personally to his household staff in a Pheidonian measure with its bottom hammered in, levelling it off strictly.[8]

(12) He makes a secret purchase from a friend who thinks he is buying something on a whim,[9] and then, once he's got it, resells it. (13) You can be sure that when he repays a debt of thirty minas, he pays four drachmas too little.[10]

(14) If his sons don't go to school because of illness,

317; Aristotle, *Rhetoric* 1401a22; Lucian, *Navigium* 12; *Paroem. Graec.* II.483.15.

[7] Literally "drags it behind him," perhaps of rough wear, but more probably delay (LSJ ἐφέλκω I.4).

[8] He personally oversees the doling out of grain, using a smaller than average cup (for Pheidonian measures see Aristotle, *Constitution of Athens* 10.2), made still smaller by pushing in its base (cf. *PCG* Aristophanes fr. 281, Pherekrates fr. 110), and scraping off any excess grain on top (Pollux 4.168).

[9] He dupes his friend into agreeing to a low price by pretending the item is something he aches to own. But the text is corrupt here, and the version translated is largely modern conjecture.

[10] He pretends he is one coin short (the *tetradrachmon* was the largest common silver coin in use in Athens), assuming his creditor will not insist on it.

διδασκαλεῖον [τὸν μῆνα ὅλον]⁸ διά τιν᾿⁹ ἀρρωστίαν ἀφαιρεῖν τοῦ μισθοῦ κατὰ λόγον· καὶ τὸν Ἀνθεστηριῶνα μῆνα <ὅλον>¹⁰ μὴ πέμπειν αὐτοὺς εἰς τὰ μαθήματα διὰ τὸ θέας εἶναι πολλάς, ἵνα μὴ τὸν μισθὸν ἐκτίνῃ.

(15) καὶ παρὰ παιδὸς κομιζόμενος ἀποφορὰν τοῦ χαλκοῦ τὴν ἐπικαταλλαγὴν προσαπαιτεῖν, καὶ λογισμὸν δὲ λαμβάνων παρὰ τοῦ χειρίζοντος. (16) καὶ φράτορας ἑστιῶν αἰτεῖν τοῖς ἑαυτοῦ παισὶν ἐκ τοῦ κοινοῦ ὄψον, τὰ δὲ καταλειπόμενα ἀπὸ τῆς τραπέζης ἡμίση τῶν ῥαφανίδων ἀπογράφεσθαι, ἵν᾿ οἱ διακονοῦντες παῖδες μὴ λάβωσι. (17) συναποδημῶν δὲ μετὰ γνωρίμων χρήσασθαι τοῖς ἐκείνων παισί, τὸν δὲ ἑαυτοῦ ἔξω μισθῶσαι καὶ μὴ ἀναφέρειν εἰς τὸ κοινὸν τὸν μισθόν. (18) ἀμέλει δὲ καὶ συναγόντων παρ᾿ αὐτῷ¹¹ ὑποθεῖναι τῶν παρ᾿ ἑαυτοῦ διδομένων ξύλων καὶ φακῶν καὶ ὄξους καὶ ἁλῶν καὶ ἐλαίου τοῦ εἰς τὸν λύχνον. (19) καὶ γαμοῦντός τινος τῶν φίλων καὶ ἐκδιδομένου θυγατέρα πρὸ χρόνου τινὸς ἀποδημῆσαι, ἵνα <μὴ>¹² προπέμψῃ προσφοράν. (20) καὶ παρὰ τῶν γνωρίμων τοιαῦτα κίχρασθαι, ἃ μήτ᾿ ἂν ἀπαιτήσαι μήτ᾿ ἂν ἀποδιδόντων ταχέως ἄν τις κομίσαιτο.

---

⁸ del. Nast.
⁹ Unger: τὴν V.
¹⁰ suppl. Bloch.
¹¹ Korais: ἑαυτῷ V.
¹² suppl. Amaduzzi.

he makes a deduction proportionally from their fees, and doesn't send them to their lessons for the whole month of Anthesterion because of its numerous shows, to avoid paying the fee.[11]

(15) When he collects tenant-rent from his slave,[12] he demands also the fee to exchange the copper,[13] as also when he settles accounts with his steward. (16) When entertaining his clan,[14] he demands a dinner for his own slaves at joint expense, yet insists that even the radish-halves left over from the meal be inventoried, to prevent the waiters from taking them. (17) When he is travelling with acquaintances he uses their servants, and hires out his own without sharing the proceeds. (18) You can be sure that when people get together at his house he makes a bill for the wood, beans, vinegar, salt and lamp-oil he's contributed. (19) When one of his friends is getting married, or marrying off a daughter, he leaves town some time before to avoid giving a present. (20) He borrows from acquaintances the sorts of things one wouldn't ask for back, or wouldn't pick up if people offered them back.

[11] In the month of Anthesterion (February-March) were celebrated the Anthesteria, the Diasia and the Lesser Mysteries at Eleusis; other months seem to have had more holidays, but our knowledge may be defective.

[12] Masters of slaves often allowed them to work for others, in return for a portion of the wages.

[13] The slave pays in copper coinage, which must be converted to silver at a bank for a fee (see *RE* Suppl. II, "agio").

[14] To celebrate the *Apatouria* (Burkert, *Greek Religion* 255).

ADDITIONAL NOTES

1. DISSEMBLING

The title is literally "irony," a notion with a long and complex history. It consists of saying what one obviously does not mean, and originally εἰρωνεία meant simply "lying" (Aristophanes, *Clouds* 499, cf. *Wasps* 174, *Birds* 1211); but it came to be applied specifically to the self-deprecating false modesty of Socrates (e.g., Plato, *Republic* 337A, cf. Aristotle, *Nicomachean Ethics* 1127b; Gregory Vlastos, *Socrates, Ironist and Moral Philosopher* [Ithaca, N.Y., 1991] 21–44). The brothers Schlegel conceived it to be a playful excess of self-confidence (Ernst Behler, *Klassische Ironie, romantische Ironie, tragische Ironie*, Darmstadt 1972); then, by way of reaction, it was viewed as a destructive force (Søren Kierkegaard, *The Concept of Irony*, tr. Lee M. Capel, New York 1965). Modern criticism considers (unconscious) irony to be an important element of tragic drama (beginning with Connop Thirlwall, "On the Irony of Sophocles," *The Philological Museum* 2 (1833) 483–536).

The εἴρων is described also by Ariston of Keos (see the Appendix); he is one of the characters of comedy according to *Tractatus Coislinianus* XII; in Aristotle, *Nicomachean Ethics* 1127a20ff., the εἴρων is opposite to the ἀλαζών

145

(see *Character* 23 below). See in general Otto Ribbeck, "Über den Begriff des εἴρων," *Rheinisches Museum* 31 (1876) 381–400.

Irony as described by Theophrastus is rather different: it is *dissimulation*—avoiding all forthright statements—with the goal of avoiding all involvement in their consequences.

2. FLATTERY

Eupolis wrote a comedy *The Flatterers* (*PCG* fr. 156–191) and there is a play *The Flatterer* by Menander (p. 93 Koerte). Theophrastus himself wrote a book *On Flattery* (fr. 547–8), the peripatetic Klearchos of Soloi did as well (fr. 19 Wehrli), and Plutarch wrote "How to Tell a Flatterer from a Friend" (*Moralia* 48e–75d).

For ancient caricatures of the flatterer see in general Otto Ribbeck, *Kolax: eine ethologische Studie* (Leipzig 1883) and H.-G. Nesselrath, *Lukians Parasitendialog* (Berlin 1985). Another character-trait relating to praising others is "Obsequiousness" (chapter 5); the difference is that the flatterer is totally fixed on the attention of a single patron, for whom he lowers himself to perform tasks usually done by slaves.

3. IDLE CHATTER

ἀδολεσχία is mentioned in Aristotle as a vice (*Nicomachean Ethics* 3.1117b35, *Rhetoric* 1390a9) and discussed in Plutarch's "On Garrulity" (*Moralia* 502b–515a). It is listed as one of the "stylistic" techniques for producing laughter in *Tractatus Coislinianus* V (p. 64 line 16 Koster); Lane Cooper, *An Aristotelian Theory of Comedy* (New York 1922) 231–233 gives many examples of long-winded comic characters from Aristophanes to Molière. See also "Garrulity" (*Character* 7).

4. BOORISHNESS

Aristotle (*Nicomachean Ethics* 1128a) uses ἀγροικία of an inability to appreciate wit, but here it is closer to its original meaning (that of English "boorish" as well), "like a farmer" (cf. Dikaiopolis or Trygaios in Aristophanes, *Acharnians* and *Peace*, and the plays entitled *Agroikos* by Anaxandrides, Antiphanes, Menander, Philemon and others). See Otto Ribbeck, "Agroikos, eine ethologische Studie," *Abhandlungen der königlichen sächsischen Gesellschaft der Wissenschaften* 23 (1888) 1–68.

It is the first of six characters portraying a general lack of tact—the others are "Shamelessness" (6), "Bad Timing" (12), "Absent-mindedness" (14), "Squalor" (19) and "Bad Taste" (20). This is a more subtle portrait than most of the others, and not entirely unsympathetic.

5. OBSEQUIOUSNESS

See the note on "Flattery" (2). Sometimes the distinction is drawn that flattery is for one's advantage, obsequiousness is not (Aristotle, *Nicomachean Ethics* 1108a26, 1127a8), and that is roughly true here, but there are differences as well: "the flatterer [in Theophrastus] . . . is the constant, fixed companion of one and the same patron, while the ob-

147

sequious man is an excessively friendly but basically insecure person, who is driven by the overpowering desire to please everyone" (Nesselrath, *Lukians Parasitendialog* 113).

All the manuscripts (even P. Herc. 1457, of the first century B.C.) make §6–10 follow immediately upon §5. Yet these sections clearly do not describe an obsequious man but an entirely different type, a show-off spendthrift rather like the Aristotelian description of vanity, *Nicomachean Ethics* 1125a27–35, or vulgarity, *Nicomachean Ethics* 1123a19–31, or "Petty Ambition" (21). The only reasonable assumption is that §6–10 belong to a different character, either because they have been displaced from the end of *Character* 21 or—more probably—because a column of text was lost at an early date containing the end of "Obsequiousness" and the beginning of another character. The same thing seems to have happened in *Character* 19.

6. SHAMELESSNESS

The title is literally "mindlessness," or "lack of good sense." The term is much rarer than any other trait-name in the *Characters*, and often a virtual synonym for shamelessness: it is applied to a parasite in *PCG* Nicolaos Comicus fr. 1.43, and to a political opponent by Demosthenes *On the Crown* 249 (where see the commentary of Hermann Wankel). R. G. Ussher, *Greece and Rome* 24 (1977) 77, compares the sausage-seller in Aristophanes, *Knights*.

Considering the low reputation of moneylending in antiquity (Paul Millett, *Lending and Borrowing in Ancient*

Athens, Cambridge 1991, 179) it is not surprising that his ultimate disgrace is to charge exorbitant interest.

6.4 ("have a ticket *or* claim . . ."): As often in this work (e.g., the next sentence), καί links *alternatives*: see J. D. Denniston, *Greek Particles* (2nd ed. Oxford 1954) 292.

7. GARRULITY

See on ἀδολεσχία (3); there we have a sustained portrait of a single man in one situation, here a series of different characteristic actions.

8. RUMOR-MONGERING

A type of political gossip known to Demosthenes, *In Timocratem* 15 and Aeschines, *De falsa legatione* 153. On the dating of its historical allusions see Introd. pp. 10–11.

9. SPONGING

Literally "shamelessness," not a term normally applied to the desire for money, although this was a common topic of ancient moralists and satirists: notable are the Pseudo-Platonic *Eryxias*, Plutarch, "On the love of money" (*Moralia* 523c–528b), the comedies entitled Φιλάργυρος (see on *PCG* Dioxippus fr. 4), Plautus' *Aulularia*, and innumerable satirists; see Gilbert Highet, *Juvenal the Satirist* (New York 1954) 282.

In his discussion of virtues and vices relating to money, Aristotle remarks (*Nicomachean Ethics* 1121b12–1122a3): "Lack of generosity (ἀνελευθερία) is incurable, since old age and any disability seem to make people ungenerous. It is also more innate in people than is extravagance [the opposite excess]; most people are more inclined to love money than to give it away. It is also widely prevalent, and diverse, since of the lack of generosity there are many varieties. Because it consists of two parts—a deficiency in giving and an excess in taking—it does not occur in its entirety in all [ungenerous people], but is sometimes separated, some being excessive in taking and some deficient in giving. The one group, called things like 'sparing,' 'sticky' or 'skinflint,' are all deficient in giving, but neither desire nor are willing to take others' possessions . . . The others are excessive in taking, because they take anything from any source . . . what is common to them all is the desire for base profit (αἰσχροκέρδεια), since they all take upon themselves disgrace for the sake of gain."

In this and the other three characters relating to money—μικρολογία (10), ἀνελευθερία (22), αἰσχροκέρδεια (30)—the terminology is differently applied, and the standard names for greed (like φιλαργυρία and φιλοχρηματία) are avoided; but the distinction between taking and keeping is maintained. This particular man is distinguished by his cheerful openness in taking extras for himself: he makes no attempt at concealment, passing off each small depredation as common courtesy or friendship.

10. PENNYPINCHING

μικρολογία is "obsession with details," but often applied to one who counts every penny (PCG Menander fr. 106, Ephippus fr. 15.10). On the types of greed in general see the Additional Notes on Character 9: this man is not concerned with taking from others, but making sure no others take from him.

11. OBNOXIOUSNESS

βδελυρία is literally "hatefulness," a strong term used to describe the most loathsome enemies (e.g., Aeschines 1.31, 189, Demosthenes 25.27). Here it has something in common with Aristotle's "buffoonery" (βωμολοχία, *Nicomachean Ethics* 1128a4), which aims to get a laugh at any price.

12. BAD TIMING

καιρός means "the proper time" (see West on Hesiod, *Works and Days* 694). This man's blunders are not always his fault—he simply does not foresee how inopportune are his actions. He might be a comic character in a farce, who manages to do something reasonable in itself at the worst possible time.

13. OVERZEALOUSNESS

περιεργία as used here is a synonym of the more common πολυπραγμοσύνη, the meddlesomeness for which Athenians were especially famous: Victor Ehrenberg, "*Polypragmosyne*: A Study in Greek Politics," *Journal of Hellenic Studies* 67 (1947) 46–67. Plutarch wrote a treatise on it (*Moralia* 515b), and πολυπράγμων was the title of comedies by Diphilus, Heniochus, and Timocles. See also H.-J. Mette, "Die περιεργία bei Menander," *Gymnasium* 69 (1962) 398–406.

14. ABSENT-MINDEDNESS

ἀναισθησία is literally "insensitivity," but comes to be used for "stupidity" (Thucydides 6.86, Demosthenes 21.153, Pseudo-Aristotle, *Physiognomica* 3.807b12), and applied especially to Boeotians (see Wankel on Demosthenes, *On the Crown* 43). When Aristotle, *Nicomachean Ethics* 1107b7, applies it to a character-trait, it is the inability to feel pleasure, a meaning not present here.

15. GROUCHINESS

The character described here and in *Character* 17 ("Griping") is better-known by the epithet "bad tempered" (δύσκολος) as described in Aristotle, *Nicomachean Ethics* 1126b11ff, and in Menander's play of that name. Cf. *Eudemian Ethics* 1221a8, *Magna Moralia* 1192b31, Ariston of Keos col. 16–17 (Appendix).

16. SUPERSTITION

δεισιδαιμονία is literally "fear of the gods," one of three character-traits relating to fear—"Mistrust" (18) is the fear of being deceived, "Cowardice" (25) is the fear of death.

"Superstition" is in some ways a poor translation, since it ascribes supernatural significance to everyday events or things; but the events listed here *could* have religious meaning in ancient Greece, so that this man merely takes a correct attitude too far. (Xenophon, *Agesilaos* 11.8 and Aristotle, *Politics* 1315a1 actually use the word δεισιδαίμων in a positive sense.) He attempts to influence the gods on his own behalf, and substitutes personal rituals for public ones. In terms of the Aristotelian mean, his is an excess of piety (εὐσέβεια, on which Theophrastus wrote a treatise, fr. 584A–588), just as atheism is the deficiency of it.

Ancient critiques of superstition in a more modern sense are found in the Hippocratic treatise *On the Sacred Disease*, chapters 1–4, Plato, *Laws* X.909a8–910e4, and Plutarch, "On Superstition" (*Moralia* 164e–171f). Menander wrote a play entitled Δεισιδαίμων (said by an ancient critic to have been modeled on a comedy called "The Reader of Omens" by Antiphanes). For Theophrastus see especially H. Bolkestein, *Theophrastos' Charakter der Deisidaimonia als religionsgeschichtliche Urkunde* (Religionsgeschichtliche Versuche und Vorarbeiten vol. 21.2, Giessen 1929).

17. GRIPING

The title means literally "finding fault with one's lot"; see the Additional Notes on 15 (αὐθάδεια). Μεμψίμοιρος was the title of a comedy by Antidotus.

18. MISTRUST

Menander wrote a play entitled "The mistrustful man."

19. SQUALOR

δυσχέρεια usually indicates "revulsion," i.e. the reaction of the viewer rather than the behavior of the character.

§8–11 do not seem to belong to the same character

as §1–7; perhaps they should be placed at the end of another character (e.g. 11, "Obnoxiousness"), or else we must assume a column of text was lost containing the end of "Squalor" and the beginning of this new character, something like "Lack of Cooperation." The same thing appears to have happened in *Character* 5.

20. BAD TASTE

ἀηδία is literally "unpleasantness"; the noun and adjective are used of disagreeable or odious people by the orators (Demosthenes 21.153, 47.28, 3.72, 164) and elsewhere (*PCG* Alexis fr. 278). Aristotle uses it simply of a man who gives others no pleasure (*Nicomachean Ethics* 1108a30, 1171b26, *Magna Moralia* 1200a15). This character is more precise than the term used: he offends others like many other characters, but mostly he is a city version of the boor, who is best viewed at home (§4–10) and resembles Trimalchio in Petronius' *Satyricon*.

21. PETTY AMBITION

μικροφιλοτιμία, a term found only here, is literally "desire for small honor." The corresponding discussion in Aristotle is not on ambition (*Nicomachean Ethics* 1107b27ff, 1125b1–25, where he concludes that the proper mean between ambition and the lack of it has no name) but on the magnanimous man, who "will reject honor that comes from just anyone, or for petty achievements" (*Nicomachean Ethics* 1124a10). With Theophrastus' man it is not the strength of the desire for honor that is in question, but error about the proper kind of it; Aristotle would have called him "vain" ($\chi\alpha\hat{v}\nu\sigma\varsigma$, *Nicomachean Ethics* 1125a27).

22. LACK OF GENEROSITY

A wealthy Athenian was expected to be generous to his family, friends and country (Dover, *Greek Popular Morality*, Oxford 1974, 230–231). This man behaves with a shabby parsimony on the very occasions (a dramatic victory, his daughter's wedding, command of a warship, contributions to charity) designed to display generosity, and does not maintain the style that suits his prosperity.

A satirist of the third century B.C. mocks the school of Theophrastus for requiring some of the very things the ungenerous man does without: "There [in Theophrastus' school] one needed to have footwear—and it couldn't be re-soled—and further a fancy cloak, a slave to attend you, a large house for dinner parties . . . this way of life was considered 'liberal' ($\dot{\epsilon}\lambda\epsilon\upsilon\theta\dot{\epsilon}\rho\iota\sigma\varsigma$, Teles p. 40.8ff Hense)." Compare also Diogenes Laertius 6.90, Hermippus fr. 51 Wehrli.

23. FRAUDULENCE

$\dot{\alpha}\lambda\alpha\zeta\sigma\nu\epsilon\dot{\iota}\alpha$ is literally "boasting"; the word may be taken from the name of a Thracian tribe (Herod. 4.17, 52; cf. the modern use of "bohemian" or "vandal"). It is defined by Aristotle as the opposite vice to $\epsilon\dot{\iota}\rho\omega\nu\epsilon\dot{\iota}\alpha$ (*Nicomachean Ethics* 1108a9–30; in between them is "being truthful"). The $\dot{\alpha}\lambda\alpha\zeta\dot{\omega}\nu$ is listed as one of the three "characters of comedy" in the *Tractatus Coislinianus*. It comes to be applied especially to soldiers, like Capitano Spavento in the commedia dell' arte, Bobadill in Jonson's *Every Man in His Humour*, Falstaff and Pistol in Shakespeare's *Henry IV* and V, and many characters in ancient comedy. See Walter Hofmann, *Der Bramarbas in der antiken Komödie* (Berlin 1973); J. Arthur Hanson, "The Glorious Military," in T. A. Dorey and D. R. Dudley (eds.), *Roman Drama* (New York, 1965) 51–85.

But its basic sense is "being an impostor," e.g. of a doctor (*De morbo sacro* 2), an ambassador (Aristophanes, *Acharnians* 109, 135), a prophet (Aristophanes, *Peace* 1045, Aristoxenus fr. 1 West), or a philosopher (Aristophanes, *Clouds* 102, *PCG* Eupolis fr. 157). Theophrastus' impostor pretends to have a financial empire, and most closely resembles the *gloriosus* vividly described in *Rhetorica ad Herennium* 4.50–51.64. Cf. Demetrius, *On Style* 119: "the fraud boasts that he possesses things that he doesn't" (ὅ τε γὰρ ἀλαζὼν τὰ μὴ προσόντα αὑτῷ αὐχεῖ ὡς προσόντα).

Plutarch wrote an essay "On extravagant self-praise" (*Moralia* 539a). On the whole theme see especially Otto Ribbeck, *Alazon: ein Beitrag zur antiken Ethologie* (Leipzig 1886).

24. ARROGANCE

For ὑπερήφανος see MacDowell on Demosthenes, *Against Meidias* 83. This man is not really hostile (as is the grouch in 15) but imperious and superior, maintaining a cool distance from everyone he deals with. Cf. Ariston of Keos, col. 20 (Appendix).

25. COWARDICE

Aristotle described the coward as one who feared even what he need not (*Eudemian Ethics* 1221a18, cf. *Nicomachean Ethics* 1115b15f, 34f, and Theophrastus fr. 449a). This coward is more developed; he not only fears danger, but attempts to disguise his cowardice with various excuses, and is pictured in two extended scenes.

26. AUTHORITARIANISM

ὀλιγαρχία is better known as a form of government than a trait of character; but Plato's sketches of human types who correspond to forms of government in *Republic* VIII include the "oligarchic" man (553a1–554b1), who equates excellence with wealth, and a character is called "oligarchic" when he denigrates large juries in Menander, *Sicyonius* 156.

Theophrastus' "oligarchic" man is a retailer of authoritarian slogans: he could as well be called "anti-democratic," as the word implies in political speeches (Andocides 4.16, Lysias 25.8). He much resembles the anonymous author (sometimes dubbed "the old oligarch") of the treatise *On the Constitution of the Athenians* ascribed (falsely) to Xenophon, but the topic was also fresh: from 322 to 318 an oligarchic government of nine thousand led by Phocion replaced the democracy at Athens. See Lawrence A. Trittle, *Phocion the Good* (London 1988) 129–140.

27. REJUVENATION

ὀψιμαθία is literally "late learning" (cf. Aulus Gellius 11.7, Cicero, *ad familiares* 9.20.2, Horace, *Satires* 1.10.22), and it is true that a part of this man's oddity consists in going to school at an advanced age; his appearance in military drills and athletic contests is as absurd as Strepsiades' enrolling himself in Socrates' school in *Clouds* (cf. the adjective παιδομαθής "having learned it in childhood," as a term of praise).

But the essential characteristic here is a general enthusiasm and recklessness of behavior that was tolerated in youths (Dover, *Greek Popular Morality* 103) but not their elders: Philokleon's re-education and rejuvenated violence at a symposium in Aristophanes, *Wasps* 1122–end, are closely parallel.

28. SLANDER

There were legal sanctions against slander in Athens (for which the more common term was κακηγορία), but this man manages to avoid them, and his techniques are in any case the stock-in-trade of the ancient orator's invective, as itemized by Wilhelm Süss, *Ethos: Studien zur älteren griechischen Rhetorik* (Leipzig 1910) 247ff; see also Severin Koster, *Die Invektive in der griechischen und römischen Literatur* (Beiträge zur klassischen Philologie vol. 99, Meisenheim am Glan, 1980) 14, and Lucian's essay *On Not Being Quick to Believe Slander*.

29. PATRONAGE OF SCOUNDRELS

φιλοπονηρία is literally "love of wickedness" (πονηρία is often applied to democratic politicians by their enemies), and one of the oddest characters. Although the word is attested (e.g., Aristotle *Nicomachean Ethics* 1165b16, Dinarchus fr. 42, Plutarch, *Alcibiades* 24.5), the type as described here is not: his interests are purely political, and he is a master of slogans, able to cast doubt on claims of virtue (χρηστός, §3) and misapply aristocratic terms (ἐλεύθερος, εὐφυής, φιλέταιρος, §4) to a demagogue. On the types of vocabulary used see especially R. A. Neil, "Political Use of Moral Terms," Appendix II (pp. 202–209) in his edition of Aristophanes, *Knights* (Cambridge 1909).

30. CHISELING

αἰσχροκέρδεια is literally "base profiteering." The αἰσχροκερδής is an avaricious man in Aristotle, *Nicomachean Ethics* 1122a3; but in Theophrastus' version he is mainly concerned with retaining as much as possible in cash. He buys no oil, accepts (and gives) as little hospitality as possible, always pays the minimum and collects the maximum in every transaction; he surpasses in his greed even the other three misers (9, 10, 22) at every point where he can be compared.

APPENDIX

FRAGMENTS OF THE
CHARACTER SKETCHES
OF ARISTON OF KEOS (III–II B.C.)

From a work "On Relieving Arrogance" quoted by Philo-
demus, *On vices* Book 10, edited by Christian Jensen,
Philodemi περὶ κακιῶν liber decimus, Leipzig 1911.[1]
I generally follow the text of F. Wehrli, *Die Schule des
Aristoteles* vol. 6: *Lykon und Ariston von Keos* (2nd ed.
Basel 1968) fr. 14–16.[2] On Ariston himself[3] see Wehrli in
H. Flashar (ed.), *Die Philosophie der Antike* vol. 3: *ältere
Akademie, Aristoteles, Peripatos* (Basel 1983) 579–582.

The characters treated are the inconsiderate man
(αὐθάδης, col. 16–17), the self-willed man (αὐθέκαστος,
col. 17–18), the know-it-all (παντειδήμων, col. 18), and
the dissembler or ironic man (εἴρων, col. 21–23). Inter-
spersed with the character descriptions are Philodemus'
tedious and contorted analyses of the disadvantages of

---

[1] Further bibliography in Kondo, "I caratteri."

[2] Note that uncertain letters, or lacunae in the papyrus text
which are filled by conjecture, are *not* indicated here: for an exact
account of these see the editions of Jensen or Wehrli.

[3] Not to be confused with Ariston of Chios, Stoic and pupil of
Zeno (*SVF* vol. 1 p. 75).

each trait. The sections I think most likely to be from Ariston are italicized in the translation; on their close similarity in form and style to Theophrastus see Pasquali, "Sui caratteri," 59–62.

(XVI.29sqq.) ὁ δ᾽ αὐθάδης λεγόμενος ἔοικε μὲν εἶναι μεικτὸς ἐξ οἰήσεως καὶ ὑπερηφανίας καὶ ὑπεροψίας, μετέχων δὲ καὶ πολλῆς εἰκαιότητος. τοιοῦτος γὰρ ἐστιν, φησὶν ὁ Ἀρίστων, οἷος ἐν τῇ μάκρᾳ θερμὸν ἢ ψυχρὸν αἰτεῖν μὴ προανακρίνας τὸν συμβεβηκότ᾽, εἰ κἀκείνῳ συναρέσκει, καὶ . . .

(XVII) . . . παῖδα πριάμενος μηδὲ τοὔνομα προσερω- τῆσαι μήτ᾽ αὐτὸς θέσθαι, καλεῖν δὲ "παῖδα" καὶ μηθὲν ἄλλο· καὶ τὸν συναλείψαντα μὴ ἀντισυναλείφειν· καὶ ξενισθεὶς μὴ ἀντιξενίσαι· καὶ θύραν ἀλλοτρίαν κό- πτων, ἐπερωτήσαντος τίς ἐστιν, μηδὲν ἀποκρίνεσθαι, μέχρι ἂν ἐξέλθῃ. καὶ ἀρρωστοῦντ᾽ αὐτὸν ἐπισκεπτο- μένου φίλου μὴ λέγειν πῶς ἔχει, μηδ᾽ αὐτὸς ἐπι- σκεπτόμενός τινα τοιοῦτό τι προσεπερωτῆσαι. καὶ γράφων ἐπιστολὴν τὸ χαίρειν μὴ προσγράψαι μηδ᾽ ἐρρῶσθαι τελευταῖον.

ὁ δ᾽ αὐθέκαστος οὐ πάνυ μὲν εἰκαῖός ἐστιν οὐδ᾽ ἄλογος ὥσπερ ὁ αὐθάδης, δι᾽ οἴησιν δὲ τοῦ μόνος φρονεῖν ἰδιογνωμόνων, καὶ πειθόμενος ἐν ἅπασιν κατ- ορθώσειν, ἁμαρτήσεσθαι δ᾽ ἂν ἑτέρου κρίσει προσ- χρήσηται, μετέχων δὲ καὶ ὑπερηφανίας· οἷος μηδενὶ προσαναθέμενος ἀποδημεῖν, ἀγοράζειν, πωλεῖν, ἀρ- χὴν μετιέναι, τἆλλα συντελεῖν· κἂν προσερωτήσῃ τις τί μέλλει ποιεῖν, "οἶδ᾽ ἐγώ," λέγειν, κἂν μέμφηταί τις, ὑπομειδιῶν, "ἐμὲ σύ;" καὶ παρακληθεὶς ἐπὶ συνεδρείαν βουλευομένῳ μὴ βούλεσθαι τὸ δοκοῦν εἰπεῖν, εἰ μὴ τοῦτο μέλλει πράττειν· καὶ πάντ᾽ ἐν ὅσοις ἀποτέτευχε . . .

(Column 16, line 29 ff.:) *The man called inconsiderate seems to be a blend of conceit, pride and scorn, with a large dose of thoughtlessness. He is the sort,* Ariston says, *who demands hot or cold water in the bath without first asking his fellow-bather whether it is all right, . . .*

(Column 17) *. . . when he buys a slave he doesn't even ask for his name, or give him one himself, but merely calls him "slave." When someone rubs him with oil, he doesn't do the same in return; if he has been invited out, he doesn't return the invitation. When he knocks at another's door and is asked "who is it?" he doesn't answer until the man comes outside. If a friend pays him a visit while he's ill, he won't say how he is feeling, and when he himself visits someone, he won't even ask such a question. When he writes a letter, he doesn't add "greetings," or "best wishes" at the end.*

The self-willed man is not exactly thoughtless or irrational like the inconsiderate one, but self-opinionated because of his conceit that he alone has any sense, and confident that he will always do the right thing, whereas if he relies on another's judgment he will make a mistake; he also has a dose of arrogance. He is the sort who seeks no one's advice before going on a trip, making a purchase or a sale, running for office, or carrying out other things. If someone asks him what he intends to do, he says "That's for me to know." If someone criticizes, he smirks "Look who's talking!" If he is called to a meeting for a man who seeks advice, he refuses to say what he thinks unless the man is definitely going to follow it. Anything in which he has failed . . .

(XVIII) . . . τελεῖν καὶ μὴ ἐπιτεθυμηκέναι γενέσθαι
φάσκειν· καὶ μὴ δυσωπεῖσθαι τοὔνομα καλούμενος ὡς
αὐθέκαστος, ἀλλὰ καὶ ἔτι παιδάρια λέγειν εἶναι τοὺς
ὡς παιδαγωγοῖς ἄλλοις προσανατιθεμένους, καὶ μόνος ἔχειν πώγωνα καὶ πολιὰς καὶ ζῆν δυνήσεσθαι
γενόμενος ἐν ἐρημίᾳ.

τούτου δ' ἔτι χείρων ἐστὶν ὁ παντειδήμων, ἀνα-
πεπεικὼς ἑαυτὸν ὅτι πάντα γινώσκει, τὰ μὲν μαθὼν
παρὰ τῶν μάλιστ' ἐπισταμένων, τὰ δ' ἰδὼν ποιοῦντας
μόνον, τὰ δ' αὐτὸς ἐπινοήσας ἀφ' αὑτοῦ. κἄστι τοιοῦτος οὐ μόνον οἷον Ἱππίαν τὸν Ἠλεῖον ἱστορεῖ
Πλάτων, ὅσα περὶ τὸ σῶμ' εἶχεν αὑτῷ πεποιηκέναι
λέγειν, ἀλλὰ καὶ κατασκευάζειν οἰκίαν καὶ πλοῖον δι'
αὑτοῦ καὶ χωρὶς ἀρχιτέκτονος· καὶ γράφειν συνθήκας
ἑαυτῷ δεομένας ἐμπειρίας νομικῆς· καὶ δούλους ἰδίους
ἰατρεύειν, μὴ μόνον ἑαυτόν, ἐπιχειρεῖν δὲ καὶ ἄλλους·
καὶ φυτεύειν καὶ φορτίζεσθαι τὰ μάλισθ' ὑπὸ τῶν
τεχνικωτάτων κατορθούμενα· καὶ ναυαγῶν ἐν ἅπασι
μηδ' οὕτω παύεσθαι τῆς ἀποπληξίας. οἷος δὲ καὶ τῶν
μαθημάτων ἀντιποιούμενος πάντων ἀσχημονεῖν· καὶ
τοὺς καταγελῶντας ἀπείρους λέγειν . . .

(XIX) . . . οὐκ ἂν δι . . . δων ἐπιτρέπειν.

τῷ μὲν οὖν αὐθάδει τά τ' ἐκ τῆς οἰήσεως καὶ τῆς
ὑπερηφανίας καὶ ὑπεροψίας εἰ μὴ καὶ τῆς ἀλαζονείας
δυσχερῆ παρακολουθεῖ, καὶ ἰδίως τὰ ἐκ τῆς εἰκαιότητος καὶ τὰ διὰ τῆς ὀργῆς τούτων οἷς οὕτω προσ-
φέρεται, καὶ τὸ τυγχάνειν ὁμοίων ἢ μηδὲ βουλομένων
εἰς ὁτιδήποτε κοινώνημα συγκαταβαίνειν, δυχρηστεῖ-

(Column 18) . . . *and has no desire to admit it happened. He is not disturbed when you call him self-willed, but says those who seek the guidance of others like nursemaids are little children, and that he is the only one with a beard and grey hair, who could survive if left on his own.*

Still worse than this one is the know-it-all, since he has persuaded himself that his knowledge is complete—some he's learned from experts, some is from merely observing them in action, some he has come up with on his own. He is not only like Plato [Hippias Minor 368B] says Hippias of Elis was, and says that he has made everything he wears, but he also builds a house and boat by himself, without an architect. He draws up contracts for himself that require legal expertise; he acts as physician to his slaves as well as himself, and tries it for others too; he works at the sort of agriculture and merchant shipping which most require experts to be successfully pursued, and if he washes out completely he does not even then stop his madness. He is the sort who makes a fool of himself by laying claim to all subjects; those who laugh at him he calls laymen . . .

(Column 19) . . . The inconsiderate man is beset by the difficulties arising from conceit, arrogance, and scorn, if not from fraudulence as well, and in particular those from thoughtlessness, and the anger of those to whom he behaves this way, and the fact that he encounters people like him, or who don't want to have anything to do with him at

σθαι, καὶ τὸ περὶ μαινομένου πάντας φέρεσθαι καὶ καθαιρεῖν, διότι τὴν κακίαν ἔχειν αὐτὸν ὑπονοοῦσιν.

τῷ δ' αὐθεκάστῳ τά τε παρὰ τὰς ἀτοπίας ἐξ ὧν μέμεικται καὶ τὸ μόνον ἀφραίνειν, ὅτι μόνος οἴεται περὶ πάντων φρονεῖν· διὸ κἂν τοῖς πλείστοις ἀποτυγχάνειν καὶ ἐπιχαίρεσθαι μετὰ καταγέλωτος ὑπὸ πάντων καὶ μηδὲ βοηθεῖσθαι· καὶ μηδὲ τῶν σοφῶν ἀναμαρτήτων εἶναι λεγόντων μηδ' ἀπροσδέκτων συμβουλίας, τοῦτον ὑπὲρ αὐτοὺς νομίζοντα φρονεῖν ἐξ ἀνάγκης κακοδαιμονεῖν· ληρεῖν δὲ καὶ διότι τὴν κοινῶς σύνεσιν οἴεται περιπεποιῆσθαι τὰ τῶν ἰδίας ἐμπειρίας ἐχόντων, καὶ μεταμεμελῆσθαι πολλῶν ἐξ ἀνάγκης ἐνκυρεῖν, καὶ λοιδορίας καρποῦσθαι καὶ προσκρούσεις ἑτέρων . . .

(XX) . . . φάσθαι . . . ἄνθρωπον ἄλλων ἀνθρώπων οὐκ ἔχειν χρείαν.

ὁ δὲ παντειδήμων ἅμα τοῖς εἰρημένοις πᾶσι καὶ μαργιτομανής ἐστιν, εἰ καὶ τὸν ὄντως πολυμαθέστατον προσαγορευόμενον οἴεται πάντα δύνασθαι γινώσκειν καὶ ποιεῖν, οὐχ οἷον ἑαυτόν, ὃς ἐνίοτε οὐδέν τι φωρᾶται κατέχων καὶ οὐ συνορῶν· ὅτι πολλὰ δεῖται τριβῆς, ἂν καὶ ἀπὸ τῆς αὐτῆς γίνηται μεθόδου καθάπερ τὰ τῆς ποιητικῆς μέρη, καὶ διότι περὶ τοὺς πολυμαθεῖς ὀσμαὶ μόνον εἰσὶ πολλῶν, οὐ κατοχαί, καὶ

all, that he does not know what to do, and that everyone rushes away and dismisses him for a madman, because they think that vice has him possessed.

The self-willed man is beset by the difficulties attendant on the strange traits of which he is comprised, and the fact that he alone is out of his mind, because of his belief that he alone is sensible about all subjects. That is why he fails in most things, and is a source of delight and ridicule for all, and receives no assistance. Whereas not even the wise claim to be without fault or in no need of advice, he, thinking he is more sensible than they, cannot avoid ill-fortune. He talks nonsense, because he imagines his basic intelligence has bestowed on him the talents of those who possess specialized knowledge, and it happens that he must regret many things, and reap the abuse and attacks of others . . .

(Column 20) He says . . . that a man has no need of other men.

The know-it-all, along with everything already said, is also as crazy as Margites,[1] if he thinks that even one truly called the greatest polymath can know and do everything—much less[2] himself, who is sometimes caught with no mastery at all, and no comprehension; the reason is that many things require practice—if they follow the same method as the elements of the art of poetry; and because around the polymaths there is only an aroma of many sub-

[1] The hero of the (now lost) comic epic of whom it was said "he had knowledge of many deeds—and he knew them all badly" (fr. 3 West).

[2] οὐχ οἷον = οὐχ ὅτι (see F. Blass and A. Debrunner, *Grammar of New Testament Greek*, tr. R. Funk, Chicago 1961, §304).

τἀποτεύγματα περίεστιν τῶν παιδευμάτων, οὐ τὰ κα-
τορθώματα, καὶ πάνθ' ὅσα τοῖς τοιούτοις συμβαίνειν
ἀνελογιζόμεθα· καὶ διότι πολλὰ γινώσκειν, ὡς Ἱππίας
ἐκαυχᾶτο, καὶ τὸ παραπλήσιον πᾶν γένος ὀνείδη μᾶλ-
λόν ἐστιν ἤπερ ἐγκώμια· καί — τί γὰρ δεῖ τἆλλα περὶ
ληρούντων λέγειν; ὡς ὅταν ἀτυχήσωσι, φωρῶνται
καταφεύγοντες ἐπὶ τοὺς τυχόντας καὶ τῶν ἐλαχίστων
ἐλάττους αὑτοὺς εἶναι προσομολογοῦσιν.

ὁ μὲν οὖν ὑπερήφανος καὶ ὑπερόπτης ἐστίν, ὁ δ'
ὑπερόπτης οὐ πάντως καὶ ὑπερηφανεῖ καὶ ἅπαντα διὰ
τὸ . . . χηρ . . . ἔστιν ὅτε τα . . . εἶναι· πέφυκε δ' οὐ . . .

(XXI) τὸν μὲν σεμνὸν ἐπαινοῦντες ὡς ἀξίαν ἔχοντα
μετά τινος αὐστηρίας, τὸν δὲ σεμνοκόπον καὶ τότε καὶ
νῦν πάντως ψέγοντες ὡς ἐπιφάσκοντα τὸν εἰρημένον
καὶ προσποιούμενον εἶναι τοιοῦτον ἐν τοῖς ὄχλοις καὶ
διὰ τῶν λόγων — ὃν σεμνομυθεῖν ἔλεγον — καὶ τῷ
σχήματι τοῦ προσώπου καὶ τῶν ὀμμάτων καὶ περι-
βολῇ καὶ κινήσει καὶ ταῖς κατὰ τὸν βίον ἐνεργείαις.
καὶ βρενθύεσθαι δὲ καὶ βρενθυόμενον ὠνόμαζον καὶ
ἔτι νῦν ὀνομάζουσιν — εἴτ' ἀπὸ τοῦ παραδεδομένου
θυμιάματος ἢ μύρου τῶν θεῶν βρένθος, ὡς καθ' ἡμᾶς
καὶ μίνθωνος ἀπὸ τῆς μίνθης, εἴτ' ἀφ' ὁτουδήποτε —
τὸν ἀπὸ τῆς εἰρημένης διαθέσεως κατεμβλέποντα
πᾶσιν καὶ παρεμβλέποντα καὶ τῇ κεφαλῇ κατασεί-
οντα καὶ κατασμικρίζοντα τοὺς ἀπαντῶντας ἢ τοὺς ὧν
ἄν τις μνημονεύσῃ, κἂν ὦσι τῶν μεγάλων εἶναι δο-
κούντων, μετὰ διασυρμοῦ καὶ μόλις που βραχείας

jects, not a mastery of them, and what remains is what they have failed to learn, not where they have succeeded, and all the rest of what we have listed as happening to such people; and because multiple knowledge in the way Hippias boasted of it, and every category like it, is more to reproach than to praise. But why say any more about windbags? Since when they fail they are caught running to anyone they can find for help, and so they admit they are at the lowest level of all.

The arrogant man is also contemptuous; but the contemptuous man is not necessarily arrogant, and . . .

(Column 21) . . . since they praised the dignified man as possessing importance combined with some austerity, but the man who makes a show of dignity both then and now alike they mock, as an impersonator of the aforementioned, who for the mob pretends to be like this in his speech (they used to say he "preached"), the cast of his face and eyes, his dress, movements and way of life. And "high-falutin"[3] behavior (*brenthuesthai*) or personality— whether from the well-known incense or perfume of the gods called *brenthos* (just as modern *minthon* from mint), or from whatever else—is what they used to call, and still do call, a man who looks down on everyone, avoids their sight, tosses his head, belittles whoever meets him or whom anyone mentions to him, even from the elite, with

[3] An Aristophanic expression for pride, of obscure origin.

ἀποκρίσεως ὑπεροχὴν ἰδίαν ἐμφαινούσης, ἄλλου δ᾽
οὐδενὸς ἀριθμὸν ἐμποιούσης· οἷον ὁ Ἀριστοφάνης
"ὅτι βρενθύει τ᾽ ἐν ταῖσιν ὁδοῖς καὶ τὠφθαλμὼ παρα-
βάλλεις" ἐκωμῴδει.

ὁ δ᾽ εἴρων ὡς ἐπὶ τὸ πλεῖστον ἀλαζόνος εἶδος . . .

(XXII) διανοεῖ . . . ος . . . ον, ἀλλὰ καὶ τἀναντία
μᾶλλον, ὥστ᾽ ἐπαινεῖν ὃν ψέγει, ταπεινοῦν δὲ καὶ
ψέγειν ἑαυτόν τε καὶ τοὺς <. . .> οἷός ἐστιν εἰωθέναι
πρὸς ὀνδήποτε χρόνον μετὰ παρεμφάσεως ὧν βούλε-
ται· συνεπινοεῖται δ᾽ αὐτῷ καὶ δεινότης ἐν τῷ
πλάσματι καὶ πιθανότης· ἔστιν δὲ τοιοῦτος οἷος τὰ
πολλὰ μωκᾶσθαι καὶ μορφάζειν καὶ μειδιᾶν καὶ ὑπ-
ανίστασθαί τισιν ἐπιστᾶσιν ἄφνω μετ᾽ ἀναπηδήσεως
καὶ ἀποκαλύψεως· μαὶ μέχρι πολλοῦ συνὼν ἐνίοις
σιωπᾶν· κἂν ἐπαινῇ τις αὐτὸν ἢ κελεύῃ τι λέγειν ἢ
μνημονευθήσεσθαι φῶσιν αὐτόν, ἐπιφωνεῖν· "ἐγὼ γὰρ
οἶδα τί πλήν γε τούτου, ὅτι οὐδὲν οἶδα;" καὶ "τίς γὰρ
ἡμῶν λόγος;" καὶ "εἰ δή τις ἡμῶν ἔσται μνεία·" καὶ
πολὺς εἶναι τῷ "μακάριοι τῆς φύσεως εἰ δή τινες" ἢ
"τῆς δυνάμεως" ἢ "τῆς τύχης." καὶ μὴ ψιλῶς ὀνο-
μάζειν, ἀλλὰ "Φαῖδρος ὁ καλός," καὶ "Λυσίας ὁ
σοφός," καὶ ῥήματ᾽ ἀμφίβολα τιθέναι, "χρηστόν,"
"ἡδύν," "ἀφελῆ," "γενναῖον," "ἀνδρεῖον·" καὶ παρεπι-
δείκνυσθαι μὲν ὡς σοφά, προσάπτειν δ᾽ ἑτέροις ὡς
Ἀσπασίᾳ καὶ Ἰσχομάχῳ Σωκράτης· καὶ πρὸς τοὺς ἐκ

ridicule and scarcely even a brief retort to express his own superiority and dismiss everyone else. Just as Aristophanes joked: "Since you act high-falutin on the street, and avert your eyes."[4]

. . . The dissembler[5] is for the most part a type of fraud . . .

(Col. 22) . . . he intends . . . but rather the opposite, so that he praises a man he finds fault with, but belittles and faults himself and those ‹. . .›[6] is the sort who is accustomed to do on all occasions, merely hinting at what he desires. In his fabrications one can discern a cleverness and persuasiveness as well. He is the sort who often mocks, grimaces, smiles, and for people in authority he rises to yield his place suddenly, with a leap and uncovering his head. With some people he remains silent, even though he has spent a long time with them. If one praises him or bids him speak or people say that he will be remembered, he responds: "What am I supposed to know, except that I know nothing?" or "Of what importance am I?" or "In the event that anyone remembers me." And he constantly calls people "Blessed, if any are, in their nature," or their "capability," or "fortune." He doesn't call people merely by their names, but "fair Phaedrus," or "wise Lysias," or uses ironic words: "good," "sweet," "simple," "noble," "brave." He shows off thoughts he thinks wise, but attributes them to others as Socrates does with Aspasia and Ischomachus.[7] To those

---

[4] *Clouds* 362, of Socrates.   [5] The literal meaning, "ironic man," is better suited to the description here than in *Character* 1 of Theophrastus.   [6] The text is corrupt; probably several words are missing.   [7] In the dialogues *Menexenus* (by Plato) and *Oeconomicus* (by Xenophon).

τῶν ἀρχαιρεσιῶν ἀπολυομένους· "ἐδοκιμ . . .

(XXIII) . . . θεων . . . μοι· πάντα γὰρ δεινὸς σὺ
κατεργάσασθαι." κἂν συνέλθῃ, τὸν καταπληττόμενον
ἐμφαίνειν τό τε εἶδος καὶ τὴν ἀξίαν καὶ τὸν λόγον
πρὸς τοὺς συγκαθημένους θαυμάζοντα, καὶ προσκα-
λούμενος εἰς κοινολογίαν φοβεῖσθαι καὶ τἀλάχιστα
φάσκειν ἄπορα καταφαίνεσθ' ἑαυτῷ, καὶ διαγελάσαν-
τος· "ὀρθῶς μου καταφρονεῖς τηλικοῦτος ὤν, καὶ γὰρ
αὐτὸς ἐμαυτοῦ." καὶ "νέος ὤφελον εἶναι καὶ μὴ γέρων,
ἵν' ἐμαυτὸν ὑπέταξά σοι." κἂν τῶν συμπαρόντων του
ὁτιδήποτε εἰπόντος ἐκδήλως, ἐκεῖνος εἴπῃ τοιοῦτον·
"διὰ τί λέγεις;" ἐπιφωνεῖν τὰς χεῖρας ἀνατείνας· "ὡς
ταχὺ συνῆκας, ἀλλ' ἀφυὴς ἐγὼ καὶ βραδὺς καὶ
δυσαίσθητος." καὶ προσέχειν μὲν διαλεγομένῳ καὶ
ἐνχάσκειν, εἶθ' ὑποκινναιδεῖν καὶ διανεύειν ἄλλοις,
ποτὲ δ' ἀνακαγχάζειν·

οἷος δὲ καὶ πρὸς οὓς ἔτυχεν ὁμιλῶν "διασαφεῖτέ
μοι τὰς ἐμὰς ἀγραμματίας καὶ τὰς ἄλλας ἀστοχίας
ὑμεῖς, ὦ φίλοι, καὶ μὴ περιορᾶτ' ἀσχημονοῦντα." καὶ
"οὐ διηγήσεσθέ μοι τὰς τοῦ δεῖνος εὐημερίας, ἵνα
χαίρω, κἂν ἄρα δυνατὸς ὦ μιμῶμαι;" καὶ τί δεῖ τὰ
πλείω λέγειν; ἅπαντα γὰρ τὰ Σωκρατικὰ μνημονεύ-
ματα . . .

(XXIV) . . . ὅμοιοι δ' εὐτελιστὴς ἢ ἐξευτελιστὴς καὶ
οὐδενωτὴς ἢ ἐξουδενωτὴς καὶ ἐπὶ ταὐτὸ φέρονται,
διαφέροντες ἀνέσει καὶ ἐπιτάσει διαβολῆς τοῦ πλη-
σίον· ὁ μὲν γὰρ ἐξευτελιστὴς ἀπόντων τινὰ φαυλότε-

who have been eliminated from the elections . . .

(Column 23) . . . *"You're adept at carrying out everything."*[8] *And if he meets him, to those sitting nearby he reveals himself awestruck with admiration of his appearance, his dignity and speech. When he is asked to share his ideas he is terrified, and says that even the smallest difficulties seem to him impossible, and when the man mocks him he says "A man like you is right to feel contempt for me—I feel it for myself." And "I wish I were young and not old, so I could sit at your feet." When someone in the group makes any sort of obvious comment, if that man says something like "What makes you say that?" he exclaims with upraised hands "How quickly you have grasped it! I've been dull, slow, stupid!" When the man converses he is intent and open-mouthed, then he talks mincingly and nods to others, and sometimes bursts out laughing.*

He is the sort who says to whoever he happens to be talking to, "Friends, you must explain to me my ignorance and other blunders, and not let me make a fool of myself"; or "Please tell me about so-and-so's happy state, so that I may have the pleasure of being like him, if I can." Why go on? All the memoirs about Socrates . . .

(Column 24) *The disparager and the utter disparager, and the vilifier and the utter vilifier are the same and amount to the same thing, differing only in whether their slander of their neighbor is relaxed or intense: the utter disparager*

---

[8] This paragraph seems to describe the dissembler's ironic treatment of one particular individual.

ρον δὴ δοκεῖν παρίστησιν, ὁ δ᾽ ἐξουδενωτὴς ἴσον τῷ
μηδενί. λοιπὸν ἔστιν μὲν ὅτε τοιοῦτοί τινές εἰσιν
ὑπεροχὴν ἐμφαίνοντες ἰδίαν ἢ τῶν ⟨καὶ τῶν⟩[1] οὓς
ἀποσεμνύουσιν, ἔστιν δ᾽ ὅτε κατατρέχοντες μόνον
ἐνίων· ὥστε τοὺς προτέρους καὶ ὑπερηφάνους εἶναι·
διὸ καὶ δῆλον ὅτι φησὶν ἐπακολουθεῖν αὐτοῖς τὰ δι᾽
ἐκείνην ἄτοπα καὶ περιττότερόν τι τῇ διαβλητικῇ καὶ
βασκαντικῇ καὶ φθονητικῇ. καὶ τὸν ὑπομνηματισμὸν
δὲ τοῦτον αὐτοῦ καταπαύσομεν, ἐπισυνάψωμεν δ᾽ αὐτῷ
τὸν περὶ τῶν ἄλλων κακιῶν ὧν δοκιμάζομεν ποιεῖσθαι
λόγον.

[1] Supplevi (ἢ τῶν οὓς papyrus).

suggests that a person then absent doesn't seem very significant; the utter vilifier, that he is worthless. Well, they are sometimes this way because they are hinting at their own superiority, or of this or that group they are praising; sometimes it is only because they run certain people down. The former are therefore arrogant as well; thus it is obvious that he[9] says they are beset by the strange things arrogance produces, and somewhat more abundantly [than the arrogant man] because of slander, malignity and envy.

And here we shall end this excerpt from him [Ariston], and append to it one about the other vices which we are attempting to treat.

[9] Ariston.

HERODAS

MIMES

EDITED AND TRANSLATED BY

I. C. CUNNINGHAM

Note to the 2002 Edition

In this reprint of Herodas' Mimes some mistakes have been corrected and the translation has been revised in some details; in particular, in damaged passages restorations suggested in the apparatus have often been included in the translation, to give the probable sense.

To the bibliography we can now add the first volume of an Italian translation and commentary by L. Di Gregorio (1997). I have read as many of the books and articles which have appeared since the last printing as were accessible; a few changes in interpretation have resulted.

INTRODUCTION

In the first half of the fourth century the city-states of
Greece continued, as for generations past, their self-de-
structive warring. Athens, Sparta, Thebes—each in turn
achieved and lost brief supremacies. When a new power
began to emerge in the north, it was regarded as something
to be used, as they had previously used the Persian and
other eastern powers, to help defeat whoever was the current chief rival. But Macedonia under Philip II proved
to be very different. With a mixture of cunning diplo-
macy and military might Philip advanced southwards into
Thessaly; by the middle of the century he was a power to
be reckoned with, a position recognised by his presidency
of the Pythian Games in 346. His progress was temporarily
impeded by an alliance led by Athens under the orator
Demosthenes. But his victory at the battle of Chaeroneia
in 339 left him overlord of all Greece. He began to organ-
ise it into a confederacy led by Macedonia, with the aim
of renewing the age-old struggle with Persia. However in
336 he was assassinated in obscure circumstances, and
the kingship and leadership of Greece passed to his son,
known to history as Alexander the Great.

After a short period spent in consolidating his position in Greece, in Thrace, and in Illyria, Alexander in 334
turned to Asia. In rapid succession he conquered Asia

Minor, defeated the Persian king Darius at Issus, overran
Syria and Egypt, advanced into Babylonia, defeated Darius again at Gaugamela, and conquered Persia itself. At the
beginning of 330 he rested briefly in the Persian palace,
then pursued Darius to Ecbatana; Darius was overthrown
in a coup and murdered. Alexander now continued east
into modern Afghanistan and Uzbekistan, spending some
time in Samarkand; then south into Pakistan. He would
have gone on but his weary army had had enough. At the
end of 324 he returned to Babylon. Six months later he fell
ill and died.

Alexander took Greek culture and language with him,
but inevitably they evolved in their new surroundings.
Greek colonists settled all over the lands of his conquests.
Cities called Alexandria were left behind as he marched.
He created the first European empire. But it scarcely survived him. In the absence of a recognised successor his
generals battled for supremacy and the empire fell apart.
India was soon given up. Macedonia, Syria and Egypt
emerged as the most powerful kingdoms, which for a century and a half re-enacted the feuding of the old city-
states. The rising power of Rome was more and more
drawn into their disputes and ended by absorbing all into
its empire.

In the fourth century, poetry in Greece was totally
overshadowed by the refined and polished prose of orators, philosophers and historians. Only comedy continued
a live verse tradition. But in the following century there
was a brief revival, mostly centred on the capital of Egypt,
Alexandria. Founded by Alexander in 331, it became the
capital of the Egyptian kingdom and dynasty of the
Ptolemies. In the 280s Ptolemy II, known as Philadelphus,

set up both the celebrated Library, into which were collected texts of all Greek literature, and the Museum, a university or research institute rather than a museum in the modern sense. To these were attracted a host of scholars and literary figures, and in this highly intellectual atmosphere flourished the poetry now known as Alexandrian or Hellenistic.

Some authors used traditional genres in a new way, such as Apollonius with his long epic the *Argonautica*. But more typical is the short poem, whether equally traditional in genre like the epyllia of Callimachus and Theocritus; or using old forms for new purposes, like the hymns and iambs of Callimachus; or introducing subjects new to poetry, like the mimiambs of Herodas and the mime-related poems of Theocritus. Common to all is the fact that this is learned poetry, composed by and intended for those who were familiar with earlier literature, recondite myths, obscure words, unusual metres. Poetry was the companion of studies in the Library and the Museum.

Herodas and His Work

No biographical information about the poet has come down from antiquity. Those who quote a few lines of his work (see under Text) variously give his name as Herodas (Ἡρώδας, a later form of Ἡρώιδας), Herodes (Ἡρώδης) or Herondas (Ἡρώνδας). The first and third are Doric, the second presumably a normalisation to the Attic form. The forms with and without the *n* are both possible, but the evidence for the latter is slightly greater.

Pliny the Younger (see end of this section) mentions him in conjunction with Callimachus, in such a way that it is possible that they were contemporaries. This is confirmed by a few internal references. The fourth mimiamb can be dated to between about 280 (as Apelles, mentioned in the past in lines 72–78, must have died before then) and 265 (as the sons of Praxiteles, mentioned in the present in lines 25–26, must have died by then). The first must be after, probably soon after, 272/1 (by which date Ptolemy II and Arsinoe, who have a shrine in line 30, were deified). The second is probably earlier than 266 (by which date the city of Ace, mentioned in line 16, had been renamed Ptolemaïs). Herodas' poetical activity can therefore be assigned to the late 270s and early 260s, exactly the period of Callimachus and of Theocritus, the high point of Hellenistic poetry.

The second mimiamb is undoubtedly set in the island of Cos in the Dodecanese, and the temple of Asclepius in the fourth may be that in Cos (though there is no coincidence between the works of art mentioned in that poem and those known to have been in that temple). The connected sixth and seventh appear to be located in Asia Minor (the month Taureon in 7.86 suggests that, as does Cerdon's origin in either Chios or Erythrae, 6.58). Egypt is highly praised in 1.26–35; and the phrase 'Attic minae' in 2.22 may indicate that this was written within the Ptolemaic empire (the Attic silver standard being universal, and the adjective therefore needless, everywhere else).

The evidence may be summarised: Doric in origin, living in the first half of the third century, connected to a greater or lesser extent with Egypt, Cos and Asia Minor.

His poems are typical of their place and time in that they combine the content of one older genre with the form of another. This is indicated by their name (recorded by several of the ancient quotations), mimiambs: they are both mimes and iambs.

The Greek mime was a popular entertainment in which one actor or a small group portrayed a situation from everyday life in the lower levels of society, concentrating on depiction of character rather than on plot. Situations were occasionally borrowed from comedy. Indecency was frequent. Ancient writers mention a great variety of subtypes, the details of which are obscure. Some had a musical accompaniment; of one such group we are told possible subjects: 'sometimes women who are adulteresses and procuresses, sometimes a man drunk and going on a revel to his lover'.[1] Some performers shared booths in the market-place with conjurers, dancers and the like; others played at private parties. Individual mimes could act several parts in a piece when necessary. The normal vehicle was prose and the spoken language.

A few fragments of or relating to such performances have been found in texts from Egypt dating from the second century B.C. to the fifth A.D.[2] Only one writer is known by name, Sophron of Syracuse, of the late fifth century B.C., whose mimes were introduced to Athens by Plato. But full texts have not survived, and most of the fragments quoted by later writers were selected for grammatical interest, so that we know little of the nature of his work.

---

[1] Athenaeus 14. 621c (Loeb edition: vol. VI, page 347).

[2] The texts of these fragments have been added to this edition. Also now included is a selection of the fragments of Sophron's mimes.

However it can be said that he wrote in his native Doric dialect and in prose, and his subjects are apparently all realistic.

The iamb was a genre of seventh- and sixth-century Ionia. Named from its characteristic metre, the iambic trimeter, it is personal and realistic, full of immediate loves and hates. Archilochus and Hipponax are the major names, but few complete poems have survived. Archilochus came from the island of Paros, Hipponax from Ephesus; both used their vernacular languages. Hipponax increased the coarse, sneering effect of his verse by using the so-called 'limping iambic' (choliambos), where the second-last element of the line is long instead of short.

Herodas took his subject-matter from the mime. Only in the case of the fifth mimiamb is there an exact parallel in the mime tradition; but the first and second have characters which are known to have figured in the tradition; and the situation of the fourth and subject of the sixth appeared in Sophron. And the treatment is invariably that of the mime: characters from the urban proletariat in realistic settings and situations, and character-depiction more important than plot.

But there is a crucial difference in the form. His language and verse are, as far as we can tell, a slightly imperfect rendering of those of Hipponax. The qualification is necessary because we have so little of the latter's work and because of the possibility of corruption in our texts of both Hipponax and Herodas and in Herodas' text of Hipponax. The imperfections in his rendering consist of a few false Ionic forms and a few non-Ionic (Attic and Doric) words; the not infrequent occurrence of common Greek (Attic) forms is almost certainly due to corruption. The most striking features of the dialect, which differentiate it from most literary Ionic, are the use of κ for π in interrogative and indefinite pronouns and adjectives (κοῦ, κοῖος etc.) and the absence of aspiration at the beginnning of words (psilosis), both of which are sporadically but unmistakably indicated by the papyrus. In his versification Herodas, probably following Hipponax, is far freer than most Greek writers in allowing a long vowel at the end of a word to be followed by one at the beginning of the next, the whole counting as only one long syllable; this may either be indicated in writing (crasis; e.g. μἤλασσον = μὴ ἔλασσον) or not (synaloephe; e.g. μέσωι ἔστω). He resolves long syllables into two shorts (creating anapaests, dactyls or tribrachs in place of iambs) not infrequently, and rarely admits anaclasis (– ∪ ∪ – for ∪ – ∪ –).

Mimes were recited either by one actor, taking several parts if necessary, or by a small troupe. There has been much discussion as to which method Herodas used. Certainty is unattainable, but it seems unlikely that a troupe with costumes and sets would be assembled for such brief pieces, whose performance would not have been frequently repeated.[3]

Herodas' work is typically Hellenistic. The poems are short. The subjects are new to poetry, remote from the experience of the intellectual audience. The language and metre are revivals of obsolete forms. It is clear from the eighth mimiamb that he met with criticism in his own day,

[3] See my review in *Journal of Hellenic Studies* 101 (1981), 161, of G. Mastromarco, *Il Pubblico di Eronda,* 1979 (English translation, *The Public of Herondas,* 1984), who takes the opposite view.

185

but the text is so badly preserved that it cannot be ascertained (if it was clearly stated in the first place) who the critics were or what they objected to.

In the same poem Herodas anticipated fame for himself, but that was not to be. Texts were still to be had in Egypt in the second century A.D., though whether these represent the end of a continuous interest or a revival is unknown. A few sententious lines were taken into the anthological tradition which we know under the name of John of Stoboe (Stobaeus) (see 1.15–16, 67–68; 6.37–39; 10; 12; 13), while one of his many proverbs is in the collection of Zenobius (see 3.10). Grammarians picked up a few unusual words or forms (see 5.32; 8.59–60; 11). But the later Greek literary and biographical sources know nothing of him. The only person known to have read him as literature is Roman: Pliny the Younger about 100 A.D. compliments his friend Arrius Antoninus on his Greek epigrams and mimiambs—'What an amount of elegance and beauty is in them, how sweet they are, and pleasing and bright and correct. I thought I was reading Callimachus or Herodes, or better if such exists.'[4] In the century since he again became known he has excited considerable interest, often for the wrong reasons: despite appearances, he is no 'ancient realist', but a highly literary writer with a similarly elite audience.

---

[4] *Epp.* 4.3.3: *quantum ibi humanitatis, uenustatis, quam dulcia illa, quam amantia, quam arguta, quam recta. Callimachum me uel Heroden uel si quid melius tenere credebam.*

INTRODUCTION

The Mimiambs

1. *A Matchmaker or Procuress.* Metriche, companion of Mandris who has been for some considerable time absent in Egypt, is alone with her slave Threissa. She is visited by her old nurse, Gyllis, the matchmaker of the title. The reason for the visit is approached obliquely: Mandris, tempted by the attractions of Egypt, has gone for good; Metriche will be old before she realises it and should enjoy herself while she can. Then she comes to the point: the athlete Gryllus is desperately in love with Metriche and will not leave Gyllis alone; Metriche should yield to him. Metriche firmly rejects the proposition: she is faithful to Mandris. This little drama is framed by the domestic scene, the arrival and the hospitality before departure.

The characterisation of the matchmaker is the purpose of the piece. This was one of the subjects of the popular mime.

2. *A Brothel-keeper.* Battarus the brothel-keeper lives in Cos, a resident alien. He claims that a sea captain Thales has attacked his house in an attempt to abduct Myrtale, one of his girls. In Greek courts complainants and defendants had to represent themselves, and the mimiamb consists of Battarus' speech to the jury. He depicts himself as poor and humble, providing a necessary service to the community, and grossly abused by Thales. But this is a charade, and the greed, shamelessness and indecency normally considered typical of his profession constantly break through. He attempts to follow the usual pattern of a legal speech (known to us from the fourth-century Attic orators), but is regularly diverted from his theme and repeats himself endlessly.

187

An incoherent orator appeared in Sophron. The brothel-keeper is a regular character in Middle and New Comedy.

3. *A Schoolmaster.* Metrotime brings her delinquent son Cottalus to the schoolmaster Lampriscus for punishment. She narrates his wrongdoings: gambling in bad company, neglect of his studies, damage to the roof of the building in which they live, generally leading a lazy and worthless life. Lampriscus agrees that a beating is required and with the assistance of other pupils proceeds to inflict it. The boy pleads for mercy and promises to reform, but when released is apparently still impudent. Metrotime angrily goes off to get fetters for him.

Despite the title Metrotime is the dominant character in the piece, as she obviously is in her household.

4. *Women dedicating and sacrificing to Asclepius.* The two women, with their slaves, come to the temple early in the morning to thank the god for curing an illness. After praying and giving the sacrificial cock to the temple attendant, they inspect the sculptures and paintings which can be seen. One of them is a stranger and exclaims excitedly at what she sees. The other acts as guide and makes a vigorous defence of the art of the painter Apelles. Finally the success of the sacrifice is announced and arrangements are made for the distribution of the sacrifice—as in 1 the central scene is placed in a frame.

The description of works of art is common in Greek literature, from the shield of Achilles in the *Iliad* on. One of Sophron's mimes was entitled 'Women watching the Isthmian Festival'. Theocritus, *Idyll* 15, roughly contemporary with this poem of Herodas and also related to the mime, includes a description of a tapestry concerning Adonis. Here the observers are poor, unsophisticated women, whose sole criterion of excellence is naturalness.

5. *A Jealous Person.* Bitinna has a sexual relationship with her slave Gastron, whom she accuses in crude terms of infidelity. Rejecting both pleas of innocence and appeals for mercy, she orders that he should be flogged, and on second thoughts tattooed also. But her anger, though vehemently expressed, is not implacable, and when another slave Cydilla, whom she regards more as a daughter, intercedes on Gastron's behalf, she is prepared to remit his punishment, at least for the present.

The situation is not dissimilar to that of the mime fragment P.Oxy. 413 verso (anonymous fragment 7 below), though Bitinna is mild by comparison with the protagonist of that violent piece.

6. *Women in a Friendly or Private Situation.* Metro visits her friend Coritto to enquire who made her the red dildo. Coritto is astonished that she knows of this and asks where she saw it. On learning that Euboule had lent it to Nossis, she complains bitterly of her false friend. Metro consoles her and again asks who made it. Coritto tells her that it was Cerdon and describes him and his skill; she explains why she was unable to get a second dildo from him. Metro further learns that more can be discovered of the cobbler from Artemis, and departs to see her.

Dildos are at least mentioned in Sophron.

7. *A Cobbler.* Metro brings some other ladies to Cerdon's shop. He shows them his stock, with elaborate praise of his wares. There is some bargaining about prices. Cerdon fits some of the ladies with shoes and tells Metro to

come back later. Cerdon has been described as the great craftsman in the previous poem; here he is the consummate salesman.

That Cerdon the cobbler of 6 and 7 is the same person can hardly be doubted; it is equally certain that the Metro of both is the same, having by the dramatic date of 7 come to know and patronise Cerdon. It is therefore an obvious question if there is not also a continuity of subject; and in fact there are clear indications that Cerdon is still selling dildos as well as shoes, in the very high prices mentioned and in various remarks throughout (especially lines 62–63, 108–112, 127–129).

8. *A Dream*. The speaker, the poet himself, wakens his household and narrates and interprets his dream. It appears that he has participated in some kind of Dionysiac festival, with the sacrifice of a goat, the appearance of the god himself, and a contest in which the participants attempt to stand on an inflated wineskin. He wins this and is threatened by an old man; he replies and calls on a young man. He interprets the dream in relation to his poetry, which is represented by the goat: it is eaten, i.e. attacked by critics; probably he predicts future fame for himself.

The mutilated condition of the text is very unfortunate; if the dream and its interpretation had been better preserved, we should know more of Herodas' view of his own work and perhaps the identity and arguments of his critics. But the damage is so great that no certainty is possible.

9. *Women at Breakfast*. Clearly a domestic scene, perhaps recalling one in Sophron, but the few surviving words give no more detail.

10. *Molpinus*. The surviving fragment advocates avoid-

ing the miseries of old age by death, a not infrequent wish in Greek literature. Here it may well be an aside rather than the subject. Molpinus will have been the main character, Gryllus another.

11. *Women working together.* The only surviving line appears to be erotic.

12 and 13, brief quotations from unknown poems, respectively describe a children's game and repeat a popular commonplace. Nothing is known of their contexts.

Text and Editions

In 1891 F. G. Kenyon published a papyrus roll which had been discovered in Egypt and purchased by the British Museum.[5] It contains the first seven mimiambs of Herodas more or less complete (though the text is damaged from time to time by abrasions or holes); the eighth and the beginning of the ninth were later put together from fragments of papyrus. Presumably the other two whose names are known from quotations, and quite possibly more, have been totally lost from the end of the roll. The scribe writes a small, clear bookhand which can be ascribed to the early second century A.D. He has the orthographical peculiarity of frequently writing ι for ει. Words are not usually separated. In some difficult passages accents, breathings or punctuation marks are added. Changes of speaker are not marked by names but by the paragraphus, a short line placed under the first few letters of the verse in the middle of or after which the change oc-

---

[5] Now British Library, Pap. 135. It is referred to as P.

curs; this indication is not infrequently omitted. The scribe made or faithfully copied many mistakes; some he corrected himself in the course of writing, many more afterwards, doubtless having looked again at his model. A corrector, probably using a different copy, wrote in about three dozen corrections or variants, mostly in the first three poems. There is a handful of later annotations.

A small fragment of a second roll from later in the second century, discovered at Oxyrhynchus in Egypt, was published by E. Lobel in 1954[6] and recognised a year later by A. Barigazzi as the ends of 8.67–75. Its text is marginally worse than that of P.

Kenyon's first edition was little more than a transcript of P. Shortly afterwards W. G. Rutherford published his, which assigned the lines to their speakers and made some correct emendations (among a host of wild conjectures). Many other scholars made suggestions in periodicals for the reading, supplementing and interpretation of the new text, including F. Blass, O. Crusius, "F. D." (an unidentified English scholar), O. A. Danielsson, H. Diels, W. Headlam, H. van Herwerden, A. Palmer, H. Richards, and H. Stadtmüller. Editions and commentaries were produced by F. Bücheler (1892), O. Crusius (1892–1914), and R. Meister (1893; fundamental for the dialect). The work of this early period is summarised in the commentary of J. A. Nairn (1904).

Walter Headlam had spent years collecting material for a definitive commentary, but was prevented by his prema-

6 *The Oxyrhynchus Papyri*, vol. 22, no. 2326; it is preserved in the Ashmolean Museum, Oxford, and is referred to as O.

ture death from finally organising and publishing it. This task was undertaken by A. D. Knox, who contributed significantly to the restoration of 8. This edition (1922) is the only one of Herodas which will certainly have a lasting value beyond its immediate sphere, but for that sphere it has major defects, in particular the absence of typographical indications of supplements in the text. P. Groeneboom's French commentary on 1–6 (1922) is also important. Knox and R. Herzog continued to struggle with the problems of 8, and each finished by producing a text with translation: Herzog a revision of Crusius's German one (1926), Knox in the first Loeb edition a very idiosyncratic and unhelpful antique English one (1929). At the same time a French translation in the Budé series was done by H. Laloy, with text by Nairn (1928).

Later editors have followed the modern tendency of keeping the text much freer of uncertain supplements: Q. Cataudella (1948; Italian translation), G. Puccioni (1950; Italian commentary), L. Massa Positano (mimiambs 1–4, 1970–3; Italian translation and commentary), I. C. Cunningham (1971; English commentary), and B. G. Mandilaras (1978 and 1986; Modern Greek translation and commentary). The present editor's Teubner edition (1987) has a full apparatus, bibliography and index. Important modern books on the dialect are those of D. Bo (*La Lingua di Eroda*, 1962) and V. Schmidt (*Sprachliche Untersuchungen zu Herondas*, 1968); on the production that of G. Mastromarco (see above, note 3).

This edition largely repeats the text of the Teubner one, but is somewhat less austere in printing supplements in damaged passages; these are to be understood as giving the likely sense, but not necessarily the exact words lost. Supplements are placed in square brackets, editorial insertions in angle brackets. The apparatus records only substantive variations from the papyrus; most corrections by the scribe and orthographical and dialectal modifications are not included.

MIMES

1. ΠΡΟΚΥΚΛΙ[Σ] Η ΜΑΣΤΡΟΠΟΣ

(ΜΗ.) Θ[ρέισ]σ̣', ἀράσσει τὴν θύρην τις· οὐκ ὄψηι
      μ[ή] τ̣[ις] παρ' ἡμέων ἐξ ἀγροικίης ἥκει;
(ΘΡ.) τίς τ̣[ὴν] θύρην;
⟨ΓΤ.⟩   ἐγῶδε.
⟨ΘΡ.⟩   τίς σύ; δειμαίνεις
      ἆσσον προσελθεῖν;
⟨ΓΤ.⟩   ἢν ἰδού, πάρειμ' ἆσσον.
5 ⟨ΘΡ.⟩ τίς δ' εἰ⟨ς⟩ σύ;
⟨ΓΤ.⟩   Γυλλίς, ἡ Φιλαινίδος μήτηρ.
      ἄγγειλον ἔνδον Μητρίχηι παρεῦσάν με.
(ΘΡ.) καλεῖ—
⟨ΜΗ.⟩   τίς ἐστιν;

    1 Θ[ρέισ]σ̣' Rutherford, Bücheler
    2 μ̣[ή] τ̣[ις] Blass
    3 τ̣[ὴν] several   ΓΤ. ἐγῶδε (= ἐγὼ ἤδε) Blass
    5 φιλαινίου in text, ·νιδος· in margin P
    7 So divided by Danielsson: ΜΗ. κάλει ('Invite her in'). τίς ἔστιν;
ΘΡ. Γυλλίς, ἀμμίη Γυλλίς Blass (but command and question should
be in the reverse order)

1. A MATCHMAKER OR PROCURESS

METRICHE

Th[reis]sa, someone is banging at the door. Go and see [if one] of our people from the country has come.

THREISSA

Who's at [the] door?

⟨GYLLIS⟩

It's I.

⟨THREISSA⟩

Who are you? Are you afraid to come nearer?

⟨GYLLIS⟩

See, I have come nearer.

⟨THREISSA⟩

But who are you?

⟨GYLLIS⟩

Gyllis, Philaenis' mother. Go in and tell Metriche that I am here.

THREISSA

There is a visitor—

⟨METRICHE⟩

Who is it?

<ΘΡ.>   Γυλλίς.

<ΜΗ.>   ἀμμίη Γυλλίς.

    στρέψον τι, δούλη. τίς σε μοῖρ' ἔπεισ' ἐλθεῖν,
    Γυλλίς, πρὸς ἡμέας; τί σὺ θεὸς πρὸς ἀνθρώπους;

10   ἤδη γὰρ εἰσι πέντε κου, δοκέω, μῆνες
    ἐξ εὖ σε, Γυλλίς, οὐδ' ὄναρ, μὰ τὰς Μοίρας,
    πρὸς τὴν θύρην ἐλθοῦσαν εἶδέ τις ταύτην.

(ΓΥ.)   μακρὴν ἀποικέω, τέκνον, ἐν δὲ τῇς λαύρῃς
    ὁ πηλὸς ἄχρις ἰγνύων προσέστηκεν,

15   ἐγὼ δὲ δραίνω μυῖ' ὅσον· τὸ γὰρ γῆρας
    ἡμέας καθέλκει κἠ σκιὴ παρέστηκεν.

[ΜΗ.]   σίγη] δὲ καὶ μὴ τοῦ χρόνου καταψεύδεο·
    οἴη τ' ἔτ'] εἰ<ς> γάρ, Γυλλί, κἠτέρους ἄγχειν.

(ΓΥ.)   σίλλ̣[α]ι̣νε· ταῦτα τῇς νεωτέρῃς ὑμῖν

20   πρόσεστιν.

<ΜΗ.>   ἀλλ' οὐ τοῦτο μή σε θερμήνῃ.

<ΓΥ.>   ἀλλ' ὦ τέκνον, κόσον τιν' ἤδη χηραίνεις
    χρόνον μόνη τρύχουσα τὴν μίαν κοίτην;
    ἐξ εὖ γὰρ εἰς Αἴγυπτον ἐστάλη Μάνδρις
    δέκ' εἰσὶ μῆνες, κοὐδὲ γράμμα σοι πέμπει,

25   ἀλλ' ἐκλέλησται καὶ πέπωκεν ἐκ καινῆς.
    κεῖ δ' ἐστὶν οἶκος τῆς θεοῦ· τὰ γὰρ πάντα,
    ὅσσ' ἔστι κου καὶ γίνετ', ἔστ' ἐν Αἰγύπτωι·
    πλοῦτος, παλαίστρη, δύναμις, εὐδίη, δόξα,

15–16 are cited by Stobaeus, *Anth.* 4.50b.52, from Herodas' Mimiambi, with minor corruptions

17 σίγη] Bücheler   δὲ Cunningham

MIME 1

<THREISSA>

Gyllis.

<METRICHE>

Mama Gyllis! Leave us, slave. What fate has persuaded
you, Gyllis, to come to us? Why are you here, a god to men?
For it's now, I think, about five months since anyone saw
you, Gyllis, coming to this door even in a dream, I swear it
by the Fates.

GYLLIS

I live far off, child, and in the lanes the mud comes up to
one's knees. And I have the strength of a fly; for old age
weighs me down and the shadow is at hand.

[METRICHE]

[Be quiet] and do not bring false charges against your age.
For [you are still able] to hug others, Gyllis.

GYLLIS

Joke away; that's typical of you younger ones.

<METRICHE>

Now don't let this heat you.

<GYLLIS>

Well, my child, how long now is it that you've been
separated, wearing out your single bed alone? It's ten
months since Mandris set off for Egypt, and not a word
does he send you; he has forgotten and drunk from a new
cup. The home of the goddess is there. For everything in
the world that exists and is produced is in Egypt: wealth,
wrestling schools, power, tranquillity, fame, spectacles,

---

[18] οἴη τ᾽ ἔτ᾽] (ε)ῖ Tucker   [20] Others give the whole line
to Gyllis, 'but this will not keep you warm'.

θέαι, φιλόσοφοι, χρυσίον, νεηνίσκοι,
30 θεῶν ἀδελφῶν τέμενος, ὁ βασιλεὺς χρηστός,
Μουσῆιον, οἶνος, ἀγαθὰ πάντ᾽ ὅσ᾽ ἂν χρήιζηι,
γυναῖκες, ὁκόσους οὐ μὰ τὴν Ἅιδεω Κούρην
ἀστέρας ἐνεγκεῖν οὐραν[ὸ]ς κεκαύχηται,
τὴν δ᾽ ὄψιν οἷαι πρὸς Πάριν κοτ᾽ ὥρμησαν
35 θ]ε[αὶ κρ]ιθῆναι καλλονήν—λάθοιμ᾽ αὐτάς
γρύξασ]α. κο[ί]ην οὖν τάλαιν[α] σὺ ψυχήν
ἔ]χο[υσ]α θάλπεις τὸν δίφρον; κατ᾽ οὖν λήσεις
γηρᾶσα] καί σευ τὸ ὥριον τέφρη κάψει.
πάπτ]ηνον ἄλληι κἠμέρας μετάλλαξον
40 τὸ]ν νοῦν δύ᾽ ἢ τρεῖς, κἰλαρὴ κατάστηθι
(.).....ις ἄλλον· νηῦς μιῆς ἐπ᾽ ἀγκύρης
οὐκ] ἀσφαλὴς ὁρμεῦσα· κεῖνος ἢν ἔλθηι
..........].ν[.] μηδὲ εἷς ἀναστήσηι
ἠ]μέας ....τοδιυα δ᾽ ἄγριος χειμών
45 ..[.............].. κοὐδὲ εἷς οἶδεν
τὸ μέλλο]ν ἡμέων· ἄστατος γὰρ ἀνθρώποις
......]..η[.]ς. ἀλλὰ μήτις ἕστηκε
σύνεγγυς ἡμῖν;
⟨ΜΗ.⟩   οὐδὲ ε[ἷ]ς.
⟨ΓΤ.⟩   ἄκουσον δή
ἄ σοι χρε[ί]ζουσ᾽ ὧδ᾽ ἔβην ἀπαγγεῖλαι·
50 ὁ Ματαλίνης τῆς Παταικίου Γρύλλος,

---

31 χρήιζη⟨ις⟩ Bücheler
32 τὴν Δεωκούρην ('daughter of Deo', i.e. of Demeter) Meister
34 τὴν δ ὀψιν P, with το δ (ε)ιδος written above by the corrector

philosophers, gold, youths, the sanctuary of the sibling
gods, the King excellent, the Museum, wine, every good
thing he could desire, women, as many by Hades' Maid as
the stars that heaven boasts of bearing and as lovely as [the
goddesses] who once hastened to Paris to be [judged] for
beauty—may they not notice [what I say]! What then, poor
girl, [is in] your mind that you are keeping your seat
warm?[1] You will [become old] before you know and ashes
will gulp your beauty. [Glance] elsewhere and for two or
three days change [your] purpose, and become cheerful
[   ] another: a ship [is not] safe riding at one anchor.
If that [dark one] comes, no one shall raise us [   ] and a
wild storm [   ], and none of us knows [the
future]; for [life is] unstable for men. But is there anyone
near us?

<METRICHE>

No one.

<GYLLIS>

Then listen to what I came here wishing to tell you:
Gryllus, son of Pataecion's Mataline, winner of five

---

[1] I.e. 'doing nothing'.

---

35 θεαὶ κρ]ιθῆναι Bücheler
36 γρύξασ]α Headlam   37 ἔ]χρ[υσ]α several
38 γηράσα] Rutherford, Blass   39 πάπτ]ηνον Weil
43 ὁ πορφύρεος] Crusius   [οὐ] μηδὲ Richards
44 -το· δεινὰ seems preferable to · τὸ δεῖνα; but with the latter
φίλη (Bell) may precede
46 τὸ μέλλο]ν several
47 beginning βίος or similar
50 ματακινης P, with λ written above κ by the corrector

ὁ πέντε νικέων ἆθλα, παῖς μὲν ἐν Πυθοῖ,
δὶς δ' ἐν Κορίνθωι τοὺς ἴουλον ἀνθεῦντας,
ἄνδρας δὲ Πίσηι δὶς καθεῖλε πυκτεύσας,
πλουτέων τὸ καλόν, οὐδὲ κάρφος ἐκ τῆς γῆς
55 κινέων, ἄθικτος ἐς Κυθηρίην σφρηγίς,
ἰδών σε καθόδωι τῆς Μίσης ἐκύμηνε
τὰ σπλάγχν' ἔρωτι καρδίην ἀνοιστρηθείς,
καί μευ οὔτε νυκτὸς οὔτ' ἐπ' ἡμέρην λείπει
τὸ δῶμα, [τέ]κνον, ἀλλά μευ κατακλαίει
60 καὶ ταταλ[ί]ζει καὶ ποθέων ἀποθνήισκει.
ἀλλ', ὦ τέκνον μοι Μητρίχη, μίαν ταύτην
ἁμαρτίην δὸς τῆι θεῶι· κατάρτησον
σαυτήν, τὸ [γ]ῆρας μὴ λάθηι σε προσβλέψαν.
καὶ δοιὰ πρήξεις· ἡδέω[ν] τε[ύ]ξ[ει] κ[αί σοι
65 δοθήσεταί τι μέζον ἢ δοκεῖς· σκέψαι,
πείσθητί μευ· φιλέω σε, να[ὶ] μὰ τὰς Μοίρας.

(ΜΗ.) Γυλλί, τὰ λευκὰ τῶν τριχῶν ἀπαμβλύνει
τὸν νοῦν· μὰ τὴν γὰρ Μάνδριος κατάπλωσιν
καὶ τὴν φίλην Δήμητρα, ταῦτ' ἐγὼ [ἐ]ξ ἄλλης
70 γυναικὸς οὐκ ἂν ἡδέως ἐπήκουσα,
χωλὴν δ' ἀείδειν χώλ' ἂν ἐξεπαίδευσα
καὶ τῆς θύρης τὸν οὐδὸν ἐχθρὸν ἡγεῖσθαι.
σὺ δ' αὖτις ἔς με μηδὲ ἔν<α>, φίλη, τοῖον
φέρουσα χώρει μῦθον· ὃν δὲ γρήιηισι
75 πρέπει γυναιξὶ τῆις νέηις ἀπάγγελλε·

64 ἡδέω[ν] τε[ύ]ξ[ει] κ[αί σοι Headlam

prizes—as a boy at Pytho, twice at Corinth over the
downy-cheeked youths, while he in wrestling brought
down men twice at Pisa[2]—quite well off, but not moving
even a straw from the earth,[3] an untouched seal as far as
Cytheria[4] is concerned, on seeing you at the Descent of
Mise[5] seethed inside, stung to the heart with love, and
neither at night nor throughout the day does he leave my
house, child, but wails at me and calls me mama and is
dying of desire. Now, Metriche my child, allow the goddess
this one fault; dedicate yourself, in case old age sees you
unexpectedly. You will gain two benefits: [you will get]
pleasure [and] something greater than you expect will be
given [to you]. Consider, do as I say; I love you, I swear it by
the Fates.

METRICHE

Gyllis, the whiteness of your hair is blunting your mind; for
by Mandris' return and dear Demeter I should not have
heard this cheerfully from another woman, but should
have taught her to sing her lame song with a limp and to
find the threshold of my door a hostile place. See that you
do not come again to me, my friend, with any such tale, but
repeat to your young girls one which suits old crones. And

---

[2] In the Pythian, Isthmian and Olympic games respectively.

[3] Proverbial expression for a quiet person; also used in 4.67.

[4] Aphrodite.   [5] Festival representing a descent (into
Hades) of this minor goddess.

67–68 are cited by Stobaeus, *Anth.* 4.50b.59, from Herodas'
Mimiambi, with γύναι for Γυλλί

73 ἔν⟨α⟩ Blass

τὴν Πυθέω δὲ Μητρίχην ἔα θάλπειν
τὸν δίφρον· οὐ γὰρ ἐγγελᾶι τις εἰς Μάνδριν.
ἀλλ' οὐχὶ τούτων, φασί, τῶν λόγων Γυλλίς
δεῖται Θρέισσα, τὴν μελαινίδ' ἔκτριψον
80 κἠκτημόρους τρεῖς ἐγχέασ[α τ]οῦ ἀκρήτου
καὶ ὕδωρ ἐπιστάξασα δὸς πιεῖν.

(ΓΤ.)   καλῶς.

(ΜΗ.)   τῆ, Γυλλί, πῖθι.

<ΓΤ.>   δεῖξον οὐ[.].....πα.[
        πείσουσά σ' ἦλθον, ἀλλ' ἔκητι τῶν ἱρῶν.

<ΜΗ.>   ὦν οὕνεκέν μοι, Γυλλί, ὦνα[

85 <ΓΤ.>   οσσοῦ γένοιτο, μᾶ, τέκνον π[.]..........
        ἡδύς γε· ναὶ Δήμητρα, Μητρ[ί]χη, τούτου
        ἡδίον' οἶνον Γυλλὶς οὐ πέ[π]ωκέν [κω.
        σὺ δ' εὐτύχει μοι, τέκνον, ἀσ[φα]λίζευ [δέ
        σαυτήν· ἐμοὶ δὲ Μυρτάλη τε κ[αὶ] Σίμη
90   νέαι μένοιεν, ἔστ' ἂν ἐμπνέη[ι] Γυλλίς.

79 In the margin is what appears to be a gloss on μελαινίδα:
κυλ(ίκων) γέ(νος) εὐ(τελές)
81 γτ. καλῶς Headlam
84–85 Division among speakers and readings are doubtful

let Metriche, daughter of Pytheas, keep her seat warm; for no one laughs at Mandris. But it is not these words, they say, that Gyllis needs; Threissa, wipe the cup clean and give her a drink, pouring in half of wine and a splash of water.

GYLLIS

No, thanks.

METRICHE

Here, Gyllis, drink.

⟨GYLLIS⟩

Show.[6] I did not come to persuade you [   ], but because of the rites.

⟨METRICHE⟩

On account of which to me, Gyllis, [   ].

⟨GYLLIS⟩

†   † may be, ah, child, [   ] sweet; by Demeter, Metriche, Gyllis has never [before] drunk sweeter wine than this. Farewell, child, [and] look after yourself; but may my Myrtale and Sime[7] remain young, as long as Gyllis breathes.

---

[6] The meaning is not clear: perhaps explained by the lost end of the verse. 'Give it me' (Knox) is an unsupported rendering.

[7] Typical names of courtesans.

2. ΠΟΡΝΟΒΟΣΚΟΣ

(ΒΑ.) ἄνδρες δικασταί, τῆς γενῆς μ[ὲ]ν οὐκ ἐστέ
ἡμέων κριταὶ δήκουθεν οὐδὲ [τ]ῆς δόξης,
οὐδ' εἰ Θαλῆς μὲν οὗτος ἀξίην τὴ[ν] νηῦν
ἔχει ταλάντων πέντ', ἐγὼ δὲ μ[η]δ' ἄρτους,
5 ....] ὑπερέξει Βάτταρόν [τι π]ημήνας·
πολλο[ῦ] γε καὶ δ(ε)ῖ· [τ]ὠλυκὸν γὰρ [ἂν] κλαύσαι
....].ιησομαστοσηιασ[..].νχωρη
....].σμε.ι. ἐστὶ τῆς [πό]λιος κἠγώ,
καὶ ζ]ῶμεν οὐκ ὡς βουλό[με<σ>]θ' ἀλλ' ὡς ἡμέας
10 ὁ και]ρὸς ἕλκει. προστάτην [ἔχ]ει Μεννῆν,
ἐγ]ὼ δ' Ἀριστοφῶντα· πὺξ [νε]νίκηκεν
Μεν]νῆς, [Ἀρισ]τοφῶν δὲ κ[ἤτι] νῦν ἄγχει·
κεἰ μ]ή ἐστ' ἀ[λη]θέα ταῦτα, το[ῦ ἡ]λίου δύντος
ἐξε]λθέτω[...]ων ἄνδρες .[..]χε χλαῖναν
15 ...] γνώσετ' οἴωι προστάτ[ηι τ]εθώρηγμαι.
ἐρεῖ τάχ' ὑ[μ]ῖν 'ἐξ Ἄκης ἐλήλ[ο]υθα
πυρ]οὺς ἄγων κἤστησα τὴν κακὴν λιμόν',

---

⁵ δίκηι] Crusius   ⁶ πολλο[ῦ] γε καὶ δ(ε)ῖ Milne   [τ]ὠλυ-
κὸν γὰρ [ἂν] κλαύσαι Knox   ⁷ supplements and word-division
are quite uncertain   ⁸ κοῦτ]ος μέτοικος F.D.
⁹ καὶ ζ]ῶμεν Headlam   βουλό[με<σ>]θ' Crusius

2. A BROTHEL-KEEPER

BATTARUS

Gentlemen of the jury, certainly you are not judges of our family or reputation; nor, if the defendant Thales has a ship worth five talents and I not even bread, shall he prevail [in his suit] by doing [some] harm to Battarus. [Far from it:] for he would weep bitterly [[1] He too is an alien] of the city, as I am, [and] we live not as we wish but as [the moment] compels us. He [has] Mennes as patron, [I] have Aristophon: Mennes has won with his fists, but Aristophon can [even] now wrestle; [if] this is not true, after sunset ( ) come out,[2] gentlemen, [ ] cloak [and] he will know by what kind of patron I am protected. Perhaps [he will say] to you, 'I came from Ace[3] with

---

[1] The meaning of line 7 is quite uncertain.

[2] This may be said to the jury, 'come out', or of Thales, 'let him come out'. [3] The later Acre.

---

10 ὁ και]ρὸς Stadtmüller [ἔχ]ει Milne

12 Μεν]νῆς Crusius [Ἀρισ]τοφῶν Headlam κ[ῆτι] Bücheler 13 κεἰ μ]ὴ Blass ἀ[λη]θέα Blass

14 ἐξέέ]λθετ' Blass, ἐξέ]λθέτω Knox ἦ[ν (ε)ῖ]χε Blass, but the first letter is rather α[15 καὶ γνώσετ' οἴωι Knox

16 ἐρ(ε)ῖ] τάχ' ὑ[μ]ῖν Crusius

17 πυρ]οὺς F.D., Crusius

ἐγὼ δ]ὲ πό[ρ]νας ἐκ Τύρου· τί τῶι δήμωι
........; δ]ωρεὴν γὰρ οὔτ᾿ οὗτος πυρούς
........]θιν οὔτ᾿ ἐγὼ πάλιν κείνην.
εἰ δ᾿ οὕνεκεν πλεῖ τὴν θάλασσαν ἢ χλαῖναν
ἔχει τριῶν μνέων Ἀττικῶν, ἐγὼ δ᾿ οἰκέω
ἐν γῆι τρίβωνα καὶ ἀσκέρας σαπρὰς ἕλκων,
βίηι τιν᾿ ἄξει τῶν ἐμῶν ἔμ᾿ οὐ πείσας,
καὶ ταῦτα νυκτός, οἴχετ᾿ ἡμῖν ἡ ἀλεωρή
τῆς πόλιος, ἄνδρες, κἀπ᾿ ὅτ‹ε›ωι σεμνύνεσθε,
τὴν αὐτονομίην ὑμέων Θαλῆς λύσει.
ὃν χρῆν ἑαυτὸν ὅστις ἐστὶ κἀκ ποίου
πηλοῦ πεφύρητ᾿ εἰδότ᾿ ὡς ἐγὼ ζώειν
τῶν δημοτέων φρίσσοντα καὶ τὸν ἥκιστον.
νῦν δ᾿ οἱ μὲν ἐόντες τῆς πόλιος καλυπτῆρες
καὶ τῆι γενῆι φυσῶντες οὐκ ἴσον τούτωι
πρὸς τοὺς νόμους βλέπουσι κἠμὲ τὸν ξεῖνον
οὐδεὶς πολίτης ἠλόησεν οὐδ᾿ ἦλθεν
πρὸς τὰς θύρας μευ νυκτὸς οὐδ᾿ ἔχων δᾶιδας
τὴν οἰκίην ὑφῆψεν οὐδὲ τῶν πορνέων
βίηι λαβὼν οἴχωκεν· ἀλλ᾿ ὁ Φρὺξ οὗτος,
ὁ νῦν Θαλῆς ἐών, πρόσθε δ᾿, ἄνδρες, Ἀρτίμμης,
ἅπαντα ταῦτ᾿ ἔπρηξε κοὐκ ἐπιδέσθη
οὔτε νόμον οὔτε προστάτην οὔτ᾿ ἄρχοντα.
καίτοι λαβὼν μοι, γραμματεῦ, τῆς αἰκείης
τὸν νόμον ἄνειπε, καὶ σὺ τὴν ὀπὴν βῦσον
τῆς κλεψύδρης, βέλτιστε, μέχρις εὖ ‹ν›είπηι,

18 ἐγὼ δ]ὲ Headlam   19 τοῦτ᾿ ἔστι; Headlam

[wheat] and checked the bad famine.' [But I] came from Tyre with girls. What [is that] to the people? For neither does he [give] the wheat [   ][4] for nothing, nor again do I give her.[5] But if because he sails the sea or has a cloak worth three Attic minas, while I live on land wearing a rough coat and shuffling along in rotten shoes, he will by force take one of my girls without my consent, and that at night, the security of your city is lost, gentlemen, and what you pride yourselves on, your freedom, will be undone by Thales. Knowing who he is and from what kind of clay he is mixed, he ought to live as I do, trembling before even the humblest of the common people. But in fact those who are the upper-crust of the city, and are puffed with pride in their family far more than he, respect the laws; no citizen has thrashed me, the alien, or come to my doors at night or with torches set my house on fire or forcibly abducted one of my girls. But this Phrygian, who is now called Thales but previously, gentlemen, was Artimmes,[6] has done all this and showed no respect for law or patron or ruler. Now, clerk, take and read me the law of assault, and you, my good fellow, stuff the hole of the water-clock until he has

4 '[to grind]' or '[to eat]' or something similar.

5 Or (with κινεῖν) 'give (her to them) to screw'.

6 Battarus alleges that Thales has changed his name to conceal his foreign (and possibly servile) origin.

---

20 δίδωσ᾽ ἀλή]θ(ε)ιν F.D., δίδωσιν ἔσ]θ(ε)ιν Crusius
κινῆν P, whence κείνην Hicks, κινεῖν Crusius

28 εχρην αυτον P, corrected by several

43 ⟨᾽ν⟩είπηι Richards

     μὴ †προστε† κῦσος φῆι τι κὠ τάπης ἦμιν,
45   τὸ τοῦ λόγου δὴ τοῦτο, ληίης κύρσηι.

(ΓΡ.) ἐπὴν δ᾽ ἐλεύθερός τις αἰκίσηι δούλην
     ἢ ἕ<λ>κων ἐπίσπηι, τῆς δίκης τὸ τίμημα
     διπλοῦν τελείτω.

(ΒΑ.)   ταῦτ᾽ ἔγραψε Χαιρώνδης,
     ἄνδρες δικασταί, καὶ οὐχὶ Βάτταρος χρήιζων
50   Θαλῆν μετελθεῖν. ἢν θύρην δέ τις κόψηι,
     μνῆν τινέτω, φησ᾽· ἢν δὲ πὺξ ἀλοιήσηι,
     ἄλλην πάλι μνῆν· ἢν δὲ τὰ οἰκί᾽ ἐμπρήσηι
     ἢ ὅρους ὑπερβῆι, χιλίας τὸ τίμημα
     ἔνειμε, κἢν βλάψηι τι, διπλόον τίνειν.
55   ὤικει πόλιν γάρ, ὦ Θάλης, σὺ δ᾽ οὐκ οἶσθας
     οὔτε πόλιν οὔτε πῶς πόλις διοικεῖται,
     οἰκεῖς δὲ σήμερον μὲν ἐν Βρικινδήροις
     ἐχθὲς δ᾽ ἐν Ἀβδήροισιν, αὔριον δ᾽ ἤν σοι
     ναῦλον διδοῖ τις, ἐς Φασηλίδα πλώσηι.
60   ἐγὼ δ᾽ ὅκως ἂν μὴ μακρηγορέων ὑμέας,
     ὦνδρες δικασταί, τῆι παροιμίηι τρύχω,
     πέπονθα πρὸς Θάλητος ὅσσα κἢν πίσσηι
     μῦς· πὺξ ἐπλήγην, ἡ θύρη κατήρακται
     τῆς οἰκίης μευ, τῆς τελέω τρίτην μισθόν,
65   τὰ ὑπέρθυρ᾽ ὀπτά. δεῦρο, Μυρτάλη, καὶ σύ·

---

44 πρόσθ᾽ ὁ Piccolomini   φησι P, corrected by Rutherford
47 ἕ<λ>κων Rutherford

spoken, lest bum say †   †[7] and our sheet, as the
saying goes, gets the spoil.

CLERK

When a freeman assaults a slave-girl or pulls her about and
belabours her, he is to pay double the fine for the crime.

BATTARUS

This was written by Chaerondes,[8] gentlemen of the jury,
and not by Battarus wanting to punish Thales. But if someone knocks at a door, he is to be fined a mina, he says; and
if he beats someone up, again another mina, and if he
burns the house or crosses the boundary, he assessed
the penalty at a thousand, and if he causes any injury, to
pay double. For he was settling a city, Thales, but you do
not know a city and how a city is governed: but today you
live in Bricindera, yesterday in Abdera, and tomorrow if
someone gives you the fare you'll sail to Phaselis.[9] But I,
gentlemen of the jury—in order not with long speeches to
wear you out by digression—I have suffered from Thales
what the mouse did in pitch:[10] I was struck with his fist,
the door of my house, for which I pay a third[11] in rent,
was broken down, the lintel roasted. Myrtale, you too,

---

[7] Probably 'lest the bum say something before'. Battaros
compares the waterclock, which had a hole and plug in its base,
to an anus about to 'speak' (similar vulgarities are found in
Aristophanes) and soil the bed (the saying about 'sheet' and 'spoil'
is not otherwise known).

[8] A lawgiver.   [9] All cities of poor reputation.

[10] Battarus recalls, but very vaguely, the proverbial mouse
which was trapped in pitch and died.

[11] Presumably 1/3 of the value of the house, a large amount to
reflect the dangers to which Battarus' profession exposed it.

δεῖξον σεωυτὴν πᾶσι· μηδέν' αἰσχύνευ·
νόμιζε τούτους οὓς ὁρῆις δικάζοντας
πατέρας ἀδελφοὺς ἐμβλέπειν. ὁρῆτ' ἄνδρες,
τὰ τίλματ' αὐτῆς καὶ κάτωθεν κἄνωθεν
70   ὡς λεῖα ταῦτ' ἔτιλλεν ὠναγὴς οὗτος,
ὅτ' εἷλκεν αὐτὴν κἀβιάζετ'—ὦ γῆρας,
σοὶ θυέτω ἐπ[εὶ] τὸ αἶμ' ἂν ἐξεφύσησεν
ὥσπερ Φίλιστος ἐν Σάμωι κοτ' ὁ Βρέγκος.
γελᾶις; κίνα[ι]δός εἰμι καὶ οὐκ ἀπαρνεῦμαι,
75   καὶ Βάτταρός μοι τοὔνομ' ἐστὶ κὠ πάππος
ἦν μοι Σισυμβρᾶς κὠ πατὴρ Σισυμβρίσκος,
κἠπορνοβόσ[κ]ευν πάντες, ἀλλ' ἔκητ' ἀλκῆς
θαρσέων λέο[ν]τ' ἄ[γχ]οιμ' ἂν εἰ Θαλῆς εἴη.
ἐρᾶις σὺ μὲν ἴσω[ς] Μυρτάλης; οὐδὲν δεινόν·
80   ἐγὼ δὲ πυρέων· ταῦτα δοὺς ἐκείν' ἕξεις.
ἢ νὴ Δί', εἴ σευ θ[ά]λπεταί τι τῶν ἔνδον,
ἔμβυσον εἰς τὴν χεῖρα Βαττρίωι τιμήν,
καὐτὸς τὰ σαυτοῦ θλῆ λαβὼν ὅκως χρήιζεις.
ἐν δ' ἔστιν, ἄνδρες—ταῦτα μὲν γὰρ εἴρηται
85   πρὸς τοῦτον—ὑμεῖς δ' ὡς ἁμαρτύρων εὔντων
γνώμηι δικαίηι τὴν κρίσιν διαιτᾶτε.
ἢν δ' οἷον ἐς τὰ δοῦλα σώματα σπεύδηι
κῆς βάσανον αἰτῆι, προσδίδωμι κἀμαυτόν·
λαβών, Θαλῆ, στρέβλου με· μοῦνον ἡ τιμή
90   ἐν τῶι μέσωι ἔστω· ταῦτα τρυτάνηι Μίνως

66 μηδέν' and μηδὲν are both possible
72 ἐπ[εὶ] Blass

come here; show yourself to all—don't be ashamed before anyone; consider that in these gentlemen you see on the jury you are looking on fathers, brothers. See, gentlemen, her plucked skin, both below and above, how smooth this "innocent" has plucked it, when he was dragging and forcing her—Old Age, let him make you a thank-offering, else he would have breathed out his blood as Philistus son of Brenx once did in Samos.[12] You laugh? I am gay and don't deny it; Battarus is my name and my grandfather was Sisymbras and my father Sisymbriscus,[13] and all were brothel-keepers, but for strength I'd boldly [choke] a lion, if it were Thales. You love Myrtale perhaps: nothing strange in that; but I love bread: give the one and you will have the other. Or by Zeus, if your passion is roused, stuff the price into little Battarus' hand, and take your own property and bash her as you want. But there is one thing, gentlemen—for this was addressed to him—you must, as there are no witnesses, decide the case with just judgement. But if he is only eager for slaves' bodies and asks them for torture, I offer myself: take me, Thales, and stretch me; only let the value be on hand.[14] Minos judging

12 The victim of a boxer falsely accused of softness.

13 Names suggesting effeminacy.

14 When a slave was tortured to obtain evidence and the accusation was not upheld, the accuser had to compensate the owner with the value of the slave.

---

73 φιλιππος corrected to φιλιστος P

78 λέο[ν]τ᾽ ἄ[γχ]οιμ᾽ ἂν Bücheler

82 Βαττάρωι Rutherford

213

οὐκ ἂν δικάζων βέλτιον διήιτησε.
τὸ λοιπόν, ἄνδρες, μὴ δοκεῖτε τὴν ψῆφον
τῶι πορνοβοσκῶι Βαττάρωι φέρειν, ἀλλά
ἄπασι τοῖς οἰκεῦσι τὴν πόλιν ξείνοις.
95 νῦν δείξετ᾿ ἢ Κῶς κὠ Μέροψ κόσον δραίνει
κὠ Θεσσαλὸς τίν᾿ εἶχε κἠρακλῆς δόξαν,
κὠσκληπιὸς κῶς ἦλθεν ἐνθάδ᾿ ἐκ Τρίκκης,
κἤτικτε Λητοῦν ὦδε τεῦ χάριν Φοίβη.
ταῦτα σκοπεῦντες πάντα τὴν δίκην ὀρθῆι
100 γνώμηι κυβερνᾶτ᾿, ὡς ὁ Φρὺξ τὰ νῦν ὑμῖν
πληγεὶς ἀμείνων ἔσσετ᾿, εἴ τι μὴ ψεῦδος
ἐκ τῶν παλαιῶν ἡ παροιμίη βάζει.

102 βραζει the corrector

this with his scales would not have decided it better.
For the rest, gentlemen, do not think that you are casting
your vote for the brothel-keeper Battarus, but for all
the foreigners living in the city. Now you will show to
what extent Cos and Merops[15] are strong, and what fame
Thessalus had and Heracles,[16] and how Asclepius came
here from Tricca,[17] and the reason for Phoebe's giving
birth to Leto here.[18] Considering all this, steer the case
with straight judgement, and you'll see that the Phrygian
will now be better for a beating, unless the saying from
men of old speaks false.

[15] Merops was a legendary king of the island, Cos his daughter.
[16] Heracles, returning from Troy, landed in Cos, and was the
father of Thessalus by the king's daughter.
[17] Town in Thessaly, original site of the cult of Asclepius.
[18] Leto, daughter of *Coeos,* is claimed to have been born in
Cos.

3. ΔΙΔΑΣΚΑΛΟΣ

(ΜΗ.) οὔτω τί σοι δοίησαν αἱ φίλαι Μοῦσαι,
Λαμπρίσκε, τερπνὸν τῆς ζοῆς τ᾽ ἐπαυρέσθαι,
τοῦτον κατ᾽ ὤμου δεῖρον, ἄχρις ἡ ψυχή
αὐτοῦ ἐπὶ χειλέων μοῦνον ἡ κακὴ λειφθήι.
5 ἔκ μευ ταλαίνης τὴν στέγην πεπόρθηκεν
χαλκίνδα παίζων· καὶ γὰρ οὐδ᾽ ἀπαρκεῦσιν
αἱ ἀστραγάλαι, Λαμπρίσκε, συμφορῆς δ᾽ ἤδη
ὁρμᾶι ἐπὶ μέζον. κοῦ μὲν ἡ θύρη κεῖται
τοῦ γραμματιστέω—καὶ τριηκὰς ἡ πικρή
10 τὸν μισθὸν αἰτεῖ κἢν τὰ Ναννάκου κλαύσω—
οὐκ ἂν ταχέως λήξειε· τήν γε μὴν παίστρην,
ὅκουπερ οἰκίζουσιν οἵ τε προύνεικοι
κοἰ δρηπέται, σάφ᾽ οἶδε κἠτέρωι δεῖξαι.
κἠ μέν τάλαινα δέλτος, ἣν ἐγὼ κάμνω
15 κηροῦσ᾽ ἑκάστου μηνός, ὀρφανὴ κεῖται
πρὸ τῆς χαμεύνης τοῦ ἐπὶ τοῖχον ἑρμίνος,
ἢν μήκοτ᾽ αὐτὴν οἷον Ἀίδην βλέψας
γράψηι μὲν οὐδὲν καλόν, ἐκ δ᾽ ὅλην ξύσηι·
αἱ δορκαλίδες δὲ λιπαρώτεραι πολλόν

8 κοῦ (i.e. καὶ οὖ) Hicks, Weil   10 The paroemiographer
Zenobius, 6.10, says that Herodes the iambic poet used the proverb

3. A SCHOOLMASTER

METROTIME

Lampriscus, as the dear Muses may give you something pleasant, and enjoyment of life, flay this boy on his shoulder, until his wretched soul is just left on his lips. He has pillaged my house, poor me, by spinning coins; for in fact the dice are no longer enough, Lampriscus, but things are now rushing to a greater disaster. Where the teacher's door is—and the woeful thirtieth seeks the fee,[1] even if I weep the tears of Nannacus[2]—he could not quickly say: but the gaming house, where the toughs and runaways live, he knows well enough to show to someone else. The wretched tablet,[3] which I tire myself out waxing each month, lies orphaned before the bed-post next the wall, except when he looks at it as if it were Hades and writes nothing good but scrapes it all smooth. But the dice, much more shiny,[4] are

---

[1] Accounts, including school fees, are paid on the last day of the month.   [2] A king in Phrygia, said to have attempted to avert the great flood by tears to the gods.

[3] Wax-tablets are the equivalent of an exercise-book.

[4] With use.

---

11 λέξειε many, unnecessarily

12 ὀκλάζουσιν Herwerden

17 κην P, corrected by Blass, Palmer

ἐν τῆισι φύσηις τοῖς τε δικτύοις κεῖνται
τῆς ληκύθου ἡμέων τῆι ἐπὶ παντὶ χρώμεσθα.
ἐπίσταται δ' οὐδ' ἄλφα συλλαβὴν γνῶναι,
ἢν μή τις αὐτῶι ταὐτὰ πεντάκις βώσηι.
τριτημέρηι Μάρωνα γραμματίζοντος
τοῦ πατρὸς αὐτῶι, τὸν Μάρων' ἐποίησεν
οὗτος Σίμων' ὁ χρηστός· ὥστ' ἔγωγ' εἶπα
ἄνουν ἐμαυτήν, ἥτις οὐκ ὄνους βόσκειν
αὐτὸν διδάσκω, γραμμάτων δὲ παιδείην,
δοκεῦσ' ἀρωγὸν τῆς ἀωρίης ἕξειν.
ἐπεὰν δὲ δὴ καὶ ῥῆσιν οἷα παιδίσκον
ἢ 'γώ μιν εἰπεῖν ἢ ὁ πατὴρ ἀνώγωμεν,
γέρων ἀνὴρ ὠσίν τε κώμμασιν κάμνων,
ἐνταῦθ' ὅκως νιν ἐκ τετρημένης ἠθεῖ
"Ἀπολλον . . . Ἀγρεῦ . . .', 'τοῦτο' φημὶ 'κἠ
    μάμμη,
τάλης, ἐρεῖ σοι—κἠστὶ γραμμάτων χήρη—
κὠ προστυχὼν Φρύξ.' ἢν δὲ δή τι καὶ μέζον
γρῦξαι θέλωμεν, ἢ τριταῖος οὐκ οἶδεν
τῆς οἰκίης τὸν οὐδόν, ἀλλὰ τὴν μάμμην,
γρηῢν γυναῖκα κὠρφανὴν βίου, κείρει,
ἢ τοῦ τέγευς ὕπερθε τὰ σκέλεα τείνας
κάθητ' ὅκως τις καλλίης κάτω κύπτων.
τί μευ δοκεῖς τὰ σπλάγχνα τῆς κάκης πάσχειν
ἐπεὰν ἴδωμι; κοὐ τόσος λόγος τοῦδε·
ἀλλ' ὁ κέραμος πᾶς ὥσπερ ἴτ<ρ>ια θλῆται,
κἠπὴν ὁ χειμὼν ἐγγὺς ἦι, τρί' ἤμαιθα
κλαίουσ' ἑκάστου τοῦ πλατύσματος τίνω·

placed in their skins and nets,[5] than our oil-flask which we use constantly. He does not even know how to recognise the letter A, unless one shouts the same thing at him five times. Two days ago when his father was teaching him to spell 'Maron' , this fine fellow made 'Maron' into 'Simon';[6] so that I said I was a fool, teaching him book-learning instead of to feed asses, thinking I would have a support for bad times. And again when either his father, an old man with sick ears and eyes, or I ask him to recite a speech as one does a youngster, then when he lets it trickle out as if from a holed jug 'Apollo . . . Hunter . . .' , 'This' I say 'even your grandmother will recite to you, wretch, and she is devoid of learning, or any passing Phrygian.' And again if we try to speak more forcibly, either for three days he does not know the threshold of the house, but fleeces his grandmother, an old lady destitute of the means of life, or stretching his legs he sits above the roof like a monkey, bending down. What do you think my heart suffers because of his wickedness when I see him? My concern is not so much for him: but all the tiling is broken like wafers, and when winter is near, I pay in tears three half-pennies for

[5] Bags of skin and net. The disturbed order expresses her agitation.

[6] The name of a throw at dice is substituted for a Homeric name normally used as an example in school.

---

[42] κάκης Meister, κακῆς most edd.

[44] ἴτ⟨ρ⟩ια Rutherford

ἐν γὰρ στόμ' ἐστὶ τῆς συνοικίης πάσης,
'τοῦ Μητροτίμης ἔργα Κοττάλου ταῦτα' ,
κἀληθίν' ὥστε μηδ' ὀδόντα κινῆσαι.
50 ὅρη δ' ὀκοίως τὴν ῥάκιν λελέπρηκε
πᾶσαν, κατ' ὕλην, οἷα Δήλιος κυρτεὺς
ἐν τῆι θαλάσσηι, τὠμβλὺ τῆς ζοῆς τρίβων.
τὰς ἑβδόμας δ' ἄμεινον εἰκάδας τ' οἶδε
τῶν ἀστροδιφέων, κοὐδ' ὕπνος νιν αἱρεῖται
55 νοεῦντ' ὅτ' ἦμος παιγνίην ἀγινῆτε.
ἀλλ' εἴ τί σοι, Λαμπρίσκε, καὶ βίου πρῆξιν
ἐσθλὴν τελοῖεν αἵδε κἀγαθῶν κύρσαις,
μήλασσον αὐτῶι—

(ΛΑ.)   Μητροτίμη, ⟨μὴ⟩ ἐπεύχεο·
ἕξει γὰρ οὐδὲν μεῖον. Εὐθίης κοῦ μοι,
60 κοῦ Κόκκαλος, κοῦ Φίλλος; οὐ ταχέως τοῦτον
ἀρεῖτ' ἐπ' ὤμου τῆι Ἀκέσεω σεληναίηι
δείξοντες; αἰνέω τἄργα, Κότταλ', ἃ πρήσσεις·
οὔ σοι ἔτ' ἀπαρκεῖ τῆισι δορκάσιν παίζειν
ἀστράβδ' ὅκωσπερ οἶδε, πρὸς δὲ τὴν παίστρην
65 ἐν τοῖσι προ⟨υ⟩νείκοισι χαλκίζεις φοιτέων;
ἐγώ σε θήσω κοσμιώτερον κούρης,
κινεῦντα μηδὲ κάρφος, εἰ τό γ' ἥδιστον.
κοῦ μοι τὸ δριμὺ σκῦτος, ἢ βοὸς κέρκος,
ὧι τοὺς πεδήτας κἀποτάκτους λωβεῦμαι;
70 δότω τις εἰς τὴν χεῖρα πρὶν χολῆ⟨ι⟩ βῆξαι.

---

53 δ' Terzaghi, τ' P   58 ⟨μὴ⟩ several
68 σκυλος P, corrected by several   70 χολῆ⟨ι⟩ Hicks

each tile; for there is one voice in the whole tenement, 'This is the work of Cottalus, Metrotime's son,' and it is true, so as not to move a tooth.[7] See how he has roughened all his back by dragging out his pointless life in the wood, like a Delian pot-fisherman[8] at sea. And he knows the seventh and twentieth of the month[9] better than the star-watchers; not even sleep overcomes him as he thinks of when you are on holiday. But if these ladies[10] are to fulfil for you good success in life and you are to obtain blessings, no less to him—

LAMPRISCUS

Metrotime, stop praying; for he shall get no less. Euthies, where are you, and Coccalus, and Phillus? Quickly lift him on your shoulders to show him to Aceses' moon.[11] I approve of your deeds, Cottalus; isn't it enough for you any longer to play flashingly with dice, like these boys, but you go to the gaming house and spin coins among the toughs? I shall make you better behaved than a girl, not moving even a straw,[12] if that is what you want. Where is my biting strap, the bull's tail, with which I mutilate those whom I've fettered and set apart? Put it in my hand before I cough with bile.[13]

---

[7] Sense uncertain.   [8] Reference uncertain.

[9] Feast days when the school would be closed.

[10] The Muses.

[11] Aceses, pilot of the ancient hero Neleus, always waited for the full moon so as not to sail in darkness. His moon therefore is the time that is ripe for action.

[12] Compare 1.54.

[13] He fears his shouting may cause bile to accumulate in his lungs and make him ill.

(ΚΟ.)   μή μ᾽ ἱκετεύω Λαμπρίσκε, πρός σε τῶν Μουσέων
         καὶ τοῦ γενείου τῆς τε Κόττιδος ψυχῆς,
         μὴ τῶι με δριμεῖ, τῶι ᾽τέρωι δὲ λώβησαι.

⟨ΛΑ.⟩ ἀλλ᾽ εἰς πονηρός, Κότταλ᾽, ὥ⟨σ⟩τε καὶ περνάς

75   οὐδείς σ᾽ ἐπαινέσειεν, οὐδ᾽ ὅκου χώρης
         οἱ μῦς ὁμοίως τὸν σίδηρον τρώγουσιν.

(ΚΟ.)   κόσας, κόσας, Λαμπρίσκε, λίσσομαι, μέλλεις
         ἔς μ᾽ ἐμφορῆσαι;

⟨ΛΑ.⟩   μὴ ᾽μέ, τήνδε δ᾽ εἰρώτα.

⟨ΚΟ.⟩ τατα⟨ῖ⟩, κόσας μοι δώσετ᾽;

⟨ΜΗ.⟩   εἴ τί σοι ζώιην,

80   φέρειν ὅσας ἂν ἡ κακὴ σθένηι βύρσα.

⟨ΚΟ.⟩ παῦσαι· ἱκαναί, Λαμπρίσκε.

(ΛΑ.)   καὶ σὺ δὴ παῦσαι
         κάκ᾽ ἔργα πρήσσων.

⟨ΚΟ.⟩   οὐκέτ᾽ οὐκέτι πρήξω,
         ὄμνυμί σοι, Λαμπρίσκε, τὰς φίλας Μούσας.

(ΛΑ.)   ὅσσην δὲ καὶ τὴν γλάσσαν, οὗτος, ἔσχηκας·

85   πρός σοι βαλέω τὸν μῦν τάχ᾽ ἢν πλέω γρύξηις.

---

78 μευ φορησαι P, corrected by Rutherford
79 τατα⟨ῖ⟩ Herwerden
82 οὐκέτι Rutherford, ουχι P

---

14 I.e. a very barren place whose inhabitants would not find much
fault with potential slaves. The reference of 'equally' is unclear.

MIME 3

COTTALUS

No, I beseech you, Lampriscus, by the Muses and your beard and poor Cottalus' life, do not mutilate me with the piercing one, but with the other.

⟨LAMPRISCUS⟩

But you are wicked, Cottalus, so that no one, even if selling you, would praise you, not even where mice eat iron equally.[14]

COTTALUS

How many, how many, Lampriscus, I beg you, are you going to inflict on me?

⟨LAMPRISCUS⟩

Ask her, not me.

⟨COTTALUS⟩

Ow! How many will you give me?

⟨METROTIME⟩

As I wish to live, as many as your wicked hide can bear.

⟨COTTALUS⟩

Stop! Enough, Lampriscus.

LAMPRISCUS

You too stop doing wicked deeds.

⟨COTTALUS⟩

I shall not do any again, I swear to you, Lampriscus, by the dear Muses.

LAMPRISCUS

What a tongue you've acquired; I'll put the gag on you quickly, if you say any more.

(ΚΟ.) ἰδού, σιωπῶ· μή με, λίσσομαι, κτείνῃς.

(ΛΑ.) μέθεσθε, Κόκκαλ', αὐτόν.

(ΜΗ.)   οὐ δ⟨εῖ σ'⟩ ἐκλῆξαι,
Λαμπρίσκε· δεῖρον ἄχρις ἥλιος δύσῃι.

88a ⟨ΛΑ. ἀλλ' . . . . ⟩

(ΜΗ.) ἀλλ' ἐστὶν ὕδρης ποικιλώτερος πολλῶι

90   καὶ δεῖ λαβεῖν νιν—κἀπὶ βυβλίωι δήκου,
τὸ μηδέν—ἄλλας εἴκοσίν γε, καὶ ἢν μέλλῃ
αὐτῆς ἄμεινον τῆς Κλεοῦς ἀναγνῶναι.

⟨ΚΟ.⟩ ἰσσαῖ.

⟨ΛΑ.⟩   λάθοις τὴν γλάσσαν ἐς μέλι πλύνας.

⟨ΜΗ.⟩ ἐρέω ἐπιμηθέως τῶι γέροντι, Λαμπρίσκε,

95   ἐλθοῦσ' ἐς οἶκον ταῦτα, καὶ πέδας ἥξω
φέρουσ' ὅκως νιν σύμποδ' ὧδε πηδεῦντα
αἱ πότνιαι βλέπωσιν ἃς ἐμίσησεν.

---

87 δ⟨εῖ σ'⟩ Danielsson, Pearson
88a added by a friend of Headlam
93 ἰσσαῖ is given to Cottalos by Crusius, the rest to Lampr. by Nairn

---

15 A line with the general sense 'But he has had enough' appears to have been lost.
16 If he pretends to study.
17 One of the Muses.
18 Rejoicing at his release and his mother's discomfiture.

MIME 3

COTTALUS

See, I'm silent. Don't kill me, I beg you.

LAMPRISCUS

Let him go, Coccalus.

METROTIME

You ought not to have stopped, Lampriscus; flay him until the sun sets.

⟨LAMPRISCUS⟩

⟨   .⟩[15]

METROTIME

But he is much more subtle than a water-snake, and he ought, even over his book,[16] the wretch, to get another twenty at least, even if he will read better than Cleo[17] herself.

⟨COTTALUS⟩

Ha-ha![18]

⟨LAMPRISCUS⟩

May you find your tongue washed in honey.[19]

METROTIME

On second thoughts, Lampriscus, I shall go home and tell the old man this; and I shall come back with fetters, so that the Ladies[20] he has hated may see him jumping here with feet tied together.

[19] I.e. be honoured by the Muses (Hesiod, *Theogony,* 83–84), something which is unlikely to happen by his own act.

[20] The Muses.

4. ΑΣΚΛΗΠΙΩΙ ΑΝΑΤΙΘΕΙΣΑΙ
ΚΑΙ ΘΥΣΙΑΖΟΥΣΑΙ

(ΚΥ.) χαίροις, ἄναξ Παίηον, ὃς μέδεις Τρίκκης
καὶ Κῶν γλυκεῖαν κἠπίδαυρον ὤικηκας,
σὺν καὶ Κορωνὶς ἤ σ' ἔτικτε κὠπόλλων
χαίροιεν, ἦς τε χειρὶ δεξιῆι ψαύεις
5   Ὑγίεια, κὠνπερ οἴδε τίμιοι βωμοί
Πανάκη τε κἠπιώ τε κἰησὼ χαίροι,
κοἰ Λεωμέδοντος οἰκίην τε καὶ τείχεα
πέρσαντες, ἰητῆρες ἀγρίων νούσων,
Ποδαλείριός τε καὶ Μαχάων χαιρόντων,
10 κὤσοι θεοὶ σὴν ἐστίην κατοικεῦσιν
καὶ θεαί, πάτερ Παίηον· ἵλεωι δεῦτε
τὠλέκτορος τοῦδ', ὄντιν' οἰκίης †τοίχων†
κήρυκα θύω, τἀπίδορπα δέξαισθε.
οὐ γάρ τι πολλὴν οὐδ' ἕτοιμον ἀντλεῦμεν,

The names of the participants and the division of the lines between them are not certain. One of the women is Cynno, but the other may be Phile or Cottale (then φίλη = 'dear'); Coccale and Cydilla are their slaves in either case

5 τε κωνπερ P, corrected by several   6 Herwerden transposed χαίροι before κηπιώ to improve the syntax
12 τοίχων P, τρηχὺν Richards, μόχθων Stadtmüller

226

4. WOMEN DEDICATING AND SACRIFICING TO ASCLEPIUS

CYNNO

Greetings, Lord Paeeon,[1] who rulest Tricca and hast settled sweet Cos and Epidaurus, and also may Coronis who gave thee birth and Apollo be greeted, and she whom thou touchest with thy right hand Hygieia, and those to whom belong these honoured altars, Panace and Epio and Ieso be greeted, and the sackers of Laomedon's house and walls, curers of cruel diseases, Podalirios and Machaon be greeted, and whatsoever gods and goddesses live at thy hearth, father Paeeon: may ye graciously come hither and receive this cock which I am sacrificing, herald of the walls of the house,[2] as your dessert. For our well is far from

[1] Epithet of Asclepius, whose parents are Apollo and Coronis, wife Hygieia ('Health'), daughters Panace ('Remedy'), Epio ('Gentleness') and Ieso ('Healing'), and sons Podalirius and Machaon, both healers, who took part in the siege of Troy (whose walls were built by Laomedon).

[2] It is not clear how the cock is herald of the *walls*. 'Harsh-voiced herald' or 'herald of the labours of the house' would be easier.

15   ἐπεὶ τάχ᾽ ἂν βοῦν ἢ νενημένην χοῖρον
        πολλῆς φορίνης, κοὐκ ἀλέκτορ᾽, ἴητρα
        νούσων ἐποιεύμεσθα τὰς ἀπέψησας
        ἐπ᾽ ἠπίας σὺ χεῖρας, ὦ ἄναξ, τείνας.
        ἐκ δεξιῆς τὸν πίνακα, Κοκκάλη, στῆσον
20   τῆς Ὑγιείης.

<ΦΙ.>   ἆ, καλῶν, φίλη Κυννοῖ,
        ἀγαλμάτων· τίς ἦρα τὴν λίθον ταύτην
        τέκτων ἐπο⟨ί⟩ει καὶ τίς ἐστιν ὁ στήσας;

<ΚΤ.> οἱ Πρηξιτέλεω παῖδες· οὐκ ὁρῆις κεῖνα
        ἐν τῆι βάσι τὰ γράμματ᾽; Εὐθίης δ᾽ αὐτήν
25   ἔστησεν ὁ Πρήξωνος.

<ΦΙ.>   ἵλεως εἴη
        καὶ τοῖσδ᾽ ὁ Παιὼν καὶ Εὐθίηι καλῶν ἔργων.

<ΚΤ.> ὅρη, Φίλη, τὴν παῖδα τὴν ἄνω κείνην
        βλέπουσαν ἐς τὸ μῆλον· οὐκ ἐρεῖς αὐτήν
        ἢν μὴ λάβηι τὸ μῆλον ἐκ τάχα ψύξει⟨ν⟩;

30 <ΦΙ.> κεῖνον δέ, Κυννοῖ, τὸν γέροντ᾽—

<ΚΤ.>   ἆ πρὸς Μοιρέων
        τὴν χηναλώπεκ᾽ ὡς τὸ παιδίον πνίγει.
        πρὸ τῶν ποδῶν γοῦν εἴ τι μὴ λίθος, τοὔργον,
        ἐρεῖς, λαλήσει. μᾶ, χρόνωι κοτ᾽ ὤνθρωποι
        κῆς τοὺς λίθους ἕξουσι τὴν ζοὴν θεῖναι.

35 (ΦΙ.) τὸν Βατάλης γὰρ τοῦτον οὐκ ὁρῆις, Κυννοῖ,
        ὅκως βέβηκεν ἀνδρ[ι]άντα τῆς Μυττέω;

---

24 αυτα P, corrected by Richards
26 ευθιης P, corrected by several   29 ψύξει⟨ν⟩ Rutherford
30 <ΦΙ.> and <ΚΤ.> Hertling   γεροντά P, divided by Knox

228

abundant or ready-flowing, else we should have made an
ox or a sow heaped with much crackling, and not a cock,
our thank-offering for the diseases which thou hast wiped
away, Lord, stretching out thy gentle hands. Coccale, set
the tablet[3] on the right of Hygieia.

⟨PHILE⟩

Oh, what lovely statues, dear Cynno; what artist made this
sculpture and who is the person who dedicated it?

⟨CYNNO⟩

The sons of Praxiteles;[4] don't you see these words on the
base? And Euthies son of Prexon dedicated it.

⟨PHILE⟩

May Paeon be gracious to them and to Euthies for their
lovely works.

⟨CYNNO⟩

See, Phile, that girl looking up at the apple: wouldn't you
say that if she doesn't get the apple she will quickly expire?

⟨PHILE⟩

And that old man, Cynno—

⟨CYNNO⟩

Oh, by the Fates, how the child chokes the goose. Certainly if it were not stone before our feet, the work, you'd
say, will speak. Ah, in time men will be able to put life even
into stones.

PHILE

Now this statue of Batale, daughter of Myttes, don't you

---

[3] With a description of the cure.   [4] Cephisodotus and
Timarchus, artists like their better-known father.

εἰ μή τις αὐτὴν εἶδε Βατάλην, βλέψας
ἐς τοῦτο τὸ εἰκόνισμα μὴ ἐτύμης δείσθω.

(ΚΤ.) ἔπευ, Φίλη, μοι καὶ καλόν τί σοι δείξω
40   πρῆγμ' οἶον οὐκ ὤρηκας ἐξ ὅτευ ζώεις.
Κύδιλλ', ἰοῦσα τὸν νεωκόρον βῶσον.
οὐ σοὶ λέγω, αὕτη, τῆι ὧδε κὦδε χασκεύσηι;
μᾶ, μή τιν' ὤρην ὧν λέγω πεποίηται,
ἔστηκε δ' εἴς μ' ὀρεῦσα καρκίνου μέζον.
45   ἰοῦσα, φημί, τὸν νεωκόρον βῶσον.
λαίμαστρον, οὔτ' ὀργή σε κρηγύην οὔτε
βέβηλος αἰνεῖ, πανταχῆι δ' ἴσῃ κεῖσαι.
μαρτύρομαι, Κύδιλλα, τὸν θεὸν τοῦτον,
ὡς ἔκ με κα⟨ί⟩εις οὐ θέλουσαν οἰδῆσαι·
50   μαρτύρομαι, φήμ'· ἔσσετ' ἡμέρη κείνη
ἐν ἧι τὸ βρέγμα τοῦτο †τωυσυρες† κνήσηι.

(ΦΙ.) μὴ πάντ' ἐτοίμως καρδιηβολεῦ, Κυννοῖ·
δούλη 'στι, δούλης δ' ὦτα νωθρίη θλίβει.

(ΚΤ.) ἀλλ' ἡμέρη τε κἠπὶ μέζον ὠθεῖται·
55   αὕτη σύ, μεῖνον· ἡ θύρη γὰρ ὤικται
κἀνεῖτ' ὁ παστός.

⟨ΦΙ.⟩   οὐκ ὀρῆις, φίλη Κυννοῖ;
οἶ' ἔργα κεῖ 'νῆν· ταῦτ' ἐρεῖς Ἀθηναίην
γλύψαι τὰ καλά—χαιρέτω δὲ δέσποινα.
τὸν παῖδα δὴ ⟨τὸν⟩ γυμνὸν ἢν κνίσω τοῦτον

---

49 κα⟨ί⟩εις Meister   51 τώσυρὲς Blass, Danielsson
52 It is not clear if the corrector intended καρδιηβολεῦ or καρδίηι
βαλεῦ: καρδιηβαλλει P   57 κοινην with ι deleted P, explained by
Diels, Richards; κεῖν' ἦν Headlam, καὶ μὴν Verdenius

see, Cynno, how it stands? Anyone who has not seen Batale
herself, looking at this likeness would not need the real
thing.

CYNNO

Come with me, Phile, and I'll show you a lovely thing such
as you have never seen in all your life. Cydilla, go and call
the temple-warden. Am I not speaking to *you,* who gape
this way and that? Ah, she has paid no heed to what I say,
but stands staring at me more than a crab. Go, I say, and
call the temple-warden. Glutton, no woman pious or im-
pure praises you as good, but everywhere you are valued
equally.[5] I make this god my witness, Cydilla, that you
inflame me though I do not wish to swell up. I make him
witness, I say: that day will come when you will scratch
your filthy head.[6]

PHILE

Don't take everything so readily to heart, Cynno; she is a
slave, and a slave's ears are blocked with sluggishness.

CYNNO

But it is day and the crush is getting worse. You there, wait,
for the door has been opened and the curtain unfastened.

⟨PHILE⟩

Don't you see, dear Cynno, what works are here! You
would say that Athena carved these lovely things—greetings, Lady. This naked boy, if I scratch him, won't he have a

[5] I.e. are equally worthless.
[6] Possibly she is to be branded.

---

[61] A second $\theta\epsilon\rho\mu\grave{a}$ is added by a late hand; $\theta\epsilon\rho\mu\langle\grave{o}\nu\ a\hat{\imath}\mu\rangle a$
Stadtmüller

60   οὐκ ἕλκος ἕξει, Κύννα; πρὸς γὰρ οἱ κεῖνται
  αἱ σάρκες οἷα †θερμα† πηδῶσαι
  ἐν τῆι σανίσκηι. τὠργύρευν δὲ πύραυστρον
  οὐκ ἦν ἴδηι Μύελλος ἢ Παταικίσκος
  ὁ Λαμπρίωνος, ἐκβαλεῦσι τὰς κούρας
65   δοκεῦντες ὄντως ἀργύρευν πεποιῆσθαι;
  ὁ βοῦς δὲ κὠ ἄγων αὐτὸν ἤ τ' ὁμαρτεῦσα
  κὠ γρυπὸς οὗτος κὠ ἀνάσιλλος ἄνθρωπος
  οὐχὶ ζοὴν βλέπουσι κἠμέρην πάντες;
  εἰ μὴ ἐδόκευν τι μέζον ἢ γυνὴ πρήσσειν,
70   ἀνηλάλαξ' ἄν, μή μ' ὁ βοῦς τι πημήνηι·
  οὕτω ἐπιλοξοῖ, Κύννί, τῆι ἑτέρηι κούρηι.

(ΚΤ.) ἀληθιναί, Φίλη, γὰρ αἱ Ἐφεσίου χεῖρες
  ἐς πάντ' Ἀπελλέω γράμματ'· οὐδ' ἐρεῖς 'κεῖνος
  ὤνθρωπος ἓν μὲν εἶδεν, ἓν δ' ἀπηρνήθη',
75   ἀλλ' ὧι ἐπὶ νοῦν γένοιτο καὶ θέων ψαύειν
  ἠπείγετ'· ὃς δ' ἐκεῖνον ἢ ἔργα τὰ ἐκείνου
  μὴ παμφαλήσας ἐκ δίκης ὀρώρηκεν,
  ποδὸς κρέμαιτ' ἐκεῖνος ἐν γναφέως οἴκωι.

(ΝΕ.) κάλ' ὑμῖν, ὦ γυναῖκες, ἐντελέως τὰ ἰρά
80   καὶ ἐς λῶιον ἐμβλέποντα· μεζόνως οὗτις
  ἠρέσατο τὸν Παιήον' ἤπερ οὖν ὑμεῖς.
  ἰὴ ἰὴ Παίηον, εὐμενὴς εἴης

---

62 πύρᾱστρον P, explained by Vollgraff
68 βλεπουσιν ημερην P, corrected by Hicks
75 ὧι = ὅ οἱ explained by Paton   θέων Ellis, θεῶν most edd.

wound, Cynno? For the flesh is laid on him in the painting,
pulsing like warm springs.[7] And the silver fire-tongs, if
Myellus or Pataeciscus son of Lamprion sees them, won't
they lose their eyes thinking they are really made of silver?
And the ox, and the man leading it, and the woman following, and this hook-nosed man and the one with his hair
sticking up, don't they all have the look of life and day? If I
did not think I was acting too boldly for a woman, I should
have cried out, in case the ox might do me some harm: he
glances sideways so, Cynno, with the one eye.

CYNNO

Yes, Phile, the hands of the Ephesian Apelles are truthful
in every line, nor would you say 'That man looked at one
thing but rejected another,' but whatever came into his
mind he was quick and eager to attempt; and anyone who
has looked on him or his works without just excitement
ought to hang by the foot in the fuller's house.[8]

TEMPLE-WARDEN

Perfectly fair, ladies, are your offerings, and looking forward to better: no one has found more favour with Paeeon
than you have. Hail hail Paeeon, mayest thou be well dis-

---

[7] Or, with Stadtmüller's conjecture, 'like warm blood'.

[8] Being hung up by a foot is mentioned as a punishment in
New Comedy. The location in the fuller's adds the suggestion of
being beaten like dirty clothing.

καλοῖς ἐπ' ἱροῖς τῆισδε κεἴ τινες τῶνδε
ἔασ' ὀπυιηταί τε καὶ γενῆς ἆσσον.
85 ἰὴ ἰὴ Παίηον, ὧδε ταῦτ' εἴη.
⟨ΚΥ.⟩ εἴη γάρ, ὧ μέγιστε, κὐγίηι πολλῆι
ἔλθοιμεν αὖτις μέζον' ἴρ' ἀγινεῦσαι
σὺν ἀνδράσιν καὶ παισί. Κοκκάλη, καλῶς
τεμεῦσα μέμνεο τὸ σκελύδριον δοῦναι
90 τῶι νεωκόρωι τοὔρνιθος· ἔς τε τὴν τρώγλην
τὸν πελανὸν ἔνθες τοῦ δράκοντος εὐφήμως,
καὶ ψαιστὰ δεῦσον· τἄλλα δ' οἰκίης ἔδρηι
δαισόμεθα, καὶ ἐπὶ μὴ λάθηι φέρειν, αὕτη,
τῆς ὑγίης †λωι† πρόσδος· ἦ γὰρ ἱροῖσιν
95 †με.ων αμαρτιησηνυγιηστι† τῆς μοίρης.

88 κοτταλη P, corrected by Rutherford

94 δωι P, λωι the corrector; neither is intelligible and no conjecture is plausible

95 μεθ ων is the likeliest reading at the beginning. The middle is unmetrical (ὑγίη). I have conjectured μετ' ὧν ἀμαρτεῖ (Meister) ἦσ⟨ίς ἐ⟩στι (deleting ἡ ὑγίη as a gloss), 'for certainly at sacrifices after which it (health) follows there is enjoyment.'

posed for their fair offerings to these ladies and to any who
are their spouses and near kin. Hail hail Paeeon; so may
it be.

⟨CYNNO⟩

May it be, o most mighty, and in good health may we come
again with our husbands and children, bringing greater
offerings.—Coccale, remember to cut carefully the bird's
little leg and give it to the temple-warden, and place the
batter reverently in the snake's hole[9] and dip the cakes; the
rest we shall feast on at the house's seat—and don't forget,
you, to carry some of the health-offering and †   †;
surely at sacrifices †   † of the portion.

[9] The gift to the god's holy animal had by this period been for-
malised into money placed in a box shaped like a snake, but the old
terminology was retained.

5. ΖΗΛΟΤΥΠΟΣ

(ΒΙ.)   λέγε μοι σύ, Γάστρων, ἤδ᾽ ὑπερκορὴς οὕτω
         ὥστ᾽ οὐκέτ᾽ ἀρκεῖ τἀμά σοι σκέλεα κινεῖν
         ἀλλ᾽ Ἀμφυταίηι τῆι Μένωνος ἔγκεισαι;

(ΓΑ.)   ἐγὼ Ἀμφυταίηι; τὴν λέγεις ὀρώρηκα
5   γυναῖκα;

<ΒΙ.>   προφάσις πᾶσαν ἡμέρην ἕλκεις.

<ΓΑ.>   Βίτιννα, δοῦλός εἰμι· χρῶ ὅτι βούληι <μοι>
         καὶ μὴ τό μευ αἷμα νύκτα κἠμέρην πῖνε.

(ΒΙ.)   ὅσην δὲ καὶ τὴν γλάσσαν, οὗτος, ἔσχηκας.
         Κύδιλλα, κοὔ 'στι Πυρρίης, κάλει μ᾽ αὐτόν.

10 (ΠΤ.) τί ἐστι;

<ΒΙ.>   τοῦτον δῆσον—ἀλλ᾽ ἔτ᾽ ἔστηκας;—
         τὴν ἱμανήθρην τοῦ κάδου ταχέως λύσας.
         ἢν μὴ κατακίσασα τῆι σ᾽ ὅληι χώρηι
         παράδειγμα θῶ, μᾶ, μή με θῆις γυναῖκ᾽ εἶναι.
         ἦρ᾽ οὐχὶ μᾶλλον Φρύξ; ἐγὼ αἰτίη τούτων,

---

[1] εἰ δ᾽ Bücheler (if accepted, read εἰς)   [4] αμφυταιην P, corrected by Jackson   [6] <μοι> Blass, Bücheler

---

[1] His penis, indicated by a gesture.

5. A JEALOUS PERSON

BITINNA

Tell me, Gastron, is this[1] so over-full that it is no longer enough for you to move my legs, but you are devoted to Menon's Amphytaea?

GASTRON

I to Amphytaea? Have I seen the woman you speak of?

⟨BITINNA⟩

You draw out excuses all day.

⟨GASTRON⟩

Bitinna, I am a slave: use me as you wish and do not suck my blood night and day.

BITINNA

You, what a tongue you've acquired. Cydilla, where is Pyrries? Call him to me.

PYRRIES

What is it?

⟨BITINNA⟩

Tie him—are you still standing there?—quickly taking the rope from the bucket. If by my ill-treatment of you I don't make you an example to the whole country, well, don't count me a woman. Is this not rather a case of the Phrygi-

15   ἐγῶιμι, Γάστρων, ἤ σε θεῖσ' ἐν ἀνθρώποις.
    ἀλλ' εἰ τότ' ἐξήμαρτον, οὐ τὰ νῦν εὖσαν
    μώρην Βίτινναν, ὡς δοκεῖς, ἔτ' εὑρήσεις.
    φέρ', εἷς σύ, δῆσον, τὴν ἀπληγίδ' ἐκδύσας.

(ΓΑ.) μὴ μή, Βίτιννα, τῶν σε γουνάτων δεῦμαι.

20 (ΒΙ.) ἔκδυθι, φημί. δεῖ σ' ὀτεύνεκ' εἰ‹ς› δοῦλος
    καὶ τρεῖς ὑπέρ σευ μνᾶς ἔθηκα γινώσκειν.
    ὡς μὴ καλῶς γένοιτο τήμέρηι κείνηι
    ἥτις σ' ἐσήγαγ' ὧδε. Πυρρίη, κλαύσηι·
    ὁρῶ σε δήκου πάντα μᾶλλον ἢ δεῦντα·

25   σύσσφιγγε τοὺς ἀγκῶνας, ἔκπρισον δήσας.

(ΓΑ.) Βίτινν', ἄφες μοι τὴν ἀμαρτίην ταύτην.
    ἄνθρωπός εἰμ', ἥμαρτον· ἀλλ' ἐπὴν αὖτις
    ἔλῃς τι δρῶντα τῶν σὺ μὴ θέλῃς, στίξον.

(ΒΙ.) πρὸς Ἀμφυταίην ταῦτα, μὴ 'μὲ πληκτίζευ,

30   μετ' ἧς ἀλινδῇ καὶ εμ...η ποδόψηστρον.

⟨ΠΤ.⟩ δέδεται καλῶς σοι.

⟨ΒΙ.⟩   μὴ λάθηι λυθεὶς σκέψαι.
    ἄγ' αὐτὸν εἰς τὸ ζήτρειον πρὸς Ἕρμωνα
    καὶ χιλίας μὲν ἐς τὸ νῶτον ἐγκόψαι
    αὐτῶι κέλευσον, χιλίας δὲ τῆι γαστρί.

35 (ΓΑ.) ἀποκτενεῖς, Βίτιννα, μ' οὐδ' ἐλέγξασα
    εἴτ' ἔστ' ἀληθέα πρῶτον εἴτε καὶ ψευδέα;

---

30 ἐμέ is likely, but the following verb uncertain: χρὴ can be read (Milne), then a line must have been omitted

32 Quoted by the *Etymologicum Magnum*, p. 411.33, for the scansion ζητρεῖον from 'Herodotus' (i.e. Herodas)

33 τον P, corrected by Rutherford, Blass

an?[2] I am the cause of this, Gastron, I am, by having set you among men. But if I was wrong then, you will no longer find Bitinna being foolish now, as you expect. Come, you by yourself, take off his cloak and tie him.

GASTRON

No, no, Bitinna, by your knees, I beg you.

BITINNA

Take it off, I say. You must realise that you are a slave and I paid three minas for you. A curse on that day which brought you here! Pyrries, you will regret this: I see you undoubtedly at everything rather than tying him. Bind his elbows tightly; saw them off with the ties.

GASTRON

Bitinna, excuse me this mistake. I am human, I went wrong; but whenever again you catch me doing anything you don't wish, tattoo me.

BITINNA

Don't make up to me like this, but to Amphytaea, with whom you roll about, and [   ] me a doormat.

⟨PYRRIES⟩

He's well tied for you.

⟨BITINNA⟩

See that he doesn't slip free. Take him to the executioner's, to Hermon, and order him to hammer a thousand blows into his back and a thousand to his belly.

GASTRON

Will you kill me, Bitinna, without proving first whether this is true or false?

2 Who is the better of a beating (2.100).

(ΒΙ.) ἃ δ᾽ αὐτὸς εἶπας ἄρτι τῆι ἰδίηι γλάσσηι,
       ‘Βίτινν᾽, ἄφες μοι τὴν ἀμαρτίην ταύτην’;
(ΓΑ.) τήν σευ χολὴν γὰρ ἤθελον κατασβῶσαι.
40 (ΒΙ.) ἔστηκας ἐμβλέπων σύ, κοὐκ ἄγεις αὐτόν
       ὄκου λέγω σοι; θλῆ, Κύδιλλα, τὸ ῥύγχος
       τοῦ παντοέρκτεω τοῦδε. καὶ σύ μοι, Δρήχων,
       ἤδη ᾽φαμάρτει ⟨τῆι⟩ σοι ἂν οὗτος ἡγῆται.
       δώσεις τι, δούλη, τῶι κατηρήτωι τούτωι
45   ῥάκος καλύψαι τὴν ἀνώνυμον κέρκον,
       ὡς μὴ δι᾽ ἀγορῆς γυμνὸς ὢν θεωρῆται.
       τὸ δεύτερόν σοι, Πυρρίη, πάλιν φωνέω,
       ὅκως ἐρεῖς Ἕρμωνι χιλίας ὧδε
       καὶ χιλίας ὧδ᾽ ἐμβαλεῖν· ἀκήκουας;
50   ὡς ἤν τι τούτων ὦν λέγω παραστείξηις,
       αὐτὸς σὺ καὶ τἀρχαῖα καὶ τόκους τείσεις.
       βάδιζε καὶ μὴ παρὰ τὰ Μικκάλης αὐτόν
       ἄγ᾽, ἀλλὰ τὴν ἰθεῖαν. εὖ δ᾽ ἐπεμνήσθην—
       κάλει, κάλει δραμεῦσα, πρὶν μακρήν, δούλη,
       αὐτο⟨ὺ⟩ς γενέσθαι.
55 (ΚΤ.)   Πυρρίης, τάλας, κωφέ,
       καλεῖ σε. μᾶ, δόξει τις οὐχὶ σύνδουλον
       αὐτὸν σπαράσσειν ἀλλὰ σημάτων φῶρα.
       ὁρῆις ὅκως νῦν τοῦτον ἐκ βίης ἕλκεις
       ἐς τὰς ἀνάγκας, Πυρρίη; ⟨σ⟩έ, μᾶ, τούτοις
60   τοῖς δύο Κύδιλλ᾽ ἐπόψετ᾽ ἡμερέων πέντε
       παρ᾽ Ἀντιδώρωι τὰς Ἀχαϊκὰς κείνας,

BITINNA

But what about what you just said with your own tongue:
'Bitinna, excuse me this mistake'?

GASTRON

I wanted to calm you down.[3]

BITINNA

Are you standing there staring, instead of taking him
where I tell you? Bash this knave's snout, Cydilla. And you,
Drechon, follow now where he leads you. Girl, will you
give some rag to this cursed fellow to hide his unmentionable tail, to avoid his being seen naked through the marketplace. For the second time, Pyrries, again I tell you, that
you are to instruct Hermon to inflict a thousand here and a
thousand here: have you heard? If you go astray in any of
my orders, you will yourself pay both principal and interest. Go on, and don't take him by Miccale's but the direct
road. But I've just remembered!—run and call, girl, call
them before they get far.

CYDILLA

Pyrries, you deaf wretch, she is calling you. Ah, you'd think
he was dragging a grave-robber rather than a fellow-slave.
Do you see how you're now forcibly pulling him to the torture, Pyrries? Ah, it's you that Cydilla will see with these
two eyes within five days at Antidorus' rubbing your ankles

3 Lit. 'extinguish your bile'.

---

41 θλῆ Headlam, Hicks, Ellis: οδη P (ΘΛΗ and ΟΔΗ are only
two strokes apart)   43 ⟨τῆι⟩ σοι ἂν Danielsson, σοι εαν P
55 αὐτο⟨ὺ⟩ς several   59 ⟨σ⟩έ Blass, Weil
60 τους P, corrected by Blass, Weil

ἃς πρῶν ἔθηκας, τοῖς σφυροῖσι τρίβοντα.

(ΒΙ.) οὗτος σύ, τοῦτον αὖτις ὧδ' ἔχων ἧκε
δεδεμένον οὕτως ὥσπερ ἐξάγεις αὐτόν,
65 Κόσιν τέ μοι κέλευσον ἐλθεῖν τὸν στίκτην
ἔχοντα ῥαφίδας καὶ μέλαν. μιῆι δεῖ σε
ὁδῶι γενέσθαι ποικίλον. κατηρτήσθω
οὗτω κατάμνος ὥσπερ ἡ Δάου τιμή.

(ΚΤ.) μή, τατί, ἀλλὰ νῦν μὲν αὐτόν—οὕτω σοι
70 ζώιη Βατυλλὶς κἠπίδοις μιν ἐλθοῦσαν
ἐς ἀνδρὸς οἶκον καὶ τέκν' ἀγκάληις ἄραις—
ἄφες, παραιτεῦμαί σε· τὴν μίαν ταύτην
ἁμαρτίην . . .

(ΒΙ.)   Κύδιλλα, μή με λύπει τι
ἢ φεύξομ' ἐκ τῆς οἰκίης. ἀφέω τοῦτον
75 τὸν ἑπτάδουλον; καὶ τίς οὐκ ἀπαντῶσα
ἔς μευ δικαίως τὸ πρόσωπον ἐμπτύοι;
οὐ τὴν Τύραννον, ἀλλ' ἐπείπερ οὐκ οἶδεν,
ἄνθρωπος ὤν, ἑωυτόν, αὐτίκ' εἰδήσει
ἐν τῶι μετώπωι τὸ ἐπίγραμμ' ἔχων τοῦτο.

80 (ΚΤ.) ἀλλ' ἔστιν εἰκὰς καὶ Γερήνι' ἐς πέμπτην.

70 μεν P, corrected by Rutherford, Blass

73 με λυπεῖ τι Palmer, λυπιτε με P

74–75 ἀφέω . . . ἑπτάδουλον is quoted by Eustathius in his commentary on the *Odyssey* 5.306

with those Achaean objects[4] you recently put off.

You there, come back here again with him tied just as you
are taking him away, and order Cosis the tattooer to come
to me with his needles and ink. At the one go you must become speckled. Let him be hung up gagged as much as His
Honour Daus.[5]

No, mama, but for the moment let him—as Batyllis may
live and you may see her going to a husband's house and lift
her children in your arms—let him be excused, I beseech
you: this one error—

Cydilla, do not vex me at all, or I shall rush out of the
house! Am I to excuse this sevenfold son of slaves? Would
not anyone who met me justly spit on my face? No, by the
Queen.[6] But since, though human, he does not know himself, he will soon know when he has this inscription[7] on his
forehead.

But it is the twentieth, and the Gerenia[8] are in four days—

---

[4] Clearly chains, though the reason for the epithet is unclear.

[5] Daus is a common slave-name in New Comedy, and we must
suppose that one suffered the fate described.

[6] Which goddess is meant is not clear.

[7] Probably γνῶθι σαυτόν, 'know yourself'.

[8] An otherwise unknown festival, obviously in honour of the
dead (84).

(BI.)   νῦν μέν σ᾽ ἀφήσω, καὶ ἔχε τὴν χάριν ταύτηι,
        ἢν οὐδὲν ἧσσον ἢ Βατυλλίδα στέργω,
        ἐν τῆισι χερσὶ τῆις ἐμῆισι θρέψασα.
        ἐπεὰν δὲ τοῖς καμοῦσιν ἐγχυτλώσωμεν
85   ἄξεις τότ᾽ ἀμελι‹τῖ›τιν ἑορτὴν ἐξ ἑορτῆς.

85 ἀμελι‹τῖ›τιν Headlam

BITINNA

For the moment I shall excuse you, and be grateful to her, whom I love no less than Batyllis, as I reared her in my own arms. But when we have poured libations to the dead, you will then keep unhoneyed[9] festival on festival.

[9] I.e. bitter. Honey was not offered to the dead.

6. ΦΙΛΙΑΖΟΥΣΑΙ Η ΙΔΙΑΖΟΥΣΑΙ

(ΚΟ.)   κάθησο, Μητροῖ. τῆι γυναικὶ θὲς δίφρον
        ἀνασταθεῖσα· πάντα δεῖ με προστάσσειν
        αὐτήν· σὺ δ' οὐδὲν ἄν, τάλαινα, ποιήσαις
        αὐτὴ ἀπὸ σαυτῆς· μᾶ, λίθος τις, οὐ δούλη
5   ἐν τῆι οἰκίηι ‹κ›εῖσ'· ἀλλὰ τἄλφιτ' ἢν μετρέω
        τὰ κρίμν' ἀμιθρεῖς, κἢ‹ν› τοσοῦτ' ἀποστάξηι
        τὴν ἡμέ[ρ]ην ὅλην σε τονθορύζουσαν
        καὶ πρημονῶσαν οὐ φέρουσιν οἱ τοῖχοι.
        νῦν αὐτὸν ἐκμάσσεις τε καὶ ποεῖς λαμπρόν
10   ὅτ' ἐστὶ χρ[εί]ῃ, λῃστρί; θύέ μοι ταύτηι
        ἐπεί σ' ἔγευσ' ἂν τῶν ἐμῶν ἐγὼ χειρέων.
(ΜΗ.)   φίλη Κοριττοῖ, ταῦτ' ἐμοὶ ζυγὸν τρίβεις·
        κἠγὼ ἐπιβρύχουσ' ἠμέρην τε καὶ νύκτα
        κύων ὑλακτέω τῆι[ς] ἀνωνύμοις ταύτηις.
15   ἀλλ' οὕνεκεν πρός σ' ἠλ[θ]ον—ἐκποδὼν ἡμιν
        φθείρεσθε, νώβυστρ', ὦτ[α] μοῦνον καὶ γλάσσαι,
        τὰ δ' ἄλλ' ἑορτή—λίσσομαί [σ]ε, μὴ ψεύσηι,

    5 ‹κ›εῖσ' Richards   μετρέω, corrected to μετρῇι, P (the correction, 'when you measure out', loses the nice point of the characterisation of Coritto as careful, if not mean, cf. 99 ff.)

6. WOMEN IN A FRIENDLY OR PRIVATE SITUATION

CORITTO

Be seated, Metro. Stand up and put out a chair for the lady.
I have to give you every instruction myself: you would do
nothing by yourself, you wretch; ah, you are a stone lying in
the house, not a slave. But if I measure out the meal to you,
you count the crumbs, and if so much should drop the
walls won't contain you as you mutter and fume the whole
day. Are you rubbing it and making it shiny now, when it's
needed, you pirate? Give a thank-offering, I tell you, to
this lady, since I would have made you taste my hands.

METRO

Dear Coritto, you have the same yoke wearing you down as
I. I too am a barking dog, snapping day and night at those
unmentionable girls. But why I've come to you—get to
hell out of our way, with your closed minds, only ears and
tongues, but otherwise idleness—I beg you, do not lie,

---

⁶ κη . . . αποσταξει P, corrected by several

¹⁰ χρ[(ε)ί]η several

¹⁶ ὦτ[α] Hicks

¹⁷ εορτηι P, corrected by Blass, Danielsson

  φίλη Κοριττοῖ, τίς κοτ᾽ ἦν ὅ σοι ῥάψας
  τὸν κόκκινον βαυβῶνα;

(ΚΟ.)   κοῦ δ᾽ ὀρώρηκας,

20 Μητροῖ, σὺ κεῖνον;

(ΜΗ.)   Νοσσὶς ε[ἶ]χεν ἠρίννης
  τριτημέρηι νιν· μᾶ, καλόν τι δώρημα.

(ΚΟ.) Νοσσίς; κόθεν λαβοῦσα;

(ΜΗ.)   διαβαλεῖς ἤν σοι
  εἴπω;

(ΚΟ.) μὰ τούτους τοὺς γλυκέας, φίλη Μητροῖ,
  ἐκ τοῦ Κοριττοῦς στόματος οὐδεὶς μὴ ἀκούσηι

25 ὅσ᾽ ἂν σὺ λέξηις.

(ΜΗ.)   ἡ Βιτᾶδος Εὐβούλη
  ἔδωκεν αὐτῆι καὶ εἶπε μηδέν᾽ αἰσθέσθαι.

(ΚΟ.) γυναῖκες. αὕτη μ᾽ ἡ γυνή κοτ᾽ ἐκτρίψει.
  ἐγὼ μὲν αὐτὴν λιπαρεῦσαν ἠιδέσθην
  κἤδωκα, Μητροῖ, πρόσθεν ἢ αὐτὴ χρήσασθαι·

30 ἡ δ᾽ ὥ‹σ›περ εὕρημ᾽ ἁρπάσα‹σα› δωρεῖται
  καὶ τῆισι μὴ δεῖ. χαιρέτω φίλη πολλά
  ἐοῦσα τοίη, κἠτέρην τιν᾽ ἀντ᾽ ἡμέων
  φίλην ἀθρείτω. τἀμὰ Νοσσίδι χρῆσαι
  τῆι μὴ δοκέω—μέζον μὲν ἢ δίκη γρύζω,

35 λάθοιμι δ᾽, Ἀδρήστεια—χιλίων εὔντων

---

³³ ταλλα P, corrected by Groeneboom χρησθαι P, interpreted
by others as χρῆσθαι
³⁴ Μηδόκεω Weil wrongly η γυνη γρυξω P, η δικη γρυζω the
corrector

dear Coritto: who was it who stitched the scarlet dildo for you?

CORITTO
And where, Metro, did you see that?

METRO
Nossis, daughter of Erinna,[1] had it two days ago; ah, what a fine gift!

CORITTO
Nossis? From whom did she get it?

METRO
Will you disparage me if I tell you?

CORITTO
By these sweet eyes, dear Metro, no one shall hear what you say from Coritto's mouth.

METRO
Bitas' Eubule gave it to her and said that no one should know.

CORITTO
Women! This woman will uproot me yet. I paid respect to her plea, and gave it her, Metro, before I used it myself. But snatching it like a windfall, she passes it on even to those who ought not to have it. Many farewells to a friend who is of such a nature; let her look on some other instead of me as her friend in future. That she should have lent my property to Nossis! To whom I do not think—I speak more strongly than is right, may Adrestia[2] not hear—if I had a

---

[1] The names of two famous poets, used maliciously.
[2] Goddess who punished any kind of excess.

ἔν' οὐκ ἂν ὅστις σαπρός ἐστι προσδώσω.

(ΜΗ.) μὴ δή, Κοριττοῖ, τὴν χολὴν ἐπὶ ρινός
ἔχ' εὐθύς, ἤν τι ρῆμα μὴ καλὸν πεύθηι.
γυναικός ἐστι κρηγύης φέρειν πάντα.

40 ἐγὼ δὲ τούτων αἰτίη λαλεῦσ' εἰμι
πόλλ', ἀ⟨λλὰ⟩ τήν μευ γλάσσαν ἐκτεμεῖν δεῖται.
ἐκεῖνο δ' εὖ σοι καὶ μάλιστ' ἐπεμνήσθην,
τίς ἔστ' ὁ ράψας αὐτόν; εἰ φιλεῖς μ', εἶπον.
τί μ' ἐμβλέπεις γελῶσα; νῦν ὀρώρηκας

45 Μητροῦν τὸ πρῶτον; ἢ τί τἀβρά σοι ταῦτα;
ἐνεύχομαι, Κοριττί, μή μ' ἐπιψεύσηι,
ἀλλ' εἰπὲ τὸν ράψαντα.

(ΚΟ.)   μᾶ, τί μοι ἐνεύχηι;
Κέρδων ἔραψε.

⟨ΜΗ.⟩   κοῖος, εἰπέ μοι, Κέρδων;
δύ' εἰσὶ γὰρ Κέρδωνες· εἷς μὲν ὁ γλαυκός

50 ὁ Μυρταλίνης τῆς Κυλαιθίδος γείτων,
ἀλλ' οὗτος οὐδ' ἂν πλῆκτρον ἐς λύρην ράψαι·
ὁ δ' ἕτερος ἐγγὺς τῆς συνοικίης οἰκέων
τῆς Ἑρμοδώρου τὴν πλατεῖαν ἐκβάντι
ἦν μέν κοτ' ἦν τις, ἀλλὰ νῦν γεγήρακε·

55 τούτωι Κυλαιθὶς ἡ μακαρῖτις ἐχρῆτο—
μνησθεῖεν αὐτῆς οἵτινες προσήκουσι.

(ΚΟ.) οὐδέτερος αὐτῶν ἐστιν, ὡς λέγεις, Μητροῖ·
ἀλλ' οὗτος οὐκ οἶδ' ἢ ⟨'κ⟩ Χίου τις ἢ 'ρυθρέων

36 λεπρος P, σαπρος the corrector   προσδωσω corrected to
προσδοιην P

250

thousand, I should not hand over one that was rotten.

METRO

Coritto, don't get bile in your nose as soon as you hear a word not to your liking. It is a good woman's place to bear everything. I am the cause of this by saying too much; <but> my tongue should be cut out. But to return to what I particularly asked you, who is the one who stitched it? If you love me, tell me. Why do you look at me with a smile? Have you just seen Metro for the first time? What is this delicacy of yours? I implore you, Coritto, don't deceive me, but tell me the one who stitched it.

CORITTO

Ah, why do you implore me? Cerdon stitched it.

<METRO>

Tell me, which Cerdon? For there are two Cerdons, one the grey-eyed neighbour of Cylaethis' Myrtaline; but *he* couldn't stitch even a plectrum for a lyre; and the other, living near Hermodorus' tenement as you go from the main street, he *was* someone once, but now he has grown old; the late Cylaethis was intimate with him—may her relations remember her.

CORITTO

It's neither of these, as you say, Metro, but this one comes from Chios or Erythrae, I don't know which; bald, small—

37–39 are cited by Stobaeus, *Anth.* 4.23.14, from Herodas' Mimiambi, with κόρη τὺ for Κοριττοῖ and ῥῖνας

38 σοφον P and Stobaeus, καλον the corrector

41 πόλλ᾽ , ἀ<λλὰ> Kaibel

55 τουτωι κυλαιθις or τουτω πυλαιθις P

57 ὦν several, unnecessarily   58 <ʼκ> Kaibel

ἥκει, φαλακρός, μικκός· αὐτὸ ἐρεῖς εἶναι
60 Πρηξῖνον, οὐδ' ἂν σῦκον εἰκάσαι σύκωι
ἔχοις ἂν οὕτω· πλὴν ἐπὴν λαλῆι, γνώσηι
Κέρδων ὀτεύνεκ' ἐστὶ καὶ οὐχὶ Πρηξῖνος.
κατ' οἰκίην δ' ἐργάζετ' ἐμπολέων λάθρη,
τοὺς γὰρ τελώνας πᾶσα νῦν θύρη φρίσσει.
65 ἀλλ' ἔργα, κοῖ' ἐστ' ἔργα· τῆς Ἀθηναίης
αὐτῆς ὀρῆιν τὰς χεῖρας, οὐχὶ Κέρδωνος,
δόξεις. ἐ[γὼ] μέν—δύο γὰρ ἦλθ' ἔχων, Μητροῖ—
ἰδοῦσ' ἅμ' ἱδμῆι τώμματ' ἐξεκύμηνα·
τὰ βαλλί' οὕτως ἄνδρες οὐχὶ ποιεῦσι
70 —αὐταὶ γάρ εἰμεν—ὀρθά· κοὐ μόνον τοῦτο,
ἀλλ' ἡ μαλακότης ὕπνος, οἱ δ' ἱμαντίσκοι
ἔρι', οὐκ ἱμάν[τες]. εὐνοέστερον σκυτέα
γυναικ[ὶ] διφῶσ' ἄλλον οὐκ ἀνευρ[ή]σ[εις].
(ΜΗ.) κῶς οὖν ἀφῆκας τὸν ἕτερον;
75 ⟨ΚΟ.⟩   τ[ί] δ' οὐ, Μητροῖ,
ἔπρηξα; κοίην δ' οὐ προσήγαγο[ν] πειθοῦν
αὐτῶι; φιλεῦσα, τὸ φαλακρὸν κ[α]ταψῶσα,
γλυκὺν πιεῖν ἐγχεῦσα, ταταλίζ[ο]υσα,
τὸ σῶμα μοῦνον οὐχὶ δοῦσα χ[ρ]ήσασθαι.
(ΜΗ.) ἀλλ' εἴ σε καὶ τοῦτ' ἠξίωσ', ἔδει δοῦ[ν]αι.
80 (ΚΟ.) ἔδει γάρ· ἀλλ' ἄκαιρον οὐ πρέπον τ' εἶναι·
ἤληθεν ἡ Βιτᾶδος ἐν μέσωι ⟨Εὐ⟩βούλη·

---

60 (ε)ικασαις P, corrected by Kenyon
63 κατοικειν P, corrected by Rutherford
65 εργοκοι P, corrected by Herwerden
67 ἐ[γὼ] Bücheler   72 ἱμάν[τες] several

252

you'd say he was just Prexinos, you couldn't liken fig to fig
so much; however when he speaks, you'll know that it is
Cerdon and not Prexinus. He works at home and sells se-
cretly, for every door now shudders at the tax-collectors—
but his work! What work it is! You would think you were
seeing the handiwork of Athena, not Cerdon; when I saw
them—for he came with two, Metro—my eyes swelled out
at first sight; men do not make stands—we are alone—so
straight; and not only that, but their smoothness is sleep,[3]
and the little straps are wool, not straps; if you look
for another cobbler better disposed to a woman, you will
not find one.

METRO

How then did you let the second go?

‹CORITTO›

Metro, what did I not do? What persuasion did I not bring
to bear on him? Kissing him, stroking his bald head, pouring him a sweet drink, calling him papa, almost giving him
my body to use.

METRO

But if he asked for that too, you should have given it.

CORITTO

Yes, I should have; but it is not decent to act unseasonably:
Bitas' Eubule was grinding near us. For by turning our

---

[3] I.e. they are as smooth as sleep.

---

[73] ἀνευρ[ή]σ[εις Headlam, Stadtmüller   [80] ἀλλ' ἄκαιρον
divided by Ellis   [81] ηληθεν γαρ P, γὰρ deleted by
Wilamowitz   ‹Εὐ›βούλη Jevons, Kaibel, δουλη P

αὕτη γὰρ ἡμέων ἡμέρην τε κα[ὶ] νύκτα
τρίβουσα τὸν ὄνον σκωρίην πεποίηκεν,
ὄκως τὸν ὠυτῆς μὴ τετρωβόλου κόψῃι.

85 (ΜΗ.) κῶς δ᾽ οὗτος εὗρε πρός σε τὴν ὁδ[ὸ]ν ταύτην,
φίλη Κοριττοῖ; μηδὲ τοῦτό με ψεύσῃι.

(ΚΟ.) ἔπεμψεν αὐτὸν Ἀρτεμεὶς ἡ Κανδάδος
τοῦ βυρσοδέψεω τὴν στέγην σημήνασα.

(ΜΗ.) αἰεὶ μὲν Ἀρτεμείς τι καινὸν εὑρίσκει,
90 πρόσω πιεῦσα τὴν προκυκλίην θα...ν.
ἀλλ᾽ οὖν γ᾽ ὅτ᾽ οὐχὶ τοὺς δύ᾽ εἶχες ἐκλῦσαι
ἔδει πυθέσθαι τὸν ἕτερον τίς ἡ ἐκδοῦσα.

(ΚΟ.) ἐλιπάρεον, ὁ δ᾽ ὤμνυ᾽ οὐκ ἂν εἰπεῖν μοι·
†ταύτηι γὰρ καὶ ἠγάπησεν Μητροῖ.†

95 ⟨ΜΗ.⟩ λέγεις ὁδόν μοι· νῦν πρὸς Ἀρτεμεῖν εἶμι,
ὄκως ὁ Κέρδων ὅστις ἐστὶν εἰδ[ή]σω.
ὑγίαινέ μο[ι, Κοριτ]τί. λαιμάτ[τε]ι κώρη
ἡμῖ[ν] ἀφ[έρπειν] ἐστί.

90 πρό σοι Kaibel   θάμνην Blass, Θαλλοῦν Meister (then
Rutherford's ποεῦσα must also be read, 'leaving Thallo behind in pan-
dering'); superscript letters largely illegible
94 is added by a later, cursive hand in the upper margin, with signs
indicating its position   ⟨ἤλω⟩ κἠγάπησέ ν⟨ιν⟩ Knox
95 εἶμι Rutherford, (ε)ιναι P
97 μο[ι, Κοριτ]τί Bücheler   λαιμάτ[τε]ι Crusius
98 ἀφ[έρπειν] Crusius
99 ν[εο]σσοπῶλι Diels
100 ἀλεκτο[ρῖ]δες Blass, Crusius   [σ]όαι Crusius, Palmer

millstone day and night she has ruined it, to avoid setting
her own for four obols.

METRO

But how did this man find his way to you, dear Coritto? On
this too don't deceive me.

CORITTO

The tanner Candas' Artemis sent him, pointing out the
house.

METRO

Artemis always finds something new, drinking further pan-
der's [wine]. But at least, when you could not save the two,
you should have found out who it was who ordered the
second.

CORITTO

I pleaded, but he swore he would not tell me; for ⟨he was
taken⟩ by her and she loved ⟨him⟩, Metro.[4]

⟨METRO⟩

Your words mean I must leave: now I shall go to Artemis,
to learn who Cerdon is. Keep well, [Coritto]; it is very
hungry[5] and it is time for us [to slip] away.

[4] Translating Knox's conjecture for the imperfect line.
[5] I.e., apparently, I need to use the dildo.

(κο.)   τὴν θύρην κλεῖσον,
αὕτη [σ]ύ, ν[εο]σσοπῶλι, κἀξαμίθρησαι
αἱ ἀλεκτο[ρῖ]δες εἰ [σ]όαι εἰσί, τῶν τ' αἱρέων
αὐτῆισ[ι ρ]ῖψ[ο]ν· οὐ γὰρ ἀλλὰ πορθεῦ[σ]ι
ὠρν[ι]θο[κ]λέ[π]ται, κἢν τρέφηι τις ἐν κόλπωι.

101 αὐτῆισ[ι ρ]ῖψον Blass
102 ὠρν[ι]θο[κλ]έπ[τ]αι Headlam

CORITTO

Shut the door, you there, [chicken]-seller, and count if the hens are safe, and [throw] some darnel to them; for undeniably the bird-thieves raid them, even if one rears them in one's bosom.

7. [Σ]ΚΥΤ[Ε]ΥΣ

(ΜΗ.) Κέρδων, ἄγω σοι τάσδε τὰς γ[υνάς, εἴ] τι
τῶν σῶν ἔχεις αὐτῆισιν ἄξιον δεῖξαι
χειρέων νοῆρες ἔργον.

(ΚΕ.)   οὐ μάτην, Μητροῖ,
ἐγὼ φ[ι]λ‹έ›ω σε. τῆις γυναιξὶν οὐ θήσεις
5   τὴν μέζον' ἔξω σανίδα; Δριμύλωι φωνέω·
πάλιν καθεύδεις; κόπτε, Πίστε, τὸ ρύγχος
αὐτοῦ, μέχρις τὸν ὕπνον ἐκχέηι πάντα·
μᾶλλον δὲ τὴν ἄκανθα[ν] ὡς ἔχ[ει ἐ]ν καλῆι
ἐκ τοῦ τραχήλου δῆσο[ν. εἶ]α δή, [.....]ψ,
10   κίνει ταχέως τὰ γοῦνα· [μ]έζον [....]..
τρίβειν ψοφεῦντα νουθ[ετημάτων] τῶνδε.
νῦν ἔκ μιν αὐτὴν λε[...... λαμπ]ρύνεις
καὶ ψ[ῆι]ς; [ἐγὼ] σευ τη.[.........]ψήσω.
ἔζεσ[θ]ε, Μητροῖ. Πίστ[ε, ...ο]ίξας
15   πυργίδα, μὴ τὴν ὧδ[ε, ...]ν.
τὰ χρήσιμ' ἔργα τοῦ τ.[.........]ος
ταχέως ἔνεγκ' ἄνωθ[εν ...... Μη]τροῖ,

¹ γ[υνάς Diels, ν[έας Crusius   εἴ] Blass, Ellis
⁸ ἔχει ἐν καλῆι (sc. δέσει) Cunningham, following Crusius and
Edmonds, ἔχ[ω]ν κλάηι Knox ('so that he may weep with it')

7. A COBBLER

METRO

Cerdon, I am bringing you these [ladies to see if] you can show them any skilled work worthy of your craft.

CERDON

I have good reason, Metro, for loving you. Will you not put the larger bench outside for the ladies? I'm speaking to Drimylus: are you asleep again? Pistus, hit his snout, until he sheds all his sleepiness; or rather tie the thorn to his neck, as he is, well bound. Come then, [ape], move your knees quickly: [did you want] to rub on objects that make more noise than these warn[ings?] Now, [smooth (*or* white) arse,] are you [polishing] and [wiping] it? I'll wipe your [posterior]. Sit down, Metro. Pistus, open the [double] chest, not this one here, [but that one up there]. The serviceable works of the [skilful Cerdon], bring them quickly down from above. [Lucky] Metro, what works you shall

---

⁹ [Κέρκω]ψ Headlam   ¹⁰ [ἴχην]ας Knox

¹¹ νουθ[ετημάτων] Headlam   ¹² λε[ιόπυγε,
λαμπ]ρύνεις Knox and Headlam, λε[υκόπυγε, φαιδ]ρύνεις
Crusius and Headlam   ¹³ καὶ ψ[ῆι]ς; [ἐγώ] Knox   τὴν
[κοχώνην ἐκ]ψήσω Knox   ¹⁴ τὴν διπλῆν ο]ἴξας Herzog

¹⁵ τὴν δ' ἄνω κ(ε)ίνη]ν Headlam, following Crusius

¹⁶ τρ[ίβωνος Κέρδων]ος Sitzler   ¹⁷ ἄνωθ[εν Blass, then
ὦ μάκαρ Headlam, οὐκ ἐρῶ Stadtmüller

οἷ᾽ ἔργ᾽ ἐπόψεσθ᾽. ἡσυχῇ [.........]ον
τὴν ⟨σ⟩αμβαλούχην οἶγ[ε.......] πρῶτον
20   Μητροῖ, τελέων ἄρη[ρε .....]εων ἴχνος.
θηεῖσθε κὺμε[ῖ]ς, ὦ γυ[ναῖκες· ἡ πτ]έρνη
ὁρῆτ᾽ ὅπως πέπηγε, [....]φην[.]οις
ἐξηρτίωται πᾶσα, κο[ὐ τ]ὰ μὲν κ[αλ]ῶς
τὰ δ᾽ οὐχὶ καλῶς, ἀλλὰ πά[ν]τ᾽ ἴσαι χ[εῖρε]ς.
25   τὸ χρῶμα δ᾽ οὕτως ὑμ[ι]ν ἡ πα[...] δοίη
 .[   ].ερ ἰχανᾶσθ᾽ ἐπαυρέσθαι
 .[ἄλ]λο τῶιδ᾽ ἴσον χρῶμα
 κ[   ]ωκουδε κηρὸς ἀνθήσει
 χ[   ]. τρεῖς ἔδωκε Κανδᾶτ[.].
30 κ[   ] τοῦτο κἤτερον χρῶμα
 β.[ὄμνυ]μι πάντ᾽ ὅσ᾽ ἐστὶ ἱρά
 κω[   ] τὴν ἀληθ[ε]ί[η]ν βάζειν
      ] οὐδ᾽ ὅσον ῥοπὴν ψεῦδος
     ἤ] Κέρδωνι μὴ βίου ὄνησις
35 μ[ηδ᾽   ]ων γίνοιτο κα[ὶ] χάριν πρός με
    οὐ γ]ὰρ ἀλλὰ μεζόνων ἤδη
     ] κερδέων ὀριγνῶνται
    ]. τὰ ἔργα τῆς τέχνης ἡμ⟨έ⟩ων
    πί]συγγος δὲ δειλαίην οἰζύν

<hr/>

18 [δὲ πρόσμειν]ον Blass (if spoken to Metro), or [σύ, λαί-
μαστρ]ον Knox ('you glutton,' if to the slave)

19 ⟨σ⟩αμβαλούχην several   οἶγ[ε· τοῦτ᾽ ὄρη Blass, · τουτό σοι
Knox   20 ἐκ μερ]έων Knox   21 γυ[ναῖκες· ἡ πτ]έρνη
Rutherford   22 χ[ὥτι σ]φηνί[σκ]οις Kenyon, but the first letter
is more like α̣[23 κο[ὐ τ]ὰ μὲν κ[αλ]ῶς Blass, Headlam

see. Quietly [wait,] open the shoe-box. [Look at this] first,
Metro, the sole is put together from perfect [parts]; look,
ladies, you also; see how the heel is fixed, and it is all
fitted [with decorative wedges], and it is not the case that
some parts are well-made and others are not, but all the
[handiwork] is equal. And the colour, as may [the Lady of
Paphos] give you [whatever] you wish to enjoy, [you will
find no other] colour equal to this, [nor] will beeswax[1]
flower [Cerdon] gave three [staters to] Candas's
[wife for] this and another colour [I swear
by] all that is sacred [and holy] that I speak the truth
[   ] nor so much of a lie [weighs down] the
balance [or] may Cerdon have no profit in
life [or trade]—and [asked] me for thanks in addition;
for undeniably [the tanners] now grasp at greater gains.
[You have] the works of our craft. But I the cobbler,
[   ] wretched woe, heat

[1] The material used in encaustic painting.

---

[24] χ[εῖρε]ς Blass   [25] Πά[φου] Knox, with μ[εδέουσ' in
26 ('the ruler of Paphos' , i.e. Aphrodite)

[26] ὅσων]περ Headlam   [27] ε[ὑρήσετ' οὐδὲν ἄλ]λο
Crusius   [28] κοὐδὲ or κοῦ δὲ may be read

[29] χ[ρυσοῦ στατῆρα]ς Knox, χ[θὲς οὖν στατῆρα]ς
Edmonds   Κανδᾶτ[ο]ς Diels (to be corrected to -αδ-)

[30] Κ[έρδων Knox, γυναικί Cunningham

[31] ὄμνυ]μι Blass   [32] κώ[σια, γυναῖκες,] Crusius, κώ[σσ'
ἐστιν ὅσια] Headlam   βαδίζειν P, corrected by Crusius

[34] beginning βρίθει Knox   ἢ] Bücheler

[35] μ[ηδ' Sitzler, ἐμπολέ]ων Knox   [36] ἤιτησεν Knox, οὐ
γ]ὰρ Bücheler   [37] οἱ βυρσοδέψαι] Crusius

[39] ἔχεις, ὁ Knox, or φέρουσ', ὁ ('They have the profits of our
skill') Herzog; πί]συγγος Blass

40   ].ναν[..]εων νύκτα κἠμέρην θάλπω

  ]. ἡμέων ἄχρι‹ς› ἑσπέρης κάπτει

  ]αι πρὸ[ς] ὄρθρον οὐ δοκέω τόσ‹σ›ον

  τὰ Μικίωνος κηρί᾽ εὐπ[   ]

  κοὔπω λέγω, τρισκαίδε[κ..... β]όσκω,

45   ὀτεύνεκ᾽, ὦ γυναῖκες, ἀργ[......]ς

  οἵ, κἠν ὕῃ Ζεύς, τοῦτο μοῦ[νον ἄιδουσ]ι,

  φέρ᾽ εἰ φέρεις τι, τἄλλα δ᾽ ἀ[.].[... ἢ]ρται

  ὅκως νεοσσο[ὶ] τὰς κοχώνας θά[λ]π[ο]ντες.

  ἀλλ᾽ οὐ λόγων γάρ, φασίν, ἡ ἀγορὴ δεῖται

50   χαλκῶν δέ, τοῦτ᾽ ἢν μὴ ὑμῖν ἀνδάνηι, Μητρ[οῖ,

  τὸ ζεῦγος, ἕτερον κἄτε[ρ]ον μάλ᾽ ἐξοίσει,

  ἔστ᾽ ἂν νόωι πεισθῆτε [μὴ λ]έγει[ν] ψευδέα

  Κέρδωνα. τάς μοι σα[μβα]λουχίδας πάσας

  ἔνεγκε, Πίστε ...αλισγ.ννηθεισας

55   ὑμέας ἀπελθεῖν, ὦ γυναῖκες, εἰς οἶκον.

  θήσεσθε δ᾽ ὑμ[εῖς·] γένεα ταῦτα πα[ν]τοῖα·

  Σικυώνι᾽, Ἀμβρακίδια, Νοσσίδες, λεῖαι,

  ψιττάκια, κανναβίσκα, Βαυκίδες, βλαῦται,

  Ἰωνίκ᾽ ἀμφίσφαιρα, νυκτιπήδηκες,

60   ἀκροσφύρια, καρκίνια, σάμβαλ᾽ Ἀργεῖα,

  κοκκίδες, ἔφηβοι, διάβαθρ᾽· ὧν ἐρᾶι θυμός

  ὑμέων ἑκάστης εἴπατ᾽, ὡς ἂν αἴσθοισθε

  σκύτεα γυναῖκες καὶ κύνες τί βρώζουσιν.

41 τί]ς Knox, τίς ἔστ᾽ ὀ]ς Edmonds   ἄχρι‹ς› Rutherford
42 ἢ πίετ]αι Knox   τόσ‹σ›ον Büccheler
43 μικρωνος P, corrected by Crusius

[   ] night and day. [Which] of us gulps till evening [or drinks] at dawn? I don't think Micion's honey is so [   ]. And I haven't yet mentioned the thirteen [whom] I feed, since, ladies, [they are all] lazy[ness], who, even if Zeus sends rain, [sing] this alone, 'Bring, if you've anything to bring'; but otherwise they [sit secure], like chicks warming their posteriors. But as it's not words, they say, the market needs but brass,[2] if you don't like this pair, Metro, he'll bring out another and yet another, till you are convinced that Cerdon does [not] tell lies. Bring me all the shoe-boxes, Pistus; you must, ladies, go back home [.] You will see for yourselves: here are all kinds: Sicyonians, little Ambracians, Nossises, plains, greens, hemps, Baucises,[3] slippers, Ionics with buttons, night-walkers, boots, crabs, Argive sandals, scarlets, youths, flats: say what is the heart's desire of each one of you; so that thus you may realise why women and dogs eat leather.[4]

---

[2] Cerdon adapts to his own situation the proverb 'the market needs not words, but deeds'. [3] Nossises and Baucises continue the malicious reference of 6.20: for Baucis was the friend of Nossis and subject of her poem 'Distaff'.

[4] Dogs proverbially never forget how to chew their leather lead; women similarly never give up using a leather dildo.

---

44 οὖς ἐγὼ Edmonds   45 ἀργ[ίη πάντε]ς Headlam

46 μοῦ[νον ἄιδουσ]ι Crusius   47 ἀ[σ]φ[αλεῖς Herzog

ἦ]ρται Headlam   48 κηχωνας P, corrected by Danielsson, Jackson   52 [μὴ λ]έγει[ν] F.D.

53 σα[μβα]λουχίδας Bücheler   54 An unsolved mystery

56 ὑμ[εῖς·] γένεα Rutherford   57 For λεῖαι Headlam conjectured Χῖαι   58 βλαυτ τια P, corrected by Herwerden

(ΜΗ.) κόσου χρείζεις κεῖν' ὃ πρόσθεν ἤειρας
65 ἀπεμπολῆ⟨σαι⟩ ζεῦγος; ἀλλὰ μὴ βροντέων
οὗτος σὺ τρέψηις μέζον εἰς φυγὴν ἡμέας.

(ΚΕ.) αὐτὴ σὺ καὶ τίμησον, εἰ θέλεις, αὐτό
καὶ στῆσον ἧς κότ' ἐστιν ἄξιον τιμῆς.
ὁ τοῦτ' ἐῶν γὰρ οὔ σε ῥηιδίως ῥινᾶι.
70 ζευγέων, γύναι, τὠληθὲς ἢν θέληις ἔργον,
ἐρεῖς τι—ναὶ μὰ τήνδε τὴν τεφρὴν κόρσην,
ἐπ' ἧς ἀλώπηξ νοσσιὴν πεποίηται[ι—
τάχ' ἀλφιτηρὸν ἐρ[γ]α[λ]εῖα κινεῦσι.
Ἑρμῆ τε Κερδέων καὶ σὺ Κερδείη Πειθοῖ,
75 ὡς, ἤν τι μὴ νῦν ἡμιν ἐς βόλον κύρσηι,
οὐκ οἶδ' ὅκως ἄμεινον ἢ χύτρη πρήξει.

(ΜΗ.) τί τονθορύζεις κοὐκ ἐλευθέρηι γλάσσηι
τὸν τῖμον ὅστις ἐστὶν ἐξεδίφησας;

(ΚΕ.) γύναι, μιῆς μνῆς ἐστιν ἄξιον τοῦτο
80 τὸ ζεῦγος· ἢ ἄνω 'σ⟨τ⟩' ἢ κάτω βλέπειν· χαλκοῦ
ῥίνημ' ὃ δήκοτ' ἐστὶ τῆς Ἀθηναίης
ὠνευμένης αὐτῆς ἂν οὐκ ἀποστάξαι.

(ΜΗ.) μάλ' εἰκότως σευ τὸ στεγύλλιον, Κέρδων,
πέπληθε δαψιλέων τε καὶ καλῶν ἔργων.
85 φύλασσε κά[ρτ]α σ' αὐτά· τῆι γὰρ εἰκοστῆι
τοῦ Ταυρεῶνος ἡκατὴ γάμον ποιεῖ

---

65 ἀπεμπολῆ⟨σαι⟩ several   69 The beginning was read by
Meister, the end by Blass; neither is fully certain
73 ἐρ[γ]α[λ]εῖα Diels   77 τονθορυξεις P, corrected by Rutherford   78 ἐξεφώνησας (Richards) would be easier
80 'σ⟨τ⟩' Headlam

264

MIME 7

METRO

For how much do you want to sell that pair which you lifted
up before? But see you, don't put us to flight with louder
thundering.

CERDON

Value it yourself if you wish and set what price it is worth.
One who allows this does not readily cheat you. Lady,
if you wish the true craftsmanship of pairs, you will say
something—yes by this ashen head, on which the fox has
made its den[5]—supplying food quickly to tool-wielders. O
Hermes of profit and profiting Persuasion,[6] if something
does not now chance into the cast of our net, I do not know
how the pot will fare better.

METRO

Why are you muttering instead of having searched out the
price with free tongue?

CERDON

Lady, this pair is worth one mina, you may look up or
down.[7] Not the least shaving of a copper would come off, if
Athena herself were the customer.

METRO

It's not surprising, Cerdon, that your little house is full of
abundant lovely objects. Guard them [carefully] for yourself; for on the twentieth of Taureon[8] Hecate holds the

[5] I.e. which suffers from the disease alopecia, by a pun with
'alopex', fox.   [6] The pun on κέρδος 'profit' and Cerdon is
untranslatable.   [7] Probably 'whether you look happy or sad'.
[8] A month in many cities of Asia Minor.

---

[85] κά[ρτ]α Blass   σ(οι) αὐτά understood by Bücheler

τῆς Ἀρτακηνῆς, κὐποδημάτων χρείη·
τάχ᾽ οὖν, τάλης, ἄ⟨ι⟩ξουσι σὺν τύχηι πρός σε,
μᾶλλον δὲ πάντως. ἀλλὰ θύλακον ῥάψαι

90 τὰς μνέας ὅκως σοι μὴ αἰ γαλαῖ διοίσουσι.

(ΚΕ.) ἤν τ᾽ ἠκατ⟨ῆ⟩ ἔλθηι, μνῆς ἔλασσον οὐκ οἴσει,
ἤν τ᾽ ἡ Ἀρτακηνή. πρὸς τάδ᾽, εἰ θέλεις, σκέπτευ.

(ΜΗ.) οὔ σοι δίδωσιν ἡ ἀγαθὴ τύχη, Κέρδων,
ψαῦσαι ποδίσκων ὦν Πόθοι τε κήρωτες

95 ψαύουσιν; ἀλλ᾽ εἶς κνῦσα καὶ κακὴ λώβη
ὥστ᾽ ἐκ μὲν ἡμέων †λιολεοσεω† πρήξεις.
ταύτηι δὲ δώσεις κε⟨ῖ⟩νο τὸ ἔτερον ζεῦγος
κόσου; πάλιν πρήμηνον ἀξίην φωνήν
σεωυτοῦ.

⟨ΚΕ.⟩   στατῆρας πέντε, ναὶ μὰ θεούς, φο[ι]τᾶι

100 ἡ ψάλτρι᾽ ⟨Εὑ⟩ετηρὶς ἡμέρην πᾶσαν
λαβεῖν ἀνώγουσ᾽, ἀλλ᾽ ἐγώ μιν ἐχθ[α]ίρω,
κἠν τέσσαράς μοι Δαρικοὺς ὑπόσχηται,
ὁτεὐνεκέν μευ τὴν γυναῖκα τωθάζει
κακοῖσι δέννοις· εἰ δ[έ σοί γ᾽ ἐσ]τι χρείη

105 φερευλαβου⟨   ⟩ τῶν τριῶν [. . . .] δοῦναι
καὶ ταῦτα καὶ ταῦτ᾽ ἦι ὑμῖν ἑπτὰ Δαρεικῶν
ἕκητι Μητροῦς τῆσδε· μηδὲν ἀντείπηις.

---

88 ἄ⟨ι⟩ξουσι Crusius   91 ἠκατ⟨ῆ⟩ Rutherford   92 τηι P,
corrected by Herwerden   96 Possibly Αἰολέως should be read
(taking εω as a correction of εο, added instead of substituted; Αἰολέος
Beare), followed by ⟨χεῖρον⟩ or ⟨μεῖον⟩
100 ⟨Εὑ⟩ετηρὶς Blass, Rutherford   104 δ[έ σοί γ᾽ ἐσ]τὶ Blass
105 If the first word is φέρ᾽, one can read with Headlam εὐλαβοῦ

marriage of Artacene, and there is need of shoes; so, wretch, perhaps with good luck, or rather certainly, they will rush to you. Have a sack stitched so that the cats won't plunder your minas.

CERDON

Whether Hecate comes, or Artacene, she will not get them for less than a mina; consider this, if you please.

METRO

Cerdon, does not good fortune grant you to touch the little feet which Desires and Loves touch? But you are an irritation and wicked disgrace; so that from us you will get ‹   ›.[9] But for how much will you give that other pair to this lady? Again blast out a word worthy of yourself.

‹CERDON›

Five staters, by the gods, is what the harpist ‹Eu›eteris comes each day asking me to take, but I hate her, even if she promises me four Darics, since she jeers at my wife with wicked reproaches. But if [you have] need, †   † to give [   ] of the three—and this and this may be yours for seven Darics for the sake of Metro here. Don't

---

[9] The sense must be 'you will get nothing'; with the conjecture suggested, 'you will fare worse than Aeoleus' , but the identity of Aeoleus is unknown.

‹σὺ› τῶν τριῶν [μιᾶι] δοῦναι, 'come, beware of giving them to one of the three' (i.e. Hecate, Artacene, Eueteris); if it is φέρεν, then λαβοῦ‹σα›· τῶν τριῶν [θέλω] δοῦναι (Blass, Bücheler), 'take them away; I wish to give you them for three Darics'. Knox's placing of a fragment ₋ον here is uncertain in itself and leads to no good result

267

δύ]ναιτό μ' ἐλάσαι σ‹ὴ› ἂν [ἰὴ] τὸν πίσ[υγγον
ἐόντα λίθινον ἐς θεοὺς ἀναπτῆναι·
110 ἔχεις γὰρ οὐχὶ γλάσσαν, ἡδονῆς δ' ἠθμόν.
ἆ, θεῶν ἐκεῖνος οὐ μακρὴν ἀπεσ[τ' ὠν]ήρ
ὅτεωι σὺ χείλεα νύκτα κἠμέρην οἴγ[εις.
φέρ' ὧδε τὸν ποδίσκον· εἰς ἴ‹χ›νος θῶμεν·
πάξ· μήτε προσθῆις μήτ' ἀπ' οὖν ἕληις μηδέν·
115 τὰ καλὰ πάντα τῆις καλῆισιν ἁρμόζει·
αὐτὴν ἐρεῖς τὸ πέλμα τὴν Ἀθηναίην
τεμεῖν. δὸς αὔτη καὶ σὺ τὸν πόδ'· ἆ, ψωρῆι
ἄρηρεν ὁπλῆι βοῦς ὁ λακτίσας ὑμ‹έ›ας.
εἴ τις πρ[ὸ]ς ἴχνος ἠκόνησε τὴν σμίλην,
120 οὐκ ἄν, μὰ τὴν Κέρδωνος ἑστίην, οὕτω
τοὔργον σαφέως ἔκειτ' ἂν ὡς σαφ‹έ›ως κεῖται.
αὔτη σύ, δώσεις ἑπτὰ Δαρικοὺς τοῦδε,
ἡ μέζον ἵππου πρὸς θύρην κιχλίζουσα;
γυναῖκες, ἢν ἔχητε κἠτέρων χρείην
125 ἢ σαμβαλίσκων ἢ ἃ κατ' οἰκίην ἕλκειν
εἴθισθε, τήν μοι δουλ[ίδ'] ὧδε ‹δεῖ› πέμπειν.
σὺ δ' ἧκε, Μητροῖ, πρός με τῆι ἐνάτηι πάντως
ὅκως λάβηις καρκίνια· τὴν γὰρ οὖν βαίτην
θάλπουσαν εὖ δεῖ 'νδον φρονεῦντα καὶ ῥάπτειν.

---

108 δύ]ναιτο Bücheler   σ‹ὴ› ἂν [ἰὴ] Knox   πίσ[υγγον Knox
109 ληθινον P, corrected by Headlam
110 ηδηνης P, corrected by Herwerden   ηθμην or ηθμιν P, corrected by Bücheler

contradict: your [voice] could drive me, the cobbler, a man
of stone, to fly to heaven; for you have not a tongue but a
sieve of pleasure; ah, not far away from the gods [is the
man] to whom you open your lips night and day. Give
me your little foot here; let's place it on the sole. Right!
Neither add nor remove anything: all lovely things fit
lovely ladies; you would say that Athene herself had cut the
sole. Give me your foot also: ah, the ox that kicked you was
equipped with a scabby hoof. If one had sharpened one's
knife on the sole, by Cerdon's hearth the work would not
have lain so accurately as it does lie accurately. You there,
will you give seven Darics for this, you who are cackling at
the door more loudly than a horse? Ladies, if you have
need of anything else, small sandals or what you are in the
habit of trailing at home,[10] you ⟨must⟩ send your slave
here to me. But you, Metro, be sure to come to me on the
ninth to get your crabs; for in truth a sensible man must
stitch inside the skin coat that gives warmth.

[10] Loose-fitting house-shoes.

---

111 ἀπεσ[τ᾽ ὠν]ήρ Blass   112 οἴγ[εις Blass
113 ἴ⟨χ⟩νος Blass   θῶμεν Hicks, better than θῶ μιν Blass
117 πόδ᾽ ἅ divided by Headlam
117–118 ψωρη . . . οπλη P, corrected by Rutherford
126 δουλ[ίδ᾽] several   ⟨δεῖ⟩ several

8. ΕΝΥΠΝΙΟΝ

ἄστηθι, δούλη Ψύλλα· μέχρι τέο κείσηι
ῥέγχουσα; τὴν δὲ χοῖρον αὐονὴ δρύπτει·
ἢ προσμένεις σὺ μέχρις εὖ ἥλιος θάλψηι
τὸ]ν κῦσον ἐσδύς; κῶς δ', ἄτρυτε, κοὐ κάμνεις
5 τὰ πλ]ευρὰ κνώσσουσ'; αἱ δὲ νύκτες ἐννέωροι.
ἄστη]θι, φημί, καὶ ἄψον, εἰ θέλεις, λύχνον,
καὶ τ]ὴν ἄναυλον χοῖρον ἐς νομὴν πέμψ[ο]ν.
τ]όρθρυζε καὶ κνῶ, μέχρις εὖ παραστά[ς σοι
τὸ] βρέγμα τῶι σκίπωνι μαλθακὸν θῶμα[ι.
10 δει]λὴ Μεγαλλί, κα[ὶ] σὺ Λάτμιον κνώσσεις;
οὐ] τὰ ἔριά σε τρύχ[ο]υσιν· ἀλλὰ μὴν στέμμ[α
ἐπ' ἱρὰ διζόμεσ[θ]α· βαιὸς οὐκ ἦμιν
ἐν τῆι οἰκίηι ἔτι μα[λ]λὸς εἰρίων. δειλή,
ἄστηθι. σύ τε μοι τ[οῦ]ναρ, εἰ θέλεις, Ἀννᾶ,
15 ἄκουσον· οὐ γὰρ νη[πία]ς φρένας βόσκεις.
τράγον τιν' ἕλκειν [διὰ] φάραγγος ὠιήθη[ν
μακρῆς, ὁ δ' εὐπώ[γω]ν τε κεὔκερως ἦ[εν.
ἐπεὶ δὲ δὴ [.].. [.......]. τῆς βήσσης

3 θαλψηι, corrected to θαλψ(ε)ι, P   4 τὸ]ν κῦσον Headlam
5 τὰ πλ]ευρὰ Headlam, Palmer   6 ἄστη]θι Diels
8 παραστά[ς Vogliano   σοι Sitzler

8. A DREAM

Get up, slave Psylla: how long are you going to lie snoring?
Drought is rending the sow. Or are you waiting till the sun
crawls into [your] bum and warms it? Unwearied one, how
have you avoided tiring [your] ribs with sleeping? The
night is nine hours gone. [Get up], I say, and light the lamp,
please, [and] send the unmelodious sow to the pasture.
Mutter and scratch yourself until I stand beside [you] and
make [your] head soft with my stick. [Wretched] Megallis,
are you too in a Latmian sleep?[1] It is [not] your wool that
wears you out: should we seek a wreath for the rites, there
is not any longer a tiny woollen fleece in the house for us.
Wretch, get up. And you, Annas, please listen to my dream,
for you do not nourish a silly mind. I seemed to be dragging
a goat [through] a long defile, and it [was] well bearded and
well horned; and when [   ] of the glen, at the

---

[1] Like the mythological sleeper Endymion, who frequented or
was buried on Mt Latmos.

---

9 τὸ] Headlam   10 δει]λὴ Palmer
11 οὐ] Palmer   13 μα[λ]λὸς Bücheler
14 τ[οῦ]ναρ Blass   16 [διὰ] Crusius
17 εὐπώ[γω]ν Crusius   ἦ[εν Knox, ἦ[ν τις Crusius
18 [ν]ιν Knox

```
      ἠο[ὺ]ς φα[ούσης ......] γὰρ ἔσσωμαι
20    συ[..............].ες αἰπόλοι πλε[
      τη[...............].ριωντεποιευ[
      κἠγὼ οὐκ ἐσύλευν [....].(.)[
      καὶ ἄλλης δρυὸς [...].ε[
      οἱ δ᾽ ἀμφικαρτα.[...]τεσ[
25    τὸν αἶγ᾽ ἐποίευν [....]π[
      καὶ [π]λησίον με.[....].ι.[
      κ[.....].νμα.[....].ω[
      σχ[....]κροκωτ[....]φ.[
      ω[....]λεπτῆς ἄ[ν]τυγος ....[
30    σ.[....]ς δὲ νεβροῦ χλαν[ι]δίω[ι] κατέζω[στ]ο
      κ[.....].ν κύπα[σσι]ν ἀμ[φ]ὶ τοῖς ὤμοις
      κο[.....] ἀμφὶ κρ[ητὶ κ]ίσσι[ν]· ἔστεπτο
      ..... κ]οθόρνου[....]η κα[τ]αζώστρηι
      .......]ωμεντο [....]σα.[.....] φρίκη.[
35    .......]ωρηνιχ[...].θι.[ ]
      .......]ο λῶπο[ς ...]κον [πε]ποιῆσθαι
      ..... Ὀδ]υσσέως ο[....] Αἰόλ[ου] δῶρον
      .........]φ.[......]το.[...]α λακτίζειν
      .........]εγ[......].εν[..] λῶιστον
40    ὥσπερ τελεῦμεν ἐν χοροῖς Διωνύσου.
      κοἰ μὲν μετώποις ἐ[ς] κόνιν κολυμβῶ[ντες
      ἔκοπτον ἀρνευτῆρ[ε]ς ἐκ βίης οὖδας,
      οἱ δ᾽ ὕπτι᾽ ἐρριπτεῦντο· πάντα δ᾽ ἦν, Ἀνν[ᾶ,
      εἰς ἓν γέλως τε κἀνίη [᾽ν]αμιχθ[έ]ντα.
45    κἀγὼ δόκεον δὶς μοῦ[νο]ς ἐκ τόσης λείης
      ἐπ᾽ οὖν ἀλέσθαι, κἠλάλαξαν ὤνθρωπ[οι
```

[appearance of] dawn [   ] for I am
[not] defeated, [   ] goatherds [   ]. And I
did not despoil [   ] and of another tree [   ].
And those around [   ] very [   ] made the
goat [   ] and near by [he wore a] yellow [dress] of
slight curve [   ]. He was girded with a stole of
[stippled] fawnskin, [   ] tunic about his shoulders,
and he was crowned with ivy [clusters] round his head
[   ] with the lace of a boot.[2] [   ] frost
[   ] cloak [   ] to have been made [   ]
of Odysseus [   ] gift of Aeolus [   ] to kick
[   ] best, as we observe in the choruses of Dionysus.[3] Some plunging with their foreheads to the dust forcibly struck the ground like divers, and others were thrown
on their backs; everything, Annas, was laughter and pain
[mingled] in one. And I [alone] of such a flock seemed to
leap on twice, and the men cried out, as they saw the skin

---

[2] Lines 29–35 are clearly a description of Dionysos.

[3] A game played at Dionysiac festivals, in which the participants tried to balance on an inflated wineskin.

---

19 ἠ[οῦ]ς φα[ούσης Knox   οὐ] γὰρ Knox
24 ἀμφὶ κάρτα Crusius
28 σχ[ιστὸν] κροκωτ[ὸν] Vogliano, ἠμ]φί[εστο Knox
30 στ[ικτῆ]ς Knox   κατέζω[στ]ο Herzog
31 κύπα[σσι]ν Crusius
32 κό[ρυμβα δ'] Knox   κρ[ητὶ κ]ίσσι[ν'] Knox
33 -ον or -ους   κα[τ]αζώστρηι Knox
36 λῶπο[ς Bücheler   [πε]ποιῆσθαι Milne
37 Ὀδ]υσσέως Bücheler   Αἰόλ[ου] Knox
40 διοννυσου P, corrected by Kenyon
44 ['ναμιχθ]έντα Knox   45 μοῦ[νο]ς Herzog
46 ὤνθρωπ[οι Crusius

ὥς μ' εἶδ[ον ‥]ως τὴν δο[ρὴ]ν πιεζεῦσαν
καὶ φ[   ]τ[
οιδε [
50 γρυπ[
ρυπ[
τ.[
τ[
[
55 [
[
[
τὰ δεινὰ πνεῦσαι λὰξ πατε[
ἔρρ' ἐκ προσώπου μή σε καίπ,ερ ὢν πρέσβυς
60 οὔλῃ κατ' ἰθὺ τῇ βατηρίῃ κό[ψω.'
κἠγὼ μεταῦτις· 'ὦ παρεόν[τες
θανεῦμ' ὑπὲρ γῆς, εἰ ὁ γέρων μ[
μαρτύρ[ο]μαι δὲ τὸν νεηγ[ίην
ὁ δ' εἶπεν [ἄ]μφω τὸν δορέα .[
65 καὶ τοῦτ' ἰ[δ]ὼν ἔληξα. τὸ ἔνδυ[τον
Ἀν]νᾶ δ[ὸς] ὧδε. τῶναρ ὧδ' ἰ[
‥‥‥‥]ν αἶγα τῆς φ[άραγγος] ἐξεῖλκον
‥‥ κ]αλοῦ δῶρον ἐκ Δ[ιων]ύσου
‥‥ αἰ]πόλοι μιν ἐκ βίης [ἐδ]αιτρεῦντο
70 τ]ὰ ἔνθεα τελεῦντες καὶ κρεῶ[ν] ἐδαίνυντο,
τὰ μέλεα πολλοὶ κάρτα, τοὺς ἐμοὺς μόχθους,

47 (ε)ἶδ[ον Knox   δο[ρὴ]ν Crusius   πιεζεῦντα Knox (a more
natural 'saw me pressing the skin')

pressing me [   ] and [   ]. And they [   ]
hooked [   ]dirt[

                                   ] to blow terribly trampling with the
foot [   ] get out of my sight, lest although ⌞I am
old⌟ I strike you straight down with my whole stick.' I then
[said], 'Spectators, I shall die for the land[4] if the old man
[   ] and I call to witness the young man [   ].'
He said that the flayer [should tie] both [in the stocks]. And
having seen this I stopped. [Annas, give] my cloak here.
[One must interpret] the dream thus. [As] I dragged the
goat from the [defile, I shall have some] gift from lovely
Dionysus; [and as the goat]herds forcibly butchered it,
carrying out their rites of communion, and feasted
on the meat, many will severely pluck the songs, my la-

---

[4] Or 'above the ground'

---

^{50} πατέ[οντα Crusius, πατέ[ων Herzog   59–60 are cited
by the scholiast on Nicander, *Theriaca*, 377, from Herodes the
hemiamb (i.e. mimiambic poet) in his 'Sleep' ("Υπνωι for
'Ενυπνίωι), as evidence for βατηρία = βακτηρία   59 ερρ
P, φ(ε)ύγωμεν schol. ^{60} κό[ψω Weil, καλύψω or -ηι schol.
     ^{64} [ἄ]μφω Crusius   ξ[ύλωι δῆσαι Herzog, or ξ[υνῆι
κτῆσθαι Pisani ('that both [should hold] the skin [in common]')
     ^{65} ἔνδυ[τον Crusius ^{66} 'Αν]νᾶ Sitzler   δòς] Knox
τοὖναρ Knox   (ε)ἰ[κάζειν δεῖ Crusius   67–75 The ends
are preserved in O ^{67} ὡς μὲν τò]ν Edmonds   φ[άραγ-
γος] Crusius ^{68} ἔξω τι κ]αλοῦ Knox   Δ[ιων]ύσου Knox
     ^{69} ὡς δ' οἱ Knox, αἱ]πόλοι Bücheler   [ἐδ]αιτρεῦντο Milne
     ^{70} τ]ὰ Crusius   κρεῶ[ν ἐδαί]νυντο Weil,]αμεδαινυντο O
(perhaps corrupt)

τιλεῦσιν ἐν Μούσῃσιν. ωδεγω[ ]το.
τὸ μὴν ἄεθλον ὡς δόκευν ἔχ[ει]ν μοῦνος
πολλῶν τὸν ἄπνουν κώρυκον πατησάντων,
75 κὴ τῶι γέροντι ξύν᾽ ἔπρηξ᾽ ὀρινθέντι
. .] κλέος, ναὶ Μοῦσαν, ἤ μ᾽ ἔπεα κ[
.εγ᾽ ἐξ ἰάμβων, ἤ με δευτέρη γν[
.μ.. ς μετ᾽ Ἱππώνακτα τὸν παλαι[
τ]ὰ κύλλ᾽ ἀείδειν Ξουθίδῃς †επιουσι[

72 ωδεγω[P,]το O (ruling out older supplements with ὧδ᾽ ἐγὼ [ ); I
have suggested ὧδέ γ᾽ ὤ[ισ]το or ὤ[λλ]υτο, 'so at least it presaged' or
'so at least they were destroyed'; ὤ[ιον]το, 'so they thought', Crane

73 ἔχ[(ε)ι]ν Knox

74 ἔμπνουν 'full of air' would give better sense. That ἄπνουν could
mean 'air-tight' seems unlikely.

76–79 The grammar and sense of the conclusion are unfortunately
not determinable. The principal verb may be at the beginning of 76
(ἔξω Vogliano) or at its end (κλήσει Knox); η . . . η may be the feminine relative pronoun or the disjunctive adverb; εξ may be preposition
or numeral; δευτερη γν[ωμη (?) may be nominative or dative; the construction of ἀείδειν is unknown

77 μέγ᾽ Knox

78 ἐμοῖς Herzog (but the sense of 'my Ionians' is not obvious)

bours, among the Muses; so [   ]. However as I seemed alone to have the prize, though many trod the wind-less bag, and I shared with the old man in his anger, fame, by the Muse [   ] verses [   ] from iambics [   ] me a second [   ] after Hipponax of old to sing limping songs to [ ] sons of Xuthus.

9. ΑΠΟΝΗΣΤΙΖΟΜΕΝΑΙ

ἔ]ζεσθε πᾶσαι. κοῦ τὸ παιδίον; δεξ[
.]αιπ[.]ος Εὐέτειραν καὶ Γλύκην .[
.]ι̣τ[. . . .]αιδρη τὴν ἕτοιμον ου[
. . . .] .ισμησε[.]ισματων[
. . . .] .ινατ[. . . .]νηνυτω[
. . . .] .η[. . . . . .]α̣χηπεπο[
. . . . . .] . .[. . . . . . .]φερεσκο .[
.ρ[. .]ο̣δ̣ .[. . . . .]α̣ δειλαίο̣ι̣ς βλε[
φερω . . .[. . . . .] .ακαιταννυ[
αυτησυ .[. . . . .] .εται νο[
ουπροσθα[. . . . .]νι̣σηξ[
τίθεσθ᾽ α .[. . . . . . . ἄ]εθλον ἐξοι[
γλήχ[. . . . .]κεῦσί σ᾽ ἤειρα

1 ἔ]ζεσθε Kenyon
2 κ]αὶ π[ρ]ὸς Crusius
3 λ]αιδρή, Knox
4 μή σε [κν]ισμάτων Crusius
5 ἀ]νηνύτω[ς Knox
10 Apparently P had φρ[εν- corrected to νο[- (Knox)
12 ἐξοι[σ- Crusius
13 το]κεῦσι Knox

9. WOMEN AT BREAKFAST

Sit down, all of you. Where is the child? Show [and to]
Euetira and Glyce; [   ], impudent girl; won't you
[   ] the one that is ready? Are you [   ]? Lest
[   ] you of scratches [   ] endlessly
[   ] bring [   ] with
wretched [   ]. Bring [   ] and [   ].
You there, [   ] mind [   ] not formerly [   ]
you make [   ] will carry off the prize [   ]
pennyroyal [to your] parents I reared you [

10. ΜΟΛΠΙΝΟΣ

ἐπὴν τὸν ἐξηκοστὸν ἥλιον κάμψῃς,
ὦ Γρύλλε, Γρύλλε, θνῆισκε καὶ τέφρη γίνευ·
ὡς τυφλὸς οὐπέκεινα τοῦ βίου καμπτήρ·
ἤδη γὰρ αὐγὴ τῆς ζοῆς ἀπήμβλυνται.

Verses 1–3 are cited by Stobaeus, *Anth.* 4.50b.56 from Herodas'
'Molpinus', verse 4 ibid. 55 from Herodas' Mimiambi; linked by
Salmasius

¹ ἥλιον = 'year' is scarcely possible; perhaps a line has been omitted, e.g. ἐπὴν τὸν ἐξήκοστον ἢ λ‹ίην πολλὸν / ἤκῃς ἔτος χρηστόν
τε σὸν β‹ίον κάμψῃς, 'when you reach your sixtieth or greater year
and come to the end of the good part of your life'

³ ὁ ὑπὲρ ἐκεῖνα Stob., corrected by Porson

⁴ αὕτη . . . ἀπήμβλυντο Stob., corrected by Salmasius

11. ΣΥΝΕΡΓΑΖΟΜΕΝΑΙ

προσφὺς ὅκως τις χοιράδων ἀνηρίτης

Cited by Athenaeus, *Deipnosoph.* 86b from Herondas' 'Women
Working Together', as an example of ἀναπίτης. The feminine
προσφῦο (Bücheler) is equally possible

10. MOLPINUS

Gryllus, Gryllus, when you have turned the post of sixty
suns, die and become ashes; for the further lap of existence
is blind; then the ray of life has been dimmed.

11. WOMEN WORKING
TOGETHER

Clinging like a sea-snail to the rocks.[1]

   [1] Apparently erotic.

12. From an unknown mimiamb

ἢ χαλκέην μοι μυῖαν ἢ κύθρην παίζει
ἢ τῆισι μηλάνθηισιν ἄμματ᾽ ἐξάπτων
τοῦ κεσκίου μοι τὸν γέροντα λωβᾶται.

Cited by Stobaeus, *Anth.* 4.24d.51 from Herodas' Mimiambi

13. From an unknown mimiamb

ὡς οἰκίην οὐκ ἔστιν εὐμαρέως εὑρεῖν
ἄνευ κακῶν ζώουσαν· ὃς δ᾽ ἔχει μεῖον,
τοῦτόν τι μέζον τοῦ ἑτέρου δόκει πρήσσειν.

Cited by Stobaeus, *Anth.* 4.34.27 from Herodas' Mimiambi
3 τούτου Stob., corrected by Schneidewin

12.

Either he plays brass fly or pot,[1] or fastens ties of my tow to cockchafers and despoils my 'old man'.[2]

[1] Children's games, similar to blind man's buff (the second without blindfold).
[2] Name for a distaff, from the old man's face put on it as ornament.

13.

For it isn't possible to find easily a house that lives without troubles; consider him who has less trouble to fare a little better than the other.

SOPHRON

MIMES

EDITED AND TRANSLATED BY
I. C. CUNNINGHAM

INTRODUCTION

Information from ancient sources on Sophron[1] is summarised in the Suda, σ 893: 'Sophron, of Syracuse, son
of Agathocles and Damnasyllis. He lived at the time of
Xerxes and Euripides. He wrote men's mimes and wom-
en's mimes; they are in prose, in the Doric dialect. And
they say that the philosopher Plato always read them, so
as even to sleep on them on occasions.' (Σώφρων, Συρα-
κούσιος, Ἀγαθοκλέους καὶ Δαμνασυλλίδος. τοῖς δὲ
χρόνοις ἦν κατὰ Ξέρξην καὶ Εὐριπίδην. καὶ ἔγραψε
μίμους ἀνδρείους, μίμους γυναικείους· εἰσὶ δὲ
καταλογάδην, διαλέκτῳ Δωρίδι. καί φασι Πλάτωνα
τὸν φιλόσοφον ἀεὶ αὐτοῖς ἐντυγχάνειν, ὡς καὶ
καθεύδειν ἐπ᾽ αὐτῶν ἔσθ᾽ ὅτε.) As the Persian ruler Xerxes (d. 464) and the tragedian Euripides (485–406) were
scarcely contemporaries, it has been suggested that the
former's name should be replaced by that of his son
Artaxerxes (d. 424). That the mimes were in a rhythmical
prose is stated by a scholion on Gregory of Nazianzus
(Testim. 19), which explains why he is sometimes described as a poet. That Plato was familiar with his work is
stated already in the third century by Duris (Testim. 5); a

[1] All the Testimonia will be found in Kassel–Austin, *Poetae
Comici Graeci* vol. 1.

variant of the above is that Sophron was under his pillow when he died; Diogenes Laertius further says that it was Plato who brought the neglected works to Athens (Testim. 6). The scholar Apollodorus of Athens (second century) wrote a commentary on them in at least four books (Testim. 22).

The division into men's and women's mimes goes back to Apollodorus and perhaps further; it indicates that, unlike Herodas and some of the papyrus fragments, Sophron did not mix male and female characters in the same mime. The surviving titles frequently show to which category a mime belongs, and fragments not ascribed to a particular mime can sometimes be recognised as men's or women's by the gender of the speaker or addressee.

The only fragment of any length is the papyrus plausibly ascribed to *The women who say they expel the goddess* (fr. 4). Only one of the citations is of more than two lines, and most are shorter; the majority are quoted to exemplify points of dialect or vocabulary. In these circumstances it is vain to expect much idea of either plots or characters.

The known titles, five or six of each category, suggest scenes of domestic or social life, not unlike those in Herodas. The women's are:

Sewing women ('Ακέστριαι), of which the two fragments give no further information (it has been suggested, for no good reason, that fr. 4d belongs to it);

The women who say they expel the goddess (Ταὶ γυναῖκες αἱ τὰν θεὸν φαντὶ ἐξελᾶν), in which one of them performs a ceremony to remove Hecate from a house (details of the preparation are in fr. 3, 4a, 75, 115 and 165, of the incantation in fr. *7 and **8, and of the result perhaps in fr. *9; Theocritus' imitation in *Id.* 2 is of one point only);[2]

The women viewing the Isthmian festival (Ταὶ θάμεναι τὰ Ἴσθμια), which began with a domestic scene and presumably moved outdoors for the spectacle, as in Theocritus' imitation in *Id.* 15,[3] while Herodas 4 is a parallel only for the viewing of an artistic spectacle;

Bridesmaid (Νυμφοπόνος), which apparently had a less than pleasant description of the celebration;

Mother-in-law (Πενθερά), domestic but without known details; and

the conjectural *The women breakfasting together* (Ταὶ συναριστῶσαι), whose fragments (identified from the occurrence of the name Coecoa and entitled by Wilamowitz) recall the similarly titled play of Menander and mimiamb of Herodas (9).

The men's are:

Messenger (Ἄγγελος), whose sole fragment is presumably the beginning of the mime and suggests that the eponymous hero is a bombastic figure;

The fisherman to the farmer (Ὡλιεὺς τὸν ἀγροιώταν), of which only fragments with names of fish, some with distinctly odd epithets, survive, though it may be guessed that

---

[2] See fr. *6. I see no reason to assume that his borrowing of the name or character Thestylis comes from this mime (argument to *Id.* 2 τὴν δὲ Θεστυλίδα ἀπειροκάλως ἐκ τῶν Σώφρονος μετήνεγκε μίμων, 'he transferred Thestylis ignorantly [or, tastelessly] from the mimes of Sophron').

[3] Argument to *Id.* 15 παρέπλασε δὲ τὸ ποιημάτιον ἐκ τῶν παρὰ Σώφρονι Ἴσθμια θαμένων, 'he fashioned the poem from the Women viewing the Isthmia in Sophron.'

the theme was the difference, even conflict, between life
at sea and on the farm;

Tunny-hunter (Θυννοθήρας), which must also have
concerned fishing, and of which unusually we know of two
characters, the hunter and his (possibly drunken) son;

You will frighten the darling boy (Παιδικὰ ποιφυξεῖς),
whose type of title is comparable to some in the anonymous mime fragment 15 below, as well as in Varro's satires,
and whose only fragment is again concerned with fish;

Promythion (Προμύθιον), whose title and subject are
equally obscure;[4] and

the conjectural *Old men* (Γέροντες), whose fragments
were brought together and named by Ahrens.

Other more or less clear parallels in Herodas and
Theocritus are noted below. Themes which occur relatively often are: food and drink, sex, excrement, games,
and money. Proverbs are employed frequently as in
Herodas.

Text

The now standard complete collection of testimonia and
fragments is R. Kassel and C. Austin, *Poetae Comici
Graeci*, vol. 1, Berlin and New York, 2001, pp. 187–253
(superseding G. Kaibel, *Comicorum Graecorum Frag-
menta*, vol. 1, fasc. 1, Berlin, 1899, 2nd ed. 1958). The
present edition gives text and translation of a selection
only, viz. most of the fragments of named mimes and those

---

4 It may be connected with the Sicilian word προμυθίκτρια =
προμνήστρια, matchmaker (Aristoph. Byz. fr. 279, Pollux 3.31);
cf. Herodas 1. Its use in the rhetorical schools of the imperial
period as 'moral preceding a myth' is unlikely to be relevant.

others with some interest for the later mime or otherwise informative. Quotation of sources and critical apparatus are also selective. The numbering and order follow Kassel–Austin (except that fr. 75, 115, 165, fr. 158, and fr. 65, 66 are placed under Ταὶ γυναῖκες, Ταὶ συναριστῶσαι, and Ὡλιεύς respectively); an asterisk before the number indicates an uncertain attribution; the order of the fragments from unnamed mimes is alphabetical by the source.

SOPHRON

ΜΙΜΟΙ ΓΥΝΑΙΚΕΙΟΙ

᾿ΑΚΕΣΤΡΙΑΙ

1 φωρτάτους ἀεὶ καπήλους παρέχεται

Philox. fr. 347 (ap. Et. Gen. s.v. μακάρτατος) μεμπτέον Σώφρονι
λέγοντι [1]· οὐδὲ γὰρ τὰ εἰς ῶρ λήγοντα σχηματίζουσιν
συγκριτικὸν καὶ ὑπερθετικόν. ᾿Εκλ. διαφ. λέξ. ΑΟ ii.456.2
(Suda κ 337) ἕτερόν ἐστιν οἰνοπώλης καὶ ἕτερον κάπηλος·
καθόλου γὰρ τοὺς πωλοῦντάς τι καπήλους ἔλεγον. ἔστιν καὶ
παρὰ Σώφρονι ἐν ταῖς ᾿Ακεστρίαις

   φωροτάτους codd., corr. Blomfield

*2 ἄκουέ νυν καὶ ἐμεῦ, ῾Ρόγκα

Apoll. Dysc., pron. p.65.13 ἐμεῦ· κοινὴ ᾿Ιώνων καὶ Δωριέων . . .
[2]. Σώφρων. Hesych. ρ 386 ῥογία· ἀκέστρια (῾Ρόγκα·
⟨Σώφρων⟩ ᾿Ακεστρίαις Kaibel)

SOPHRON

WOMEN'S MIMES

SEWING WOMEN

1 He/she always makes merchants the greatest thieves

Philoxenus (cited in the Etymologicum Genuinum): 'Sophron is to be criticised for saying [1]; for words ending in -or [such as the Greek for thief] do not form comparative or superlative.' *Selection of differing words* (also in the Suda): 'Wine-seller means one thing, merchant another; for they called those who sell a thing in general merchants. It occurs in Sophron in the *Sewing Women*'

*2 Listen now to me also, Rhonca

Apollonius Dyscolus, *On pronouns*: 'of me, common to Ionians and Dorians . . . [2]. Sophron.' Hesychius: 'rhogia, sewing woman' (perhaps to be corrected to: 'Rhonca, Sophron in the *Sewing Women*')

SOPHRON

ΤΑΙ ΓΤΝΑÎΚΕΣ ΑÎ ΤΑΝ ΘΕΟΝ ΦΑΝΤΙ ΕΞΕΛΑΝ

3 ὑποκατώρυκται δὲ ἐν κυαθίδι τρικτὺς ἀλεξιφαρμάκων

Athen. xi.480B κυαθίς· κοτυλῶδες ἀγγεῖον. Σώφρων δ' ἐν τῷ ἐπιγραφομένῳ μίμῳ Γυναῖκες αἱ τὰν θεόν φαντι ἐξελᾶν· [3]

τρίκτοι cod., corr. Schweighäuser (τρικτύα Jahn, Ahrens)

4a

> τὰν τράπεζαν κάτθετε ὥσπερ ἔχει·
> λάζεσθε δὲ ἁλὸς χονδρὸν ἐς τὰν χῆρα
> καὶ δάφναν πὰρ τὸ ὦας.
> 5 ποτιβάντες νυν πὸτ τὰν ἱστίαν θωκεῖτε.
> δός μοι τὺ τὤμφακες·
> φέρ' ὦ τὰν σκύλακα.
> πεῖ γὰρ ἁ ἄσφαλτος;
> – οὖτα. –
> 10 ἔχε καὶ τὸν δάιδιον καὶ τὸν λιβανωτόν.
> ἄγετε δὴ πεπτάσθων μοι ταὶ θύραι πᾶσαι.
> ὑμὲς δὲ ἐνταῦθα ὁρῆτε καὶ τὸν δαελὸν σβῆτε ὥσπερ
> ἔχει.
> 15 εὐκαμίαν νυν παρέχεσθε
> ἇς κ' ἐγὼν πὸτ τάνδε πυκταλεύσω.
> πότνια, δείπνου μέν τυ κα[ὶ ξ]ενίων ἀμεμφέων
> ἀντά[   ]ν ̣ ̣ν· καὶ κα ̣αμῶν δέ π ̣[

(traces of the following line, with no certain letters, and of the beginnings of 4 lines from the next column, with no more than 1 letter each, survive)

WOMEN'S MIMES

THE WOMEN WHO SAY THEY EXPEL THE GODDESS

3 The sacrifice for warding off poison has been buried
below in the cup

Athenaeus: 'kyathis, a cup-shaped vessel. Sophron in the mime
entitled *Women who say they expel the goddess* [3]'

4a

Set down the table as it is;
take a lump of salt in your hand
and bay at your ear.
Now approach the hearth and sit down.   5
You, give me the sword;
bring the dog here.
But where's the bitumen?
– Here. –
Hold both the torch and the incense.   10
Come then, let's have all the doors open.
Look there all of you and put out the torch as it is.
Now keep quiet   15
while I fight against this one.
Lady, food and perfect gifts
you will [receive in plenty] and reeds [

b

25 περρα.[
μυχοδ[
Μορμολύ[καν
κογχουαι[
κυναναιδ[ὲς
30 μισητάτα[

c

.[....].ιαδεσ[
θύραν τὰν αὐτὸς ἐ..[
ἐκ Στυέλλας
ἴκω σ.[.....]ọ.[
35 ετεθ.[

d

οὐδέ χ' ὔδ[ω]ρ ....ειοσ...ε.[   ] δοίη καταρρυφῆσαι·
τὸ γὰρ κακὸν γλυκύπικρον ἐὸν ἐπεπείγει.
σπατιλοκολυμφεύμες δὲ θαμὰ χοδέοντες·
40 ὁ γὰρ τῖλος ἀστα‹κ›τὶ κοχυδεύων ἀποτοσίτους ἄμ'
ἐπεποιήκει.
τ[.....].ακος στ.[..]ν [.....]μες ἀσκοὶ πεφυσ-
αμ[έ]νοι.
.....]δ' ἐπανδὺς βιῆται
45 .....]αμερον ὅπερ ἦς [.....]υδρηρον δρυψον[
.....].ṿ ἐκεραύνω[σ]εν

296

b

Mormolu[ca
shell
dog-shameful
most lewd [woman   30

c

door which he himself [knocked at
from Styella
I come [

d

nor would he/she give water [   ] to gulp down;
for the wickedness, bitter-sweet, was pressing.
And we are plunged in dung with frequent shitting;
for the diarrhoea, pouring out in floods, had made us with-   40
   out food or drink.
[The sacks/trousers   ] blown-up wineskins.
        ] rising up uses force
        ] short living which was [   ] watery tear [45
        ] struck with thunderbolts

27 Apollodorus, *On the Gods*: (Gorgyra invented as wife of
Acheron) 'just as his nurse was named as Mormolyca by Sophron'
33 Styella was a fort of Megara in Sicily

SOPHRON

(traces of 2 further lines, with no words legible)

1–49 A papyrus of the 1st century A.D., published in *Papiri della Società Italiana* (vol. 11, 1935, ed. M. Norsa and G. Vitelli: PSI 1214). 7 Schol. Lycophr. 77 καὶ γὰρ Σώφρων ἐν τοῖς μίμοις φησὶν αὐτῇ (scil. Ἑκάτῃ) κύνας θύεσθαι. 8 Ammon. adf. voc. diff. 423 τὸ . . . πεῖ τὴν ἐν τόπῳ σχέσιν δηλοῖ. Σώφρων φησί· πεῖ—ἄσφαλτος. [74], ἀντὶ τοῦ ποῦ. This line is cited without ascription by Ioann. Alex. de accent. p.32.14 and by Apoll. Dysc. adv. p.132.27 and elsewhere. 13 Et. Gen. s.v. δαλός· λέγεται δὲ καὶ δαλὸς καὶ δαελὸς παρὰ Σώφρονι. 16 Et. Orion. p.62.31 Σώφρων φησὶν ἀπὸ τοῦ πυκτεύω πυκταλεύω. 27 Apollod. Π. θεῶν xx (244 F 102a Jac.) (Gorgyra invented as wife of Acheron) καθὸ δὴ καὶ αὐτοῦ τούτου τιθήνην ὁ Σώφρων Μορμολύκαν ὠνόμασεν. 29 Schol. (Ge) Hom. Il. 21.394 (compounds of κυών) ὡς παρὰ Σώφρωνι κυναναιδές (κυνάπαιδες cod.). 30 Eust. in Od. p.1651.1 ἄλλοι δὲ μισήτην βαρυτόνως πρὸς διαστολὴν τῆς ὀξυτονουμένης τὴν κοινὴν καὶ ῥᾳδίαν, λέγοντες καὶ χρῆσιν αὐτῆς εἶναι παρὰ Κρατίνῳ (fr.354) καὶ Σώφρονι

18–19 ἀντά[σεις χα]ν[δό]ν Latte   καλαμῶν Koerte
30 [γύναι Gallavotti   32 ἔκο[πτε Olivieri
39 -κολυμφεύμες Gallavotti   θαμὰ Kerényi   χοδιτεύοντες Pohlenz   40 ἀστα‹κ›τὶ several   42 τ[ὸς θυ]λάκος ed. pr.   45 ἐπ]άμερον Kerényi   46 ὑδρηλὸν Olivieri
⟦α⟧δρυψον pap.

*6 ὑπό τε τὸν [στρ]όφιγγα ὀρρο[. .] ποτὲ βληθέν

Schol. Theocr. 2.60 τὴν δὲ τῶν φαρμάκων ὑπόθεσιν ἐκ τῶν Σώφρονος (Εὐφορίωνος codd., corr. Adert) μίμων μεταφέρει· [6]

298

*6 Once thrown below the pivot

Scholiast on Theocr.: 'He takes the plot of the drugs from the mimes of Sophron: [6]'

SOPHRON

*7 νερτέρων πρύτανιν

Schol. (1) Theocr. 2.12 τὴν Ἑκάτην χθονίαν φασὶ θεὸν καὶ [7], καθὰ καὶ Σώφρων; Schol. (2) ib. χθονίαν δὲ τὴν Ἑκάτην φησί, παρόσον Περσεφόνης τροφός, ἢ παρόσον ⟨νερτέρων⟩ πρύτανιν αὐτὴν τέθεικε Σώφρων

**8 αἴτε κα ἀπ' ἀγχόνας ἀίξασα,
αἴτε κα λεχοῦν διακναίσασα,
αἴτε κ' ἂν νέκρος μολοῦσα πεφυρμένα ἐσέλθῃς,
αἴτε κα ἐκ τριόδων καθαρμάτεσσιν ἐπισπωμένα
τῶι παλαμναίωι συμπλεχθῆις

Plut. de superst. 170B (after Timoth. fr.3) καὶ μὴν ὅμοια τούτοις καὶ χείρω περὶ Ἀρτεμίδος οἱ δεισιδαίμονες ὑπολαμβάνουσιν· [8]

Superficial corruptions corr. by Wilamowitz, who ascribed to this mime

*9 κύων πρὸ μεγαρέων μέγα ὑλακτέων

Epimer. Hom. μ 64 μέγαρον μέγαρος. ζητεῖται τὸ παρὰ τῷ Σώφρονι [9], οὐ γὰρ ἐπὶ τῆς πόλεως τὰ Μέγαρα ὁ Μεγαρεύς καὶ οἱ Μεγαρεῖς, τῶν Μεγαρέων, ἀλλ' ἀντὶ τοῦ πρὸ τῶν οἴκων· καὶ γὰρ δῆλον ὅτι πρὸ τῶν οἴκων ὑλακτοῦσιν οἱ κύνες. ἔστιν οὖν ἀπὸ τοῦ μέγαρος μεγάρεος κτλ.

*7 ruler of the dead

Scholiast on Theocr.: 'They say that Hecate is a chthonian deity and [7], as also Sophron'; id. 'He says that Hecate is chthonian, inasmuch as she was nurse of Persephone, or inasmuch as Sophron made her ruler ⟨of the dead⟩'

**8 Whether having darted from the hanging,
    or having worn out the woman in childbirth,
    or having come as a sullied corpse you enter,
    or attracted by off-scourings from the crossroads
      you are entwined with the murderer

Plutarch, *On superstition*: 'Indeed similar to these, and worse, the superstitious suppose about Artemis [mistake for Hecate?] [8]'

*9 A dog barking loudly before the house

Homeric parsings, on 'megaron': 'The line in Sophron [9] requires investigation, for it does not refer to the city Megara, inhabitant(s) Megarian(s), but means 'before the house'; for it is obvious that the dogs bark before the house. It is therefore from 'megaros' etc.'

    Cf. Theocr. 2.35

75 πῦς ἐς μυχὸν καταδύηι;

Ammon. adf. voc. diff. 423 (after other fragments of Sophron) ὅταν δὲ εἰς τόπον θέλῃ εἰπεῖν, φησί· [75], τουτέστιν ἀντὶ τοῦ εἰς τίνα μυχόν

Ascribed to this mime by Wuensch

115 φέρε τὸ θαύμακτρον κἠπιθυσιῶμες

Et. Gen. s.v. θαύμακτρον· παρὰ τὸ θαυμάζω . . . Σώφρων· [115]

Ascribed to this mime by Blomfield   θύμακτρον Kaibel

165 ἀεὶ δὲ πρόσω φύλλα ῥάμνου κραστιζόμεθα

Schol. Nic. Ther. 861 ἀλεξιάρης δὲ ῥάμνου, ὅτι οὐ μόνον ἀπαλέξειν ἐστὶν ἀγαθὴ ἡ ῥάμνος εἰς φάρμακα, ἀλλὰ καὶ εἰς φαντάσματα, ὅθεν καὶ πρὸ τῶν θυρῶν ἐν τοῖς ἐναγίσμασι κρεμῶσιν αὐτήν. . . . μέμνηται δὲ τῆς βοτάνης . . . καὶ Σώφρων ὁμοίως [165]

Ascribed to this mime by Blomfield   κρατιζόμεθα codd., corr. Bussemaker

ΤΑΙ ΘΑΜΕΝΑΙ ΤΑ ΙΣΘΜΙΑ

**10 φέρ᾽ ὦ τὸν δρίφον

Et. Gen. s.v. δρίφος Συρακοσσίων· [10]. δίφρος γὰρ καὶ δρίφος

Ascribed to Sophron and this mime by Valckenaer

75 Where do you go down into a corner?

115 Bring the censer and let's offer incense

165 And always hereafter we graze on leaves of
       buckthorn

Scholiast on Nicander, *Poisonous creatures*: 'protective twigs of
buckthorn, for buckthorn is a good defence not only against poi-
sons, but also against phantoms; hence they hang it in front of
doors in offerings to the dead. . . . The plant is mentioned by . . .
and likewise Sophron [165]'

THE WOMEN VIEWING THE ISTHMIAN FESTIVAL

**10 Bring the chair here

   Cf. Herodas 6.1, Theocr. 15.2

SOPHRON

ΝΥΜΦΟΠΌΝΟΣ

11 κἤπειτα λαβὼν προῆχε, τοὶ δ᾽ ἐβάλλιζον

βαλλίζοντες τὸν θάλαμον σκάτους ἐνέπλησαν

Athen. viii.362C (βαλλίζειν) καὶ Σώφρων δ᾽ ἐν τῇ ἐπιγραφομένῃ Νυμφοπόνῳ φησίν· [11.1] καὶ πάλιν· [11.2]

12 πατάνα αὐτοποίητος

Poll. x.107 καὶ πατάνη δὲ καὶ πατάνιον τὸ ἐκπέταλον λο-
πάδιον . . . ἡ μὲν πατάνη Σώφρονος εἰπόντος ἐν Νυμφοπόνῳ
[12] . . . ; sim. vi.90

ΠΕΝΘΕΡΆ

13 συμβουλεύω τιν ἐμφαγεῖν· ἄρτον γάρ τις τυρῶντα
τοῖς παιδίοις ἴαλε

Athen. iii.110C καὶ τυρῶντος δ᾽ ἄρτου μνημονεύει ὁ Σώφρων
ἐν τῇ ἐπιγραφομένῃ Πενθερᾷ οὕτως· [13]

τιν Cobet, Wilamowitz: τ᾽ cod.

ΤΑῚ ΣΤΝΑΡΙΣΤῶΣΑΙ (?)

14 πάρφερε, Κοικόα, τὸν σκύφον μεστόν

Athen. ix.380E (παραφέρειν) Σώφρων δ᾽ ἐν γυναικείοις κατὰ
⟨τὸ⟩ κοινότερον κέχρηται λέγων· [14]

BRIDESMAID

11 And then he took it and held it out, and they were
    dancing

    While dancing they filled the bedroom with shit

12 A homemade dish

MOTHER-IN-LAW

13 I advise you to eat; for someone has sent a cheese
    loaf for the children

THE WOMEN BREAKFASTING TOGETHER (?)

14 Coecoa, serve the cup full

Athenaeus (discussing 'serve'): 'Sophron in the women's mimes
uses it in the more common way [14]'

15 τάλαινα Κοικόα, κατὰ χειρὸς δοῦσα ἀπόδος ποχ᾽
  ἁμὶν τὰν τράπεζαν

Athen. ix.408F Ἀριστοφάνης δὲ ὁ γραμματικὸς ἐν τοῖς πρὸς
τοὺς Καλλιμάχου πίνακας (fr. 368) χλευάζει τοὺς οὐκ εἰδότας
τὴν διαφορὰν τοῦ τε κατὰ χειρὸς καὶ τοῦ ἀπονίψασθαι. παρὰ
γὰρ τοῖς παλαιοῖς τὸ μὲν πρὸ ἀρίστου καὶ δείπνου λέγεσθαι
κατὰ χειρός, τὸ δὲ μετὰ ταῦτα ἀπονίψασθαι. . . . καὶ Σώφρων
ἐν γυναικείοις· [15]

  Κοικόα Dindorf: καί κοα cod.

*17 πίμπλη δέ, Κοικόα

Herodian, Π. παθῶν ap. Et. Gen. οἱ . . . Δωριεῖς λέγουσι
πίμπλη, οἷον [17]· καὶ γὰρ τὸ ὄρα ὄρη λέγουσιν, οὕτως
πίμπλα πίμπλη

  Ascribed to Sophron by Valckenaer

*158 ἦρ᾽ ἔσθ᾽ ὕδωρ;

Schol. Dion. Thr. p.290.11 ὁ ἀρα ἐρωτηματικὸς ὢν μηκύνει τὸ
ā, συλλογιστικὸς δὲ βραχύνει. τρέπεται δὲ ἑκατέρου τὸ ā εἰς
ῆ, τὸ μὲν μακρὸν παρ᾽ Αἰολεῦσιν οὕτως [Sapph. fr. 107], [158]
Σώφρων (σῶφρον cod.) παρὰ Δωριεῦσι, καὶ παρ᾽ Ἴωσι [Call.
hy. 4.114], . . . ; sim. Apoll. Dysc. coni. p.223.24

  Ascribed to Sophron and this mime by Wilamowitz

15 Wretched Coecoa, pour the water over our hands
    and at last give us the food

Athenaeus: 'Aristophanes the grammarian in his book on
Callimachus' catalogues mocks those who do not know the difference between "water over the hands" and "washing"; for among
the ancients what was done before breakfast and dinner was called
"over the hands" and what after them "washing." . . . Sophron in
the women's mimes [15]'

Cf. Herodas 6.3

*17 Fill up, Coecoa

*158 is there water?

SOPHRON

Unnamed Women's Mimes

18 αἱ δὲ μὴ ἐγὼν ἔμασσον ταῖς αὐταυτᾶς χερσίν

Apoll. Dysc. pron. p.62.23 μόνη διπλασιάζεται παρὰ Δωριεῦσιν ἡ αὐτός ἐν τῷ αὐταυτός· [18] Σώφρων

ἔμασσον Kaibel after Valckenaer, μαθον cod.

19 ἔτι μεθὲν ἁ καρδία παδῆι

Apoll. Dysc. pron. p.66.3 ἐμέθεν. πυκνῶς αἱ χρήσεις παρὰ
Αἰολεῦσιν . . . ἀλλὰ καὶ παρὰ Συρακουσίοις· [19] Σώφρων
γυναικείοις, p.76.29 τὸ [19] ἐγκέκλιται

20 ἁ δ᾽ ἄρ᾽ ἅμ᾽ ἐλωβῆτο

Apoll. Dysc. pron. p.100.4 ἁμὲ Δωριεῖς· [20] Σώφρων γυναικείοις

*21 ἦ ῥα καλῶς ἀποκαθάρασα ἐξελεπύρωσεν

Apoll. Dysc. adv. p.169.22 (εἰς ῶϛ λήγοντα ἐπιρρήματα) παρὰ
Δωριεῦσιν ἔνια ὀξύνεται, ὥστε κατ᾽ ἔγκλισιν ἀνεγνώσθη· [21]

Ascribed to Sophron by Bast

*22 αὐτῶ ὁρῆις, Φύσκα;

Apoll. Dysc. adv. p.190.17 τὰ τῷ ō παρεδρευόμενα παρὰ
Δωριεῦσι τῶν ἐπιρρημάτων ἀπειράκις ἐν ἀποκοπῇ γίνεται
τοῦ θεν καὶ ἐν μεταθέσει τοῦ ō εἰς ῶ, καθὼς προείπομεν

WOMEN'S MIMES

Unnamed Women's Mimes

18 And if I wasn't kneading with my own hands

19 Still my heart is jumping

> Cf. Plato, Ion 535c, Symp. 215e

20 And then she was mutilating us

> Cf. Herodas 3.69, 73, 12.1

*21 Certainly she has nicely purged and stripped (him)

> Probably sexual, cf. for the first verb Aristoph., *Eccl.* 847 and Theocr. 5.119, for the second Catullus 58.5

*22 Are you looking here, Physca?

SOPHRON

αὐτόθεν αὐτῷ· [22], . . .

Ascribed to Sophron by Valckenaer

23 τίνες δ᾽ ἐντί ποκα, φίλα, τοίδε τοὶ μακροὶ
      κόγχοι;—σωλῆνές θην
      τοῦτοί γα, γλυκύκρεον κογχύλιον, χηρᾶν
      γυναικῶν λίχνευμα

Athen. iii.86E Σώφρων δ᾽ ἐν μίμοις· [23]. Demetr. eloc. 151 (after fr. 52) ὅσα τε ἐπὶ τῶν γυναικῶν ἀλληγορεῖ, οἷον ἐπ᾽
ἰχθύων [23, σωλῆνες to end], καὶ μιμικώτερα τὰ τοιαῦτά ἐστι
καὶ αἰσχρά

24 ταί γα μὰν κόγχαι, ὥσπερ αἴ κ᾽ ἐξ ἑνὸς
      κελεύματος
      κεχάναντι ἁμὶν πᾶσαι, τὸ δὲ κρῆς ἑκάστας ἐξέχει

Athen. iii.87A (κόγχαι λεγόμεναι θηλυκῶς) καὶ Σώφρων γυ-
ναικείοις· [24, αἴ to end]. Philox. fr.378 ap. Et. Gen. κέλευμα . . .
Σώφρων· [24, 1]

      αἴ γα μὰν κόγχαι Athen., οἴ γε μὰν κόγχοι Philox.

25 ἴδε καλᾶν κουρίδων, ἴδε καμμάρων, ἴδε φίλα·
      θᾶσαι μὰν ὡς ἐρυθραί τ᾽ ἐντὶ καὶ λειοτριχιῶσαι

Athen. iii.106D κουρίδας δὲ τὰς καρῖδας εἴρηκε Σώφρων ἐν
γυναικείοις οὕτως· [25], vii.306C (κάμμοροι) καὶ Σώφρων δ᾽
ἐν γυναικείοις μίμοις αὐτῶν μέμνηται

23 Whatever are they, my dear, these big male mussels?
    —Surely these ones are tubes,
a sweet-fleshed little shell, licking for solitary women

Athenaeus: 'Sophron in mimes [23]'; Demetrius, *On Style* 151:
(following fr. 52) 'and his metaphors on women, such as on fish
[23, "surely" to end], are more suited to mimes and are disgusting'

    Dildos, cf. Herodas 6–7

24 Then the female mussels, as if from one command
    they are all agape at us, and each one's flesh stands
      out

    Female genitalia, as in Plautus, *Rudens*, 704

25 See the fine shrimps, see the lobsters, see my dear;
    look how red they are and smooth-haired

    Dildos again, cf. Herodas 6.19, 71

26 δεῖπνον ταῖς θείαις κριβανίτας καὶ ὁμώρους καὶ
   ἡμιάρτιον Ἑκάται

27 τίς σταιτίτας ἢ κλιβανίτας ἢ ἡμιάρτια πέσσει;

28 εἰς νύκτα με †αἰτιαι σὺν ἄρτωι πλακίται

Athen. iii.110BC (types of bread) ὧν καὶ Σώφρων ἐν γυναικείοις μίμοις μνημονεύει λέγων οὕτως· [26]. οἶδα δ᾽ . . . ὅτι
Ἀττικοὶ μὲν διὰ τοῦ ρ στοιχείου λέγουσι καὶ κρίβανον καὶ
κριβανίτην, Ἡρόδοτος δ᾽ ἐν δευτέρᾳ τῶν ἱστοριῶν ἔφη (92.5)
κλιβάνῳ διαφανεῖ, καὶ ὁ Σώφρων δὲ ἔφη [27]. ὁ δ᾽ αὐτὸς
μνημονεύει καὶ πλακῖτα τινὸς ἄρτου ἐν γυναικείοις· [28]

   28 μ᾽ ἐσίτισεν Blomfield, μελιτίταν σὺν Kaibel

29 τῶν δὲ χαλκωμάτων καὶ τῶν ἀργυρωμάτων
   ἐγάργαιρεν ἁ οἰκία

Athen. vi.230A Σώφρων δ᾽ ἐν γυναικείοις μίμοις φησί· [29].
Cf. Schol. Ar. Ach. 3a.i (Suda ψ 22) καὶ παρὰ Σώφρονι δέ· ἁ δὲ
οἰκία τῶν ἀργ. γάργαιρε

   ἐγάργαιρεν Blomfield (cf. schol.), ἐμάρμαιρε Athen.

30 τρίγλαν γενεᾶτιν

Athen. vii.324F (after fr. 49) κἂν τοῖς γυναικείοις δὲ ἔφη [30]
. . . 325C γεν. δ᾽ ἔφη τὴν τρ. Σώφρων ἐπεὶ αἱ τὸ γένειον
ἔχουσαι ἡδίονές εἰσι μᾶλλον τῶν ἄλλων

26 As a meal for the divine ladies pan bread and sweet
breads and a half-loaf for Hecate

27 Who is baking spelt or pan breads or half-loaves?

28 Towards night he/she entertained (?) me with a flat
loaf

29 And the house was full of copper and silver objects

30 Bearded mullet

Athenaeus: 'and in the women's too he said [30] . . . And Sophron
called the mullet bearded, since those with beards are more pleasant than the others'

31 θᾶσαι ὅσα φύλλα καὶ κάρφεα τοὶ παῖδες τοὺς
ἄνδρας βαλλίζοντι·
οἱόνπερ φαντί, φίλα, τοὺς Τρῶας τὸν Αἴαντα τῶι
παλῶι

Demetr. eloc. 147 (παραβολή) Σώφρων δὲ καὶ αὐτὸς ἐπὶ τοῦ
ὁμοίου εἴδους φησί· [31]. καὶ γὰρ ἐνταῦθα ἐπίχαρις ἡ παραβολή ἐστι, καὶ τοὺς Τρῶας διαπαίζουσα ὥσπερ παῖδας

παῖδες ⟨εἰς⟩ Ahrens

32 πρὶν αὐτὰν τὰν νόσον εἰς τὸν μυελὸν σκιρωθῆναι

EM 718.1 σκιρωθῆναί φαμεν ἐπὶ τοῦ ῥύπου τοῦ σφόδρα
ἐμμένοντος καὶ δυσεκπλύτου. Σώφρων ἐν τοῖς γυναικείοις
τροπικῶς· [32]

33 ὑγιώτερον κολοκύντας

Philox. fr. 351 ap. EM 774.41 ζητεῖται τὸ παρὰ Σώφρονι [33]
πῶς οὐ λέγει ὑγιέστερον· ῥητέον οὖν ὅτι ἑκοντὶ ἥμαρτε τὸ
ἄκακον τῆς γυναικείας ἑρμηνείας μιμούμενος.

31 Look what leaves and sticks the boys are throwing at
the men,
just as they say, my dear, the Trojans did to Ajax with
the clay

Demetrius, *On Style* 147: (comparison) 'And Sophron himself
says in a similar style: [31]. For there the comparison is charming,
laughing at the Trojans like boys'

Possibly refers to throwing leaves on athletes (e.g. Pindar,
Pyth. 9.123) (then from *The Women viewing the Isthmian Festival*) or to wedding ceremonies (Stesichorus fr. 187) (then from
The Bridesmaid). An alternative version of Ajax' death (the common version being suicide after madness) was that the Trojans
killed him with lumps of clay (so that the comparison, *pace*
Demetrius, is bizarre)

32 Before the disease itself is ingrained into the marrow

Etymologicum Magnum: 'we say 'to be ingrained' of dirt that
sticks firmly and is hard to wash out. Sophron in the women's
metaphorically: [32]'

The disease may be love, cf. Theocr. 30.21

33 More healthy than a gourd

Philoxenus cited in the Etymologicum Magnum: 'It is asked with
regard to the phrase in Sophron [33] why he used the form 'hygio-
teron' and not (the normal) 'hygiesteron'. It must be said then
that he made an intentional mistake, imitating the innocence of
women's expression'

This explanation is doubtful: such variation in comparative
formation is not unknown and the same form as here is a possible
reading in Epicharmus fr. 152

34 τατωμένα τοῦ κιτῶνος, ὁ τόκος νιν ἁλιφθερώκει

Philox. fr. 351 ap. EM 774.41 (after fr. 33) ὃν τρόπον κἀκεῖ ἐσολοίκισε· [34, τ. τοῦ κ.], ἀντὶ τοῦ ἐνέχυρα θεῖσα, [34, ὁ τ. νιν ἀ.]

35 ἅμα τέκνων θην δευμένα

Plut. de E ap. Delph. 5, p.386D τοῦ εἴθε τὴν δευτέραν συλλαβὴν <ὥσπερ καὶ τὸ θην Bernadakis, larger loss assumed by Paton> παρέλκεσθαί φασιν, οἷον τὸ Σώφρονος [35]

ἅμα] ὁμᾶι Ahrens, ἀλλὰ Wilamowitz, ἁ μάτηρ Paton

36 ὁ μισθὸς δεκάλιτρον

Poll. iv.173 καὶ μὴν οἵ γε Δωριεῖς ποιηταὶ τὴν λίτραν ποτὲ μὲν νόμισμά τι λεπτὸν λέγουσιν, οἷον ὅταν Σώφρων ἐν τοῖς γυναικείοις μίμοις λέγῃ· [36]

37

Poll. x.175 καὶ βαίτας δὲ τὰς τῶν ἀγροίκων διφθέρας ἐν τοῖς γυναικείοις μίμοις ὁ Σώφρων ἐκάλεσεν

38 ἁ δ᾽ ἀμφ᾽ ἄλητα κυπτάζει

Schol. Ar. Ach. 263b περισπωμένως δὲ τὸ Φαλῆς ἀναγνωστέον, ὡς Ἑρμῆς. οὕτως δὲ Ἀττικοί. παρὰ Δωριεῦσι δὲ βαρυτόνως· [38]. Cyrill. AP iv.179.16 ἄλειαρ· τὰ ἀπὸ πυρῶν ἄλευρα, τὰ δὲ ἀπὸ κριθῆς ἄλφιτα . . . τὰ ἀλήατα καὶ ἄλητα, ἔνθεν ὁ μιμογράφος ἔπαιξεν· [38]. Herodian Π. παθῶν ap. Et.

34 Being deprived of my tunic, the interest has
    wrecked it

Philoxenus (after fr. 33): 'in this way too he made a mistake here,
"being deprived of my tunic" instead of "having pledged," "the
interest has wrecked it"'

Again doubtful: the grammarian demands literalness (if one
could further accuse him of not knowing or misunderstanding the
context, one of the other senses of τόκος might be better, 'child' or
'childbirth')

35 At the same time then being without children

36 The price is ten pence

Pollux: 'Further the Doric poets use "litre" for a small coin, as
when Sophron in the women's mimes says: [36]'

37 baetae

Pollux: 'Sophron in the women's mimes called the jerkins of country people "baetae"'

Cf. Herodas 7.128

38 And she keeps stooping about the meal

The ambiguity between ἀμφ' ἄλητα, 'about the meal', and ἀμ
φάλητα, 'about the phallus' is doubtless intentional

SOPHRON

Gen. α 457 ἄλητα. Σώφρων· ἀμφ' ἄλητα. ἀλήατα κατὰ συγκοπὴν ⟨ἄλητα⟩

ἡ δ' or ὁ δ' Schol., ἀλλ' Cyrill.   ἀμφ' ἄλητα, ἀμφάλητα, ἀμφάλιτα codd.; Schol. originally must have had ἀμ Φάλητα

40 ἐνθάδε κυπτάζοντι πλεῖσται γυναῖκες

Schol. Ar. Lys. 17 κυπτάζειν ἐστὶ τὸ περί τι πονεῖσθαι καὶ διατρίβειν. κομψῶς δὲ τῇ ἀμφιβολίᾳ καὶ χαριέντως ⟨ἐχρή-σατο⟩, καθὰ καὶ Σώφρων· [40]

ΜΙΜΟΙ ΑΝΔΡΕΙΟΙ

ἌΓΓΕΛΟΣ

41 ἐξ Ἑστίας ἀρχόμενος καλέω Δία πάντων ἀρχ-
αγέταν

Schol. Arat. Phaen. 1 (ἐκ Διὸς ἀρχώμεσθα) ζητεῖται διὰ τί ἐκ τοῦ Διὸς ἤρξατο καὶ οὐκ ἀπὸ τῶν Μουσῶν, ὡς Ὅμηρος. οἰκειότερον ἡγήσατο ἀρχὴν τῶν Φαινομένων ποιήσασθαι, ἀπὸ τοῦ Διός, ἐπειδὴ καὶ τῶν Μουσῶν ἀρχηγέτης αὐτός ἐστιν. οὐ φαίνεται δὲ Ἄρατος μόνος οὕτως ἦρχθαι, ἀλλὰ καὶ Κράτης ὁ κωμικὸς εἰπών (fr. 44)· ἐξ Ἑστίας ἀρχόμενος εὔχομαι θεοῖς, καὶ Σώφρων· [41]. Schol. German. *non solus autem ita coepisse videtur Aratus, sed et Crates comicus . . . et Sophron in mimo qui Nuntius inscribitur: a Vesta incipiens {omnes} invoco Iovem omnium principem*

318

40 Here a great many women stoop

Scholiast on Aristoph.: '"to stoop" is to take pains and be occupied about something. He (Aristoph.) used it cleverly with ambiguity and elegantly, as also Sophron [40]'

  Possibly also sexual

MEN'S MIMES

MESSENGER

41 Beginning from Hestia I invoke Zeus as creator of all

Scholium on Aratus, *Phaenomena* 1 ('Let us begin from Zeus'): 'It is questioned why he began from Zeus and not from the Muses like Homer. He thought it more fitting to make the beginning of the Phaenomena from Zeus, since he is actually the creator of the Muses too. Aratus does not seem to have been the only one to begin thus, but Crates the comic poet said "Beginning from Hestia I pray to the gods," and Sophron [41].' Scholium on Germanicus' Latin translation of Aratus: ' . . . Sophron in the mime entitled Messenger . . . '

SOPHRON

ὉΛΙΕῩΣ ΤῸΝ ἈΓΡΟΙΏΤΑΝ

42 βλέννωι θηλαμόνι

Athen. vii.288A βλέννος. τούτου μέμνηται Σώφρων ἐν τῷ
ἐπιγραφομένῳ Ὡλιεὺς τὸν ἀγρ‹ο›ιώταν· [42]. ἔστι δὲ κωβιῷ
τὴν ἰδέαν παραπλήσιος

65 βαμβραδόνι †ραφεια†

Athen. vii.287C (βεμβράδες) καὶ Σώφρων ἐν ἀνδρείοις· [65]

> Ascribed to same context as fr.42 by Botzon and Kaibel.
> ῥαφίδι Casaubon, τρυφεραῖ Kaibel

66 τριγόλαι ὀμφαλοτόμωι

τριγόλαν τὸν εὐδιαῖον

Athen. vii.324E Σώφρων δ' ἐν τοῖς ἀνδρείοις τριγόλας τινὰς
ἐν τούτοις ὀνομάζει [66.1] καὶ [66.2]

² τριγόλαι cod., corr. by Musurus

43 χηράμβας

Athen. iii.86A (Σώφρων) ἐν τῷ ἐπιγραφομένῳ Ὡλιεὺς τὸν
ἀγροιώταν χ. ὀνομάζει

44 κωθωνοπλύται

Athen. vii.309C (κωβιοί) καὶ Σώφρων ἐν τῷ Ἀγροιώτῃ κ. φησὶ
. . . Σικελιῶται δ' εἰσὶν οἱ τὸν κωβιὸν κώθωνα καλοῦντες, ὡς
Νίκανδρός φησιν ὁ Κολοφώνιος ἐν ταῖς Γλώτταις (fr. 141)
καὶ Ἀπολλόδωρος ἐν τοῖς περὶ Σώφρονος (244 F 217 Jac.)

MEN'S MIMES

THE FISHERMAN TO THE FARMER

42 For gudgeon the nurse

65 For sprat the needle

66 For piper the umbilical cutter
Fair weather piper

43 Scallops

44 Gudgeon-cleaners

SOPHRON

ΘΥΝΝΟΘΉΡΑΣ

45 ἁ δὲ γαστὴρ ὑμέων καρχαρίας, ὅκκα τινὸς δῆσθε

Athen. vii.306D Σώφρων Θυννοθήρᾳ· [45]

46 Κωθωνίας

Athen. vii.309C (after fr. 44) τὸν τοῦ θυννοθήρα δὲ υἱὸν Κωθωνίαν προσηγόρευσεν

47 ἐγκίκρα, ὡς εἴω

EM p.423.23 ἔστιν εἴω τὸ πορεύομαι, διὰ διφθόγγου, ὥς φησι Σώφρων ἐν Θυννοθήρᾳ· [47]. Choerob. in Theod. can. p.104.34 εἴω . . . τὸ πορεύομαι, ὡς παρὰ Σώφρονι· [47], τουτέστι κέρασον ἵνα πορευθῶ. Eust. in Il. p.234.39 κιγκρῶ, οὗ χρῆσις τὸ [47], ἤγουν κίρνα ὡς ὁδεύω

48 λοξῶν τὰς λογάδας

Soran. ap. EM p.572.36 λογάδες· ἐπὶ τῶν ὀφθαλμῶν τὰ λευκά . . . εἴρηται δὲ . . . ἢ ὅτι λοξοῦνται ἐν τῷ βλέπειν κατὰ τὰς ἐπιστροφάς. Σώφρων ἐν Θυννοθήρᾳ· [48]

ΠΑΙΔΙΚᾺ ΠΟΙΦΥΞΕῖΣ

49 τρίγλας μὲν γένηον, τριγόλα δ᾽ ὀπισθίδια

Athen. vii.324F (after fr. 66) ἐν δὲ τῷ ἐπιγραφομένῳ Παιδικὰ ποιφυξεῖς φησί· [49], again soon after Τρύφων φησὶν ἐν τοῖς περὶ ζῴων (fr. 121) τὸν τριγόλαν τινὰς οἴεσθαι κόκκυγα εἶναι διά τε τὸ ἐμφερὲς καὶ τὴν τῶν ὀπισθίων ξηρότητα, ἣν σεσημείωται ὁ Σώφρων λέγων· [49]

TUNNY-HUNTER

45 But your stomach is a shark, when you want something

46 Cothonias

Athenaeus: (after fr. 44) 'and the son of the tunny-hunter he called Cothonias'

The context in Athenaeus suggests the meaning 'gudgeon-like,' but it might also suggest 'drinker' (cf. fr. 47)

47 Mix it, so that I can go

48 Glancing with the whites of his eyes

Cf. Herodas 4.71

YOU WILL FRIGHTEN THE DARLING BOY

49 The beard of a mullet, but the rear of a piper

Athenaeus: (after fr. 66) 'and in *You will frighten the darling boy* he says [49] . . . Tryphon says in his work on animals that some think the piper is the cuckoo fish because of both the resemblance and the dryness of its hind parts, which Sophron has marked [49]'

Possibly Tryphon's statement is derived from the following words, now lost

SOPHRON

ΠΡΟΜΥΘΙΟΝ

50 κοντῶι μηλαφῶν αὐτὸ τυψεῖς

Prov. Par. (Corp. Paroem. Gr. suppl. i.82 nr.94) κοντ[ῳ μηλα-
φᾶς]· κατὰ τῶν τὰ ἄδηλα τελέως τεκμαιρομένων, ὡσπερεὶ
λέγοι τις· κοντὸν κ[α]θ[εὶς] δι᾽ α[ὑτοῦ] ψηλαφᾶς. Σώφρων ἐν
Προμυθίῳ· [50]. ἔοικε δὲ διαφ[έρειν] τὸ ψηλαφᾶν τοῦ μηλα-
φᾶν, ἤτοι ὅτι τὸ μὲν τὸ δι᾽ ἑτέρου ἅπτεσθαι, τὸ δὲ ψηλαφᾶν
[   ] ἐστι ταῖς χερσὶ θιγεῖν

51 βλεννόν

Antiatt. p.85.24 (Phot. β 157) β.: τὸν νωθῆ καὶ μωρόν. Σώφρων
Προμυθίῳ

ΓΈΡΟΝΤΕΣ

52 ἐνθάδε ὢν κἠγὼ παρ᾽ ὑμὲ τοὺς ὁμότριχας
    ἐξορμίζομαι πλόον
    δοκάζων· †ποντίναι† γὰρ ἤδη τοῖς ταλικοῖσδε ταὶ
    ἄγκυραι

Demetr. eloc. 151 ἔχουσι δέ τι στωμύλον καὶ ἀλληγορίᾳ τινές
. . . καὶ τὰ Σώφρονος δὲ τὰ ἐπὶ τῶν γερόντων· [52].

πόντιον· ἀρτέαι γὰρ Kaibel

PROMYTHION

50 Hitting with a pole, you'll strike it

Proverb collection: 'you hit with a pole, of those who bear witness completely to what is unclear, as if one were to say, having dropped a pole you hit by means of it. Sophron in the Promythion [50]. . . .'

51 Slimy

The (so-called) Antiatticist: 'slimy, dull and stupid. Sophron in the Promythion'

OLD MEN (?)

52 Here then I too put to sea beside you of similar hair,
        waiting for the time
     to sail; for the anchors are already prepared for men
        of such age

Demetrius, *On Style* 151: 'Some have a certain wordiness even in metaphor . . . so too the lines of Sophron on old men [52]'

53 κινζοῦμαι δὲ οὐδὲν ἰσχύων· ἁ δὲ ξυσμὰ ἐκ ποδῶν
    εἰς κεφαλὰν ἱππάζεται

Epimer. Hom. κ 125 εἴρηται δὲ κινζοῦν καὶ τὸ ξύειν παρὰ
Δωριεῦσι . . . ὡς Σώφρων· [53]. Herodian. ap. Et. Gen. τὸ δὲ
κινζῶ σημαίνει πολλάκις τὸ ξύειν, ὡς παρὰ Σώφρονι ἐν
μίμοις, οἷον· [53]; id. ap. Eust. in Od. 1766.33

54 τὸ γὰρ ἀπεχθόμενον γῆρας ἀμὲ μαραῖνον
    ταριχεύει

Stob. iv.50b.65 (ψόγος γήρως) Σώφρονος [54]. Schol. Aesch.
Cho. 296 (ταριχευθέντα) καὶ ὁ Σώφρων· [54]

55 τί μὰν ξύσιλος;—τί γάρ; σύφαρ ἀντ᾽ ἀνδρός

Et. Gen. σύφαρ· οὐχ ἁπλῶς τὸ γῆρας ἀλλ᾽ ὡς ἐπιγέννημα
γήρως . . . τὸ κατερρυσωμένον, τουτέστι τὸ δέρμα. καὶ
Σώφρων ἐν τοῖς ἀνδρείοις δεδήλωκε μίμοις εἰπών· [55]. τὸν
ἀνακρινόμενον γέροντα ξύσιλον παίζων εἴρηκεν ἀπὸ τοῦ
κνᾶσθαι καὶ ξύειν τὸ δέρμα, κἄπειτα ἀποκρινόμενον σ. ἀντ᾽
ἀ., δέρμα ψιλόν, ὡς τῶν ἄλλων ἤδη δεδαπανημένων

    Preceding words ξύσιλος τύ γ᾽ ἐσσί (or the like) Kaibel

56 καθαιρημένος θην καὶ τῆνος ὑπὸ τῶ χρόνω

Apoll. Dysc. pron. p.59.12 Δωριεῖς τῆνος [56]. Σώφρων

53 I'm scratching without strength; and the itch gallops
from head to foot

54 For hateful old age withers us and dries us up

55 ⟨You are scratchy.—⟩
What do you mean, scratchy?—What else?
Wrinkledness instead of a man

Etymologicum genuinum: "'suphar" not simply old age, but the result of old age . . . that which has become wrinkled, i.e. the skin. Sophron in the men's mimes has made this clear, saying [55]. He jokingly said the enquiring old man was scratchy from itching and scratching the skin, then replying wrinkledness instead of a man, dry skin, the rest having already been consumed'

56 So that man too is overpowered by time

Cf. Herodas 1.15–16

SOPHRON

Unnamed Men's Mimes

57 ὦ οὗτος, ἦ οἴηι στρατείαν ἐσσεῖσθαι;

Apoll. Dysc. pron. p.57.18 (οὗτος κατὰ τὸ δεύτερον πρόσωπον)
[57] Σώφρων ἀνδρείοις

58 οὐχ ὁ δεῖν τυ †επικαζε†

Apoll. Dysc. pron. p.59.21 ὁ δεῖνα . . . παρὰ δὲ Συρακουσίοις
δίχα τοῦ ᾱ· [58] Σώφρων ἀνδρείοις

ἐπε<κή>καζε; Cunningham (after Lobeck), ἐπύγιζε; Blomfield

59 Ἡρακλῆς τεοῦς κάρρων ἦς

Apoll. Dysc. pron. p.74.21 τῇ μὲν οὖν ἐμοῦ σύζυγος ἡ σοῦ . . .
καὶ τῇ ἐμοῦς Δωρίῳ ἡ τεοῦς· [59] Σώφρων

60 ὑμὲς δὲ ἐπεγγυάμενοι θωκεῖτε

Apoll. Dysc. pron. p.93.22 ὑμεῖς. Δωριεῖς ὑμές· [60] Σώφρων

61 ἐμὲ δ᾽ Ἀρχωνίδας ἴαλλε παρ᾽ ὑμέ

Apoll. Dysc. pron. p.100.10 ὑμᾶς . . . Δωριεῖς ὑμέ· [61]
ἀνδρείοις Σώφρων

MEN'S MIMES

Unnamed Men's Mimes

57 You there, do you think there will be a war?

58 Did not so and so revile/fuck you?

59 Heracles was stronger than you

The scholar Chamaeleon quoted this line to Seleucus I, when in 271 the king threatened an embassy from Heracleia Pontica, of which he was a member

60 All of you promise and sit down

61 Archonidas sent me to you

62 λιχνοτέρα τᾶν πορφυρᾶν

Athen. iii.89A Ἀπολλόδωρος δ' ὁ Ἀθηναῖος ἐν τοῖς περὶ
Σώφρονος (244 F 216 Jac.) προθεὶς τὸ [62] φησιν ὅτι παροιμία ἐστὶν καὶ λέγεται, ὡς μέν τινες, ἀπὸ τοῦ βάμματος· οὐ
γὰρ ἂν προσψαύσῃ ἕλκει ἐφ' ἑαυτὸ καὶ τοῖς παρατεθειμένοις
ἐμποιεῖ χρώματος αὐγήν. ἄλλοι δ' ἀπὸ τοῦ ζῴου

63 καταπυγοτέραν τ' ἀλφηστᾶν

Athen. vii.281E Ἀπολλόδωρος ὁ Ἀθηναῖος ἐν τῷ τρίτῳ περὶ
Σώφρονος τῷ εἰς τοὺς ἀνδρείους μίμους (244 F 214 Jac.)
προθεὶς τὸ [63] φησιν· "ἰχθῦς τινες οἱ ἀλφησταὶ τὸ μὲν ὅλον
κιρροειδεῖς, πορφυρίζοντες δὲ κατά τινα μέρη. φασὶ δὲ αὐτοὺς ἁλίσκεσθαι σύνδυο καὶ φαίνεσθαι τὸν ἕτερον ἐπὶ τοῦ
ἑτέρου κατ' οὐρὰν ἑπόμενον. ἀπὸ τοῦ οὖν κατὰ τὴν πυγὴν
θατέρῳ τὸν ἕτερον ἀκολουθεῖν τῶν ἀρχαίων τινὲς τοὺς
ἀκρατεῖς καὶ καταφερεῖς οὕτω καλοῦσιν"

64 κέστραι βότιν κάπτουσαι

Athen. vii.286D Σώφρων δ' ἐν μίμοις ἀνδρείοις βότιν καλεῖ
τινα ἰχθὺν ἐν τούτοις· [64]. καὶ μήποτε βοτάνην τινὰ λέγει;
id. vii.323A καὶ Σώφρων ἐν ἀνδρείοις· [64]

65, 66 see under Ὠλιεύς

67 Ἠπιάλης ὁ τὸν πατέρα πνίγων

Demetr. eloc. 156 ἐν δὲ τοῖς πράγμασι λαμβάνονται χάριτες
ἐκ παροιμίας. φύσει γὰρ χαρίεν πρᾶγμά ἐστιν παροιμία, ὡς
ὁ Σώφρων μὲν ἐπίης, ἔφη, ὁ τ. π. π.

 Ἠπιάλης from fr.68

62 (She is) more greedy than the purple fish

Athenaeus: 'Apollodorus of Athens in his work on Sophron, quoting [62], says that it is a proverb and is derived, some say, from the dye; for whatever it touches it draws to itself and creates the gleam of colour in what is placed beside it. Others derive from the creature'

63 (her) and more lecherous than coupling fish

Athenaeus: 'Apollodorus of Athens in his third book on Sophron, which deals with the men's mimes, quoting [63], says: "Alphestae are a kind of fish, on the whole yellowish but purplish in some parts. It is said that they are caught in pairs and appear to follow one after the other by the tail. Therefore from the fact that the one follows the other by the rump, some of the ancients so call the unrestrained and dissolute"'

64 Cestrae gulping down a botis

Athenaeus: 'Sophron in the men's mimes mentions a fish botis in [64]. And perhaps he means a plant'

67 Epiales who chokes his father

Demetrius, *On Style* 156: 'Among these things delights are taken from a proverb. For a proverb is a thing delightful by its nature, as Sophron says [67]'

Epiales (Epialos, Epialtes) was the name given to the cause of the choking sensation felt in some fevers (e.g Aristoph., *Wasps* 1037–9). Heracles is strong enough to overcome it (fr. 68; cf. fr. 59)

68 Ἡρακλῆς Ἠπιάλητα πνίγων

Eust. in Il. p.561.17 ἐν δὲ ῥητορικῷ λεξικῷ (Ael. Dion. η 12) φέρεται ὅτι Ἐπιάλτην Ἀττικοί φασι δαίμονά τινα . . . ἑτέρωθι δέ, ὅτι ἐπιάλτης ὁ πνιγαλίων ὑπό τινων, ὁ δ᾿ αὐτὸς καὶ ἠπίαλος. ἐν δὲ τοῖς Ἡρωδιανοῦ (i.69.13) κεῖται καὶ ἠπιάλης ἠπιάλητος, οὗ χρῆσις, φησί, παρὰ Σώφρονι, οἶον· [68]

69

Et. Gud. = Et. Orion. p. 101.30 μαστροπός· παρὰ τὸ μαίεσθαι τοὺς τρόπους τῶν πορνευουσῶν γυναικῶν. οὕτως ἐν ὑπομνήματι τῶν Σώφρονος ἀνδρείων

71 σῶσαι δ᾿ οὐδὲ τὰς δύο λίτρας δύναμαι

Poll. iv.174 (after fr. 36) καὶ πάλιν ἐν τοῖς ἀνδρείοις· [71]

72 Ἡράκλεις, πνίγεις γύλιόν τι

Schol. Ar. Pac. 527b (γύλιος) ἔστι δὲ καὶ ζῷον, οὗ μέμνηται Σώφρων· [72]. ἔστι δὲ ὁ καλούμενος ὑπό τινων χοιρογρύλλιος

*73 μωρότερος εἶ Μορύχου, ὃς τἄνδον ἀφεὶς ἔξω τᾶς οἰκίας κάθηται

Zenob. vulg. V 13 μωρότερος εἶ Μορύχου· αὕτη ἡ παροιμία λέγεται παρὰ τοῖς Σικελιώταις, ἐπί τῶν εὔηθές τι διαπρασ-

68 Heracles choking Epiales

Eustathius: 'In the rhetorical lexicon it is recorded that Attic writers call a certain demon Epialtes . . . and elsewhere, that Epialtes is the choker, also called Epialos. In the works of Herodian is found Epiales, genitive Epialetos, an example of which, he says, is in Sophron, as [68]'

69

Etymologicum Gudianum: 'procuress, derived from procuring the ways of women prostitutes. So in the commentary on Sophron's men's'

Doubtless Apollodorus' commentary. The word in the title of Herodas 1

71 I can't save even the two pence

Pollux: (after fr. 36) 'and again in the men's [71]'

72 Heracles, you're choking a hedgehog

Scholiast on Aristoph., *Peace* 527 (gylios, a soldier's wallet): 'It is also an animal, which Sophron mentions [72]; it is what is called by some choerogryllios'

Possibly 'Heracles' is vocative and there is a link with fr. 68; but it may be an exclamation (cf. fr. 134), and the dangerous feat is being done by someone else

*73 You're more stupid than Morychus, who sits outside the house neglecting affairs within

Zenobius: 'You are more stupid than Morychus. This proverb is current among Sicilians, about those who carry out some foolish

333

σομένων, ὥς φησι Πολέμων ἐν τῇ πρὸς Διόφιλον ἐπιστολῇ
(fr. 73). λέγεται δὲ οὕτως· [73]. Μόρυχος δὲ Διονύσου ἐπίθε-
τον ... καταγνωσθῆναι δὲ αὐτοῦ εὐήθειαν παρόσον ἔξω τοῦ
νεὼ τὸ ἄγαλμα αὐτοῦ ἐστι, παρὰ τῇ εἰσόδῳ ἐν ὑπαίθρῳ; sim.
Suda μ 1343 = Phot. μ 652, and (omitting ref. to Sicily and
Polemo) Zenob. Ath. III 68

Ascribed to Sophron by Ahrens   εἶ Zen., Sud.: εἰμι Phot.
(then κάθημαι Kaibel)   Μορ- Zen. vulg., Sud. codd. GM:
Μωρ- Zen. Ath., Sud. codd. AFV, Phot.

MIMES OF UNCERTAIN TYPE

74 πεῖ ἐσσι, λειοκόνιτε;

Ammon. adf. voc. diff. 423 (see fr. 4.8)

A variant reading in Ammon. is ποῖος εἰλισκοπεῖται: Kaibel,
knowing only this reading, ingeniously but wrongly corrected it to
πῦς Θεστυλί, σκοπῆι τύ; on the basis of the statement in the
argument to Theocr. 5, τὴν δὲ Θεστυλίδα ὁ Θεόκριτος
ἀπειροκάλως ἐκ τῶν Σώφρονος μετήνεγκε μίμων

75 see under Ταὶ γυναῖκες

77 ἐγὼν δέ τυ καὶ πάλαι ὤψεον

Apoll. Dysc. pron. p.50.9 Δωριεῖς ἐγών. Σώφρων· [77].
Choerob. in Theod. can. p.56.31 τὸ δὲ ὀψείω, ὅπερ σημαίνει τὸ
ἐπιθυμίαν ἔχω τοῦ θεωρῆσαι, ὀφεῖλον εἶναι ἐν τῷ παρα-
τατικῷ ὤψειον διὰ τῆς ει διφθόγγου, ἐπειδὴ καὶ ὁ ἐνεστὼς
τὴν ει δίφθογγον ἔχει κατὰ τὴν παραλήγουσαν, ἐγένετο

action, as Polemon says in his letter to Diophilus. It is stated thus [73]. Morychus is an epithet of Dionysus . . . His foolishness is proved inasmuch as his statue is outside the temple, beside the entrance in the open air'

The person of the first clause (you or I) is uncertain; that of the second may, but need not, be the same

MIMES OF UNCERTAIN TYPE

74 Where are you, total dust-heap?

77 I've long been wanting to see you

ὤψεον παρὰ Σώφρονι κατὰ ἀποβολὴν τοῦ ῑ, οἷον· [77], ἀντὶ
τοῦ ἐγὼ καὶ πάλαι ἐπεθύμουν θεωρῆσαι

τοι codd., corr. by Bekker

79 ἐκπεφάναντί τεος ταὶ δυσθαλίαι

Apoll. Dysc. pron. p.74.28 τῇ ἐμέος ἡ τέος κατ᾽ ἔγκλισιν
σύζυγος· [79]. Σώφρων. τὸ γὰρ ὀρθοτονούμενον κτητικὴν
σημαίνει

82 μόνον ἐμίνγα τὸ τοῦ γόγγρου τέμαχος

Apoll. Dysc. pron. p.81.20 Δωριεῖς ἐμίν καὶ ἔτι ἐμίνγα.
Σώφρων· [82]. Et. Gen. (EM 732.36) ἐπ᾽ αὐτοῦ δὲ τοῦ γε
τρέπεται (ε to α in Doric)· [82]

μόνον ἐμίνγα Apoll. Dysc., τοῦτό γα Et. Gen.

86 ὁ δ᾽ ἐκ τῶ σκότεος τοξεύων αἰὲν ἕνα τινὰ ὧν
  ζυγαστροφεῖ

Apoll. Dysc. pron. p.96.15 ἐν ἴσῳ τῷ αὐτῶν παρὰ Συρακουσίοις τίθεται τὸ ὧν. Σώφρων· [86]

87 ὅσα κα ὗμιν αἰνέσω

Apoll. Dysc. pron. p.97.28 ὑμῖν . . . παρ᾽ Ἴωσι ‹προ›περι-
σπᾶται ἐγκλινομένη, καθὸ συστέλλει τὸ ῑ. καὶ ἔτι παρὰ
Δωριεῦσιν· [87] Σώφρων

79 Your misfortunes have been displayed

82 Only the slice of eel for me

86 And he, shooting his arrow in the dark, always . . .
        some one of them

   The meaning of the verb is quite uncertain, and no proposed
correction is any better

87 What I should advise you

88 οὐ μάν τοι δίφρον ἐπημμένον ὑμίν

Apoll. Dysc. pron. p.98.1 (ὑμῖν, after fr. 87) καὶ ἐν ὀρθῇ τάσει·
[88]

91 τίς μοι τὰ λᾶια ἐκτίλλει;

Apoll. Dysc. adv. p.157.8 λήϊος, ἀφ᾽ οὗ λάϊος καὶ λάϊον καὶ
λάϊα καὶ ἐν συναιρέσει . . . τοῦ ᾶ λᾶια· [91]. Σώφρων

*93 ταυτᾶι ταὶ θύραι, μᾶτερ

Apoll. Dysc. adv. p.180.6 τὸ . . . οἱ τοί φασι Δωριεῖς, καὶ τὸ αἱ
ταί· [93]

Ascribed to Sophron by Bast, to the Women's Mimes by
Kaibel

94 ὕδωρ ἄκρατον εἰς τὰν κύλικα

Athen. ii.44B ὅτι καὶ ἐπὶ τοῦ ὕδατος ἔταττον οἱ παλαιοὶ τὸ
ἄκρατον. Σώφρων· [94]

Ascribed to the Θυννοθήρας (after fr.47) by Hauler

95 στρουθωτὰ ἑλίγματα ἐντετιμημένα

Athen. ii.48C Σώφρων δὲ σ. ἑλ. φησιν ἐν.

88 Not indeed a chair laid hold of by you

91 Who's stripping my crops?

Perhaps cf. fr. 167

*93 Here are the seats, mother

94 Neat water into the cup

Athenaeus: 'The ancients used 'neat' also in relation to water. Sophron [94]'

95 Bird-adorned, highly valued wraps

SOPHRON

96 μελαινίδες γάρ τοι νισοῦνται ἐμὶν ἐκ τοῦ μικροῦ
λιμένος

Athen. iii.86A παρὰ Σώφρονι δὲ {οἱ} κόγχοι μελαινίδες
λέγονται· [96]

Ascribed to Ὡλιεύς by Kaibel

99 βόες δὲ λαρινεύονται

Athen. ix.376B λαρινεύεσθαι, ὅπερ ἐστὶν σιτίζεσθαι, Σώφρων
[99]

100 κατάστρεψον, τέκνον, τὰν ἡμίναν

Athen. xi.479B (ἡμίνα = κοτύλη) καὶ Σώφρων· [100]

101 ἐκρατηρίχθημες

Athen. xi.504B (κρατηρίζειν) καὶ ὁ τοὺς μίμους δὲ πεποιηκώς
. . . λέγει που κηκρατηριχημες ἀντὶ τοῦ πεπώκειμεν

Corr. by Wackernagel

***103** φαλακρότερος εὐδίας

Demetr. eloc. 127 τοῦ δὲ αὐτοῦ εἴδους (τῆς ὑπερβολῆς) ἐστὶ
καὶ τὸ [103] καὶ τὸ κολοκύντης ὑγιέστερος (cf. fr.33)

96 For black shells come to me from the Little Harbour

One of the two harbours of Syracuse

99 The cattle are being fattened

100 Turn the cup over, child

101 We've been bottled

Athenaeus: 'The author of the mimes says somewhere [101] instead of "we are drunk"'

***103** Balder than a calm

Demetrius, *On Style* 127: 'Of the same kind (of hyperbole) are [103] and "healthier than a gourd"'

104

Demetr. eloc. 153 ἤδη μέντοι ἐκ δύο τόπων ἐνταῦθα ἐγένετο ἡ
χάρις· οὐ γὰρ παρὰ προσδοκίαν μόνον ἐπηνέχθη, ἀλλ' οὐδ'
ἠκολούθει τοῖς προτέροις. ἡ δὲ τοιαύτη ἀνακολουθία καλεῖται γρῖφος, ὥσπερ ὁ παρὰ Σώφρονι ῥητορεύων Βουλίας·
οὐδὲν γὰρ ἀκόλουθον αὐτῷ λέγει. καὶ παρὰ Μενάνδρῳ δὲ ὁ
πρόλογος τῆς Μεσσηνίας

105 ἐκ τοῦ ὄνυχος γὰρ τὸν λέοντα ἔγραψεν. τορύναν
   ἔξεσεν. κύμινον ἔπρισεν

Demetr. eloc. 156 (χάριτες ἐκ παροιμίας, after fr. 67) καὶ
ἀλλαχόθι πού φησιν· [105]. καὶ γὰρ δυσὶ παροιμίαις καὶ
τρισὶν ἐπαλλήλοις χρῆται, ὡς ἐπιπληθύωνται αὐτῷ αἱ χάρι-
τες· σχεδόν τε πάσας ἐκ τῶν δραμάτων αὐτοῦ τὰς παροιμίας
ἐκλέξαι ἔστιν

ἔσπειρεν cod., corr. Hemsterhuys

****106** λαδρέοντι δὲ τοὶ μυκτῆρες

Epimer. Hom. δ 78 (from Herodian, Π. παθῶν, cf. Et. Gen. λ 8)
. . . καὶ τὸ παρὰ τῷ Συρακουσίῳ [106]. ἔγκειται γὰρ τὸ λ‹α›
ἐπιτατικὸν ‹καὶ τὸ› ῥέω, ‹λα›ρέοντι ἀντὶ τοῦ μεγάλως
ῥέουσι (πλεονασμῷ τοῦ δ added in Et. Gen.)

Ascribed to Sophron by Ahrens   πλαδαρέοντι Wilamowitz

115 see under Ταὶ γυναῖκες

104

Demetrius, *On Style* 153: 'Now however here (in Aristophanes, *Clouds* 178–9) the delight has come from two places: for not only is it introduced unexpectedly, but it is not even consistent with what goes before. Such lack of consistency is called "griphos," as Boulias who makes a speech in Sophron; for he says nothing that is self-consistent. And in Menander the prologue of the *Messenia*'

Cf. Battarus in Herodas 2

105 For he drew the lion from the nail. He polished the ladle. He bit the cummin.

Demetrius, *On Style* 156: (delights from a proverb, after fr. 67) 'And elsewhere he says [105]. For he uses two and three proverbs after each other, so that the delights are multiplied; and it is possible to pick almost all proverbs from his dramas'

*106 His/her nostrils are running

Sophron is also recorded as using an unusual word ($\pi\lambda\acute{\epsilon}\nu\nu\alpha$) meaning 'discharge from the nose' (fr. 144)

SOPHRON

121 πῶ τις ὄνον ὠνασεῖται;

Et. Orion. p.137.12 τὰ τῷ ō παραληγόμενα ἐπιρρήματα ἀποκοπῇ τοῦ θεν καὶ ἐπεκτάσει τοῦ ō εἰς ω γίνεται παρὰ
Δωριεῦσιν, οἷον . . . πόθεν πῶ. Σώφρων ἐν τοῖς μίμοις· [121];
sim. Et. Gen., Apoll. Dysc. adv. p.190.21

122 κινησῶ δ᾽ ἤδη καὶ τὸν ἀφ᾽ ἱαρᾶς

Suet. ap. Eust. in Il. p.633.59 παροιμία κινεῖν τὸν ἀφ᾽ ἱερᾶς ἐπὶ
τῶν ἐν ἀπογνώσει δεομένων βοηθείας ἐσχάτης. χρῆσις δὲ
ταύτης καὶ παρὰ Σώφρονι ἐν τῷ [122], ἔνθα λείπει τὸ πεσσὸν
ἢ λίθον

124 δειπνήσας ὠστίζεται τοῖς τρηματιζόντεσσι

Eust. in Od. p.1397.22 λέγει δὲ ὁ ταῦτα παραδιδοὺς (Suet.) καὶ
ὡς οἱ τῇ παιδιᾷ ταύτῃ (κυβείᾳ) χρώμενοι ἀπὸ τῶν ἐν τοῖς
κύβοις τρημάτων τρηματῖται ἐλέγοντο, παράγων καὶ χρῆσιν
Σώφρονος τὸ [124]

Suet., Poll., Hesych. have τρηματίκται, which Kaibel thinks
occurred in Sophron

134 Ἡράκυλον

Hesych. η 855 Ἡρύκαλον· τὸν Ἡρακλέα Σώφρων ὑποκορι-
στικῶς

Corr. by Latte; ⟨μὰ τὸν⟩ Ἡ. Crusius

121 From where will one buy an ass?

122 I shall now move also the (piece) from the holy
         (line)

Suetonius in Eustathius: 'the proverb "move the piece from the
holy line" on those who in despair need the utmost help. An example of it also in Sophron in [122], where "piece" or "stone" is to be
understood'

The reference is to a board game where the central line was
called 'holy'; rules and object are obscure

124 After dinner he jostles among the pippers

Eustathius: 'The recorder of these matters (Suetonius) says also
that those who play this game (dice) are called "pippers" from the
pips in the dice, adducing an example from Sophron [124]'

134 ⟨By (?)⟩ little Heracles

SOPHRON

*136 νῦν τ᾽ ἦνθες εἰς χορόν, νῦν τ᾽ ἔπραδες

Hesych. ν 734 [136]· νῦν εἰς χορὸν ἦλθες, καὶ νῦν ἔπαρδες.
Suda ν 606 [136]

Ascribed to Sophron by Kaibel   ἐς κόρον Meineke

139 πεῖ εἶ; — εἶ τὰ τῶν χοιραγχᾶν

Ioann. Alex. De accent. p.32.14 [139] Σώφρων (followed by fr.
4.8). Apoll. Dysc. in several places quotes the second half of the
line without author

147 αἴ τις τὸν ξύοντα ἀντιξύει

ὁ χοραγὸς ξύεται

Suda ξ 91 = Phot. p.310.12 τὸ κνῆν οἱ Δωριεῖς ξύειν λέγουσιν,
ὡς καὶ Σώφρων [147.1] καὶ πάλιν [147.2]

152 τὰς ἐν Ἅιδου τριακάδας

Prov. Par. in Corp. Paroem. Graec. Suppl. i.71 [152] . . . λεχθείη
δ᾽ ἂν ἡ παροιμία ἐπὶ τῶν περιέργων καὶ τὰ ἀποκεκρυμμένα
ζητούντων γινώσκειν. ταῦτα καὶ παρὰ Σώφρονι ἐν μίμοις

154 τῆτέ τοι· κορῶναί εἰσιν

Schol. Ar. Ach. 204a(i) (τῇ) σημαίνει δέ ποτε καὶ ῥῆμα
προστακτικόν . . . ἐχρήσατο δὲ καὶ τῷ πληθυντικῷ ὁ Σώφρων
εἰπών [154]

346

*136 Now you went to the dance, and now you farted

Cf. anonymous mime no.6 below

139 Where are you?—Where the pork-butchers' shops
are

147 If one scratches the scratcher in return

The producer is scratched

'Mutual back-scratching' is the English equivalent, but the
Greek may be used of harm as well as benefit

152 The thirtieths in Hell

Proverb collection: '[152] . . . the proverb would be said of busy-
bodies and those seeking to know what is hidden. This also in
Sophron in mimes'

154 Here they are; they are crows

Possibly one of the crow-shaped objects so named rather than
birds (Sophron used it of hair ornaments, fr. 162)

SOPHRON

156 ἰλλοτέρα τᾶν κορωνᾶν

Schol. Ar. Thesm. 846 (ἰλλός) τυφλός, διεστραμμένος τὴν ὄψιν. Σώφρων· [156]. Gal. in Hipp. epid. 3 τὸ ἰλλός, ἀφ' οὗ καὶ ὁ Σώφρων δοκεῖ πεποιηκέναι τὸ συγκριτικὸν ὀνομαζόμενον παρὰ τῶν γραμματικῶν· [156]

ἰλλοτερά sch. Ar., ἰλλότερον Gal.   τᾶν κορώναν sch. Ar., τὰν κύονα Gal.

158 see under Ταὶ συναριστῶσαι

165 see under Ταὶ γυναῖκες

167

Tzetz. ad Ar. Ran. 516 κἄρτι παρατετιλμέναι· νεοξυρεῖς τὸν δορίαλον, τὸ μύτον, τὸν χοῖρον, τὸν κύσθον, καὶ ὅσα τοιαῦτα ὁ Σώφρων καὶ ὁ Ἱππῶναξ καὶ ἕτεροι λέγουσι

168 μοῖτον ἀντὶ μοίτου

Varr. De ling. Lat. v.179 si datum quod reddatur, mutuum, quod Siculi moetum: itaque scribit Sophron [168]. Hesych. μ 1557 [168]· παροιμία Σικελοῖς. ἡ γὰρ χάρις μοῖτον· οἷον χάριν ⟨ἀντὶ χάριτος⟩

moeton antimo Varr., μοιτοὶ ἄντιμοι Hesych., corr. Huschke and Kaibel

156 More squinting than the crows

Cf. Herodas 4.70–1

167

Tzetzes on Aristoph., *Frogs* 516 (women just plucked) 'newly shaved in the spear, the dummy, the pig, the cunt, and similar words used by Sophron, Hipponax and others'

Cf. Herodas 2.68–70

168 Like for like

Varro, *Latin Language*: 'If what is to be returned is given, it is *mutuum*, "like," which the Sicilians call *moeton*; and so Sophron writes [168].' Hesychius: '[168] a proverb among the Sicilians. For *moeton* means favour; so "favour for favour"'

SOPHRON

169

Zenob. Ath. I 58 ἀληθέστερα τῶν ἐπὶ Σάγραι· ταύτης (τῆς παροιμίας) μέμνηται Μένανδρος (fr.32) καὶ Σώφρων καὶ Ἄλεξις (fr.306)

*170

A Sicilian proverb, γραῦς ἔριθος (or ἔριφος or σέριφος), of an old maid, connected with grasshoppers, was discussed by Apollodorus, prob. in his comm. on Sophron. Zenob. vulg. II 94, Suda γ 431, Schol. Theocr. 10.18a

169

Zenobius: 'Truer than events at Sagra. This (proverb) is mentioned by Menander, Sophron, and Alexis'

Sagra was a river in South Italy, site of a victory of Locri over Croton in the sixth century, reports of which were not believed at Sparta

POPULAR MIME

EDITED AND TRANSLATED BY
I. C. CUNNINGHAM

INTRODUCTION

The popular mime in ancient Greece, succinctly described by an anonymous Greek source quoted by the Roman grammarian Diomedes[1] as 'imitation of life comprising both what is acceptable and what is unacceptable' (μίμησις βίου τά τε συγκεχωρημένα καὶ ἀσυγχώρητα περιέχων), was almost always subliterary (the exception is Sophron) and the subject of strong disapproval by literary critics and moralists alike. It is not surprising that few actual fragments of it have survived, and in fact (again excluding Sophron) no more than sixteen papyrus texts, of varying length, have been with any plausibility assigned to mimes.

It is scarcely possible to assign these accurately to the various genres mentioned in ancient sources, mime, magodia, hilarodia, etc., some in prose, some in verse; and some have but a weak claim to be included at all. The sixteen fragments are here arranged chronologically by the date of writing (which can be assumed in this instance to be close to that of composition), as in the appendix to my Teubner edition of Herodas (1987), with the addition of one (3a) first published after that edition was completed. A fuller bibliography and apparatus will be found there.

[1] Keil, *Gramm. Lat.* i.491; Kaibel, *Com. Graec. Fragm.*, i.61.

A brief description of the source and content of each of these pieces follows.

1 A papyrus of the 2nd century B.C., published by B. P. Grenfell (*An Alexandrian Erotic Fragment and Other Greek Papyri*, 1896: P.Grenf. 1 v.). It contains a dramatic monologue by a young girl, in love but deserted by her lover. It is in verse (not divided by metra in the papyrus; hence only in its first column, lines 1–40, where the text is complete, can the structure be determined): dactyls, iambics, dochmiacs, anapaests in various combinations; a full list, based on analyses by Wilamowitz and West, may be found in the Teubner edition.

2 From a papyrus anthology of about 100 B.C., published in *The Tebtunis Papyri* (vol. 1, 1902: P.Tebt. 2d v., ed. B. P. Grenfell, A. S. Hunt, J. G. Smyly). That there are several speakers is indicated by paragraphi, but how many there are and how the lines are to be distributed among them is unclear. The subject again is thwarted love.

3 This incomplete text is inscribed on an ostracon of the 2nd or 1st century B.C., published by O. Reinach (*Papyrus Grecs et Démotiques*, vol. 1, 1905: O.Rein.1). There are two speakers, one of whom is drunk and in love.

3a From a papyrus which has other scraps in the same hand mentioning the year 48–49 A.D., published in *The Oxyrhynchus Papyri* (vol. 53, 1986: P.Oxy. 3700, ed. M. W. Haslam). The text is a dialogue; one speaker is indicated as ETE( ) or ETEP( ) (lines 6, 7), presumably meaning 'The Other', another by an uncertain abbreviation (line 14); the symbol ∪ which precedes these may be musical, cf. no. 6 below, or indicate the change of speaker. A man seems to visit a woman (comparing himself to Heracles visiting Omphale), but details are very obscure. Several lines are iambic trimeters.

4 A papyrus in a cursive hand, found among documents of the 1st century A.D., published in *The Oxyrhynchus Papyri* (vol. 2, 1899: P.Oxy. 219, ed. B. P. Grenfell, A. S. Hunt). The speaker laments the loss of his fighting cock which has apparently yielded to the attractions of a hen. Some scholars claim to see traces of metre, but no conclusion has been reached on this.

5 A papyrus written at Heptacomia in 117 A.D., published by E. Kornemann (*Griechische Papyri zu Giessen*, 1910: P.Giss. 3). The god Phoebus announces the succession of the emperor Hadrian, and this is welcomed by a spokesman of the people. This was possibly the introduction to some kind of performance.

6 From the recto, with col. 4 of the verso, of a papyrus written in the mid 2nd century A.D., published in *The Oxyrhynchus Papyri* (vol. 3, 1903: P.Oxy.413, ed. B. P. Grenfell, A. S. Hunt; edition by Stefania Santelia, *Charition liberata*, Bari, 1991). The text, apparently incomplete at the beginning, is of a mime, but it is not the full text, rather a summary which would be expanded in performance; possibly, given the frequency of musical notes, it was the musician's copy. The verso column, written rather later, gives a fuller version of lines 30–50. The plot concerns a Greek girl, Charition, who has been captive in an Indian temple and is rescued by her brother; it resembles in many ways the *Iphigenia in Tauris* and *Helen* of Euripides, and also the adventures of Odysseus in *Odyssey* 9; the difference of genre is typified by the presence of a buffoon who routs the Indians by farting and giving them neat wine. The Greek speakers are indicated by letters: A

(Charition), B (buffoon), Γ (Charition's brother), Δ (ship's captain), and ⵝ (lookout); while some Indians are treated likewise—Z and ⵝ are women—most are more explicitly indicated: ΒΑΣ(ιλεύς), ΓΥΝ(ή), ΑΛ(λη), and ΚΟΙ(νῇι). Stage directions and musical notes occur throughout (not distinguished in the papyrus; italicised in the translation below). The Indians speak in their own tongue; although this has been shown to have affinities to real languages, it is probably largely an *ad hoc* construct, intended to amuse the audience rather than be understood by them; and no attempt to translate it has been made. The Indian king, at least, also speaks Greek, and indeed when drunk declaims in sotadean verse (lines 88–91). The finale is in iambic and trochaic verse (lines 96–106).

7   The text on columns 1–3 of the verso of the same papyrus which preserves no. 6 above. Again it is a mime in an abbreviated form, for use by the cast: apart from the last scene, we have only the words of the principal, female, character; in that scene those only of two male characters. In the papyrus each speech, represented below as a paragraph, is concluded by an oblique line. Lacking the other scripts, we must guess at what was said or done between each speech. The divisions into scenes are inferred from the text. Some of the characters are unnamed: the mistress and master of the household, and the parasite; the slaves Aesopus and Apollonia, Spinther and Malacus are mentioned by name. The main outline of the plot is clear, though many details are obscure because of the nature of our text; it bears a strong resemblance to that of Herodas 5. The mistress has been rejected by Aesopus in favour of Apollonia. In the first scene she rails against him, and orders the pair to be taken away and killed. Next it seems that

they have escaped, but the girl is recaptured; Aesopus is to be sought and killed. Then he is present, seemingly dead. Next she announces a plan to poison the 'old man' (presumably her husband) and sell the property; the parasite is to be summoned for discussion. He comes (along with a covered-up man and woman, doubtless Aesopus and Apollonia) and is told to fetch the old man for a reconciliation and lunch. Malacus is praised for preparing the poison; the parasite behaves strangely. The final dialogue between the parasite, Spinther, and the master appears to show that the plot has been discovered; someone (Malacus?) is to go the stocks; others (Aesopus and Apollonia?) are safe. The fate of the mistress is unknown.

8   A papyrus written towards the end of the 2nd century A.D., published by H. J. M. Milne (*Catalogue of Literary Papyri in the British Museum*, 1927: P.Lit.Lond. 51 v.), who characterised it as the 'rough illiterate cursive hand of an unintelligent scribe'. The text is a lament, perhaps by a mother for her son; but others have thought it to be mythological (the Sun for Phaethon, or a series of goddesses for their mortal sons). It may be a school exercise.

9   A papyrus written in a cursive hand in the 2nd century A.D., published in *Catalogue of the Greek Papyri in the John Rylands Library* (vol. 1, 1911: P.Ryl. 15 v., ed. A. S. Hunt). It seems to be in verse, possibly ionics. The very fragmentary text is a lament by a woman for a gladiator.

10   A papyrus of the 2nd century A.D., written (?) by Heraclides and owned by Prasias, published by A. Koerte (*Archiv für Papyrusforschung* 6, 1913, 1: P.Lit.Lond. 97). It is in many respects similar to no. 6 above. Only the end survives, apparently a recognition scene of the type famil-

iar from New Comedy, where a supposed courtesan is shown to be the lost daughter of a citizen. The characters are designated as A (female), B (buffoon?), Γ ('father Ion'), Δ (male), and KOI(νῆι). There is a stage direction *Finale* (line 16), in the papyrus not distinguished from the text. This and no. 13 below recall the statement of Aristoxenus (fr. 110) that magodia adopted plots from comedy.

11   A papyrus of the 2nd century A.D., published by G. Manteuffel (*Papyri Varsovienses*, 1935: P.Varsov. 2). No connected text remains. There are two character designations, E and B, which led the first editor to conclude that this is a mime (cf. nos. 6, 10, 12); but this method is now known from other genres.

12   A papyrus of the 2nd century A.D., published by G. Manteuffel (*De Opusculis Graecis Aegypto e Papyris, Ostracis, Lapidibusque Collectis*, 1930, no. 16: P.Berol. 13876). There is only slightly more text than in no. 11, but also slightly more justification for thinking it to be from a mime. There were many characters, but only A and Γ appear singly in what survives, while ς, Z, and H speak one line together. Γ possibly quotes Homer: 36–7 ἀλλὰ τὰ μὲν πρ[οτετύχθαι ἐάσομεν] ἀχνύμενοί π[ερ] (*Iliad* 18.112, 19.65).

13   A papyrus written in a cursive hand in the 3rd century A.D., published by H. J. M. Milne (*Catalogue of Literary Papyri in the British Museum*, 1927: P.Lit.Lond. 52). It is in verse: the papyrus is written in long lines, with the verses marked by a diagonal line: 1–7 anapaests (partly ἀπόκροτα, where the final foot is ∪–), 8–12 either ionic or iambic, 13–17 hexameters μείουροι (where again the final foot is ∪–). Changes of speaker are not indicated; it is pos-

sible that they coincide with change of metre. A girl begs to be left alone; her brother and nurse plead with her to tell them whatever it is that is troubling her; a young man's conduct is described. It is a reasonable inference that she is pregnant as a result of meeting the youth at a παννυχίς; parallels with New Comedy plots, e.g. Menander's *Epitrepontes*, are readily found (cf. above on 10).

14   A papyrus of the 4th century A.D., published in *Papiri della Società Italiana* (vol. 2, 1913: P.S.I. 149, ed. G. Vitelli). The texts on recto and verso are in different metres (iambic and dactylic) but in the same hand; some have thought they are parts of one piece, others that they are separate (perhaps tragedy and epic).

15   A papyrus of the 5th century A.D., published by G. Manteuffel (*De Opusculis Graecis Aegypto e Papyris, Ostracis, Lapidibusque Collectis*, 1930, no.17: P.Berol. 13927). It contains a list of titles of seven mimes; then the props required for another one and for these seven; a unique, if fitful, light is cast on the staging of these performances. The orthography has been corrected to classical norms.

POPULAR MIME FRAGMENTS

1

ἐξ ἀμφοτέρων γέγον᾽ αἵρεσις·
ἐζευγνίσμεθα· τῆς φιλίης Κύπρις
ἔστ᾽ ἀνάδοχος. ὀδύνη μ᾽ ἔχει,
ὅταν ἀναμνησθῶ
5 ὥς με κατεφίλει 'πιβούλως μέλλων
με καταλιμπάν[ει]ν
ἀκαταστασίης εὑρετὴς
καὶ ὁ τὴν φιλίην ἐκτικώς.
ἔλαβέ μ᾽ ἔρως,
10 οὐκ ἀπαναίναμαι, αὐτὸν ἔχουσ᾽ ἐν τῆι διανοίαι.
ἄστρα φίλα καὶ συνερῶσα πότνια νύξ μοι
παράπεμψον ἔτι με νῦν πρὸς ὃν ἡ Κύπρις
ἔκδοτον ἄγει με καὶ ὁ
πολὺς ἔρως παραλαβών.
15 συνοδηγὸν ἔχω τὸ πολὺ πῦρ
τὸ ἐν τῆι ψυχῆι μου καιόμενον.
ταῦτά μ᾽ ἀδικεῖ, ταῦτά μ᾽ ὀδυνᾶι.
ὁ φρεναπάτης,
ὁ πρὸ τοῦ μέγα φρονῶν, καὶ ὁ τὴν Κύπριν οὐ
20 φάμενος εἶναι τοῦ ἐρᾶν μεταιτίαν

362

POPULAR MIME FRAGMENTS

1

The choice was made by both:
we were united; Aphrodite
is surety for our love. Pain holds me,
when I remember
how he kissed me while treacherously intending   5
to leave me,
inventor of inconstancy
and creator of love.
Desire has seized me,
I do not deny it, having him in my thoughts.   10
Loving stars and Lady Night who shares desire with me,
escort me even now to him to whom Aphrodite
delivers and drives me, and the
great desire that has taken hold of me.
As guide I have the great fire   15
that burns in my heart.
These things hurt me, these things pain me.
The mind-deceiver,
he who formerly had high thoughts, and he who denies that
    Aphrodite
shares responsibility for desire,   20

οὐκ ἤνεγκε νῦν
τὴν τυχοῦσαν ἀδικίην.
μέλλω μαίνεσθαι· ζῆλος γάρ μ' ἔχει,
καὶ κατακα<ί>ομαι καταλελειμένη.
25 αὐτὸ δὲ τοῦτ[ό] μοι τοὺς στεφάνους βάλε,
οἷς μεμονωμένη χρωτισθήσομαι.
κύριε, μή μ' ἀφῆις ἀποκεκλειμένην·
δέξαι μ'· εὐδοκῶ ζήλωι δουλεύειν.
†ἐπιμανουσοραν† μέγαν ἔχει πόνον.
30 ζηλοτυπεῖν γὰρ δεῖ, στέγειν, καρτερεῖν.
ἐὰν δ' ἑνὶ προσκάθει μόνον ἄφρων ἔσει.
ὁ γὰρ μονιὸς ἔρως μαίνεσθαι ποιεῖ.
γίνωσχ' ὅτι θυμὸν ἀνίκητον ἔχω
ὅταν ἔρις λάβηι με· μαίνομ' ὅταν ἀναμ[νή]σωμ'
35 εἰ μονοκοιτήσω,
σὺ δὲ χρωτίζεσθ' ἀποτρέχεις.
νῦν ἂν ὀργισθῶμεν, εὐθὺ δεῖ
καὶ διαλύεσθαι.
οὐχὶ διὰ τοῦτο φίλους ἔχομεν
40 οἳ κρινοῦσι τίς ἀδικεῖ;
νῦν [ἂ]ν μὴ ἐπι[
ἐρῶ, κύριε, τὸν [
νῦν μὲν ουθε[
πλυτης ο[
45 δυνήσομαι [
κοίτασον ἧς ἐχ[
ἱκανῶς σου εν[
κύριε, πῶς μ' α.[

has not now borne
the present hurt.
I am about to go mad; for jealousy holds me,
and I am burning at being deserted.
For this very reason throw the garlands to me,   25
with which I shall be bedded in my loneliness.
My lord, do not exclude me and put me away;
receive me; I accept to be a slave to jealousy.
To be madly in love (?) brings great trouble.
For one must be jealous, conceal, endure.   30
And if you devote yourself to only one man, you will be
     senseless.
For single-minded desire makes one mad.
Recognise that I have an undefeated spirit
when strife takes me: I am mad when I remember
that I shall sleep alone,   35
while you go off to be bedded.
Now if we have quarrelled, we must at once
also be reconciled.
Is it not for this that we have friends
who will judge who is at fault?   40
Now if not [
I desire, my lord, the [
now [
     [
I shall be able [45
sleep with whom [
sufficiently of you [
my lord, how [do you put] me away [

50 πρῶτος μεπειρ[
κύρι᾽ ὃν ἀτυχῶς ου[ͺ] ͺ[
ὀπυασθώμεθ᾽ ἐμὴν [ͺ ͺ]εδε[ἐπι-
τηδείως αἰσθέσθω μ[ͺ ͺ]ταν[
ἐγὼ δὲ μέλλω ζηλοῦν τω[
55 δουλ[ͺ ͺ ͺ ͺ]ταν διαφορου. η[
ἀνθρ[ωπο ͺ]ς ἀκριτῶς θαυμάζεις [
με ͺ[   ] ͺ[ͺ]φ[ͺ]ρη. προσίκου δω[
θαν[μα   ] ͺχριαν κατεῖδεν ο[
σχω[   ]τωι τοιͺντͺα η ετυ[
60 κου[ἐ]νόσησα νηπία· σὺ δέ, κύρ[ιε
και[   ]μμεν ͺ[
λελαλ[ηκ   ]ριεμη ͺ[

---

7 Alternatively punctuate after εὑρετής (Maas)
10 ἀπαναίνομαι Schroeder   19 καὶ deleted by West to improve
metre   20 μ᾽ ἐρᾶν West   28 ζηλῶ Scott   29 ἐπιμανῶς
ἐρᾶν Diels, Rohde   34 ἔρως Vollgraff   48/9 (verse formerly
divided after κύριε) ἀφ[ῆις, 50 μ᾽ ἐπείρ[ασας Crusius
62 πε]ρὶ ἐμὴν [ψυχήν Powell, κύ]ριε, μή μ᾽ [ἀφῆις Manteuffel

2

—   ] ͺ ͺ[
—   ] ͺονπ ͺ[
—   ] ͺ ͺ ͺ[ͺ] ͺ[
            ] ͺω κυριατ[ͺ] ͺ[
5 —   ]ν φίλων   [
            ] ͺ μὴ σχεῖν ετ[

366

you were the first to seduce me [50
my lord, whom unfortunately [
that we be married my [
let him fittingly perceive [
but I am going to be jealous [
slave[ ] different [55
men uncritically you admire [
approach [
admir[ ] he(?) saw [
    [
I was sick like a child; but you, my lord, [60
   [
spoke [

2

[_
[_
[_
        ] my lord/lady [
[_   ] of friends [5
        ] not to have [

].[.]....ακις μονοκ[ο]ι[τ

].με..[.].α[.]ες   [

π]αράκυψον ἱκετῶ Κλευπατ[ρ

10   ].ν..ον απηλιτριωμεν δοκ[

].τα μεταπεσεῖν ἀδύ(νατον) μή μου.[

]...πέπλευκας μετα[

...(   )..καὶ απλι(   ) αρυ(   )[

ἐρῶ μαίνομαι κατ‹έ›αγμαι εμ[

15 —   κρο(ῦσον) τὰς θύρα(ς) μὴ μέγα φωνεῖ τ.[

—   ἐξαναστατοῦμαι καὶ π.[

—   δός μοι τὸν τρίβω(να) καὶ β.ν.ε.[

κύριε καθεύδεις κα[.].[

—   ἐγὼ δὲ στρέφομαι καὶ ...[

20 —   μεθύων ἔρχεται ὁ μέγα..[

ὁ κελεης σου γέμει καλεῖ καὶ [

1–3, 5 Presence of paragraphi shown by greater line spacing
7 πολλάκις ed. pr., τοσουτάκις Crusius   9 Κλευπάτ[ρα ed.
pr., Κλεύπατ[ρε Crusius   11 π[ειρῶ Crusius   14 Correction by
Crusius   21 Perhaps κέλης

3

A.   γ]έγονεν μεθύων κατα τρο-

]μων. πρόσεχε, πρόσεχε.

B.   ]ν Ναΐδες ἁβρόσφυροι

]ὑπὸ γὰρ τῶν πολλῶν προπόσεων

5   ]λλομαι.

A.   ].ν. B. ἐπὶ δέ τινα κῶμον ὁπλίζομαι

] often sleep alone [
            ]
    ] look, I beg you, Cleopat[ra/ros
            ]   10
        ] impossible to change, do not [
        ] you have sailed [
                    [
    I am in love, I am mad, I am broken [
—   Knock at the door, do not shout [15
—   I am driven out and [
—   Give me the old cloak and [
    my lord, you are asleep [
—   But I am turning and [
—   Drunk, the great [   ] is going[20
    your horse groans, calls and [

                    3

[A.   ] he has become, drunk [
[   ] Look, look.
[B.   ] neat-ankled Naiads [
[   ] for from many toasts
        I am [falling].   5
[A.   ]. B. I'm armed for some revel.

φ]ιλίης ἔχω τι παρὰ Κυπρίδος ἄδηλον

]ς ὁ γόης εἰς τὴν ψυχήν μου εἰσπε-

σὼν   ]ε παραφρονεῖν.

10 A.   ].ρα σαυτοῦ κράτει μή τι πάθηις.

     B.   ].ι μή με περίσπα. ὁμολογῶ φιλεῖν ἐρᾶν

          ]δικω οὐ πάντες ἁπλῶς τὸ Παφίης

          ] ἐν ἀκρήτωι μᾶλλον ἀνακέκαυκέ με

           ]....μου......ως οἷς οὐκ ἀντι-

. . . .

1–2 τρόπον Reinach   2 εὐθ]υμῶν Crusius, ὀρχεῖσθαι
ἐπιθ]υμῶν Wilamowitz   5 σφά]λλομαι Wilamowitz
7 κέντρον φ]ιλίης Reinach   8 ἔρω]ς Cunningham   9 ποιεῖ
μ]ε or ἐποίησ]ε Reinach   12 τί δ' ἀ]δικῶ Wilamowitz
14–15 ἀντι[σχεῖν Reinach, then ἔξεστι Beazley

3a

     ].ς Ἡρακλέα νικηφόρον

     ] Ὀμφάλης θῆλυν λάτριν

     ]την θύραν.

     ] δᾶιδα φαῖνε. τίνα βλέπω;

5   ] ΕΤΕ( ) οὐκ οἶδασημα..ερ[

     ]ν θέλει. ∪ κατάμαθ' ἀκρ.[

     ]με. ∪ ΕΤΕΡ( ) ἀγνοῶ.

     ]ς ὅ ποτε λαμπρός σου φίλ[ος

     ].η ταῖς θύραις ὅθεν παρει[

10   ]ε.ω μὴ λάβηις ὕβριν ταλ[

     ] πάλιν ὅπου μοι..[.]εις εἰδου[

I have an unclear [goad] to love from Aphrodite.
[Desire] the magician has fallen on my heart
and [made me] insane.
[A.   ] get control of yourself lest you come to some harm.   10
[B.   ] don't divert me. I admit I'm in love and full of desire.
[But what am I doing] wrong? Do not all simply [   ] the
       [   ] of Aphrodite?
[   ] in neat wine [ ] has kindled me more [
[   ] which [cannot be] resisted

3a

] victorious Heracles [
] female servant of Omphale [
] door. [
] show a torch. Whom do I see? [
] OTHER. I do not know you (*or*: You do not know us) [5
] is willing. Learn [exactly
] OTHER. I don't know [
] your once distinguished friend [
] (at?) the doors whence appear[
] I [wish] that you should not take violence [10
] again where [

] ἄκουσόν μοι ἵνα μὴ φανῇις
] δός μοι φίλημα κα[ὶ] ὑγίαινε
]ν ἐκποδών. ∪ ( ) ἰδού. ὔ.
15] ἀσυμπαθῆ μή τί μοι λέγεις
]ελήθης ὅταν ἀπέλθω
]υλεῦσαι.
]. ἄνδρες, ἰταμὸς των δύο
]ς πτωχὸς ὢν φιλεῖν θέλει
20]της οιπερ οἶδας πρός με νῦν
].ς μοι πολλὰ πρὸς ταῦτα τί λέγ[
].ινος ἐστιν, ἐγὼ δ' εἰμὶ πένης
].ις παρὰ δαπάνημα οὐ μὴ ζ.[
]τευε, ἀλλὰ δουλεύσω ἐκειν[

5 οἶδά σ' or οἶδας ἡμᾶς ed. pr.   6 ἀκρ[ιβῶς ed. pr.
10 λ]έγω or θ]έλω ed. pr.   18 τῶν or τ' ὢν ed. pr.

4

(a) . . . .

(12 lines in which the only words which can be identified are 4
καλλονήν, 5 ἐν τῆ[ι ὁ]δῶι, 9 ἀλέκτορά μου [δ]υνάμεθα, 10
ἐκ περιπάτου, and 11 δρόσοις)

π]αιδὸς ἐφύλασσεν ὁ φίλος μου τρυφῶν
τέ]κνον τη[ρ]ῶν ἐν ταῖς ἀγκάλαις
15 ἀπορο]ῦμαι ποῦ βαδίσω. ἡ ναῦς μου ἐρράγη.
τὸν κ]α[τ]α[θ]ύμιον ἀπολέσας ὄρνιθά μου κλαίω
φ]έρε τὸ ἐρνίο[ν] τροφὴν αὐτοῦ περιλάβω

372

] listen to me so that you may not appear [
] give me a kiss and farewell [
] away. See. Ugh! [
] lest you say anything unsympathetic to me[1] [15
] when I leave [
]   [
] men, eager [ ] two [
] being a beggar he wishes to love [
] you know to me now [20
] to me much against this why do[ ] say [
] is, but I am poor [
] for expense not [
] but I shall be enslaved [ ] that [

[1] Or: unsympathetic. Won't you say something to me?

4

(12 lines in which the only words which can be identified are 4 'beauty', 5 'in the street', 9 'my cock we can', 10 'from the walk', and 11 'with water')

] of the boy, my dainty friend defended
] the child, holding it in his arms
I'm uncertain where to go. My ship is wrecked.   15
I've lost my darling bird and weep for it
] come let me embrace his offspring, brood

τοῦ μ[αχ]ίμου τοῦ ἐπεράστου τοῦ Ἑλληνικοῦ.
χάρ[ιν τ]ούτου ἐκαλούμην μέγας ἐν τῶι βίω[ι]
20 καὶ [ἐ]λεγόμην μακάρι[ο]ς, ἄνδρες, ἐν τοῖς
  φιλοτροφί(οις).
ψυχομαχῶ· ὁ γὰρ ἀ[λ]έκτωρ ἠστόχηκέ μου
καὶ θακαθαλπάδος ἐρασθεὶς ἐμὲν ἐγκατέλιπε.
ἀλλ' ἐπιθεὶς λίθον ἐμαυτοῦ ἐπὶ τὴν καρδίαν
καθ[η]συχάσομαι. ὑμε[ῖ]ς δ' ὑγιαίνετε, φίλοι.

(b)   . . . .
        ]ωφ[
        ].μμ[
        ]υσυμ[
        ]ις νοσο[
5   ]ναν[
        ]πολι.[
        ]τεμ[
        ]ταψυχ[

8 πολλὰ [στέ]νων ed. pr.   10 τηρήσας ed. pr.
  (b) Uncertain whether this is from same column as (a) or from foot
of previous one

5

ἅρματι λευκοπώ[λ]ωι ἄρτι Τραϊαν[ῶι
συνανατείλας ἥκω σοι, ὦ δῆμ[ε,
οὐκ ἄγνωστος Φοῖβος θεὸς ἄν[α-

of the fighter, the beloved, the Greek.
On account of him I was called great during his life
and I was said to be blessed, men, among the breeders.   20
I fight for my life; for my cock is missing
and in desire for his hen has left me.
But setting a stone on my own heart
I shall find rest. Farewell to you, friends.

5

PHOEBUS Having recently risen in my white-horsed chariot
          along with Trajan, I have come to you, People,
          the not unknown god Phoebus,

κτα καινὸν Ἀδριανὸν ἀγγελ[ῶν
5 ὧι πάντα δοῦλα [δι'] ἀρετὴν κ[αὶ
πατρὸς τύχην θεοῦ.

χαίροντες
τοιγ]αροῦν θύοντες τὰς ἑστίας
ἀνάπτωμεν, γέλωσι καὶ μέ-
θαις ταῖς ἀπὸ κρήνης τὰς ψυχὰς
10 ἀνέντες γυμνασίων τε ἀλείμ-
μασι, ὧν πάντων χορηγὸν τὸ
πρὸς τὸν κύριον εὐσεβὲς τοῦ στρα-
τηγοῦ φιλότιμόν τε τὸ πρὸς

. . . .

¹ <ΦΟΙΒΟΣ> ed. pr.   ⁴ Supplied by Wilcken
⁶ <ΔΗΜΟΣ> Wilcken, Croenert   ¹⁴ [ἡμᾶς Wilcken

6

]ωθης πορδὴν βάλε
]. β. πορδὴν
]αι δοκοῦσι ἀποτροπαὶ
]ν ἐπιτήδειον ὄντα
5]ασην. τοσαῦτα γὰρ
].οτι ἐν τῶι πρωκτῶι μου
]ν περιφέρω. κυρία Πορδή, ἐὰν διὰ
]ν ἀργυρᾶν σε ποιήσας
]
10].οὗτοι παραγίνονται. τυμπ.

to announce a new ruler, Hadrian,
to whom all is subject because of the virtue and   5
fortune of his divine father.
PEOPLE   Gladly
therefore let us kindle the hearths in sacrifice,
with laughter and drinking
from the spring relaxing our minds
and with oils of the gymnasia.   10
Of all these the patron is the
piety of the general towards the emperor
and the goodwill towards [us   ].

6

so that you may be] saved send a fart
                        ] B. A fart
                        ] preventions seem
                  bum] being fit
                        ] For such great things   5
                        ] in my bum
              ] I carry around. Lady Fart, if
I am saved   ] having made [a model] of you
    in silver

                        ]
                        ] They're here! *Drums*   10

---

1 ἵνα δὲ διασ]ωθῆις Sudhaus
4 πρωκτὸ]ν Crusius
6 δῆλ]ον ὅτι Sudhaus
7–8 δια[σωθῶ ed. pr.

```
                    ]. κοι. αβορατον Z
                  ]μαλαλαγαβρουδιττακοτα
                  ]ρασαβαδιναραπρουτιννα
                    ]..[....]ακρατιευτιγα
15                     ]μα
                  ]οσαδω[.]χαριμμα Z
    B.          ὁ πρω]κτός μου ἀπεσφήνω-
ται                 ἐν τ]ῶι πελάγει χει-
μών                   ]αι ἐρεγμὸν
20                   κ]ατεῖδαν αὐτῶν
    κοι.            ]λαβαττα κροτ.
                   ]τυμπ. πέρδ(εται) B.
                   ]ον πορδὴν
                   ]μενω
25                 ]ην σου ποιήσας
                   ]ασαι μοι εἰπεῖν
              εἰς τὸν Ψωλι]χον ποταμὸν
                   ].μος τῆς πορδῆς
                   ] κεκρυμμένος
30          κυρία Χαρίτιον, σύ]γχαιρέ μοι λελυμέν(ωι)
                   ] γ. λάλει βα-
                   ]α. ζ. λεανδα
                   ]ομαι αὐτὰς
                   ]
35                 ]αλεμμακα κροτ.
                   ]ν κροτ.
      τὸ εἴσω ἢ ὡς μεν[
    B.   δοκῶ χοιριδίων θυγατέρες εἰσί· ἐγὼ καὶ ταύτας
```

378

	] ALL. aboraton Z	
	]malalagabroudittakota	
	]rasabadinaraproutinna	
	]akratieutiga	
	]ma	15
	]osado[ ]charimma Z	
B.	] my bum is fully compressed	
	] a storm at sea	
	] bellowing	
	] they've seen their	20
ALL	]labatta *Cymbals*	
	]*Drums. He farts* B.	
	] fart	
	]	
	] having made of you	25
	] to say to me	
	to the Psoli]chos river	
	wind] of the fart	
	] hidden	
	Lady Charition,] rejoice in my release	30
	] G. Speak	
	] Z. leanda	
	] I [ ] them	
	]	
	]alemmaka *Cymbals*	35
	] *Cymbals*	

Below or as [

B.   I think they are daughters of pigs; I shall remove

---

17 B. supplied by Crusius, 21 KOI. by Knoke

27 cf. 40, 129

28 ὁ ἀν]εμὸς Sudhaus   30 cf. 107

ἀπολύσω. _τυμπ_. _πορδ(ή)_ ΚΟΙ. αἱ ἁρμινθι _κροτ_.
τυμπ.

40 Β.   καὶ αὗται εἰς τὸν Ψώλιχον πεφεύγασι.

Γ.   καὶ μάλα, ἀλλὰ ἑτοιμαζώμεθα [ἐ]ὰν σωθῶμεν.

Β.   κυρία Χαρίτιον, ἑτοιμάζου ἐὰν δυνηθῆι τι
τῶν ἀναθημάτων τῆς θεοῦ μαλῶσαι.

Α.   εὐφήμει· οὐ δεῖ τοὺς σωτηρίας δεομένους με-

45   θ᾽ ἱεροσυλίας ταύτην παρὰ θεῶν αἰτεῖσθαι.
πῶς γὰρ ὑπακούουσι ταῖς εὐχαῖς πονηρίαι
τὸν ἔλεον μέλλοντες παρ[ασπᾶ]σθαι; τὰ τῆς
θεοῦ δεῖ μένειν ὁσίως.

Β.   σὺ μὴ ἅπτου· ἐγὼ ἀρῶ. Α. μὴ παῖζε, ἀλλ᾽ ἐὰν
παρα-

50   γένωνται διακόνει αὐτοῖς τὸν οἶνον ἄ[κ]ρατον.

Β.   ἐὰν δὲ μὴ θέλωσιν οὕτως πίνειν;

Γ.   μωρέ, ἐν [τ]ούτοις τοῖς τόποις οἶνος [. .] ων . .[
λοιπὸν [δὲ] ἐὰν τοῦ γένους δράξω[ν]τα[ι] ἀπειρ[ί]αι
[πο-
θοῦντ[ες] ἄκρατον πίνουσιν.

55 Β.   ἐγὼ αὐτοῖς καὶ τὴν τρυγίαν διακο[ν]ῶ.

Γ.   αὐτοὶ δὲ οὗτοι λελουμένοι μετὰ τῶν [. . . . . .]
παραγίνονται. _τυμπ_. _ἀναπεσ( )_ _τυμπ_. δ. . . . . .
[. .] . . . . . .[

ΒΑΣ. βραθις. ΚΟΙ. βραθεις. Β. τί λέγου[σι;

Γ.   εἰς τὰ μερίδιά φησι λάχωμεν. Β. . . . .[.] . . .

60 ΒΑS. στουκεπαιρομελλοκοροκη. Β. βάσκ᾽, ἄλαστ̣ε.

ΒΑΣ. [.]ραθιε Ζ _τυμπ_. βερη· κονζει· δαμυν· πετρεκιω
πακτει· κορταμες· βερη· ϊαλερω· δεπωμενζι

them too. *Drums. Fart* ALL. ai arminthi *Cymbals Drums*

B. They too have fled to the Psolichos. 40

G. Yes indeed, but let us get ready for our escape.

B. Lady Charition, get ready if you can
to sneak off some of the dedications to the goddess.

A. Quiet! Those seeking safety ought not
to ask that of the gods along with robbing a temple. 45
For how will they heed prayers
if they are about to be detached from mercy by
    wrongdoing?
The goddess's property must be left piously.

B. Don't you touch it; I'll take it. A. Don't joke, but if they
    appear
get the neat wine ready for them. 50

B. What if they don't want to drink it thus?

G. Fool, in these parts wine is [not for sale];
so if inexperience has a grip on the people,
in desire they drink it neat.

B. I'm preparing the dregs too for them. 55

G. But here they come, washed with the [
    Drums [   ] *Drums* [

KING Brathis. ALL. Bratheis. B. What are they saying?

G. He says, let's draw lots for shares. B. [   ]

KING Stoukepairomellokoroke. B. Get off, curse you. 60

KING [ ]rathie Z *Drums* Bere; konzei; damun; petrekio
paktei; kortames; bere; ialero; depomenzi

---

39 ἀπολούσω Knoke   46 ὑπακούσουσι 141   47 cf. 142
49 For A. Wiemken would read Γ.
52 [οὐ]κ ὤνει[ος ed. pr.
53 end supplied by Manteuffel

πετρεκιωδαμυτ· κινζη· παξει· ζεβης· λολω
βια· βραδις· κοττως. ΚΟΙ. κοττως.

65 Β.   κοττως ὑμᾶς λακτίσαιτο. ΒΑΣ. ζοπιτ τυμπ.

Β.   τί λέγουσι; Γ. πεῖν δὸς ταχέως.

Β.   ὀκνεῖς οὖν λαλεῖν; καλήμερε, χαῖρε. κροτ. τυμπ.

ΒΑΣ.   ζεισουκορμοσηδε. τυμπ. Β. ἆ, μὴ ὑγιαίνων.

Γ.   ὑδαρές ἐστι, βάλε οἶνον. τυμπ. πολ.

70 ϛ.   σκαλμακαταβαπτειραγουμι.

Ζ.   τουγουμμι κροτ. νεκελεκεθρω. ϛ. ειτουβελλετρα
χουπτεραγουμι. Β. αἴ κροτ. μὴ ἀηδίαν· παύσασθε.
τυμπ. κροτ.
αἴ κροτ. τί ποιεῖτε; Ζ. τραχουντερμανα.

ϛ.   βουλλιτικαλουμβαϊ πλαταγουλδα κροτ. βι[

75 Β.   απυλευκασαρ. τυμπ. Β[ΑΣ.] χορβονορβοθορβα[
τουμιωναξιζδεσπιτ πλαταγουλδα κροτ. βι[
σεοσαραχις. τυμπ. ΒΑΣ. [.̣.̣.]ορ̣αδω κροτ. σατυρ[

ΒΑΣ.   οναμεσαρεσυμψαραδαρα κροτ. ηι κροτ. ια κροτ.
δα[

Β.   μαρθα κροτ. μαριθουμα εδμαϊμαϊ κροτ. μαϊθο[
80   θαμουννα μαρθα κροτ. μαριθουμα. τυμπ. .[.̣.̣.̣.]τυγ[

ΒΑΣ.   μαλπινιακουρουκουκουβι κροτ. καρακο [.̣.]ρα. [

ΚΟΙ.   αβα. ΒΑΣ. ζαβεδε κροτ. ζαβιλιγιδουμβα. ΚΟ[Ι.]
αβα ουγ[

ΒΑΣ.   πανουμβρητικατεμανουαμβρητουουενι.   [

ΚΟΙ.   πανουμβρητικατεμανουαμβρητουουενι   [
85   παρακουμβρητικατε[μ]ανουαμβρητουουενι   [

petrekiodamut; kinze; paxei; zebes; lolo
bia; bradis; kottos. ALL. Kottos.

B.   May kottos kick you. KING. Zopit *Drums*   65

B.   What are they saying? G. Give them drink quickly.

B.   Are you reluctant to speak? Bringer of good days, greetings. *Cymbals Drums*

KING Zeisoukormosede. *Drums* B. Ah, not willingly.

G.   It's watery, pour in wine. *Many drums*

F.   Skalmakatabapteiragoumi.   70

Z.   Tougoummi *Drums* Nekelekethro. F. Eitoubelletra
choupteragoumi. B. Ah! *Cymbals* No unpleasantness!
stop! *Drums Cymbals*
Ah! *Cymbals* What are you doing? Z. Trachountermana.

F.   Boullitikaloumbaï platagoulda. *Cymbals* Bi[

B.   Apuleukasar. *Drums* KING. Chorbonorbothorba[75
toumionaxizdespit platagoulda. *Cymbals* Bi[
seosarachis. *Drums* KING. [. . .]orado *Cymbals* satur[

KING Ouamesaresumpsaradara *Cymbals* ei *Cymbals* ia *Cym-*
bals da[

B.   Martha *Cymbals* marithouma edmaïmaï *Cymbals*
maïtho[
thamouna martha *Cymbals* marithouma *Drums*   80
[. . . . .]tun[

KING Malpiniakouroukoukoubi *Cymbals* karako [. . .]ra.[

ALL   Aba. KING Zabede *Cymbals* zabiligidoumba. ALL Aba
oun[

KING Panoumbretikatemanouambretououoeni.   [

ALL   Panoumbretikatemanouambretououoeni.   [
Parakoumbretikate[m]anouambretououoeni.   [85

---

68 ὑγίανον Knoke
82 ου⟨ε⟩ν[ι ed. pr., cf. 83–5

ολυσαδιζαπαρδαπισκουπισκατεμαναρειμαν[
ριδαου <u>κροτ</u>. ουπατει[ ]α <u>κροτ</u>. <u>τυμπ</u>. ε΄   [

ΒΑΣ. [βά]ρβαρον ἀνάγω χόρον ἄπλετον, θεὰ Σελή[νη,
πρὸς ῥυθμὸν ἀνέτωι βήματι βαρβάρω[ι ∪––

90   Ἰ_νδῶν δὲ πρόμοι πρὸς ἱ[ε]ρόθρουν δότε <u>κροτ</u>.
    [∪∪––

[Σ]ηρικὸν ἰδίως θεαστικὸν βῆμα παρα̣λ[.]..[
<u>τυμπ</u>. <u>πολ</u>. <u>κροῦσ(ις)</u> ΚΟΙ. ορκισ[.]. Β. τί πάλι
    λέγουσι; [

Γ.   ὄρχησαί φησι. Β. πάντα τὰ τῶν ζώντων. <u>τυμπ</u>.
    <u>πορδ(ή)</u>

[Γ.] ἀναβαλόντες αὐτὸν ταῖς ἱεραῖς ζώναις
    κατα[δήσα]τε.

95   <u>τυμπ</u>. <u>πολ</u>. <u>ΚΑΤΑΣΤΟΛΗ</u>   [

Β.   οὗτοι μὲν ἤδη τῆι μέθηι βαροῦνται.   [

Γ.   ἐπαινῶ. σὺ δέ, Χαρίτιον, δεῦρο ἔξω.   [

Α.   δεῦ[ρ᾽, ἀδ]ελφέ, θᾶσσον. ἄπανθ᾽ ἕτοιμα τυγχάν[ει;

Γ.   πάντα γ[ά]ρ. τὸ πλοῖον ὁρμεῖ πλησίον. τί μέλλετε;
    [

100   σοὶ [λέ]γω, πρωρεῦ, παράβαλε δεῦρ᾽ ἄγων
    τη[– ∪ –

Δ.   ἐὰν π[ρ]ῶτος ἐγὼ ὁ κυβερνήτης κελεύσω.   [

Β.   πάλι λαλεῖς, καταστροφεῦ;   [
    ἀπο[λ]ίπωμεν αὐτὸν ἔξω καταφιλεῖν πύνδ[ακα.

Γ.   ἔνδον ἐστὲ πάντες; ΚΟΙ. ἔνδον. Α. ὦ
    τάλαιν[∪ – ∪ –

105   τρόμος πολύς με τὴν παναθλίαν κρατεῖ. [

Olusadizapardapiskoupiskatemanareiman[
ridaou *Cymbals* oupatei[ ]a *Cymbals* 5 *drums*

KING Barbarian and immense is the choir I conduct, Goddess
Moon.

In rhythm with slack barbarian step [dancing].

Chiefs of the Indians, give to the holy sound of [cymbals]   90
Cymbals

A Chinese god-like step severally [in turn].

Many drums, Stamping. ALL. orkis[ ]. B. What are they
saying again?

G.   He says, dance! B. All like living things! *Drums. Fart.*

[G.]   Trip him up and [tie] him with the holy belts.
Many drums. FINALE   95

B.   They are now heavy with drink.

G.   Good. Charition, come out here.

A.   Come, brother, more quickly. Is everything ready?

G.   Everything. The ship is anchored close by. Why do you
delay?

I mean you, bow man, bring the [ship quickly] here and   100
come alongside.

D.   If I the helmsman first give the order.

B.   Are you speaking again, ruin man?
Let's leave him out to kiss the bottom.

G.   Are you all on board? ALL We are. A. O wretched [
A great trembling overcomes me, most troubled   105
woman. [

---

89 χορεύων Sudhaus   90 κροταλισμόν Winter
91 [Σ]ηρικὸν and παραλ[λ]άξ Crusius
98 ⟨ἆρ⟩α πάνθ' ed. pr.   100 τ[ὴν ναῦν ταχύ ed. pr.
101 πρώτως ed. pr.   103 ⟨τὸν⟩ π. ed. pr.

εὐμενής, δέσποινα, γίνου· σῶζε τὴν σὴν
πρό[σπολον.

ϛ. κυρία Χαρίτιον, σύγχαιρε τουτ[
λελυμένωι. [

A. μεγάλοι οἱ θεοί. [

110 B. ποῖοι θεοί, μωρέ; <u>πορδή</u> [

A. παῦσαι, ἄνθρωπε. [

ϛ. αὐτοῦ με ἐκδέχεσθε, ἐγὼ δὲ πορ[ευ-
θεὶς τὸ πλοῖον ἔφορμον [
ποιήσω. [

115 A. πορεύου. ἰδοὺ γὰρ καὶ αἱ γυναῖκες
[
αὐτῶν ἀπὸ κυνηγίου παραγίνοντα[ι.

B. οὔ, πηλίκα τοξικὰ ἔχουσι. [

ΓΥΝ. κραυνου. ΑΛ. λαλλε. [

ΑΛ. λαιταλιαντα λαλλεαβ...αιγμ[

120 ΑΛ. κοτακως αναβ.ιωσαρα. [

B. χαίρετε. Z [

ΚΟΙ. λασπαθια. <u>κροτ.</u> [

B. αἲ κυρία, βοήθει. [

A. αλεμακα <u>κροτ.</u> ΚΟΙ. αλεμακα[

125 B. παρ' ἡμῶν ἐστι †τουκηλεω† μὰ τὴν Ἀ[

A. ταλαίπωρε, δόξασαί σε πολέμι[ο]ν [
εἶναι παρ' ὀλίγον ἐτόξευσαν. [

B. πάντα μοι κακά. θέλεις οὖν κα[....].[
εἰς τὸν Ψώλιχον ποταμὸν [;

Be favourable, mistress, save your [servant.

F.	Lady Chariton, rejoice with this [	
	released.	
A.	Great are the gods.	
B.	Which gods, fool? *Fart*	110
A.	Stop, man.	
F.	Wait for me here, and I shall go	
	and get the ship	
	anchored.	
A.	Go. Look, here come their women also	115
	from the hunt.	
B.	Oh, what big bows they have.	
WOMAN	Kraunou. OTHER Lalle.	
OTHER	Laitalianta lalleab aigm[	
OTHER	Kotakos anab iosara.	120
B.	Greetings. Z	
ALL	Laspathia. *Cymbals*	
B.	Oh, lady, help.	
A.	Alemaka. *Cymbals* ALL Alemaka[	
B.	On our part there is ‹no(?) › by A[thena / A[rtemis	125
A.	Wretch, taking you for an enemy	
	they almost shot you.	
B.	Everything's bad for me. Do you wish me then [to drive	
	them too away]	
	to the Psolichos river?	

---

107 τούτ[ωι Crusius
125 Ἀ[θήνην ed. pr., Ἄ[ρτεμιν Crusius
128 κα[ὶ ταύ]τ[ας and 129 [ἀπελάσω Crusius

130 A.　ὡς θέλεις. τυμπ.　B. <u>πορδ(ή)</u> [

　　KOI.　μινει.

　　ϛ.　κυρία Χαρίτιον, καταρχην[
　　　　ἀνέμου ὥστε ἡμᾶς πε[
　　　　τὸ Ἰνδικὸν πέλαγος ὑπ[

135　　　ὥστε εἰσελθοῦσα τὰ σε[αυτῆς ἆρον
　　　　καὶ ἐάν τι δύνηι τῶν ἀν[αθημάτων
　　　　τῆς θεοῦ βάστασον.　[

　　A.　σ[ω]φ[ρό]νησον, ἄνθρωπε· ο[ὐ δεῖ τοὺς σω-
　　　　τηρία[ς] δεομένους μετ[ὰ ἱεροσυλίας

140　　　ταύτην ἀπὸ θεῶν αἰτε[ῖσθαι.
　　　　πῶς γὰρ ὑπακούσουσιν αὐ[τῶν πονη-
　　　　ρίαι τὸν ἔλεον ἐπισπωμ[ένων;

　　B.　σὺ μὴ ἅπτου, ἐγὼ ἀρῶ. [

　　ϛ.　τοίνυν τὰ σεαυτῆς ἆρον. [

145 A.　οὐδ᾽ ἐκείνων χρείαν ἔχω, μόν[ον δὲ τὸ πρόσω-
　　　　πον τοῦ πατρὸς θεάσασθ[αι.

　　ϛ.　εἴσελθε τοίνυν. σὺ δὲ ὄψομ[
　　　　διακονήσηις ἀκρατέστερ[ον τὸν οἶνον
　　　　διδούς, αὐτοὶ γὰρ οὗτοι πρ[οσέρχονται.

132 καταρχὴ ν[ῦν ἀγαθοῦ Sudhaus
133 πε[ράσαντας and 134 ὑπ[οφυγεῖν ed. pr.
135 cf. 144
136 cf. 43
138–42 cf. 44–8

A.	As you wish. B. *Fart* [	130
ALL	Minei.	
F.	Lady Charition, there is the prospect [now of a good]	
	wind for us [to cross]	
	the Indian ocean and [escape.]	
	Therefore go in and [pick up your belongings]	135
	and if you can, lift some [of the dedications]	
	of the goddess.	
A.	Be sensible, man: those who seek safety	
	ought not with robbery	
	to ask for this from the gods.	140
	For how will they heed to those	
	who try to attract mercy with wrongdoing?	
B.	Don't you touch them, I'll pick up.	
F.	Then pick up your own things.	
A.	I don't need even those, but only	145
	to see my father's [face].	
F.	Go in then. But you [ ]	
	prepare the [wine] with less water	
	and give it to them, for here they are [coming.]	

7

(c.22 lines totally lost, then 7 with only a few letters, then c.15 lost)

[   ]ζωσωμαι.

ἐρῶ νῦν παιδ( ).

[αὐ]τὸν ἵνα με βινήσηι.

τί οὖν [μά]στιγας.

5   δοῦλε, προσελθὼν [   ].

φαιδρόν.

μαστιγία, ἐγὼ ἡ κυρία [ ]ητου. κελεύω καὶ οὐ
γίνεται;

οὐ θέλεις [   ]δινεσ( ) ποιησ( ).

μ..[..]ν τὰς μάστιγ(ας) [   ]στ( ) ποησ( ).

10   οὐδὲ σὺ θέλεις; παῖδες, τοὺς [   ] οὐδὲν
γίνεται; δὸς ὧδε τὰς μάστιγ(ας).

[   ]έστηκεν Αἴσωπ(ος) ὁ τὴν δούλ(ην)
καταδεξό(μενος) [ ]ιον [τοὺς ὀδό]ντας
ἀράσσ(ουσα) αὐτ(ῶι) ἐκτινάξ(ω). ἰδού. ⌣⌣

[κ]υρί' εἰ δέ σ[ε] σκάπτειν ἐκέλευο(ν);

εἰ δὲ ἀροτριᾶν;

[εἰ] δὲ λίθ[ους] βα[σ]τάζ(ειν);

15   πάντων οὖν τῶν ἐν τῶι ἀγρῶι ἔργων γινομέν(ων)
ὁ ἐμός σοι κύσθ(ος) σκληρότερ(ος) ἐφάνη τῶι
γυναικε(ίωι) γέν(ει) συντεθραμμ(ένωι).

[ἀ]λόγιστ(ε), πονηρί(αν) τινὰ μέν(εις) καὶ
αὐχ(εῖς), καὶ τοῦτ(ο) σὺν τῆι πώλ(ωι)

7

[gap of about 44 lines]

    [   ] that I may [   ].
    I now desire the boy.
    [   ] him to fuck me.
    What then [   ] whips.
    Slave, having approached [   ].   5
    Cheerful.
    Wretch, I your mistress [   ]. Do I give orders and
      it does not happen?
    You do not wish [   ] do.
    [ ] the whips [   ] do.
    Are you not willing either? Boys, the [   ] Is nothing 10
      happening? Give here the whips.
    [   ] Aesop stands expecting to receive the slave
      girl [ ] I'll hit his teeth and shake them out. See.
    Sirrah, if I ordered you to dig?
    And if to plough?
    And if to lift stones?
    So compared with all the things that have to be done on 15
      the farm, my cunt has appeared harsher to you who
      were raised in womanly fashion. Idiot, you're waiting
      for some wickedness and boasting of it, and that with

---

2 παιδ(ίου) ed. pr., παιδ(ός) Crusius
6 Φαῖδρον Winter
7 [α]ὑτοῦ ed. pr., [το]ύτου Crusius
11 [τοὺς ὀδό]ντας Manteuffel   End explained by Robert
15 συντεθραμμ(ένωι) Cunningham, -(ένε) Sudhaus

Ἀπολλ(ωνίαι). ὥστε, παῖδ(ες), συλλαβόντ(ες)
τοῦτον ἕλκετε ἐπὶ τὴν πεπρωμένην. προάγετε
νῦν κἀκείνην ὡς ἐστὶν πεφιμωνένη.
ὑμῖν λέγω, ἀπαγαγόντες αὐτοὺς κατὰ ἀμφότερα
τὰ ἀκρωτήρι[α].. τὰ παρακείμενα δένδρα
προσδήσατε, μακρὰν διασπ[ά]σαντες ἄλλον
ἀπ' ἄλλου, καὶ βλέπετε μὴ πο[τε] τῶι ἑτέρωι
δείξητε μὴ τῆς ἀλλήλων ὄψεως [πλ]ησθέντες
μεθ' ἡδονῆ[ς] ἀποθάνωσι. σφαγιάσαντες δὲ
αὐτοὺς πρός με ε.. ἀντᾶτε. εἴρηκα. ἐγὼ δὲ
ἔνδον εἰσελεύσομα[ι].

τί λέγετε ..[...]; ὄντως ο[ἱ] θεοὶ ὑμῖν ἐφαν-
τάσθ(ησαν);
[κ]αὶ ὑμεῖς ἐφοβήθ[ητ]ε;
κα[ὶ] ἐκεῖν(οι) ..[.]..( ) γεγόνασι;
[ἐ]γὼ [ὑ]μῖν καταγγέλ[λω].
ἐκεῖνοι εἰ καὶ ὑμᾶ[ς] δ[ιέ]φυγεν τοὺς
ὀρε[ο]φ[ύλ]ακας οὐ μὴ λάθωσι. νυνὶ δὲ τοῖς
θεοῖς ...αρασαι βούλομαι, Σπινθήρ.
ὄμοσον.
επιπ.σ.....ινομενα.
λ[έγ]ετε τὰ πρὸς τὰ[ς] θυσίας.
ἐπειδὰν οἱ θεοὶ καὶ ἐπ' ἀγαθῶι ἡμῖν φα[ί]νεσθαι
μέλλω(σιν) ὡς προσέχ(οντας) ὑμνήσ(ομεν)
τοὺς θεού[ς].
μαστιγία, οὐ θέλ(εις) ποιεῖν τὰ ἐπιτασσόμε(να);
τί γέγονε[ν; ἢ] μαίνηι;

the filly Apollonia. So, boys, seize him and drag him to
his fate. Now bring her forward too, gagged as she is.
I'm speaking to you, take them away and tie them by
both extremities [to] the neighbouring trees, dragging one a long way apart from the other, and see that
you don't show one to the other, in case being full of
the sight of each other they should die happy. And
when you have slaughtered them, meet me [inside].
I've spoken. And I shall go within.

What are you saying [   ]? Did the gods really appear to
you?
And you were terrified?
And they became [   ]?
I declare to you.   20
They, if he has escaped you, will not evade the mountain
guards. But now I wish to [pray?] to the gods,
Spinther.
Swear.
[   ]
Say the words for the sacrifices.
When the gods are going to appear to us for our good   25
too, we shall praise the gods as being attentive.
Wretch, are you not willing to do what is commanded?
What has happened? are you mad?

---

16 κ]αὶ ed. pr., πρ]òς Crusius   ἔσω ed. pr.
17 ὑμ[εῖς ed. pr.
21 διέφυγον Crusius
25 End explained by Sudhaus
27 γέγον[εν ἤ] Sudhaus

εἰσελθόντ(ες) ἴδετε τίς ἐστιν.
τί φησιν; [.] . . .ν ἆρα;
30 ἴδετε μὴ [κ]αὶ ὁ ὑπερήφανος ἔσω ἐστί.
ὑμῖν λέγω, ἀπαλλά[ξα]ντες ταύτην παράδοτε
τ[οῖς] ὀρεοφύλαξι καὶ εἴπατε ἐν πολλῶι
σιδήρωι τηρεῖν ἐ[π]ιμελῶς.
ἕλκετε, σύρετε, ἀπάγετε.
κ̣α̣ὶ̣ ὑ̣[μ]ε̣ῖ̣[ς δ]ὲ̣ ἐκεῖνον ἀναζητήσαντες ἀποσφά[ξατε   ]ε προβάλετε, ἵνα [ἐγ]ὼ̣
αὐτὸν νεκρὸν ἴδω. [Σπι]νθήρ, Μάλακε,
μετ᾽ ἐ̣μ̣οῦ.

———

ἐξιοῦσα [ἀκρ]ιβῶς νῦν ἰδεῖν πειράσομαι εἰ
τέθηκε[ὅ]πως μὴ πάλιν πλανῆι μ᾽ ἔρις.
35 ὧδε μεν[   ].μαι τὰ ὧδε. ἑέ.
ἰδ[ο]ῦ οὗτος· αἲ ταλαί[πωρε .....] ἤθελες
οὕτω ῥιφῆναι μᾶλλον ἢ ἐμὲ [......; κε]ί̣μ̣ε̣ν̣ο̣ν̣
δὲ κωφὸν πῶς ἀποδύρομαι; νεκρῶι
[   ].ε̣ γέγ̣ο̣νεν, ἦρται πᾶσα ἔρις.
ἀνάπαυσον.
[   ]..[.].μενας φρένας αρω. Σπινθήρ,
πόθεν σου ὁ ὀφθαλμὸς ἡμέρωται;
ὧδε ἄνω συνείσελθέ μοι, μαστιγία, ὅπως οἶνον
διυλίσω.
εἴσελθε, εἴσελθε, μαστιγία.
40 ὧδε πάρελθε.
ποταπὰ περιπατεῖς; ὧδε στρέφου.
ποῦ σού τὸ ἥμισυ τοῦ χιτωνί(ου);

Go in and see who it is.

What does he say? [   ]

30

Look lest the boaster is inside.

I tell you, take this woman away, hand her over to the
  mountain guards, and say they are to watch her carefully in many irons.

Pull, drag, take away.

And you, seek him out and kill him [   ] bring him forward, so that I may see him dead. [Come, Spi]nther,
  Malacus, with me.

Coming out [   ] I shall now try accurately to see if he is
  dead [   ] so that jealousy shall not deceive me again.

Here [   ] things here. Ah!

35

You, look! Ah wretch [   ] did you wish rather to be
  thrown out thus than [to fuck] me? As he lies dumb
  how do I mourn him? To a corpse [   ] has become,
  all jealousy is removed. Stop.

[   ] I shall lift thoughts. Spinther, whence has your
  eye been tamed?

Come in up here with me, wretch, so that I may strain
  the wine.

Come in, come in, wretch.

Come here.

40

What is this wandering about of yours? Turn here.

Where is the half of your shirt?

---

29 [ἤ]δ' ἦν Crusius, [π]οῖον Manteuffel   33 ἀποσφά[ξατε
σπάσατ]ε Sudhaus   [ἔλθετε ed. pr.   34 ἐξιοῦσα taken as
stage direction by Wiemken   τέθνηκε]ν ἐκεῖνος Sudhaus
36 [βινεῖν Cunningham   37 ἀρῶ ed. pr., ἄρω Sudhaus

τὸ ἥμισυ. ἐγώ σοι πάντα περὶ πάντων ἀποδώσω.

οὕτω μοι δέδοκται, Μάλακε. πάντας ἀνελοῦσα
καὶ πωλήσασα τὰ ὑπάρχοντά πού ποτε
χωρίσεσθαι.
45 νῦν τοῦ γέροντ(ος) ἐγκρατὴς θέλω γενέσ(θαι)
πρίν τι τούτ(ων) ἐπιγνοῖ. καὶ γὰρ εὐκαίρως
ἔχω φάρμακον θανάσιμον ὃ μετ᾽ οἰνομέλιτος
διηθήσασα δώσω αὐτῶι πεῖν. ὥστε πορευθεὶς
τῆι πλατείαι θύραι κάλεσον αὐτὸν ὡς ἐπὶ
διαλλαγάς.
ἀπελθόντες καὶ ἡμεῖς τῶι παρασίτωι τὰ περὶ τοῦ
γέροντος προσαναθώμεθα.

παιδίον, παῖ.
τὸ τοιοῦτόν ἐστι, παράσιτε.
οὗτος τίς ἐστι(ν);
50 αὕτη δέ;
τί οὖν αὐτῆι ἐγένετο;
ἀ[ποκ]άλυψον ἵνα ἴδω αὐτήν.
χρείαν σου ἔχω.
τὸ τοιοῦτόν ἐστι, παράσιτε.
55 μετανοήσασ(α) θέλ(ω) τῶι γέροντ(ι) διαλ-
λαγ(ῆναι).
πορευθεὶς οὖν ἴδε αὐτὸν καὶ ἄγε πρὸς ἐμέ, ἐγὼ
δὲ εἰσελθοῦσα τὰ πρὸς τὸ ἄριστον ὑμῖν
ἑτοιμάσ[ω].

The half. I shall repay you in full for everything.

This is what I've decided, Malacus. Having destroyed
    everyone and sold the property to go away some-
    where.
Now I wish to get control of the old man before he gets 45
    to know anything of this. For by good luck I have a
    deadly drug which I'll mix with wine and honey and
    give him to drink. So go in by the main door and invite
    him as if to a reconciliation.
We too shall go and consult with the parasite about the
    matter of the old man.

Boy, boy.
That's how it is, parasite.
Who is this man?
And this woman? 50
So what happened to her?
Uncover her so that I may see her.
I have need of you.
That's how it is, parasite.
I've changed my mind and wish to be reconciled with 55
    the old man.
So go and see him and bring him to me, and I shall go in
    and get things ready for lunch for you.

ἐπαινῶ, Μάλακε, τὸ τάχος. τ[ὸ] φάρμακον ἔχεις
    συγκεκραμένον;
καὶ τὸ ἄριστον ἕ[τοι]μόν ἐστι;
τὸ ποῖον;

60   Μάλακε.

λαβὲ ἰδοὺ οἰνόμελι.
τάλας, δοκῶ Πανόλημπτος γέγονεν ὁ παράσιτος.
τάλας, γελᾶι. σ[υν]ακολουθήσ[α]τε αὐτῶι μὴ καί
    τι πάθηι.
τοῦτο μὲν ὡς ἐβ[ο]υλόμην τετ[έ]λεσται. εἰσελ-
    θ[όν]τες περὶ τῶν λοιπῶν ἀσφαλέστερον
    βουλευσώμεθα.

65   Μάλακε, πάντα ἡμῖν κατὰ γνώμην προκεχώρηκε,
    ἐὰν ἔτι τὸν γέροντα ἀνέλωμεν.
παράσιτε, τί γέγονεν;

ἀγών(ισμα)

αἲ πῶς;
μάλιστα. πάντων γὰρ ν[ῦ]ν ἐγκρατὴς γέγονα.
ἄγωμεν, παράσιτε.

70   τί οὖν θέλεις;

(ΠΑΡ.) Σπινθήρ, ἐπίδος μοι φαιὸν ἱμάτιον.
(ΣΠ.)   παράσιτε, φοβο[ῦ]μαι μὴ γελάσω.
(ΠΑΡ.) καὶ καλῶς λέγεις.
(ΠΑΡ.) λέξω τί με δεῖ λέγειν.

---

[71] Read by Knox

Congratulations, Malacus, on your quickness. Do you
    have the drug mixed together?
And is lunch ready?
What?
Malacus!   60
See, take the wine and honey.
Wretch, I think the parasite has become panic-stricken.
Wretch, he's laughing. Follow him in case he has an acci-
    dent.
This has been completed as I wished. Let's go in and
    plan more safely about the rest.
Malacus, everything has proceeded as we intended, if 65
    we still destroy the old man.
Parasite, what's happened?   *conflict*
Ah, how?
Certainly. For I've now gained control of everything.
Let's lead on, parasite.
What then do you want?   70

(PAR.) Spinther, give me also a grey cloak.
(SPI.) Parasite, I'm afraid I shall laugh.
(PAR.) And you are right.
(PAR.) I shall say what I must say.

75 (ΠΑΡ.) πά[τ]ερ κύριε, τίνι με καταλείπεις;
   (ΠΑΡ.) ἀπολώλεκά μου τὴν παρρησ(ίαν).
   (ΠΑΡ.) τὴν δόξ(αν).
   (ΠΑΡ.) τὸ ἐλευθέριον φῶς.
   (ΠΑΡ.) σύ μου ἧς ὁ κύριος.
80 (ΠΑΡ.) τούτωι μόνον – ἀληθῶς οὐ λέγω; – ἄφες. ἐγὼ
         αὐτὸν θρηνήσω.
   (ΔΕΣ.) οὐαί σοι, ταλαίπωρε, ἄκληρε, ἀ[λγ]εινέ, ἀναφ-
         ρόδιτε· οὐαί σοι, Ξ´ οὐαί μοι.
   (ΔΕΣ.) οἶδα γάρ σε ὅστισπ[ε]ρ εἶ, μισο<ύ>μενε.
         Σπινθήρ, ξύλα ἐπὶ τοῦτον.
   (ΔΕΣ.) οὗτος πάλιν τίς ἐστιν;
   (ΣΠΙ.) μένουσι σῶοι, δέσποτα.

   ⁸² π[ε]ρ Crusius

8

ἤδη σέ περ ὄντα πρὸ τοῦ πολλοῦ
κλαύσω τάφον οἷα θανόντι
πρὸ τοῦ θανάτου στήσας
τέκνον ἄρματα πάντα·
5 φαοσφόρος σὺ καλεῖ παῖ καὶ σὸν περὶ
τύμβον ἱερὸν φυτεύσω δένδρεα
χρύσεα.
πτεδάσω νάμασιν ορ...νους[
στενάξω δεύτερον ἥλιον ὡς Κλυ-

(PAR.) Father and lord, to whom do you abandon me?   75
(PAR.) I've lost my freedom of speech.
(PAR.) My reputation.
(PAR.) The light of freedom.
(PAR.) You were my lord.
(PAR.) This man alone – do I not speak truly? – acquit. I shall
          lament him.
(MAS.) Woe to you, wretched, poor, suffering, unloved; woe to
          you X woe to me.
(MAS.) I know what you are, hateful man. Spinther, the stocks
          for him.
(MAS.) This man again, who is he?
(SPI.) They're waiting safely, master.

8

Although you are now alive before much time (?)
I shall lament your grave as for a dead man
having before your death set in place,
my child, all the furnishings.
You are called light-bringing, son, and around your   5
sacred tomb I shall plant trees
of gold;
I shall make it gush (?) with springs [   ]
I shall groan for a second sun as

10 μένη γῶον Ἠριδανοῦ. Κυβέλ[η
σύ με †δευοδο† δίδασκ᾽ ὅτε
νάπαις γαμέτην Φρύγα πῶς νεάγαμ[ον
ἔτεμες περὶ τύμβον ἱερὸ[ν
καὶ μέλος ἔλεγον ὅτε παρὰ π-
15 αππᾶν γεγόνει γυνὴ Παφίη σ...
...[...]εκαι ...πτεδασω
16a ἔχουσα τὸν Ἄδωνιν ..ουσα νυ[   ]σπε..[
γόους Βυβλιάσιν ἔλεγον αἰαῖ βρα-
χὺς ὑμὴν τὰ ν..... τὰ ἔντιμα
μέλη σεῖστρον καλεῖ σ᾽ ὑφ᾽ ἁρ..
20 ταληθη νυχίαν ἤδη ....
.πας παρα κορη . φύγε φέγγος
ἐμὸν σπευσιν ἐμάγευον ἀλλὰ
μενε κλαίω τέκνον ἔλεγον
ἐμὸν δεύτερον ἤλιον ὡς Κλυ-
25 μένη γῶον Ἠριδανοῦ.

¹ πολλοῦ read by Manteuffel   ⁵ καλεῖ read by Croenert
⁸ πιδάσω Keydell   ¹² End supplied by Manteuffel
¹⁸ Νείλου Schubart   ²⁰ -τα λήθη⟨ς⟩ . . . ἐς εὐνήν Manteuffel

Clymene for the monument (?) of Eridanus. Cybele,   10
teach me [   ] when
in the glades how you cut your newly wed Phrygian husband
around the sacred tomb
and when a song of mourning from
ancestors the Paphian lady sang (?) [   ]   15
I shall make gush (?)
having Adonis [   ]
laments for women of Byblos an elegy alas
a short wedding song (?) the honoured lays of [the Nile]
the rattle calls you below [   ]
[ ] of night now [   ]   20
[   ] flee from my light
[   ] I bewitched but
[   ] I weep for my lamented child
a second sun as Clymene
the monument of Eridanus.

9

]συναις μορβίλλων ὦν ... νου
]ν ἅμα κρατῶν ἐν παλάμαις
]. κρατεραῖς ξίφος ὅπλον αἰαῖ
]ις μόνην μ' ἔλιπες.

———————

5

]. ς ῥοδίνους πυκάζησ . ε
]με . [.]ν παιδὶ κυρεῖ κακοῖς
]μονομαχήσειν ἀνέπεισαν
] . . . . . νου μηδὲ λάθοι.

———————

]σης γὰρ ἔχεις χρυσὸν παῖ
10

κ]αρ[τ]ερόθρουν βριαρ . [. .]ε
]ομενην πορφυρ[ε]ω[. . . . .]
] . λη[.]φερει[.]κα[
] . χρ . ο[. .]θα

. . . .

(From col. 2 the opening letters, up to 5 in number, of 16 lines
survive)

5 στεφάνο]υς ed. pr.   πυκάζη<ι> σε or πυκάζησθε
10 βριαρό[ν τ]ε Murray

10

A.   ποῦ τὸ δίκαιον;   [
B.   παρὰ τοῖς ἀλλήλους [.]υτίζουσι. [

9

    ] being a gladiator [
    ] together strong among hands
    ] that are strong a sword a weapon alas
    ] you have left me alone.

                ————

garlands] of roses you deck [5
       ] for a boy he meets with evil
     ] they persuaded (you? him?) to engage in single
combat
       ] nor may it be unobserved.

                ————

    ] for you have gold, boy
    ] strong-voiced and powerful   10
    ] purple

10

A.   Where is justice?
B.   Among those who rend (?) each other.

Δ.　ἄγε, περὶ ταύτης σ[υνή]κα τὴν γνώμ[ην
　　τῶν κοσμίων [　　　　　　] τί βουλεύεσθ[ε
5 Γ.　ε[( )]ται [　　　　　]ινα　　　　　[
ΚΟΙ.　δικαι[ ]]　　　　　　　　　　　[
Δ.　πάτερ Ἴων, οὐ χρῶμαί σοι οὔτε κριτῆι [
　　παρακρήτωι. [Δ.] παρακλήτωι.　　　[
Γ.　διὰ τί;　　　　　　　　　　　　[
10 D.　ὅτι ὅλος ἐξ ἐκ[εί]νο[υ το]ῦ μέρους εἶ. ο[
　　οὐδ᾽ εἰς β[.....]ν ἁ[ρ]πάζομα[ι
Γ.　συγγνώμην μ[.....]κομψος [
　　αὐτοῦ γέγονα φ[ίλ]ος ἀναγκαῖος [
　　ὡς ἀκούσας τὴ[ν] μεταλλαγὴ[ν
15　　τούτωι συλλυπηθησόμενος.　　[
Δ.　καταστροφή λέγ[ε] μοι, πάτερ Ἴων, [
　　πατέρα ἡμῶν ἤιδεις;　　[
Γ.　τὸ[ν] τούτου ἤιδειν.　　[
Δ.　αγ [ ] .... ατὴρ ην[
20 Γ.　οὐ μὰ τὴν ἐμὴν σω[τ]ηρίαν [
Δ.　πῶς ρε εγ ο [
Γ.　[ ] ... εκείνη γυνὴ ἀξιω[　　　　προσφι-
　　λεστάτη.
Δ.　]οιχ[ ]ντ[...].. [
25　　ὅμοιός εἰμι.
Γ.　τυχόν.
Δ.　οὐκ ἀρέσκει μοι ουτ[
　　σάπρ᾽ ἄλμεια.

(A second fragment continues the dialogue between Δ, Γ, Δ,

D.	Come, concerning this woman I [understood] the opinion
	of the honest [ ] what you plan
G.	[ ] 5
ALL	Just[ ]
D.	Father Ion, I do not treat you either as judge [or as
	arvocate. [A.] Advocate.
G.	Why?
D.	Because you are wholly of that part [10
	nor to [ ] am I seized [
G.	Excuse [me] skilled. [Of the father
	himself I have become a close friend [
	since having heard of the change [I've come
	to sympathise with him. 15
D.	*Finale* Tell me, father Ion [
	did you know our father?
G.	I knew the father of this man.
D.	Come, [ ] father [
G.	No by my safety [20
D.	How [
G.	[ ] that woman worth[
	most loved.
D.	Adulteress (?) [
	I am similar. 25
G.	Perhaps.
D.	I do not like either [adultery or
	rotten pickles.

. . . .

(A second fragment continues the dialogue between A, G, D and

and B; the fifth and seventh lines each begin ναί, ἀλλ[ὰ?, the eighth σ̣ο̣ῦνται[)

² [σκ]υτίζουσι ed. pr.   ³ Supplied by Bell   At end τὴν Crusius, περὶ ἅ ed. pr.   ⁴ [· ἀλλὰ] Crusius, [τούτων] ed. pr.   ⁵ ἑταίρ[αν παρε]ῖνα[ι Crusius, ἔ[σ]ται τ[αῦτα δε]ινά Knox   ⁶ δίκαι[ον ed. pr., δικαί[ως Bell   ⁷ [οὔτε Bell   ¹⁰ Supplied by Bell   ¹² μ[οι ἔχε Bell   τ[οῦ πατρὸς Srebrny   ¹³ φ[ίλ]ος Hunt   [καὶ νῦν ed. pr.   ¹⁴ At end ἥκω ed. pr.   ¹⁶ [σὺ γὰρ τὸν Crusius   ¹⁹ ἄγ' ε[ἰ] ed. pr., then ἐμὸς Manteuffel   ²²⁻³ ed. pr.   ²⁴ μ]οιχ[ο]υ ed. pr., μ]οιχ[ε]υτ[ρία]ν Srebrny   ²⁷ οὔτε μοιχικὰ οὔτε Manteuffel   ²⁸ ἅλμια ed. pr.   ³⁹ λα]βὲ Bell

11

    ]. βροντην[
    ]ιποι τις ἀνουτ[
    ]ειπανειταυτα[
    ]λειν κατάρατε [
5   ] μηδενὶ τῶν [
    ] ἵν' εὑρήσει[
    ] ε. οὐδαμοῦ π[
    ] β. τῆς ἐπεμψ[
    ]πειθεις ἀπηλθο[
10]που πρέσβεων [
    ]...νεξα ....[

B; the fifth and seventh lines each begin 'Yes, but(?) . . .', and the
eighth 'They are rushing'

11

    ] thunder[
    ] anyone [
    ]   [
    ] cursed man [
    ] to no one of the [5
    ] so that [ ] will find [
    ] E. No where [
    ] B. Of the [
    ]   depart [
    ] of the elders [10
    ]   [

12

]μέλλομεν
επ]εμψεν
]πλατος ἐστί

(ends of 21 lines, of which only 4 have a few letters surviving
and 2 have the musical note τυμπ.)

(1 line missing)

25   .].[
        .].. ω[
        καὶ ψυχαγω[γ

  Γ.   καλῶς ὡς οιη[
        μάχοντο.   [
30 ϛ.ζ.η. οὐά· οὐά· ο[
  Γ.   οὗτοι δὲ .α.[

        οὐ θέλετ᾽ ἐξελ[
           διώκει. τυμπ. .[
  Γ.   οὐδὲν ἀργοτερ[
35 Α.   καθ[..]ον λοιπὸν [
  Γ.   ἀλλὰ τὰ μὲν πρ[
        ἀχνύμενοι π.[
        καὶ ισισιο. Α. κ[
  Γ.   τί τοῦτο ἐποιησα[
40   οὐκ ἀρτίως σου α[

12

            ] we are about to
            ] he sent
            ]

        18, 22 *Drums*

] [25
] [
and soul-lead[
———

G.	Well as [	
	they fought. [	
F.Z.E.	Ah. Ah. A[h.	30
G.	But they [	

———

You do not wish [to go out
      He pursues. *Drums*

G.	Nothing more slow[	
A.	All remaining [	35
G.	But theses things [	
	They grieving [	
	and Isis Io (?) A.[	
G.	Why have [they (?)] done this [	
	Not recently your [	40

A. οὐ ἄνθρωπε . . . [
    ἐξέπεσεν καὶ [
    φίλησα ουτ [
Γ. τοῦτ' ἐστι μ[
45 ἀνάγειν α[

3 Read by Cunningham   30 ο[ὑά ed. pr.   31 πάν]τες ed.
pr.   32 Perhaps ἐξελ[θεῖν   35 καθ' [ὅλ]ον ed. pr.
38 Ἴσις Ἴο ed. pr.   43 οὕτω ed. pr.

13

        ] ρατε σώματα, μαινόμεναι,
    καὶ μὴ καθυβρίζετε τρόπον ἐμόν.
    τί περὶ σφυρά μου δέματ' [ἐ]βάλετε;
    ἐμέ, σύγγονε βάρβαρε, παρακαλεῖς;
5   ἱκέτις, τροφέ, ναί, πέπτωκας ἐμοῦ;
    φιλάδελφε, πρόνοια λόγων ἀνέχηι.
    πειραζομένη βασανίζομαι.

    οὕτω τι [.....] ν ....μενη ναί,
    καὶ πρόσωπα τύπτει κ[αὶ] πλοκάμους
        σπαράσσει.
10 νῦν ἔμαθον ἀληθῶς ὅτ[ι πλ]εῖον οὐ ποθεῖς
        μετελθοῦσά τι λέξαι.
    ἔδει σ' ἐμὲ λιτ[αν]εῦσαι
    καὶ οὐ παρῆν ἐμοὶ ποεῖν πάντα κελεῦσαι.

A.   No, man, [
     he has fallen out [
     I loved [
G.   This is [
     to lead up [

13

(GIRL) Do not flay] your bodies, mad women,
          and do not insult my habits.
          Why have you put ropes round my ankles?
          Is it I, barbarian brother, whom you exhort?
          As a suppliant, nurse, yes, have you fallen before me?   5
          Dear brother, let the foresight of words sustain.
          I am tested and tortured.

(NURSE) Thus [   ] being [   ], yes,
          she both strikes her face and rends her hair.
          Now I have learned truly that you do not long to seek me   10
            out and say any more.
          You ought to have entreated me
          and ordered me to do everything where it was possible
            for me.

θρῆνον ὑπερθεμέ̣ν̣η λέγε, παρθένε, μή τινα
    ποθεῖς;
εἰπέ, κόρη, φανερῶς ἀλγηδόνα μηδ᾽ ἐ̣[μὲ] φοβοῦ.

15 εἰ θεός ἐστιν ὁ σὰς κατέχων φρένα[ς οὐ]δὲν
    ἀδικεῖς.
κοὐκ ἔχομεν γενέτην ἀγριώτατον· ἥμερα φρονεῖ.
καὶ καλός ἐστιν ἔφηβος ὁ σὸς τάχα, καὶ σὺ δὲ
    καλή.

ἐπικωμάζει καὶ μεθύει.
κοινῆς δὲ φέρων πόθον Ἀφροδίτης
20 αὐτός τ᾽ ἐφηβῶν ἄγρυπνον
ὑπὸ κάλαμον ἄνομα λέγει.
καὶ τοῦτον ἐῶ. βραχύτατον ἦν
ζήλωμα, πάτερ, γινώσκω.
ἕτερον ....ρον
25 παρὰ παννυχίσι̣ν̣ ....
το κατελθὼ̣ν̣ ἐπι[

14

r ..]δη.[
   ..]δεν ξ[
   τωιμ[
   τοναι[
5 ἑκατε[

(BROTHER) Rising above your lament, say, maiden, do you de-
    sire some one?
    Speak, girl, clearly of your pain and do not be afraid of
    me.
    If it is a god who possesses your mind, you do no wrong.   15
    And we do not have a very brutish parent; he has gentle
    thoughts.
    And your boy is probably lovely, and you are lovely.

(GIRL) He comes revelling and is drunk.
    Having a desire for common love
    and being himself a youth, beneath the wakeful   20
    flute he talks unlawfully.
    And him I give up. It was a very short
    infatuation, father, I recognise.
    An other [
    at night festivals [25
    coming down [

14

(The first 7 lines have no recognizable words. There is a para-
graphos after the fifth.)

π ...[
αμ ...[..].ν[.].[....]η[
τὸν [ε]ὐσεβῆ τοι̣ν̣δ̣[..]..[
ὃς ο[ὐ]δὲν ἄλλο πλὴν .[
10 καὶ τῶν ἀδελφῶν ὑ̣.[
αὔταρκες εἰς ε...[
σώζει δὲ τοῦτο πρ.[
ἡ συμφυὴς ὁμόνοι[α
τῆς εἰς ἅπαν[τας

15 τὰ μὲν καθη[
μακρηγορεῖ[
ἔαρ χελιδὼν [

v   (the first 7 lines have only a few letters surviving)

25   ]το.εστι...[
        ]τα κεκοινωνηκ[.].[
        ] χάριτες τῆς πατρίδο̣ς [
        ]υτοι πέφρασται̣] ν̣.ε....[
        ].βη.ας ἐστι καλη..η.[
30   ]νε σαόπτολίς ἐστιν α...[
        ].ων βλάστησεν ἑορτ̣[
        ] εἰ θέμις ἄρτι χορευ[
        ]ου τεὸν αὐχένα ...[
        ]μο̣[.] ἐξεναρ[

15 καθή[κοντα Koerte   16 μακρηγορεῖ[ν δ' οὐ βούλομαι
Heitsch   17 [οὐχὶ ποιήσει μία ed. pr.   32 χορεύ[ειν Koerte

416

the pious [
who nothing else except [
and of the brothers [10
self-sufficient to [
and he saves this [
the natural agreement [
of the towards all [

———

The fitting [15
speak(s) at length [
summer [is not made by one] swallow

(7 lines with no recognizable words)

]is [25
] has/have made common [
] graces of one's country [
] they have supposed [
]   is
] is saviour of the city [30
    ] has grown fest[ival
    ] if it is right now to dance [
    ] your neck [
    ]   [

. . . .

α´]   σοι με πόλιν διζε[

β´   σχημάτι‹ο›ν τολ[. . .]ιμ[. .]ατος

γ´   οὐ χρ‹ε›ία ῥημάτων

δ´   τὸ τῶν μαλακῶν

5 ε´   τὸ τοῦ ἡλίου

ϛ´   τιβιάζεσθ(αι) μετὰ τῆς παρθ(ένου) [. . . .].ι

ζ´   τὰ τῶν Γόθθων

      .].. ε ---

      τὸ ὑπομνηστικὸν χορηγίας

10   Λευκίππης

      ἐ]ργαστήρ(ιον) κουρέως

             κουρικά

             ‹ε›ἴσοπτρον

             φασκίας

15   κιβάρια γ´ τῆ‹ι› γραΐδ(ι)

      ζωνοβαλλάντι‹ο›ν

      γλωσ‹σ›όκομον χάρτ(ου)

      τὰ τοῦ χαλκέως

      σφῦραν σπάθην

20   τὸ ‹ε›ἰκόνι‹ο›ν α´

      σινδόνι‹ο›ν προμ .( )

      η...[

           ]πολ ...[

      ὑπομ]νη‹σ›τικὸν χορηγιῶν παραγρα( )

25   ]θη οὕτως---

15

1. That I seek the city for you
2. Little figure [   ]
3. No need of words
4. That of the soft ones
5. That of the sun   5
6. Flute-playing with the maiden
7. Those of the Goths

The memorandum of props
   of Leucippe   10
Barber's shop
   scissors
   mirror
   bandages
   3 rations for the old woman   15
   belt-purse
   papyrus box
Things for the smith
   hammer   blade
   1 small picture   20
   cloth ?

Memorandum of props written
was agreed] thus: 25

$]$ον τῆς πόλεως

$]$.χε̣διν

β′ <ε>ὶϲ ….δαιμε καὶ ταῖϲ τεταιϲ[

φαλητάρια β′

30 $[σ]$φύραϲ β′

ἄρμενον. πλοῖον

λύχνον. κοϲούλλια [

κώπαϲ. κουρικόν

φάγι<ο>ν. χόρτον

35 γ′ <ε>ὶϲ τὸ οὐ χρ<ε>ία ῥημάτων

κιθάρα. δελφάκι<ο>ν

κυνάρι<ο>ν. ζωμάρυϲτρα

δ′ <ε>ὶϲ τὸ τῶν μαλακῶν

περιζώματα φαϲκίαϲ

40 ε′ <ε>ὶϲ τὸ τοῦ ἡλίου

ἀκτῖναϲ

ϛ′ <ε>ὶϲ τὸ τιβιάζεϲθαι

οὐδέ[ν]

ζ′ <ε>ὶϲ τὸ τῶν Γόθθων

45 χλωρὰ <ε>ὶϲ τὸν ποταμό(ν)

τριβυνάρι<ο>ν τῶ<ι> ποταμῶ<ι>

ϲχήματα Γόθθων

καὶ Γοθθιϲϲῶν

---

[1] End read by Maehler   [2] should be, but is not, the same as 28
    [6] τιβιάζεϲθαι recognised by Maehler   παρθ(ένου) read by
Schubart   [21] προμ( ) read by Maehler
[24-5] παραγρα(πτὸν) [ἐτάχ]θη ed. pr.   [26] Beginning α′ <ε>ὶϲ
Cunningham   [27] Perhaps ϲχέδι<ο>ν   [42] cf. 6

1. For '   ] of the city'
   ]
2. For '. . . and the . . .'
   2 small phalluses
   2 hammers   30
   rigging. ship
   lamp. ?
   oars. cutting
   glutton. grass
3. For the 'no need of words'   35
   cithara. little pig
   little dog. soup ladles
4. For that of the soft ones
   girdles bandages
5. For that of the sun   40
   rays
6. For the flute playing
   nothing
7. For that of the Goths
   green stuff for the river   45
   small cloak (?) for the river
   dresses of male and female Goths

Composed in ZephGreek and ZephText by
Technologies 'N Typography, Merrimac, Massachusetts.
Printed and bound by Edwards Brothers, Ann Arbor, Michigan
on acid-free paper made by Glatfelter, Spring Grove, Pennsylvania.